"DON'T WORRY, LITTLE ONE. I WON'T SEDUCE YOU ... UNLESS, OF COURSE, THAT'S WHAT YOU WANT."

Jessica gasped sharply and began to struggle for release once more, trying desperately to get away while keeping her hold on the quilt. "You . . . !"

"Me what?" he asked casually, keeping her firmly in place. The reaction he'd received had been exactly what he'd expected, but he wasn't through. "Does that mean you want more?"

"Never!"

His eyebrows shot up in mock surprise as he looked down into her sparking eyes. "So vehement? And here for a moment I thought you were actually enjoying yourself. Was I wrong?"

Struck temporarily silent, she stammered, sputtering for words. He was impossible! "I . . . I hate you!"

"Do you? Should I show you how much?"

Other Leisure Books by Kim Hansen:

REBECCA McGREGOR

KIM HANSEN

LEISURE BOOKS NEW YORK CITY

A LEISURE BOOK®

May 1991

Published by

Dorchester Publishing Co., Inc.
276 Fifth Avenue
New York, NY 10001

Printed in the United States of America.

Chapter 1

The chair shattered the window and the cool night with unexpected clatter as it bounced from the boardwalk into the dusty street.

From the porch of the hotel Jessica Wescott turned startled eyes toward the sound and watched in speechless awe as a man followed the chair through the broken window and into the street.

Loud voices accompanied by piano music and high-pitched laughter poured out after the fallen man who, staggering to his feet, replaced a wide-brimmed hat on his head and wove a crooked path back up the stairs and into the saloon where he disappeared into the crowd as if he'd never left.

Jessica let out the breath she had unknowingly held and smiled to herself. Independence, Missouri! How different it was from Boston!

Pulling her shawl more closely about her shoulders, she turned from the noise of the saloon to look down the street to where the waters of the Missouri River lay gleaming like silver in the moonlight. She walked slowly to the porch steps, and the same glow bathing the shifting waters reached out from the night sky to touch her, too. It illuminated the gold of her hair and played across her face.

Her smile faded to a small frown. So peaceful and quiet on one end of the street, but so chaotic and loud on the other. She sighed. Would she ever get used to it? Would she ever get used to the contrasts?

The contrasts began with the river's restlessly flowing current and extended to the restless faces of the people surrounding it. The faces were many, but the likenesses were few. Hard men, gentle women, experienced fighters, timid farmers. They were all here and were all busy going somewhere. Oregon or California, New Orleans or Texas. This was the jumping off point for countless journeys to any number of places, and it was reflected everywhere one looked. Constant motion. Constant change.

No matter how often she saw the same river or the same people or the same streets, somehow they were always different. Each day was new. Each day brought complete change to a strange sameness that was nothing like the sights, sounds or people she'd seen and known all her life in the land known as the "East." But the East was behind her. West was where she was.

She had arrived only ten days before with the intent of leaving immediately for Santa Fe, but her guardian had suddenly fallen ill. Precious time had passed while recovery was sought, and Jessica had been patient. She had waited. However, she would wait no longer. It was time to go to Santa Fe. It was time to see him. He was waiting for her.

She glanced inside the dimly lit hotel lobby. Mrs. Abbott would not approve of her being out here alone. The older woman wouldn't allow either Jessica or Aggie to leave the hotel without the other's company. The two young women had to go everywhere together, escorting each other because their intended chaperone could not.

But, for once, having a companion forced on her did not bother Jessica. For once, she actually enjoyed the company. This was in part due to Aggie's being close to her own age, not quite twenty, but mostly it was due to Aggie's finding this entire trip as exciting as Jessica did. They were both awed by the life here compared to that at home, between civilization and the edge of it where Independence lay.

Every day found both young women eager to rise and explore, eager to satisfy their curiosity about this "West" that up to now they had only seen through pictures painted in their minds by journalists who told stories of savage Indians and wild outlaws who committed murder every day.

Mrs. Abbott hated the West already, hated the thought of going farther into it—especially when it was to see him. She declared the trip was too dangerous and the men who surrounded them, wearing guns on their hips and sporting unshaven chins and rough cotton clothes, were "barbaric."

But despite her guardian's constant warnings against the men, Jessica found herself fascinated by them and the country they lived in. They were like no men she had ever seen or met before. Rugged, independent and proud as this land they had chosen to live in, there were few—if any—gentlemen among them.

Oh, they held doors and tipped their hats and gave

motion to the usual pleasant treatment of women, but there was something different in their behavior. The respect was shown, but there was an unyielding quality, a strength that took the "gentle" away from the "man."

Jessica tipped her head back to look up at the ink-black sky studded with countless stars. There was an undercurrent of something here, something that made her wake up each morning filled with anticipation and excitement. How could she have waited so long to come? Why had she allowed her grandparents to keep her away? The deep green of her eyes glinted with new-found determination, and her slender chin jutted into a firm line. She would wait no longer. She lowered her gaze to the street. Tomorrow she was leaving.

The reflection of the moon on the Missouri again drew her attention. She had never been down to the docks at night. It looked so peaceful. Glancing up and down the dark street, the town seemed deserted. There was no one but her on the boardwalks.

Jessica smiled and, gathering her skirts, descended the stairs to the street. Independence just wasn't as bad as Mrs. Abbott believed. It was a city like Boston. There was no harm in taking a short stroll, and besides, she was tired of asking for permission all the time.

As she began to walk, the echo of shouting and laughter from the saloon drew her attention once more. She cast an anxious, yet disbelieving glance over her shoulder toward the building. This morning the desk clerk had told her and Aggie that a man had been killed there while playing a game of cards the night before.

"He was supposed to be cheating," the young, dark-haired clerk had told them, straightening the wire-rimmed glasses perched on his nose.

"Supposed to be?" Jessica had repeated. "You mean they weren't sure he was?" Beside her Aggie had listened with wide brown eyes.

"Didn't have to be sure," had come the response. "Just had to think so."

Jessica gave her head a slight shake of incredulity. She remembered reading an article about the West. It had said men here made the law themselves, using the guns they wore strapped to their hips instead of police officers. At the time she had thought the writer of the article must have been exaggerating. Surely people didn't shoot each other whenever they had a disagreement . . . or at least she had believed that before arriving here. Now, after watching the quick tempers and seeing the rough-and-tumble lifestyle of those living here, it wasn't difficult to believe in such swift justice.

Lost in thought, she looked up to see the ripples of the mighty river as it stretched down toward a distant horizon. She was much closer now and could see the wide variety of ships and boats tied to the docks. Her imagination sparked with wonders of where these vessels and their cargo might be going. Some would travel down the shores to the Mississippi River and New Orleans. Others would sail further—around Florida to the East Coast, or perhaps even brave the width of the Pacific Ocean to reach Europe.

Abruptly Jessica's thoughts were shattered as a man appeared, stepping directly into her path from one of the dark alleys lining the street.

"Lost, ma'am?"

Jessica started visibly at his unexpected appearance but quickly recovered and raised her chin in defiance at any thoughts he might have of the type of woman who walked the streets alone at night. "No. I was only walking down to the docks."

With his face in the shadow of his hat and the moon to his back, the man nodded as he watched her closely. The motion made her uneasy. "Alone?" he asked.

"I would think that's obvious," she retorted in sharp annoyance. "Now, if you'll excuse me . . ."

She should have been warned by the smile that suddenly broke upon his face, his teeth showing white in the moonlight. She should have known his sudden presence meant he had been watching her. Waiting for her. Hoping she would walk into his trap. But it was too late to think. Someone grabbed her from behind.

She opened her mouth to scream, but a foul-smelling rag dipped in chloroform was clamped over her mouth. She staggered back under the assault, and a wave of dizziness shook her as rough hands tried to harden their hold on her.

"Hold her still!" her captor hissed, one hand attempting to restrain her while the other tried to bury her nose in the rag.

But her hands were still free, and Jessica jerked her head away and swung blindly. She grabbed at the rag threatening to take consciousness from her and with desperate strength brought her heeled shoe down on the instep of her captor's foot.

The rag dropped to the dirt as the man released her with a howl of pain. She turned to run. But it was no use. A strangled cry escaped her lips as his partner brutally caught her. His fingers dug into her arms, and she was dragged against him. For an eternal second of terror she stared up into cold, merciless eyes. His grip tightened.

But then, she was free! Her attacker fell swiftly backwards as he was yanked from her by some unseen force which sent her to her knees in the dirt. The sickening sound of flesh meeting flesh echoed in the night as she watched her assailant reel backwards from the impact of a blow from a shadowy stranger.

The second man who had held the lethal rag charged at her savior's back, and she screamed a warning. The stranger easily sidestepped the attack, kicking the feet from under his new opponent to send him sprawling in the dirt beside his partner.

The two did not join for a second attack against the lone man. Instead they chose the safer route of flight and ran rapidly back toward the dark alleys from where they had come.

Jessica watched them go, her breath coming quickly and her heart hammering harshly against her ribs. Turning to the stranger as they disappeared, she looked up at him from the street where she still knelt. He seemed to tower above her. The width of his shoulders and the length of his long legs were highlighted by the moon which hung suspended in the night sky behind him.

He looked away from the alley and down at her. For a moment the image she made kneeling in the street, her blonde hair turned white in the moon's glow, made him hesitate. Recovering himself swiftly, though, he moved forward, extending his hand to her. "You all right, ma'm?"

Jessica accepted the strong hand that reached down to help her rise and nodded as she gained her feet. "Yes,

I . . . I think so.''

He released her hand immediately and watched as
she tried to brush some of the dirt from her skirt. Anger
raged within him, but it was tempered by a strong desire
to reach out and comfort her. She seemed so small now
standing before him. No longer a distant image viewed
from a porch where he'd been hiding. She was lovely.
He crushed the thought and his feelings abruptly. ''You
shouldn't be out by yourself at night.''

The statement was spoken harshly, underlined with
impatience. Any concern he may have held for her
safety was obviously now gone. Jessica blinked at his
change in manner, and her gratitude dissolved under a
surge of independence. ''I was only going for a walk.''

''Why?''

The question flustered her momentarily, and she
stammered uncertainly. ''Because . . . because it's a
nice night,'' she defended herself. ''And, because I
wanted to,'' she added with a flare of defiance.

A heavy sigh escaped his lips, and his head dropped
briefly before immediately lifting again. He stared down
at her, his face veiled from her by the broad-brimmed
hat he wore and by the shadows of night. Finally, he
motioned toward the alley. ''You know what those men
were going to do to you?''

Jessica felt her face burn hotly at his bluntness but
straightened her slender shoulders to face him with a
voice that only trembled slightly. ''I can guess.''

''Can you? I doubt it.'' Stepping away from her, he
bent down to pick up her shawl from where it had fallen
into the street before continuing. ''They were going to
shanghai you, sell you down the river as they say.''

''Sell me . . .''

"You probably would have ended up in some whore house down in New Orleans or maybe after a long trip you might have made it to San Francisco." His voice was cold and hard as he faced her, the tone as merciless as her assailant's eyes had been.

"I didn't know . . ."

"I didn't think you did. But now you do, I think you better get back to that hotel."

Accepting the shawl from him, she looked in vain at the face she could not see and felt fear vibrate through her at the words he'd spoken. Her gaze swung to the alley where her attackers had disappeared but returned quickly to him. She bit her lip hesitantly. She was more than willing to go, but she felt she had to say something before leaving. But what? She looked away. What could she say? She looked up again. "I . . . thank you."

For a moment she didn't think he'd heard her. He didn't move, didn't acknowledge her words. Then, silently, he raised a hand to touch the brim of his hat lightly. He did not speak again.

Curiosity and fear mingled in a quick conflict before fear and his advice to leave made her turn and hastily retreat to the hotel. She paused there on the porch, though. She had to look back. Her breath caught in her throat. He was still there, standing tall and unknown in the moon's glowing light.

Who was he? Where had he come from? She did not stop to think of him more, however. The threat of the darkness around her was more powerful than her wonder. She hurried inside and up the stairs to the safety of her room where Aggie sat sewing on the bed.

"There you are!" Aggie greeted her as the door

opened. "I was wondering . . . Miss Jessica! Your dress . . ."

Jessica ignored the worried cries of her maid and hurried to the window to look back out into the street. He was gone.

"Are you all right?" Aggie asked coming to stand beside her.

Jessica glanced absently at the young maid who had been with her family for as long as she could remember. They had grown up together, she and Aggie, had shared childhood secrets even though they hadn't shared the same social position. "Yes, I'm fine," Jessica answered turning back to the window. Where had he gone? It had only taken her a moment to reach her room.

"Your dress . . ."

Jessica moved to look down at the dress she wore. It was now covered with dirt. "I fell. That's all. Will you help me out of it?"

As soon as the words were out, Jessica wondered at herself. Why had she lied? She could not remember ever lying to Aggie before. They knew everything about each other and were great friends. Mrs. Abbott didn't approve of the relationship—pointing to the difference in classes. But the stranger . . . she didn't want to share him, at least not yet. She wanted to think about him. Think about what had happened. It had all happened so fast! Had it really even happened at all?

Jessica managed a forced smile as she accepted her wrap from Aggie. It had happened, and he had been there. She had almost been kidnapped, sold into slavery—a slavery different from the type the United States had just finished a war over.

She sank down on the bed and tried to listen to

Aggie's senseless chatter, but Jessica could not keep her thoughts from wandering to the stranger and the fate he had saved her from. Who was he? Would she ever see him again? And, how had he known she had come from this hotel? He must have seen her leave, but he hadn't been outside, had he? She hadn't seen him. But, then, she hadn't seen the men who had attacked her either.

A chill ran down her spine, and she shook her head at her thoughts. She should just be thankful he had come along when he had. She smiled. Mrs. Abbott would be happy to hear there was at least one gentleman in this town. Unfortunately, his existence would have to be kept from her. If she heard of or suspected anything like this night's events victimizing her ward, she would never allow the two young women to leave tomorrow. She wasn't convinced she should let them go as it was.

However, Jessica's mind was made up. Not even what had almost happened only moments before could stop her now. If anything, it had strengthened her resolve. She was going. Before anything else could happen, before anyone else could try to stop her, she was going to leave. She was going to Santa Fe. She was going to meet him at last.

Outside Nick Driscoll returned to the alley from where he had been watching the hotel for almost four hours. But, as he returned, he was not thinking about the hotel or the man inside who called himself Anson Jessop. He was thinking about the woman, the one he had rescued from kidnapping only moments ago.

Abruptly his anger returned with renewed force. He shouldn't have left the alley. He could have been seen. He gritted his teeth silently and his blue-gray eyes reflected irritation. Damn women anyway! They were more trouble than they were worth.

What had she been doing walking around in the middle of the night alone? She should have known better. He sighed impatiently. How could she have known? She wasn't from Missouri. Her cultured voice told him she was probably from the East. Boston? Philadelphia? What was she doing here?

Leaning against the building beside him, he doggedly forced his thoughts away from her. It didn't matter who she was or where she'd come from. He'd never see her again. Besides, he had more important things to think about than some damn fool woman. He shook his head silently.

Anson Jessop. Thomas Franklin. One and the same man. Why was he in Independence?

"He disappeared at the end of the War," Evans had told them earlier that day. "No one has heard from or seen him until recently, and when they did, he'd changed his name and occupation." Evans paused to light a cigar, the match flaring up brightly to illuminate the lines time and worry had etched onto his face.

As usual when he met Evans, Nick found himself wondering about the man, wondering who he really was. Nick and his friend, Diego, along with several others, knew him only as Curtis Evans and only saw him when the United States Government needed something done.

"Franklin was a big plantation owner before the War. His plantation was one of the largest in southern Virginia and one of the best. He was a settled family man with a wife and two children, but when the War broke out, he became an officer in the Confederate Army." Evans stopped to puff on the cigar momentarily. "He was one of the Union's nightmares. He was a brilliant tactician. Because of him, the Rebels outfoxed us more than once, but when the War ended and he didn't come home, it was assumed he was dead. The government forgot about him until one day, his family just up and disappeared, too."

Nick and Diego exchanged doubtful looks.

"Disappeared. You're using that word a lot tonight," Nick commented. "People don't just disappear."

"Not usually," Evans agreed. "But that family did. One day they were at their house in Virginia. The next, they were gone."

"No one saw them leave?" Diego queried.

"Let's say if anyone saw them go, no one's telling us about it. It's no secret that the South is still resisting Union law," Evans answered gravely. "And if someone's neighbor wants to leave quietly, everyone in the district is liable to help him do so."

"There is no idea as to where they are going?" Diego asked.

"Mexico," Nick replied before Evans could. "There's a lot of Southerners going over the border."

"People aren't the only things going over the border," Evans countered. "And that's why you're here."

"I knew we could not be so lucky to be here only for a social call," Diego grinned, his teeth flashing brightly in his golden brown face, his complexion reflecting the Spanish heritage flowing in his blood.

Evans ignored Diego and reached for some papers before him. He was used to dealing with men such as Nick and Diego. It was his job. He was the middle man.

He sent others out to gather information or to perform tasks. When the gathering or performing was done, he then passed the results on to whomever had requested the work in the first place. He'd been functioning in this position for a long time—since the War with Mexico years before. He was good at what he did—as were the men and women who followed his orders.

Nick and Diego had proven to be a great asset to him during the War with the South. They'd both grown up and lived in the southwest territories and had provided Evans with a ready source of knowledge. Evans had used them to scout for him, to run messages, to execute intricate plans and missions that had aided in the victory of the United States Government over the Rebels.

Yes, he was used to dealing with Nick and Diego or those like them and so did not respond to Diego's attempt at humor. For Evans it was necessary to avoid any contact that bred familiarity or encouraged unwanted questions. The only answers he wanted to provide were facts surrounding assignments. Who Curtis Evans was and why he was could be of no concern to any who worked under him.

Evans continued, "Thomas Franklin and his family could have gone to Mexico like the others, but we don't think they did. We think they're here in Missouri, but only for a short stop. We think they're getting ready to go to Texas or, more likely, the New Mexico Territory."

"Lots of people go to New Mexico," Diego put in with an expressive shrug. "It is a place with much land to be settled. People go there to find some."

"Franklin's not looking for land. He's looking for

Maximilian and a new South.''

Nick and Diego's eyes met in surprise. Maximilian and Mexico. Another war—one that wasn't yet over. The French held Mexico now. Maximilian was their leader and the Mexican President. However, for the past few years, Mexico and the Mexican people had been fighting the French and their supposed president. The people wanted a Mexican leader and a Mexican president and independence from France.

The revolution in Mexico was not unlike the one fought in the United States one hundred years before when the thirteen colonies had risen against England, and because of the similarity, the revolution had captured the American interest in the Mexican cause—at least partially.

When the Civil War had ended and the Confederate soldiers had returned to their homes, many had found themselves penniless and their plantations burned to the ground. Instead of trying to rebuild what they had lost, entire families had packed the few possessions they had remaining and began the long journey west to California or Oregon. Some preferred the closer territories of New Mexico and Arizona. But there were others still who had gone and were continuing to go into Texas and then south.

There had been strong rumors of Southerners finding sympathy with the French in Mexico. The French were welcoming them with open arms, and so they should. They needed all the support they could get. The French were losing steadily to a Mexican revolutionary leader named Juarez.

Juarez was strong and had the Mexican people behind him, but more often than not, the Mexican revolutionaries were low on supplies and weapons which made their progress slow. Mexican sympathizers in the United States were running the needed materials over the border. However, unfortunately, so were French sympathizers. The Civil War might be over, but in this new cause, the United States was still divided.

Nick knew General Sheridan had arrived in Texas only months ago to find Southerners going into Mexico by the hundreds. They were taking everything they owned with them, including whatever Confederate weaponry they could find.

"Gunrunning?" Nick asked. "I thought General Sheridan was handling that."

"He is. In Texas."

"New Mexico," Diego whispered. "Instead of going south, they are going west into New Mexico."

"We think," Evans agreed. "General Sheridan telegraphed Washington two weeks back. He's worried the movement may be more organized than we think. While questioning some of the Confederate men, it seems one slipped and mentioned the name Franklin. A few days later one of our men thought he recognized a man, but when the trooper asked, the man identified himself as Anson Jessop. Thinking he was mistaken, our soldier let him go. It wasn't until later that he was able to give a name to the face. Thomas Franklin. But it was too late. Jessop-Franklin was gone."

"You've found him again?" Nick asked, sitting back in his chair and stretching his long legs out in front of him.

"We've traced him through hotel registers and by a very vague but definite trail. He's arriving here today on the noon stage."

Diego frowned. "Alone?"

"No. Gabe Ramsey is with him. As soon as the stage stops, Ramsey leaves and you two take over. I want you to follow him, find out where he's going and why. If he's running guns, we want him stopped—immediately."

"You want him alive?" Nick queried quietly, watching Evans closely. But the older man gave nothing away. His face remained impassive.

"I want him stopped," Evans replied evenly. "No matter what you do with him, the operation can't be allowed to continue. If it does, we risk bad relations with Mexico. The revolution down there is far from over, but we think the Mexicans are going to win this war, and when they're done defeating the French, we don't want them coming back at us. We've already had one war with them. We don't want another."

A sound from behind Nick made him turn, and his hand slid the gun on his hip smoothly and swiftly from its holster. A low whistle greeted him. "Come on in, Diego."

Diego appeared, a poncho over his clothes to keep out the cool night air and his mouth spread in its customary grin. "How goes it, *amigo*?"

"Quiet. He hasn't moved since dinner."

Diego nodded, his gaze locked on the hotel across the street. "He has booked himself on the stage for tomorrow morning. Looks like we are going to Fort Dodge."

"The sooner the better," Nick retorted sourly.

"What's wrong, *amigo*? You don't like this town?"

"Let's just say I like the wide open spaces where a

man can walk without worrying about his pocket or his life whenever he passes an alley.''

Diego grinned. ''Fort Dodge is not so much better, but at least it is closer to home.''

Chapter 2

"I'm going and there is nothing more to be said about it," Jessica insisted as she turned to view herself for one last time in the mirror on the vanity.

"But Jessica . . ." the older woman protested feebly from where she sat on the edge of the bed, knowing even as she battled verbally with her young ward that the outcome was predetermined. When Jessica Wescott made up her mind to do something, there was no stopping her.

"There are no buts, Mrs. Abbott. None at all," Jessica interrupted in the same firm tone, but when she moved from the vanity and saw her guardian's distressed expression, her eyes softened and she smiled warmly. "Don't worry. Everything has been pre-arranged so nothing can go wrong. Aggie and I have our tickes to Santa Fe, so all we have to do is make sure we meet the stage schedules and get safely on board. My

father will be waiting in Santa Fe for us and will take
care of everything once we arrive."

Mrs. Abott snorted emphatically, her graying head
tilting disdainfully. "Why should he bother to take care
of you now when he couldn't be bothered with you up
to this time? What right does he have to suddenly
demand your presence in that God-forsaken territory
somewhere west of Texas?"

Jessica sat on the bed beside the older woman and
put a comforting arm around the aged shoulders. "My
father did not demand my presence. He merely wrote a
letter."

"The first in how many years?"

"And I decided to go," Jessica continued as if Mrs.
Abbott had not spoken. "As it is, he'll be wondering
what's happened to us because of our delay here in
Independence. We've waited over a week for you to
recover, and we'll be at·least ten days later than I wrote
him. It wouldn't be right to leave him worrying about
us, now would it?"

Mrs. Abbott sniffed slightly, regretting the
necessity to agree with her ward's logic. But she was not
ready to give up yet. "But what would your grandparents say to your going off by yourself like this?"

"No doubt they would agree with me," Jessica
answered unconcerned. "Obviously you cannot make
the trip and will have to return to Boston, and just as
obviously I must go on to prevent my father any need-
less anxiety. And, furthermore," she continued rising to
her feet to walk to the hotel room window. "I'll not be
traveling alone. Aggie will be with me."

"She's only two years older than you!" Mrs.
Abbott waved her hands helplessly. "Two young

females, both under twenty-five, should not be wandering about on their own.''

Jessica sighed and reluctantly turned from the view outside the window. Even after days of seeing the same street day after day, the people and way of life beyond the pane fascinated her. There was so much to learn about the West, and her father's letter had said so much and yet so little about it. ''We will not be wandering about. We'll be riding on the stage until we reach Santa Fe where my father will meet us and take us on to his ranch.''

''But when you each Santa Fe, how will you know him? You've never even seen him . . . at least not since you were a baby.''

''I won't know him, but I expect he'll know me. You've often told me how much I look like my mother.''

Mrs. Abbott looked forlornly at Jessica. It was true. She did look much like her mother and was fast proving once again she had her mother's temperament and strong will. It was no use. There was no swaying her.

A knock on the door brought the conversation to an abrupt end.

''That will be Aggie,'' Jessica announced, the note of excitement in her voice barely suppressed. ''We must go now. The luggage has already been sent ahead of us to Santa Fe, and the cases we'll be carrying on the stage are already at the station.'' She picked up her purse which held her father's carefully folded letter and turned to face Mrs. Abbott one last time. ''Now you mustn't worry. We'll be fine, and I promise to write as soon as we arrive.''

Mrs. Abbott rose to her feet, realizing she must accept the inevitable. "I can see you're determined to go." Jessica nodded decisively, and with a heavy sigh, the older woman held out her arms and wrapped them around the girl she had watched grow from a long-limbed, skinny child to a blossoming and lovely young lady.

Jessica was released with a firm but gentle shake.

"Now you be careful. All those stories I've heard about wild Indians and no-good men." She grimaced. "You stay to yourself and look out for that Aggie. She has a knack for getting into trouble."

Jessica smiled brightly, her green eyes shining with anticipation. "Thank you, Mrs. Abbott. Take care of yourself and stay here until you're sure you feel strong enough to make the trip back to Boston." She planted a kiss on the woman's soft cheek. "Give my best to Grandma and Grandpa."

Before Mrs. Abbott could answer, the door closed and Jessica was gone, her soft voice echoing momentarily in the hall as she and Aggie made their way downstairs to the street.

"Oh, I'm so excited, Miss Jessica!" Aggie exclaimed when they reached the boardwalks outside. "Imagine us going West!"

Jessica nodded quick agreement. This dream had been a long time coming. She felt as if she'd been waiting for this moment all her life. As a child, knowing her father was somewhere far beyond the reaches of Boston had meant little. She had been secure with her grandparents and her Nanny and a houseful of servants. But adolescence had given root to curiosity and day-dreaming and wondering about the parent she'd never known . . . "I know. Me, too. But now we're away from Mrs. Abbott, don't you think you can call me just Jessica?"

Aggie grinned, her dark eyes dancing mischievously. It was like being children again going off on a forbidden adventure. "All right . . . Jessica."

Jessica returned the conspiratorial grin. She had never felt so free! At last she was on her own, but her thoughts were soon diverted from her newfound independence by the high activity on the streets.

Even at such an early hour the walks were filled with people. Shopkeepers were beginning to open their doors, and men and women were moving inside to make necessary purchases. Wagons rolled past with a jangle of harness and were followed by small clouds of dust. Neighbors greeted each other. Women stopped to exchange talk, and children ran in and out from between anyone or anything which temporarily blocked their paths. Dogs barked, horses snorted. There was not a corner left untouched by the myriad of action around them.

All these sounds combined with the shouts of workmen on the docks and the blaring of a ship's horn on the Missouri River. The blowing wail reminded Jessica of the night before, and she smiled. Exposed to the light of day, her near-abduction had lost its touch of reality. If it were not for the bruises on her arms where the men had gripped her so tightly, she could easily have believed it had all been a bad dream—bad, except for him.

Without realizing she was doing so, she scanned the street, looking at all the men present a little more carefully than she normally would. Was he here now?

She frowned. Even if he were, she would never be able to recognize him.

With what little light there had been at his back and with his hat shadowing his features, she had never seen his face. Size was all she had to go by, and thinking back now, she was not sure of even that. In the dark and against the glow of the moon, she was certain he had appeared much taller than he really was.

She shrugged her slender shoulders carelessly. It was no use wondering. She would never see him again, and that was probably for the better. A man who could handle himself so well in a fight had probably had more than one occasion to practice such brawling. And, his manners . . .

While coming to her rescue, he could hardly be termed a gentleman in the true sense of the word. He had been blunt, none too tolerant of her innocent motives, and rude and arrogant in telling her what she should or shouldn't do. Unconsciously, Jessica raised her chin in defiance of him. No, it was better she didn't know him. But still . . .

"There's the stage," Aggie interrupted, grasping Jessica's arm in excitement.

Jessica forced her own elation down to a smile, though her heart jumped suddenly against her ribs. "It doesn't look like our coaches back East." But, look alike or not, a thrill of unbridled anticipation swept through her. She was finally going. She was finally on her way. and this sober wooden coach pulled by six strong and high-strung horses would take her.

"The coach'll be leavin' in about ten minutes, miss," the attendant at the window told Jessica. "You can climb on board now or wait for a bit.''

"Thank you."

" 'Welcome. Have a good trip.''

Jessica turned to Aggie and began to lead the way back to the door. She had to suppress the urge to rush outside and jump into the waiting coach. It would only be a few more minutes. She moved to step out onto the porch, but suddenly faltered in mid-step as a broad shadow unexpectedly fell across the entrance and a man barged through its width and straight into her.

Hard hands caught her as they collided, but the touch was momentary and gruff as the big man recovered his balance and pushed her from him. He glowered fiercely down at the two women before moving brusquely away to the ticket window without a word. "Anson Jessop. I'm to ride the stage today."

Jessica glared at Jessop's well-clad back and then looked at Aggie. "Mr. Jessop may dress like a gentleman, but he certainly doesn't act like one."

"I hope you will not think that of all of us you ride with, *señorita*."

Jessica turned to find Diego standing in the doorway behind her with his hat courteously held in his hand.

He flashed her a bright smile. "I, too, am riding the stage today. My name is Diego Terez."

"I'm Jessica Wescott, and this is Aggie Morrison. We're traveling together."

"And with me," Diego declared gallantly, grinning widely at Aggie who colored immediately. "And I was afraid this would be a boring trip."

"Excuse me," a voice interrupted them.

Diego turned to look up at the man waiting to enter the station office. "Excuse me, *señor*! We did not mean to block the way."

Nick nodded, stopping only briefly to look first at Diego and then at the two women, his eyes first passing and then locking in surprise with Jessica's. He turned away shortly. Damn! What was she doing riding the stage? Why this one? Why now? And muttering darkly to himself, he wondered why he should care if she came along.

It wasn't long before everyone was called to board the coach, and the rugged carriage began its long trek from the streets of Independence to the towns and plains that lay between the Missouri River and Santa Fe. For Jessica and Aggie, the beginning hours were lost to the excitement of a new journey and new scenery, but it wasn't long before the excitement began to wane in the face of a continuing series of relay stations.

Stopping and going every ten miles or so, the stage pulled into a station where the horses were changed and where the passengers were allowed a brief stretch of their legs or the opportunity to purchase a quick meal. And, then there was the dust.

It followed the steady rocking and rolling of the constantly moving carriage and floated through the windows to coat the floor and the clothes of the passengers. It was an endless siege, and Jessica silently tried to ignore it and the stiffening ache of her muscles and the grimy taste of dirt in her mouth. She was determined to endure and made herself as comfortable as possible on the hard seat where she was wedged between Aggie and Anson Jessop. Diego and the tall stranger sat across from her.

Talk within the confines of the coach was infrequent at best, the majority of it coming from Diego who had obviously taken a liking to a flustered but flattered Aggie. So with little but the passing scenery and an occasional town or farm to capture her attention, Jessica repeatedly found her mind wandering ahead to the journey's end.

What would it be like to meet her father? What would it be like to meet this man she knew only through occasional letters and gifts? What would she say to him? How would she greet her father, a stranger?

Her grandparents were not overly fond of Nathan Wescott. He'd taken their daughter from them, something they could never forgive him for. Her grandfather, in particular, was fierce in his dislike of his son-in-law and had, Jessica was wise enough to realize, passed some of his prejudice on to her. Because of this, Jessica tried to examine her own true feelings toward her father, but it wasn't easy.

Whenever she thought of him, a variety of complex emotions surged to life—confusion, loneliness, frustration, but most of all, there was anger. Anger because he had sent her away when her mother had died, anger because he would not write more often, anger for his disinterest in her, for the attempts he'd never made to come out East to see her, and anger because she had let him get away with all these things until now.

But even in her anger, there were times when she could almost understand his reasoning. For a man in the middle of a nearly unpopulated territory to raise a child by himself would have been difficult. And as for is infrequent letters and occasional gifts . . . did the scarcity of letters and presents mean he didn't care, or was it, as her grandmother had often gently suggested, he didn't know what to write or what to send?

Even though they were father and daughter, they were complete strangers. How could he write her without knowing what she was interested in? And, choosing gifts would be no easier. He was totally unaware of her likes and dislikes—as she was of his. When she was able to overlook her anger with him and confront her feelings honestly, she had to admit she had the same trouble relating to him. Talking to strangers was no simple matter. How did she write to one?

However, all that was in the past, a past they could have shared if he'd only taken the time over the years to come and see her. Jessica gave an inward sigh of frustration. Why had he never come to see her? Could he be that busy, that committed to the ranch he owned? Was there so much to do in New Mexico that he never had a chance to think of his only child? Didn't he wonder about her as she did about him?

She closed her eyes to the thoughts and the rolling of the stage. There were no answers here. She would have to wait until she reached Santa Fe to ask him these things. And, ask them she would.

"Last stretch you'll be gettin' before nightfall, folks," the driver announced as once again the passengers climbed from the stage while the horses were changed. "Next stop will be for the night, and that's about three hours away."

"Thank you, Diego," Jessica smiled as he assisted her from the coach.

"It is nothing, *señorita*," he answered with a grin.

"A pleasure even though our *Señor* Jessop would not agree."

Jessica laughed, flexing stiff muscles and relishing the feel of solid earth beneath her feet. "I can't imagine anything pleasing *Señor* Jessop."

"Perhaps he will be leaving the stage before us."

"Perhaps," she agreed, falling into step beside him as they wandered toward the station cabin.

"How far do you travel?"

"To Santa Fe."

He grinned widely. "Santa Fe! I know it well. I lived not far from there as a child. You will like it, I think. You have friends there?"

"My father."

"His name is Wescott, too?"

She nodded agreement.

"I am afraid I do not recognize the name. I think perhaps I have heard it before, but I do not think I have met this man."

"Perhaps because he doesn't live in Santa Fe. He has a ranch farther south on the Pecos River."

"Ah! Maybe this is the reason." Aggie emerged from the cabin to join them, and Diego smiled brightly at her and then at Jessica. "You will excuse me for a moment?"

Nodding agreeably, he walked away toward the corrals which lay around the corner of the station building. Anson Jessop would not be able to see him meet Nick there if Jessop came out of the cabin to return to the stage.

Nick was waiting by the enclosures, leaning on the top rail of the nearest corral fence. "Jessop?" he asked looking away from the land beyond the yard.

"Inside. Not a friendly man, *amigo*."

Nick glanced at his friend, a slow smile playing with his lips. "You mean he's not a gentleman to your ladies?"

Diego grinned but sobered quickly. "Yes and no. There is something about him . . ." He shrugged expressively.

"I know. I have the same feeling. What about the women?"

"They are going to Santa Fe. The golden-haired one has a father there."

Nick nodded and moved back from the corral fence. "We'll be gone long before then." And indicating the yard where the horses and coach now stood ready. "We better go."

Seated inside the stage once more with the landscape rolling past the windows, Jessop struck a match to a cigar. Beside him Jessica wrinkled her nose and shared a look of disgust with Aggie. There was no end to this man's rudeness. From the time he'd almost bowled her over at the station, through lunch and the hours in the stage, Jessop's actions could be called anything but polite. He was concerned only with his own comforts. He cared nothing for anyone else's.

Within moments the draft carried in from the windows brought the cigar smoke around and to both the women, leaving them struggling not to choke.

"I wonder, *señor*, if perhaps you could not be more careful with your cigar," Diego suggested after a short hesitation. "The smoke is not agreeing with the ladies."

Jessop looked shortly at Diego before turning indifferently to flick some ash from the cigar out the window.

Jessica smiled feebly at Diego before a fresh gust of smoke caught her fully, and she started to cough.

Suddenly the silent stranger moved, his right arm abruptly flashing to his side and then extending to show the six gun held firmly in his fist. The cold metal touched Jessop's throat. "I think the ladies would like you to put that cigar out, mister. I'm sure you wouldn't mind obliging them."

The color in Jessop's face receded rapidly as he stared down the gun's barrel. He looked up to meet the threat of the weapon echoed in Nick's eyes, and tension filled the coach. What if he refused? Jessop's face hardened and flushed angry red, but left with no choice and feeling the pressure against his throat increase slightly, he relented and hastily threw the cigar out the window.

Not flinching from the murderous glare Jessop focused on him, Nick nodded graciously and withdrew the gun, sliding it smoothly back into its holster. He looked away from the still red-faced but silent Jessop, and his eyes met Jessica's. Her expression was a mixture of astonishment and relief.

Caught watching him, Jessica's gaze quickly fell from his but soon lifted again to seek out the gun strapped snugly to his hip. When she looked up once more, it was to find the stranger's eyes still on her, their cool bluish-gray depths revealing nothing. How could he appear so calm after threatening a man's life? It didn't seem to have affected him at all. Suddenly she saw his lips twitch as an indulgent smile touched his mouth. She was staring but hadn't realized it.

Irritation flooded through her accompanied by hot embarrassment, and she turned away quickly as angry color burned her cheeks. He was amused by her curiosity and surprise! Setting her jaw firmly, she stared determinedly out the window. Arrogance! It seemed to run in the men west of the Mississippi. They appeared to take pleasure in observing other people's ignorance.

She thought again of the man who had saved her the night before. She wondered if he was smiling now, too.

Chapter 3

Before the sun's rays even began to glow on the eastern
horizon, breakfast was served to the passengers while
the station master and his son harnessed the team to the
stage in the cold gray of early morning.

Jessica picked at her food, pushing the scrambled
eggs across her plate. She was more tired than hungry,
and some of the enthusiasm she had felt earlier for the
journey to Santa Fe was beginning to fade with the
prospect of at least another week spent sitting in the
jostling stage which stood waiting outside the cabin
door. She grimaced inwardly. It was not a pleasant
prospect and not one she looked forward to.

"Time to be rollin', folks," the driver announced,
pausing to drain his cup of coffee before leading the
way out the door.

The passengers rose slowly to follow him into the
yard where the sky above was beginning to turn to a
lighter gray. Sleep was still uppermost in everyone's

mind, and talk had so far consisted of little more than mumbled morning greetings. But, hitched to the stage, the horses were far from tired. They tossed their heads restlessly as the people approached, and their hooves pawed at the hard ground as if anxious to be off.

Jessica smiled at their high spirits and felt some of the lethargy clinging to her slip away. It was a new day, a new beginning. She looked out at the miles of open country around her. It stretched endlessly in every direction in an expanse of unsettled, yet fertile land. Excitement stirred again within her. This was the unknown, and it was waiting for her to come and explore.

Slow to board because of looking around her, Jessica climbed into the coach to take her seat beside Aggie and was surprised to find herself facing Anson Jessop's big-boned frame across the stage.

As if reading her thoughts, Diego, who was now seated next to Jessop and opposite Aggie, shrugged lightly. His grin was still wide in the early morning, but his eyes looked heavy from want of sleep.

The stranger climbed on board last, closing the door behind him as the whip cracked above them and the driver gave a shout to urge the team forward.

A quick glance at Jessop seated beside Diego was the only acknowledgement he made to the change in seating arrangements. But, as he eased himself onto the seat next to her, Jessica wondered if it was only her imagination or a trick of the rising sun that made her think a brief smile had momentarily brushed his lips.

His arm brushed hers as he settled himself, and Jessica's pulse unexpectedly quickened at the contact. Her eyes dropped hastily to the floor of the stage as it bounced its way onto the well-worn road. What was happening to her? Her nerves were suddenly tingling with an awareness she'd never felt before. It was almost as if he was touching her even though he was not. It was a kind of hidden power, a magnetism she could sense but not see. She wondered about him.

Tall and lean in build, his movements were smooth and easy. He kept to himself and usually only spoke when spoken to. But, despite his unobtrusive manner, there was an alertness about him. It showed in his ever-watchful eyes. It reminded Jessica of a cat waiting to spring.

Last night when she had gone outside for a breath of fresh air before retiring to the hard bunk provided for her at the stage station, she had seen him in the yard. For a startling moment, standing tall and silent in the starlight, she had thought he was the man who had rescued her from her would-be assailants in Independence.

She smiled lightly now, putting her head back against the wall of the stage and closing her eyes to try to shut out the scene around her. The world was small, but not so small as to throw her together with the same man twice in twenty-four hours.

She was just not used to the men out here yet. They all looked alike with heavy guns on their hips and broad-brimmed hats. Both things combined to make them seem much taller and bigger than the men back East who wore derby hats and finely tailored clothes.

The smile lingered on her lips. Somehow she could not imagine the tall stranger beside her wearing a derby hat with a suit coat and carefully arranged tie.

Jessica woke with a jolt some time later as the stage lurched over a rut in the road. Startled from an amazingly sound sleep, she was shocked to find herself laying heavily against the stranger. Of all people to use as a pillow!

She rapidly retreated from the warm strength of his body and straightened in her seat. A guilty flush burned her cheeks as she glanced quickly around the coach at the other passengers.

Thankfully all three men and Aggie appeared to be sleeping. But, when Jessica glanced hopefully back up at the stranger to assure herself that he really was asleep, it was to find his solemn but warm blue-gray eyes on her.

"I'm sorry," she stammered in a low voice, her cheeks flushing hotly. "I didn't mean to . . ."

The stranger moved, easing himself up in the seat and pushing the hat he had tilted over his eyes back on his head. For a moment, he didn't speak, choosing instead to look steadily into Jessica's eyes before responding. "Nothing to be sorry about, ma'am. It seems everyone's tired."

She followed his nod towards the two men across from them who were both breathing deeply with their eyes closed. "Yes . . . it's been a long trip."

"It'll get longer," he replied staring out the window at the passing land. "By this afternoon we'll be getting into the plains. It'll be hot there this time of year."

"You've been here before, Mr. . . ." she asked, already sure of his answer. He was too at ease here, too confident and accepting of his surroundings not to have traveled this way before.

"Driscoll," he provided and turned his head to look down at her. "Many times, Miss . . ."

"Wescott. Jessica Wescott," she supplied. "You must like it here then."

"Usually."

"Usually?"

His eyebrow arched slowly as he watched a small frown touch her face. He hadn't realized until now how green her eyes were. "I don't suppose most people like a place all the time."

"What makes you not like it here—sometimes?"

He shrugged. "The days are hot, the nights cold. It's not an easy life here. People die every day, killed by bandits or Indians. Livestock is stolen, crops won't grow." He moved his shoulders again.

"Then why do you stay?" she asked in amazement.

"Because I like it, prefer it to the East." He smiled faintly at her look of doubtful surprise. "Yes, I've been there. But I wouldn't want to stay. Life's too set there. Everything's arranged by rules and laws—unwritten as well as written. There's too many things you have to do or aren't supposed to."

"But you have to have law. Otherwise . . ."

"Otherwise people would steal from and cheat each other?"

"Well, yes, but . . ."

"But that happens every day—here and back there. It's just that back East people are more subtle in the taking. They hide behind lawyers and pieces of paper."

"And here?"

"If a man steals from his neighbor, his neighbor shoots him."

"You make it sound so simple, so right," she protested.

"It is simple. Simple and quick."

"And just?"

"Not always. East or west of the Mississippi, the strong still prey on the weak."

Jessica's eyes clouded thoughtfully. "Are you saying that only the strong survive then? That the weak can never win?"

"I'm saying survival *is* the law, at least out here, and anyone can win if they want to and if they find others who believe the same."

"Democracy," she responded softly. She looked up to find him watching her. It seemed strange to suddenly confront an idea she had always merely accepted as fact. "It's more than a word."

"Mr. Lincoln thought so."

"You fought in the War?"

His expression darkened, and he looked away. Unwanted memories rushed back unexpectedly. He'd seen so much senseless waste. Senseless death. "Yes."

Jessica felt him withdraw from her, but she didn't want him to. "Would you mind if I asked what you do now? For a living, I mean."

"Drift."

"Drift?" she asked in confusion.

"I don't stay in one place long. I move around quite a bit."

"But how do you live? I mean, don't you have a job?"

"I've had a lot of jobs, mostly working for ranchers."

Jessica started slightly, hope springing to life inside her as she turned to face him more directly. Perhaps he knew her father. "Have you ever worked in New Mexico?"

"Some," he answered, seeing her sudden interest and again struck by how small she seemed sitting next to him. It'd been a long time since he'd spent any time with a woman such as she. The War, the aftermath, drifting from state to state . . .

"Have you ever heard of Nathan Wescott?"

Nick shook his head. "Can't say as I have." He watched her sag back into her seat, disappointment clearly reflected in the green depths of her eyes. "You know him?"

"He's my father."

The defensive note in her voice challenged Nick, dared him to ask the obvious question, but he didn't ask and his face remained solemn. "You've been here before then."

"No. Well, yes . . . when I was little." She looked away from him, seeking refuge from her confusion in the view beyond the window.

Nick watched her, his eyes narrowing. Expressions passed over her face as rapidly as the pages of a book could be turned, and despite himself, he felt his curiosity grow. She was coming to see her father, apparently for the first time in several years. Why?

His eyes slid over her carefully and expensively dressed form. What was an obviously well-educated and fairly wealthy, if not rich, young woman doing coming across the frontier alone in search of her father?

Suspiciously his mind went to Jessop, and his eyes turned to the man sleeping across from him. She didn't know him. He was certain she didn't. Or, was he? Where was the family Jessop was supposed to meet?

"You coming out from Boston?" he hazarded a guess.

She nodded absently, not really listening. "Yes."

"You planning on staying?"

She frowned, her attention returning to him once more. "I don't know." Her gaze fell for a moment before she looked up to meet his eyes. The question was there. He wanted to know what she meant. She hesitated. She could almost tell him . . . almost. Pride intervened, and her chin tilted defiantly. "Don't you have any family?"

"Not out here. My mother died when I was quite young. My father just a few years back."

Immediately regretting her brashness, she faltered. "I'm sorry . . . my mother's dead, too. She died when I was only a baby."

"Sister?" he asked indicating Aggie.

Jessica smiled quickly. "No. Companion, or chaperone if you like." He looked harder at Aggie, and Jessica's smile deepened. She knew he was thinking of Aggie as too young for such a position. "Our intended chaperone is probably on her way back to Boston by now. She wasn't well enough to make the trip." She paused, her eyes shining at a mental picture he could not see. "It was probably for the better, too. She hated it here as soon as she got off the train."

"And you don't?"

"No. Not at all." She paused, trying to find the words to express how she felt about this new land she had come to. "It's so different here. The people, the places . . . it's exciting."

"Exciting?" Nick repeated. "This trip might seem exciting and the life and people here more interesting than back East, but you're going to need a better reason than that to stay. This is a hard place for a woman.''

"For me, you mean,'' she retorted, her temper flaring in her own defense.

"For any woman, but yes, it would be especially hard for someone like you—fresh from the East and cities and plumbing and paved streets and friendly neighbors. Santa Fe is an old Spanish town. It's been part of this territory for more years than you or I can remember, but it's nothing like Boston. It's in the middle of the New Mexico Territory, a territory, mind you, not a state. There's no law.''

"They have a governor . . .''

"Who stays in a town far from the hardships life in a territory can offer.'' He saw her frown. "If you want to stay, Miss Wescott, you have to like it here. You can't mind the dust and the heat. You can't care if your nearest neighbor is a day's ride away and the nearest town is farther still. You have to get used to people carrying guns wherever they go, and you have to be prepared to wake up some morning and find your livestock gone, stolen by Indians or bandits.''

He paused to stare down at her, his eyes narrowing. "Yes, it's exciting here, but a good part of the time, the excitement is something you'd rather do without. You'd best remember that before you decide if you want to stay.''

Jessica met his hard stare. For a moment she'd thought he'd been trying to frighten her, but she realized now that was not his intent. His words were hard but honest. They described and warned of trials and discomforts, possible heartbreak and pain. They tried to give her an accurate picture of what this land he loved was like, and Jessica was surprised to find she was not discouraged by what he said. She really wanted to stay . . .

Before this moment she had never allowed herself to truly think about her reasons for coming west. She had never examined her feelings too closely. She had never told anyone or even admitted to herself that when she left Boston, she had left for good. She had no intention of returning. She had come west to find her father, yes. But, more, she had come west to find her home, and it didn't matter what difficulties lay ahead or what obstacles would be set in her path. She had come to find her family, her origins, her roots.

She wanted to be part of this land, to be part of him—the parent she did not know. She wanted to prove to herself and to him that she did belong, could belong in the home he had sent her away from. She wanted to know him, know what she had lost, what she could have had, what she could still have if she was willing to try.

So, defiantly, her eyes shone brightly at the challenge this stranger presented. "I want to stay."

A slow smile formed on Nick's mouth as he looked down at her, but there was no humor in his expression. She might be small, but there was iron in her. She wouldn't bend easily. It might be enough. It could be if her determination lasted, if she was willing to continue to listen and learn. After a long moment, he nodded slightly and softly agreed, "Miss Wescott, I believe you will."

A teeth-rattling bump broke the link between them and woke the rest of the passengers. They all hurriedly regained their balance and looked through the windows to see yet another stage station ahead with a team of fresh horses already harnessed and waiting in the yard.

Jessica felt the private moment she had shared with this stranger regretfully disappear. But her regret puzzled her. Why did she feel so drawn to this man? Why did he fascinate her so?

The stage pulled to a stop in front of the low-set cabin, and the driver called a greeting to the waiting men standing in the yard. The coach door opened immediately, and Anson Jessop and Diego climbed out first. The stranger followed but stopped to assist Aggie to the ground. Then he turned to help Jessica.

Jessica accepted his hand and moved to step down. However, before she was halfway out of the coach, it unexpectedly lurched forward, and her hand was jerked from his grip. She started to fall. A cry caught in her throat. The ground loomed before her, but suddenly she was safe. Nick caught her, his arms locking firmly around her and pulling her away from the danger of the large wheels of the carriage.

Held securely against him, Jessica stared into the blue-gray of his eyes. From somewhere she heard the driver yell, "Watch them horses!" But the cry seemed far away. All she could see was Nick. All she could feel was the strength of his hands and the warmth of his gaze.

Nick released her slowly, lowering her gently to the ground. His eyes didn't leave hers. Not even when he reluctantly took his hands from her when she was standing securely on the ground before him.

Suddenly breathless, her skin burning from the brief contact with his hard body, Jessica managed to find her voice. "Thank you, Mr. Driscoll."

Nick nodded and raised a hand to touch the brim of his hat.

Jessica watched the gesture and felt her heart turn over as time faded back to a moonlit street where another stranger had acknowledged those same words with the same silent answer.

The rest of the day passed through a succession of stage stations, a rushed lunch, and slowly rising temperatures. The land around them was beginning to turn from rolling green grasslands where an occasional farm could be seen to low and long-running flat lands. And, as the miles disappeared behind them, the terrain did not improve.

The second night out they stayed at a station where a grove of trees lined a flow of water called Cottonwood Creek. It was an open place with rolling meadows and tall grass, but when they left it behind the next morning, it was to enter another world barren of water and civilization.

Two days came and went while the temperature continued to soar, and the dust became even worse than it had before. With the land baked dry under a constant siege from the sun, the dust was thicker and more constant. It followed in the wake of the coach in a huge cloud and clung to their clothes like a second skin.

Settlements soon ceased to exist, and farms were rare. The only sign of human life was an occasional herd of cattle which seemed to spread for miles over the flat plains.

None of the traveling conditions or surroundings gave root to much conversation, and the passengers spoke little. They merely endured. Each day became a duplicate of the last, bringing with it the same rocking coach, the same rutted road, and the same stagnant air of grime and heat. It was numbing.

Only the night brought a type of relief. When the coach pulled to a stop for the night, it meant a chance to flee from the stuffy confines of the stage. It meant escaping to fresh air—even if it was still hot, and as the stage drew into a yard for yet another night and everyone eagerly climbed out, Jessica stepped to the ground and breathed deeply of the almost dust-free air. She stretched and brushed absently at the accumulated powdered dirt on her skirt. The fading light of afternoon was coloring the sky with brilliant colors of pink, purple and orange. It was a constant source of amazement to her when she saw the glowing sun set here. The sky seemed so much larger here than back East.

She turned reluctantly to follow the others toward the station house, only half-listening to the talk of the driver and the station master behind her.

"Early today, Hank. No trouble I hope?"

The driver shook his head, raising his forearm to wipe the sweat from his brow. "No, just good horses, I reckon. That and the wantin' of havin' some of your Lil's cookin' again."

At that moment the station door opened, and a middle-aged woman wearing a faded gingham dress appeared. "Hank, you devil, you're early."

"He was just sayin' he couldn't wait to get here to taste your cookin' again," her husband explained with a grin.

Jessica smiled at the woman who blushed happily at the compliment. Few of the relay stations had women living in them. It was good to see another of her own sex, especially someone so at ease and used to living in this country. Jessica licked her dry lips and moved forward to meet her.

Dinner was served shortly after their arrival and was all their driver had implied it would be. Liz buzzed happily around the table, depositing a plate before each person that was covered by a large steak and a huge helping of mashed potatoes and steaming carrots. Words immediately died away as everyone picked up their forks in favor of food. Talk came again only after the hunger pangs of all were appeased and no one could eat any more.

Satisfied sighs echoed around the table, and even Anson Jessop's face was less grim on a full stomach. It didn't take long for the men to push their chairs back and drift outside to smoke and exchange news, but Jessica and Aggie stayed behind to help collect the numerous plates left from the meal. Liz would not let them remain in the kitchen to assist with the washing, though. Instead she hurried them out.

"I'm used to doing this," she told them with a warm smile. "You two go on out and stretch your legs and get some fresh air. Just don't wander too far from the cabin."

Thus relieved of the cleaning, Jessica began to lead the way to the door but abruptly and purposely hesitated before reaching it. "I'll meet you outside, Aggie. I want to get something from our room."

The statement was only an excuse, but Aggie accepted it eagerly as Jessica knew she would. Diego was outside, and Aggie wanted to be with him. The two had been spending a considerable amount of time together at night during the past few days, wandering off together to take strolls when Aggie didn't think Jessica would notice.

Jessica smiled as she stepped out the door into the cool evening air moments later, for off to her right she could see two figures disappearing around the corner of the cabin. Mrs. Abbott had told her to keep an eye on Aggie, but Jessica did not think that responsibility should touch on a fleeting romance with a polite and charming gentleman, even if the gentleman was wearing a gun.

She wandered slowly toward the stone wall surrounding the station, taking deep breaths of the clean, sharp air that was tinged with so many unknown scents and sounds.

Above her the sky was partly obscured by clouds, and the stars and moon shed only dim light through the denseness of the floating masses. Because of this, Jessica found it difficult to see farther than a few feet out into the blackness beyond the gate. She had never realized how dark it could be at night with no street lamps to show the way.

"I wouldn't wander about by yourself, ma'm."

At the sound of the voice Jessica started sharply and swung around to face Nick, her heart leaping abruptly into her throat to hammer madly.

"It's not safe."

"Whyever not?" she asked, attempting to recover control of her scattered senses. Where had he come from? She had not heard him come up behind her.

He gestured to the wall. "Haven't you noticed this wall?"

"Yes, but what of it?" she inquired harshly, her temper rising at the stupidity of the question and at the tone of authority in his voice.

"It's there for a purpose. To keep Indians out."

"Indians!"

"That's right, ma'm. Indians. The fence was built for the defense of the station in case of an attack."

Jessica looked away into the blackness beyond the wall and unconsciously took a step backward. "I didn't think Indians would come so close."

"They will if they want something."

She looked up at him uncertainly. His face was hidden in the shadows of his hat. Was he mocking her? She didn't think so. She moved uneasily, frightened but unwilling to admit it. She attempted instead to use his presence in her defense. "If it's not safe, Mr. Driscoll, why are you out here?"

"Two reasons," he answered quietly, pushing his hat back on his head. "The first is because I know what can happen and am armed to defend myself. The second is because I saw you out here and didn't figure you knew any better."

"Know any better . . . Mr. Driscoll, I appreciate your concern, but I can take care of myself. If I heard or saw an Indian, I can assure you I wouldn't stand here waiting for him to come closer."

"If you saw or heard him before he reached you, I doubt you would. But you wouldn't see or hear him first."

"How can you be so sure?" she retorted hotly.

"You didn't hear me, did you?"

Chapter 4

The next morning Jessica awakened to the quiet stirrings of Aggie's movements in the room.

"Is it time to get up already?" Jessica moaned stretching her arms above her head while the golden length of her hair flowed over her pillow in a thick cascade.

"Not if you don't want to," Aggie answered with a shy smile. "The driver found a pin missing from the wheel or some such thing, and we can't leave until they fix it."

"A reprieve," Jessica sighed. As old and hard as the bed was, it was too comfortable to get out of just yet.

"Liz will fix you breakfast whenever you get up, so if you want to lay in bed for awhile . . ."

"I think I will, if only for a few minutes."

The two women exchanged understanding smiles. It was nice to be able to walk on solid ground again for a time and to enjoy a leisurely rising rather than the hurried pace set so that the stage was on the road by dawn. Riding the coach was getting them where they wanted to go, but it was not the most comfortable way to travel—with a schedule that was demanding and difficult to get used to.

Aggie slipped from the room, and Jessica lay listening to the various sounds coming from both inside and outside of the station cabin walls. None of them were very familiar sounds, however, so despite the bed's warm comfort, curiosity urged her to rise and explore.

It only took a few moments to dress in a skirt and blouse she had brought for traveling, but instead of taking the time to pin her hair on top of or behind her head as she had been doing, she quickly braided it into a long strand and let it trail casually down her back.

Liz was in the kitchen when Jessica emerged from the small room she and Aggie had shared, and the other woman was quick to set a plate of scrambled eggs and bacon in front of her. But after eating, once again there was no helping Liz in the kitchen. Jessica was urged to go outside and leave Liz behind. It made her feel guilty, but her guilt was quickly forgotten as she stepped outside into the bright morning light.

She raised a hand to shade her eyes and looked out over the yard. The day was still crisp and cool from the night, and the sun was still low on the eastern horizon. The uncomfortable heat of the later hours was a long way off yet, and with the blue sky above spotted with large white clouds, it seemed to her to be the beginning of a beautiful day.

She breathed in the fresh air deeply and sought out

the winding length of the Arkansas River where it lay beyond the yard. From where she stood by the station house, it was a glimmering mass of moving water. For the past few days the coach had been following the river's course. It was a welcome and much-needed supply of water, but unfortunately, its presence did little to curb the heat and dust of the land surrounding it.

Abruptly Jessica's eyes fell on the long stone wall encircling the station yard, and some of the sunshine immediately faded. She quickly raised her gaze again to scan the open land beyond the fence for movement. There was none. And there probably wouldn't be any either, she thought with a shrug of disgust. Indians, indeed.

Turning sharply away from the sight of the wall, she moved toward the corner of the cabin where she could hear a whip humming. She didn't want to think about last night, or him. He disturbed her in a way she couldn't define. When he was near, her senses seemed to heighten their activity, and her confidence seemed to desert her.

A horse's frightened cry greeted her as she rounded the cabin wall, and she stopped in surprised horror as she saw a large man swing a whip back and then bring it crashing down on the back of a horse tethered helplessly to a pole in the center of the corral.

The whip was brought back again, and without thinking Jessica broke into a run. A frantic glance around her showed there was no one else in sight. The man was alone with the trapped animal. The whip fell once more as she reached the gate and burst inside.

"Stop it! What are you doing?" she demanded

angrily, her breath coming rapidly from between her lips as she squared herself to confront the horse's tormentor.

The man stopped, bringing the arm he had cocked for yet another swing down to his side. "You speakin' to me?"

"Yes, I am," she retorted sharply. "What do you think you're doing, beating that horse like this?"

He looked from her to the horse. "I'm teachin' him some manners, you might say. He ain't learned to be polite yet."

"If by polite you mean he hasn't learned to obey you, beating him won't make him understand what you want. You'll only hurt him, break him, but you won't train him." Her grandfather was a great admirer of horse flesh and, in fact, had a large stable where Jessica had spent more than a fair share of her time. Being there so often, she had watched horses being broken to ride many times. But not like this. Never like this. There were no whips . . .

His eyes narrowed on her. "And just how would you happen to know so much? You ever broke a horse?"

"No, I haven't," she answered, stammering angrily for words. "But . . ."

"Then leave it to people who know how." His hard expression chilled her, but then it changed subtly. His eyes dropped to roam over the soft contours of her body with slow insolence. His lips twisted into a leering smile. "If you'll excuse me now, ma'm, much as I like the company of pretty women, I ain't got time for you at the moment."

Frustrated rage flared in Jessica as he turned his back on her and prepared to strike again. She wouldn't let him do it! She leapt forward and grabbed the corded whip, yanking on it with all her strength.

Caught off balance, the man staggered back. He stumbled awkwardly, but managed to keep a strong hold on the length of woven rawhide. It remained firmly in his grasp as he caught himself and swung to stare at her. His look was one of disbelief. But the disbelief was swept away in a wave of quivering anger.

The whip Jessica still held on to was ripped suddenly and roughly from her hands, tearing the soft skin of her fingers and palms. She winced at the unexpected pain, but fear wiped the pain away as she found herself confronting a now hostile madman.

Angered beyond reason, his eyes were wild and his chest was heaving. She took a faltering step backwards. What had she done? Abruptly she became aware of how quiet it was in the enclosure. There was only the nervously dancing horse to see her here with him. He advanced a step. She retreated. But, there was no place to run.

In petrified silence she watched his arm go back to a cocked position once more. This time, though, his intended victim was not the horse. It was her. The whip started to move, and with a fluttering heart Jessica braced herself for the blow.

Suddenly a shot rang out. It broke the still morning with its sharp retort and the black whip dropped to the ground like a writhing snake.

With pounding eardrums Jessica stared in stunned amazement at the man who, grimacing in pain, now held his bleeding wrist.

A hand touched her shoulder, and she looked up to see Nick beside her. His face was a cold mask, his eyes icy gray with suppressed fury. But he wasn't watching her. He was watching the wounded man, and his gun was locked firmly in his fist to insure the man did not move. "Are you all right?"

It took a moment to respond. Her mouth and lips were unusually dry, and it was difficult to make her muscles work. All her joints seemed paralyzed. She finally managed a quick nod and pointed a shaking finger toward the horse. "He was . . . he was beating that horse."

Nick threw a sidelong glance at the white-eyed, prancing animal before returning his attention to the bleeding man before him. "You work here?"

"He did," a voice responded as Liz's husband entered the corral from behind them. He looked gravely from the whip on the ground to the horse's back. "He ain't no more."

"Wait a minute . . ." the man began in blustering protest.

"You don't got no minute. I hired you to break horses into harness for the stage, not to break them with a whip until they couldn't stand. They ain't good to anyone dead."

The man stiffened, anger once again distorting his face. He glared at the men confronting him. He wasn't backing down, and tense silence descended on the corral. No one moved.

Jessica shifted nervously, glad Nick was standing beside her. She glanced hurriedly up at him, but his face was expressionless.

Abruptly the man stiffened. He jerked forward to lean down and snatch up his whip. As he straightened, his eyes caught Jessica's. She flinched at the hate she met there, but then he was striding away and into the barn. It wasn't long before the pounding beat of hooves echoed on the stable floor, and the man emerged from the building, driving his horse at a full run.

As he raced onto the plains beyond the station yard, the station master turned to Jessica. "I'm sorry, ma'm. Did he hurt you?"

"No. No, he didn't. But the horse . . ."

He moved to the terrified animal with the confidence and skill of years of experience, muttering soothing sounds and firmly but gently catching the lead rope. "He should be okay after a bit. We can fix his back . . ."

"Can't you let him go?" Jessica blurted, surprising even herself with her question.

"Let him go?" he echoed in confusion.

"Yes . . . I mean . . . I think he deserves his freedom." She watched him look doubtfully up at the horse. "I'll pay for him."

"Ma'm, I couldn't let you . . ."

"I will, and then if he's mine, I can do what I want with him. Isn't that right?"

"Yes, ma'm, but I really didn't pay to get him. I caught him right off the range."

"Then you can send him back with profit as if you'd sold him to the stage line."

"Yes, ma'm, I reckon, but . . ."

"Aggie," Jessica said turning to the fence where all the others had come to stand. "Pay him whatever he says the horse is worth."

"Yes, Miss Jessica," Aggie quickly responded,

habit making her respectfully agree to the note of authority in Jessica's voice. She hurried away toward the cabin.

"Will you turn him loose?" Jessica asked.

Flabbergasted, the man turned to look helplessly at Nick who had been watching her in silent appraisal the entire time. His gun was back in his holster now, and his gaze was a warm blue rather than stormy gray. He hesitated for a moment but then nodded and moved forward to help hold the horse until it was freed of the halter.

With whooping yells and swinging their hats, the men drove the startled horse out the gate. The liberated animal charged from the enclosure as if demons were chasing it and stampeded away from captivity to the freedom of the land beyond. Everyone stayed to watch it go, waiting until it vanished into the brush beyond before moving once more.

Shaking his head incredulously, the station master went by Jessica with a sheepish grin while those who had viewed the scene from the fence made their way back to the cabin. Diego sent Jessica a bright smile, as did Liz. Anson Jessop merely shuffled off without change in expression.

"You sure are one headstrong woman," Nick said from behind her, but a ghost of a smile was playing across his lips. He was the only one who had remained except her.

Jessica looked back to where the horse had gone. "I'm glad he's free." She turned to face Nick, brushing her hands down her skirt as she did so. She winced in pain immediately. The whip had been pulled from her hands . . . But before she could look herself, Nick had trapped her wrists within the strong circle of his fingers. The skin of her palms was badly burned, some skin being partially torn away.

An exasperated sigh escaped Nick, and he grasped her one arm tightly and pulled her out of the corral to the nearby water trough. "Put your hands under there."

Jessica meekly moved to obey, sensing a return of his anger. She somehow knew he wasn't in the mood to argue. She put her stinging hands under the spout, and he began to pump the handle. Water gushed out in a burst, hitting the sensitive skin with considerable force. She cried out and jerked back, but he immediately shoved her hands back under the cleansing liquid.

"You deserve to hurt after pulling a damn fool stunt like that," he told her sharply. He still couldn't believe it. What had she thought she was doing trying to face down a man twice her size who was holding a whip? She had more courage than sense!

"What was I supposed to do?" she snapped back just as sharply, gritting her teeth against the pain. "Stand there and watch him beat the poor animal?"

"You could've come got me."

"I didn't know where you were. And besides, how did I know you'd help?"

He glared down at her. "How'd you know I wouldn't?" He jerked her hands from under the water to look at them critically. "You better get up to the house and have Liz put some ointment on them before we go. They're almost done fixing that wheel."

She turned to leave but stopped when he started to follow. "I can find the way by myself. I'm not helpless."

His eyes narrowed, and he stopped to gaze solemnly down at her. He raised his hands to rest them on his hips. "Maybe I want to make sure you get there. I wouldn't want you fainting from the sight of blood."

"I don't faint."

He drew himself up to his full height. "Maybe you should. It might mellow that stubborn streak in you that gets you into so much trouble."

"I'm not stubborn," she protested unreasonably, not liking his condescending tone or manner. "And I don't get myself into trouble."

His eyebrows shot up, and the beginnings of a small grin tugged at his mouth. She really was full of surprises. "Then what would you call that little incident in the corral?" he drawled casually, crossing his arms over his chest.

Jessica glared back up at him and then at the empty corral, knowing he was right and hating him for it. She frowned fiercely, needing an answer that would support her. It took a moment to find one. "A difference of opinion."

Nick watched her swing away, his jaw dropping slightly at the absurdity of her answer. Then, he began to laugh.

She spun around to face him again. "What are you laughing at?"

He sobered slightly, pushing his hat back on his head to meet her sparking eyes across the yard. "You."

"I am not an object of amusement," she retorted hotly and stamped her foot. She started to turn away but stopped. "However, even if you happen to think so, you could at least behave like a gentleman and wait until I'm gone to give into your . . . beliefs." Once more she started to turn away. "But then, on the other hand," she continued, spinning back. "I forget. There's no such thing as a gentleman west of the Mississippi."

With a righteous swish of her skirts, she whirled away with her head aloft. And, he had to give her credit, her steps only faltered slightly as she swallowed more angry words when he started laughing again.

The twilight beyond the stage windows darkened into night, and with the going of the sun, the temperature began to fall. Prepared for the worst, Nick handed Jessica a rough woolen blanket. "Wrap this around yourself and your friend. Your combined body heat and this blanket will keep off most of the cold."

"What about you?" Jessica asked in concern, coloring as she forced herself to continue. "We could share . . . I mean . . ."

The small smile she was beginning to know too well touched his mouth. "It's all right, ma'm. I'm more used to this weather than you are and, I have my coat."

Nodding quick agreement, she turned away to Aggie, and they began wrapping the blanket around them as the men shrugged into coats to protect themselves from the cold of the night plains.

The last of the rays from the setting sun vanished behind the horizon, and the only light came from the lanterns hung on either side of the coach and from the few hearty stars that managed to blink through the heavy cloud banks that had been gathering in the sky during the day.

For Jessica it seemed odd to be traveling at night, and she was struck by how empty the land seemed with no light shining upon it. During the day it was so wide

and endless. At night, it was so cold and lonely. She
wondered if her father felt the same way. When the day
was done and he was alone in the house he had built for
himself and his family, did he get lonely? Or, was the
land enough?

Under the cover of darkness, Jessica glanced up at
Nick Driscoll as he sat silently beside her. The lanterns
were casting shadows across his face. What was he
thinking? Feeling? He belonged here. She could feel it,
but did the night hold any secrets for him? Any hidden
fears? She couldn't imagine this man being afraid. But
everyone was afraid of something. Weren't they?

From outside the cold slowly seeped in, working its
way through the blankets and coats they hid behind to
relentlessly finger their skin. It was difficult to ignore it
for there was nothing to distract their attention from it.

"How far do you go, *amigo*?" Diego inquired of
Nick in an effort to turn thoughts in the couch from the
cold. "This is, if you don't mind me asking?"

"Fort Dodge."

"Fort Dodge? Me also. I hear there is work there
for a man who has run down on his luck."

"So goes the talk," Nick agreed casually. "I've
friends there to put me up if what's being said isn't
true."

"It is good," Diego commented nodding, "to have
friends or family about when one travels so much. I,
myself, wish I could travel on to Santa Fe for I have a
sister who lives not far from there, but there is no
money here to make this possible." He pulled emphatically at his empty pockets in the shadows of the coach.

"Diego, if I could help . . ." Jessica offered.

Diego held up a hand. "No, no, *señorita*, I would

not hear of such a thing.'' He touched his heart. ''Pride is too strong. And, besides, I do not think it would look so good for you to come home to your father with a stranger who has nothing in his pockets.''

Jessica smiled. She was familiar with male pride from bouts with her grandfather. ''If you're sure?''

''I am certain, kind lady. I could not impose,'' Diego told her. ''However, I will accept an invitation to visit you next time I make the trip to Santa Fe.''

''You have one.''

Diego laughed, his teeth flashing brightly in the dark coach. ''And I accept.''

Silence settled on the stage once more as it continued to rock over what Jessica was sure was a barely visible road, and soon, despite the more than occasional jolts, the cold, and the discomfort, she found herself growing tired as time carried them on into the night. The wheel had delayed their usual early morning departure, and then there had been all the excitement with the horse.

She closed her eyes. Her hands still stung a little. A small smile curved her lips as she remembered Nick's laughter. He was right about her always managing to get into trouble. Her grandmother had constantly reminded her of that fact . . .

A hand on her shoulder brought her slowly back to consciousness, and Jessica lifted a weary head to look up into Nick's deeply shadowed face.

''We're at the next station,'' he told her quietly. ''We'll only be here for a few hours and there's not much room for all of us to lay down, but at least we can stretch our legs.''

Jessica nodded absently, blinking away the sleep

that had claimed and still drugged her senses, and turned to wake Aggie as he slipped out of the coach.

Inside the cabin the station master gave up his cot and room for the two women before leading the men to the only other room available for them to sleep in.

"We'll be arriving in Fort Dodge just about noon tomorrow," the driver told everyone as he followed the other men toward the room. "For those of you going on to Santa Fe, you'll be able to rest up there some before we push on."

Jessica nodded at his words and sank down onto the hearth by the fire to warm herself, leaving Aggie to go to their room alone. She didn't feel like moving another step.

"You should try to get some sleep," Nick told her, stopping to stand over her instead of following the rest of the men to the room where they were to sleep. The soft crackling of the flames was lighting her hair to a golden glow. It reminded him of the first time he'd seen her. The moon had done the same thing.

"What's the use of going to bed when you'll only be getting up again in two or three hours?"

He shrugged and looked across the room to where a pot-bellied stove stood. "Coffee?"

"Please." She stared into the fire, watching it finger the burning logs as he crossed the room silently to rummage for some cups and the hot brew. How far away Boston seemed now. She could almost believe she'd been traveling on a stagecoach her entire life.

"This'll help," Nick announced, handing her a tin cup and easing his lean frame down onto the hearth beside her. He watched as she took a long drink of the black liquid. The firelight was playing across her features. He could see her fatigue there. "Why don't you stay in Fort Dodge for a day or two to catch up on your rest before going on to Santa Fe?" he asked softly.

She lifted her head to smile at him, his face fully revealed to her now with his hat off and the shimmering glow of the fire dancing around them. His hair was dark and thick. She'd never really noticed before. But then, except for mealtime, he always had his hat on. "I almost wish I could, but I can't. I've waited for too long as it is."

He sipped his coffee for a moment. "It means that much to you to see your father?"

She hesitated, thinking over past time, lost time, and to the time ahead. "Yes. Yes, it does. I should have come back here to live with him years ago."

He waited for her to continue, but she did not. Instead she retreated into thoughts that were beyond him, and again he found himself wondering what she was doing here alone and seeking a man she claimed as her father. Still suspicious, willing to believe the worst, he asked, "Have you ever been south?"

She looked up at him absently, taking a moment before realizing he required an answer to his question. "South? You mean to the Confederate states?"

He nodded.

"No," she answered with a small, indifferent shrug. "I almost went to Richmond once, but the War broke out and we never went. I'm afraid while you're well traveled, the only places I've been other than Boston are all cities north of the Mason-Dixon line."

"Europe?"

"Only a dream."

She reminded him of a dream in that moment, her

hair glowing in the light, her eyes shiny with melancholy and memories. A man could get lost in those eyes, could bury his hands in the richness of her hair. She was beautiful.

Shaking himself mentally he abruptly rose quickly to his feet. Obviously she wasn't the only one who was tired. "You should try to get some sleep," he told her gruffly. "You've got a long trip ahead of you yet."

Jessica sighed reluctantly and stood. She was too tired to notice the change of tone in his voice. "I suppose you're right." She set her cup aside and stepped forward to go to the waiting room, but unexpectedly her foot caught. She tripped over the length of her skirts and was in his arms before she realized what happened. She tilted her head back in surprise to look up at him.

For a long moment he stared down into her eyes. Then, slowly, his head lowered to hers. It seemed so natural. It was as if she'd been waiting for him all this time. Their lips met.

Unconsciously Jessica moved closer into the security of his arms and felt the pressure of his mouth on hers increase. She didn't resist but trembled against him, feeling the raw strength of his muscles beneath her fingers.

The embrace deepened, and Nick drew her closer until the soft contours of her body were pressed to him. She yielded to his touch readily, almost as if she was melting into him. It was a heady sensation, and his heartbeat quickened.

Time and reality ceased for Jessica. Her mind and body flooded with sensations she had never experienced before, and her head spun with the dizzying effects he was loosening within her. It felt as if he was drawing her very essence from her, draining her until she was sure she could give no more.

Uncounted moments slipped past, and Nick lifted his mouth from hers to feel her sag weakly against him. He buried his hands in the golden thickness of her hair and pulled her head back to look down into her face. He could feel the fatigue in her body and see it reflected in the depths of her eyes. But there was more than weariness shining there. "You need your sleep." He bent to brush his lips against hers once more, but the intended briefness lingered and they clung together once more. It was a strong inner battle he fought in order to release her. "And you better go now while the going's good."

She felt his hands take hold of her arms and push her gently away, innocence blocking the meaning of his words and showing in the eyes she raised to him.

He groaned at the enticing feminine sight she made and quickly propelled her toward the bedroom door. She was beautiful and, at the moment, vulnerable. Too tired to resist and perhaps too trusting to try. He watched her go. She stopped at the door and turned to look back at him. He held his breath, hoping she would stay and yet praying she would go. The door closed behind her, and he turned away.

Desire and anger collided head on within him, and he muttered darkly to himself. He'd known she'd meant trouble when he'd first seen her. He'd known it! He cursed himself severely and ran a hand through his hair. Tonight shouldn't have happened. It would't have happened if she'd just gone to bed like she was supposed to.

He swore softly. He wasn't going to let himself get

more deeply involved than he was already. He didn't have the time, and she wasn't ready. She was young and inexperienced at life. She hadn't been over as many roads as he had. Hadn't seen the things, done the things—even heard of some of the things he'd been through.

Growing up in an unsettled territory, following a father who roamed the wildernesses of this new nation at will and struggling to survive, then fighting through a war that had pitted brother against brother as well as state against state. It hadn't been an easy way to live. It had taken him through things people should never have to see. Especially not someone like her. She was too lovely, too fine—a lady.

He hadn't much experience with ladies. The only woman he had known well who could qualify as one had been his mother, and since her death when he had been so young, the women he had spent time with could not be called ladies in the social sense of the word.

But now was not the time to be regretting the past or thinking about changing company. His eyes moved to the closed door where the other men were sleeping. There was no time to think of anything except a man named Jessop and tomorrow. For tomorrow they reached Fort Dodge.

Chapter 5

"I've finally figured out what it is that bothers me about our Mr. Jessop," Nick told Diego as they stood at a distance watching the men hitch the team to the coach the next morning.

"And that is?"

"He's not Anson Jessop."

Diego turned to look at him in surprise. "He is what?"

"Think about it, Diego. Listen to his voice, the way he speaks. Does he sound like an educated Virginian? And what about his manners? No self-respecting Southern gentleman would treat the women on this stage the way he does. And, he carries a gun and wears it like he knows how to use it." Nick shook his head. "No, he's not Anson Jessop."

"If he is not Anson Jessop, who is he?"

"The man Thomas Franklin hired to pretend he's Anson Jessop. Franklin must have suspected he would be followed so he found this man to take his place and muddy the trail.''

"But Evans . . .''

"Evans said Gabe was following a vague but definite trail. That trail was found mostly through hotel registers, not through visual contact.''

"So Gabe was following Thomas Franklin under the name of Anson Jessop until . . .''

"Franklin found someone else to become Jessop for him.''

Diego nodded slowly. "Where do you think this man is taking us?''

"Eventually, back to Franklin,'' Nick answered. "Right now I'd say he's just making sure his tail is clear.''

"Of us?''

Nick shrugged. "I don't know. He might not even suspect us.''

"But then again, he might.'' Diego crossed his arms over his chest. "You think this one has friends in Fort Dodge?''

"Probably.''

"Maybe Franklin is there.''

Nick shook his head dubiously. "I don't think so. New Mexico is more likely. There was some Confederate action there during the War. They took Santa Fe, remember? We had to make them give it back.''

Diego's grin was lopsided as he nodded. Remember? How could he forget? It was there that he and Nick had met. In the midst of the fighting. Both of them came from a life of wandering. Nick had traveled further, reaching the west coast and even Montana while Diego had stayed in Texas and the New Mexico and Arizona Territories, choosing to remain closer to Santa Fe where he'd grown up, the only child of Mexican peasants. Both men, however, had come forward to defend the Union, and that conflict was what brought them together.

It was January 1862 when the Confederate forces left Texas to invade the New Mexico Territory. The Rebels wanted to cut the southwest off from the Union and gain control of the routes to the gold fields in Nevada. They marched in and took Fort Craig which lay in the Rio Grande Valley, and from there went north through Albuquerque until they reached Santa Fe.

The Confederates dug in there, ready to occupy the old Spanish city for the duration of the War. But the United States Army regulars were already moving to stop the Southern advance, joined by New Mexico militia units and Colorado volunteers.

It was a two-day battle—"The Gettysburg of the West"—and the Rebel soldiers retreated. However, it wasn't until August of the same year that all Confederate forces were beaten back from the Territory, leaving New Mexico as Union land for the remainder of the War. For Nick and Diego those months had been spent together, scouting or raiding or fighting skirmishes. They'd fallen together by chance but had stayed together by choice.

"We drove the Confederates out, though," Diego protested. "How could they still be there?"

"How can we be so sure we drove them all out? There's a lot of ground between Santa Fe and Fort Bliss."

"You think Franklin was there during the fighting?"

"Maybe. If he was, he probably got a good layout of the land."

"And he probably knows exactly where he wants to go, no?"

Nick nodded and looked up as the cabin door opened. He watched Jessica emerge. In the cool gray of the morning, she pulled the shawl on her shoulders more closely around her, and he felt something inside of him tighten as a primitive urge to protect stirred to life. She looked too fragile to be out here alone. Any father who would let a daughter like her ride the frontier without a male escort deserved to be shot. There wasn't something quite right there.

Again he wondered about this man she called Nathan Wescott. He evidently owned a ranch in New Mexico, somewhere on the Pecos from what Diego said. What was the mystery between him and his daughter? Or, was there a father and daughter?

He swung away, hardening his thoughts against her. She was no concern of his unless she got in his way, and that was unlikely to happen. They'd be parting company today. For good.

Inside the coach Jessica sat silently between Aggie and Nick. He hadn't spoken to her yet, and it didn't appear he was going to. She closed her eyes to block out her thoughts, but her mind wouldn't obey. He had kissed her last night. She had been in his arms, wrapped against him. It was so real for her—even now in the light of day. How could he act as if it had never happened?

She moved restlessly in her seat and thought darkly of the trip still ahead. It seemed endless. Day after day of this uncomfortable, dirty travel. Why hadn't they built the railroad all the papers back East had been clammering for? It would've been so much faster and more convenient to come by rail.

Irritation flamed through her. Damn her father anyway! If he hadn't sent her away, she wouldn't be going through this now. She couldn't wait until she saw him. Oh, did she have a thing or two to tell him!

She stared, unseeing, through the window at the view outside. Land, land and more land. Was that all there was to the West?

She closed her eyes once more and put her head back against the coach wall. Stubbornly she forced her thoughts aside, willing her mind to empty and contriving to still her restlessness. She was only tired. Once she reached Santa Fe, she'd forget anything had ever happened. It wouldn't matter any more. It wouldn't matter that the man sitting beside her had held her in his arms and kissed her—and she had let him!

Fuming darkly she opened her eyes and rolled them sideways to look at Nick. He was staring out the window, and the strong angle of his jaw was in profile to her.

What was so fascinating about him anyway? He was just a man. Why should she care what he did or thought? He was a stranger. She didn't even like him, nor he her. He thought she was a headstrong, stupid female, and she thought he was an arrogant, egotistical . . .

Unexpectedly the stage lurched into the air as it bounced over a series of ruts and chasms in the road. Everyone was thrown off their seat and scrambled madly to maintain their balance until the coach returned to a smoother section of road.

Somehow Jessica found herself locked firmly

against Nick as with one arm wrapped tightly around her waist and the other looped out the window to hold onto the stage wall, he stopped them both from falling.

For an endless moment Jessica was imprisoned by his grip. Their faces were inches apart. Their eyes locked and held. The heat of their bodies burned together, and their breath mingled.

The violent rocking stopped as abruptly as it had begun, and the coach returned to its customary swaying. With a thudding heart, Jessica felt Nick's arm slowly slip away from around her to let her back down onto her seat.

Neither of them spoke as everyone in the stage resettled themselves, but until they reached Fort Dodge, Jessica was unable to forget the contact. She was unable to think of anything but his touch and of the limber strength of him beside her.

She had no way of knowing that he was thinking of her, too, cursing himself silently. For, because of her, he could not keep his mind on the danger waiting ahead. And he knew not being able to concentrate more often than not got a man killed.

"He's inside the saloon with his friend, *amigo*," Diego told Nick as he joined Nick down the street from the noisy building Jessop had just entered.

Nick nodded, not moving from where he leaned against a boardwalk pole with his thumbs looped in his gun belt. It was night now. Hours had passed since the stage had arrived and dropped them off before continuing on with the rest of its passengers. Since then Nick and Diego had been spelling each other in their surveillance of Jessop. He had to make a contact here, and it was vital they not miss the meeting when it came.

"You think this man he is with is a messenger of Franklin?"

Nick straightened. "Let's hope so, *amigo*. He's the only lead we've got."

Diego grinned. "You first?"

"Me first. You stay where you can see anyone coming or going, and I'll see if I can find out which way the wind'll be blowing."

Diego watched his friend start off, watched the easy, long-legged strides carry Nick rapidly toward the saloon where their quarry lay. As Nick disappeared inside, Diego moved his fingers over his chest in a lone, silent cross. He was not a very religious man, but he knew Nick Driscoll. The man was daring to the point of being reckless, and too many times Diego had seen him walk away from situations that would have left other men dead.

The still swinging doors to the saloon were set in motion again by the entrance of a group of rowdy cowhands, and Diego pulled his hat more firmly down over his eyes. Time had a way of catching up with men who took chances. He hoped Nick's time hadn't come now.

Time was not Nick's concern, however, as he entered the gambling hall. He was only concerned with finding his adversary and through him some answers and, eventually, Thomas Franklin.

The saloon was crowded. Men were massed around the gaming tables, placing hard-earned wages on a number or a drop of a card while hoping to double their money, and they were lined up at the bar, exchanging silver coins for a glass or bottle of whiskey.

Except for the dealers, all the men present were

dressed for the range. Their dull-colored shirts and
pants made a somber background for the bright,
glittering dresses of the saloon hall women who
wandered among them, throwing smiles and well-
practiced winks at gullible strangers.

Nick made his way slowly through the thronging
crowd to the bar and ordered a whiskey. While he
waited for his drink, the mirror behind the counter
provided the opportunity to find Jessop. He was
standing further down the bar next to the man he had
met shortly after getting off the stage. The man was
wearing an old Confederate Army shirt. Now all Nick
had to do was wait, and waiting was a game he'd played
many times before.

"Like some company, stranger?"

Nick turned to look down at a young, dark-haired
woman. He smiled as he appraised the full figure
wrapped vividly in sparkling yellow. She presented an
attractive package. "I was never one to turn down the
company of a pretty lady." And to the bartender,
"Give the lady whatever she likes."

"Whiskey," she told the small, balding man
behind the counter and waited until the glass was in her
hand before speaking again. "You passing through or
staying on?"

"Depends."

She smiled. "I like a man who can make up his
mind."

Nick arched an amused eyebrow and raised his
glass to her. The game had begun. At least while the
clock was running this time, the company would be
pleasant. He shifted into a more comfortable position at

the bar, one where he could talk to her and watch Jessop, too. It was Jessop's move.

The night deepened, and whiskey flowed freely up and down the bar. Glasses clinked. Laughter echoed throughout the room. Men spun the brightly dressed women around the floor to the tunes played on an old piano, and talking and singing grew in volume as spirits soared, and the minutes raced on.

From the other end of the bar, Nick was conscious of rising voices as the drinks consumed took effect, but he never appeared to be listening. He merely continued to stand and watch quietly while the woman called Samantha clung possessively to his side and attempted to entertain him.

By midnight, though, the merrymaking began to subside. The saloon started to empty. Men either walked, staggered or were thrown out the swinging doors to the street. But still, Jessop and the man in gray stayed on.

The early morning hours crept in, and the crowd dwindled to the poker players and those lining the bar. The would-be dancers no longer whirled across the floor, and the laughter which had echoed through the hall hours before had been reduced to smothered smiles and occasional loud exclamations.

One of the few men left standing at the bar, Nick allowed each glass of whiskey to last a long time as if he were savoring every swallow. His stance was set. His gun arm was free. Whatever was going to happen would happen soon, and he was prepared for any action called for.

Neither of the men at the other end of the long

counter had made a move to leave, but the end was nearing. They were spending this night, holding onto it, as if it would be the last night of pleasure they would enjoy for some time. But, with a new day already upon them, they would have to leave soon, and their going would tell Nick which direction to take.

Suddenly a bottle was flung to the floor. It shattered across the boards, and Jessop let out a roar. "Bartender! Where the hell are you? Bring me another bottle."

The man hurried to do Jessop's bidding, and it was when the bartender stopped to pull a bottle from beneath the counter near Nick that Jessop saw and recognized the man he had ridden with on the stage.

"You!" Jessop bellowed. "You down there!"

Samantha moved nervously beside Nick.

"Sam. I think you'd best get on the other side of me," Nick told her without glancing up and raised his glass to his mouth to toss the remainder of his whiskey between his lips. She did as she was told, moving casually to stand on his left and putting Nick between Jessop and herself. Nick waited until she stopped beside him before looking down the bar.

"That's right. I'm talking to you, mister," Jessop spit, his large frame supported by legs spread aggressively beneath him while his hand lingered malevolently near the butt of the gun strapped around his bulky waist.

Nick shifted so his left elbow leaned casually on the bar, but he was careful not to let his gun hand fall from the counter. He motioned to the bartender to refill his glass. His expression didn't change.

The bartender's hand shook violently as the liquid

splashed from the bottle into the glass, but Nick's was steady as he tossed the man his money.

"Best get yourself out of the way."

"Yes, sir," the bartender hastily agreed and rapidly scurried away to the far end of the room.

Nick turned to face Jessop once more. "You want something, mister?"

"Yeah, I want something," Jessop agreed thickly, taking a heavy step forward. "You dead."

Nick lifted the glass to his lips to sip the whiskey slowly. He studied Jessop over its rim, letting a long, tense moment pass before speaking again. "I've got no fight with you."

"I got one with you."

Nick frowned into his glass and put it down. The stage and the cigar. Damn! Fool that he was for not remembering the incident until now. He glanced down the bar. The man in the Confederate shirt was looking worried. Good. A frightened hen ran home to the coop faster than a calm one, and he'd be plenty frightened when the shooting started.

Nick's eyes locked with Jessop's. There was no other path open to him. He would have to kill Jessop. Or, Jessop would have to kill him. "You can't fight alone," he said, making one final attempt to avoid the showdown which now seemed inevitable.

"You sayin' you won't fight me?" Jessop demanded, his voice slurred with drink.

"I'm saying I don't want to."

"Want to or not, mister, you're going to fight."

Nick watched Jessop throw his coat jacket behind his gun to leave it free for drawing. There was no avoiding it. He was going to have to fight. He turned slightly to address the woman at his side. "Sam, you better get out of the way."

She looked up into his face. She could read no sign of fear there. "I'll stay where I am."

Nick moved his head to look down at her in mild surprise. She had grit, but in this instance, he knew it was misplaced. "I'd sure hate to see you get hit by a stray bullet."

"Then how about if I go fix us a room for the night?" she asked, running her tongue with forced calm over her painted lips. "Room four upstairs?"

Nick nodded, a slow smile touching his mouth. She'd made the evening pleasant. She'd been good but undemanding company. "I'll be there."

Silence reigned supreme as she moved with swishing skirts across the room to the stairs. But no one was watching her. They were watching the two men at the bar.

Nick straightened, finally letting his hand drop to his side to hang loosely by his gun. His eyes were cold, hard gray as they looked across the floor at Jessop. "It's your move, mister."

Jessop's face broke into a wide grin. He'd never lost a fight yet. Abruptly his hand flashed, a blur of motion as it reached for his gun. His weapon cleared its holster, and a blast shattered the silence. But the explosion of lead had not come from his gun. No, unfired, it tipped and fell, slipping from his fingers to clatter to the floor.

Jessop staggered blindly from the deathblow dealt to his chest. His expression was confused as he stared down at the weapon at his feet. He faltered, took a step forward, and then followed the gun to the floor.

As the big man hit the boards with a decisive thud, Nick slid his gun smoothly back into its holster. The man in the Confederate shirt was staring in disbelief at the still figure laying before him, but the others in the room were beginning to move.

"Fair fight, mister," one man told Nick. "Mortician will see to the body. Sheriff will be told."

Nick nodded. "Thanks." He turned away toward the doors, reaching in his pocket to throw the bartender a silver dollar as he passed. "See that a bottle of whiskey gets sent up to room four, and tell the lady I'll be with her shortly. I've got to see to my horse."

"Yes, sir!"

Nick continued out the door and turned down the street. He hadn't gone far when Diego called to him from the shadows.

"Jessop?"

"Dead. He didn't give me a choice," Nick told him in disgust and stepped into the alley. He would have preferred that the night had ended differently. "And in a few minutes you'll see our new friend come running out that door. He'll be going south. You follow him outside of town and pick up his trail. I'll meet you there in a few hours."

"Few hours? Where are you going?"

Nick looked down at his friend's shadowed face. "I've got a little business to attend to."

Diego shrugged. "Whatever you say, *amigo*. You don't want to stay too close?"

Nick shook his head. "Give him a chance to get away. If he's running scared, he might go in the wrong direction for awhile.''

Diego nodded and then motioned to the saloon doors. "Here he comes."

Nick stood silent as the man in the Confederate shirt raced down the steps to his horse. In a matter of seconds he was spurring his way out of town—south. When Nick moved again, Diego was gone.

Chapter 6

Jessica stared out the window of the stage as it rolled on across the plains. Rugged and free, the land continued to run unbroken by the tools of man. It wove and wound around cliffs and dipped into gullies, stretching on as far as the eye could see.

She sighed and leaned back from the window. Hours before they had left the small stage station where they had spent the night after leaving Fort Dodge. They had started out in the cool gray of dawn, traveling swiftly over the dusty road, but they could not outrun the heat. It had once again risen with the sun, climbing with the glaring orb to its summit and then increasing even more as time passed into late afternoon. She raised her hand to brush back the hair clinging damply to her face. It was more oppressing today for some reason, she felt. It seemed night would never come.

Across from her and Aggie were two men who had joined the stage in Fort Dodge for the trip to Santa Fe.

Both wore dusty range clothes and had kerchiefs knotted around their throats. As was normal for the men of the west, the standard guns were strapped to their hips. Neither of them spoke much, which was perhaps for the better. Jessica did not feel like talking.

On reaching Fort Dodge the day before, she and Aggie had said their goodbyes to Diego. He had smiled merrily and promised to come visit them in New Mexico when he managed to get there once more, but despite his carefree manner and charming grin, Jessica had felt sad.

At first she had put it down to being tired and to losing the company of such a friendly companion as Diego. But that night, alone in the bunk provided her at the stage stop, she had admitted the truth to herself. She was not being honest. It was Nick. It was the loss of his presence that was bothering her, not the departure of Diego.

Getting off the stage, Nick had stopped to help her down. He hadn't spoken, hadn't smiled. He had only tipped his hat and, with one last intense look, walked away. Now the seat next to her was oddly empty. She missed him. But why? He was only a stranger. One she didn't understand. How could he be so warm and gentle one moment and so cold and brusque the next? She shook her head silently at her thoughts. She would never know why because she would never see him again. And, knowing that, she felt a heavy and unexplainable sorrow.

A call that sounded like a person shouting interrupted her musings, and she looked up to find the two men across from her staring in tense silence out the windows.

Another call echoed to them, and one of them gasped, "Oh, my God! Indians!"

And as if in confirmation to his words, the air suddenly split with a series of bloodcurdling cries. The sound sent chills down Jessica's spine, and she turned to watch in petrified silence as the once empty plains seemed to fill with horses ridden by half-naked men with flowing black hair. Their horses plunged over the plains at breakneck speed while the warriors fired bullets from stolen rifles and released arrows from taut bows.

One arrow thudded into the stage door, and one of the men grabbed Jessica and Aggie and shoved them to the floor yelling, "Get down!" Both he and the other passenger immediately drew their weapons and opened fire as a rifle shot rang out from the coach seat outside and above them.

Terrified beyond reason, Jessica and Aggie clung together on the floor. The stage lunged forward as the whip cracked, and the horses strained into a fresh burst of speed. For the two women, it was as if chaos had descended upon them. Guns roared, men swore, and smoke from the firing weapons burned their nostrils. The coach bounced beneath them and swerved, plunging and jerking over the rutted ground as the Indians closed in.

Jessica looked up at the men shooting out the windows. Her mind was clogged with disbelief. This couldn't be happening. This wasn't real. It was only a nightmare—a chapter out of one of the many books she had read back in Boston about the West. Suddenly, though, reality became blatantly clear as a feathered arrow drove through the window and lodged in one of the men's neck. She screamed as he collapsed back onto the seat, blood spurting from his throat. Then the world turned upside down.

The stage unexpectedly pitched straight into the air. Jessica was torn free from Aggie and thrown violently against the wall. Her head cracked the edge of the seat, and the last thing she heard was Aggie screaming as the stage hit and rolled over on its side.

Consciousness came back slowly. Unfamiliar sounds filtered through the black oblivion to touch her numbed mind. What had happened? Where was she? She tried to move, but it was so hard. She struggled inwardly. She had to wake up.

Jessica tried to force her eyes open and groaned at the throbbing pain in her head. She tried to clear her blurry vision. There was something directly in front of her face. What was it? Two moccasined feet . . .

Abruptly she was grabbed, jerked to her feet and shaken. Her teeth crashed together, and she flopped limply back and forth under the power of the grip on her arms. She wanted to cry out, but she had no voice. Her head snapped back once more and abruptly the shaking stopped. She staggered on her feet and looked up at her tormentor. It was an Indian!

A scream rose and lodged in her throat, terror and shock robbing her of any type of speech. He let out an unintelligible shout as she stared at him, and his coal-black eyes shone with the light of victory. He gave her one final harsh shake and spun her around. She was too stunned to react so didn't resist when the warrior roughly lifted and threw her astride a waiting pony.

She landed in a heap and clung to the pony's mane for support. Her head was reeling and she stared out at the scene around her in disbelieving horror. The stage was over on its side, and the horses were now free of their harness and huddled in a group. Nearly naked Indians were walking and calling in the area, whooping as they sifted through the contents of the cases the passengers had brought that were now scattered over the ground.

Jessica's eyes turned from the wreck and her captors to the bodies scattered among the debris. A small cry escaped her throat as she saw Aggie stretched out in the sand, her neck cocked at a grisly angle. She was dead. Gone. Helpless tears burned Jessica's eyes, and nausea rose in her throat as her gaze wandered helplessly on to absorb every grim detail.

Not far from Aggie was the twisted body of Hank, their driver. The hair had been ripped from his head and a spear was driven through his body. The other two men were also dead, left scalped and staring sightlessly into the sky above. There was blood everywhere.

The Indian who had waked her leapt onto the pony behind her, clutching her roughly as she sagged in sick horror and pain. Smoke began to rise from the stage, and he let out an earsplitting yell. The others echoed his cry and waved their spears in the air as the fire caught. Then the horse beneath them jerked forward, and the air filled with the victorious calls of the red men as they drove the stage ponies before them, south towards a distant camp and a profitable rendezvous.

Jessica held tightly to the pony's mane as it broke into a run, desperately trying to comprehend what had happened even while she shied away from the terrifying truth. Aggie was dead, the stage destroyed, Santa Fe was still far away, and she was the captive of a band of renegade Indians . . .

* * *

Two days out of Fort Dodge, Nick and Diego stopped to look down at the tracks leading southwest into the New Mexico Territory.

"Indians," Diego announced dismounting to examine the unshod hoof prints in the sand. "They are moving in a hurry but stopped to rest here."

Nick scanned the horizon in all directions. The tracks came from the north. "Raiding party probably." Since the Civil War had taken most of the soldiers out of the western posts, the raiding by Indians had become a problem once more. With no regular patrols and no manpower to fight for the white settlers, the recently-attained friendly relations between all white and red men had crumbled.

Diego studied the tracks more closely. "They are driving horses." He frowned at a mark in the dirt and moved nearer to see it more clearly. His mouth thinned as he recognized the sign. "They have at least one captive—a white woman."

Nick felt his stomach tighten. A white woman? Could it be . . . ? "How long ago were they here?"

"A few hours. They must have been the cause of the dust we saw."

Nick looked away to the north. There wasn't much between them and the north. Very few ranches. Damn few. Them and the stage line. He looked south. It had been three and a half days since he'd seen her leave again on the stage in Fort Dodge. In another two to three days she'd be in Sante Fe. Or, she would be if nothing interferred with the coach's schedule.

"Think we might follow? Just for a short time?" Diego ventured as if reading Nick's mind. "We know where our man is going. There is but one town near here."

Nick did not answer for a moment, instead continuing to stare silently to the south. They shouldn't leave their man. They could lose him—however slight the chances. He removed his hat to wipe the sweat from his forehead.

It might not be her. Chances were it wasn't . . . But it could be. Golden hair that shone brightly in the light. He wouldn't want to see that hair hanging from some pole outside a brave's teepee. "Let's go. Thomas Franklin has waited this long. He can wait a little longer."

The raiding party's tracks were not hard to follow at a fast pace, but the two men chose to trail them slowly. Any dust raised was one way of alerting the warriors that they weren't alone, and if they even suspected they were being followed, the result could well be the death of any captives they held. For at a run, captives only slowed the Indians down.

Gradually the scorching afternoon sun dipped westward and sank into a rainbow of vivid colors. It hovered on the horizon and lit the desert plains with a glowing red hue. When the little remaining light began to fade into dusk, Diego stepped down from his horse once more to examine the tracks.

"They are slowing down, *amigo*. I think maybe they will be stopping for the night."

Nick nodded thoughtfully. "If they've been traveling for two or three days, they'll have to. Their horses will be tired."

"Yes, the horses will need rest. That or these warriors will be walking back to their tepees and squaws.''

An odd note had entered Diego's voice and made Nick look up from his contemplation of the tracks. "Something bothering you?"

Diego shook his head and searched the rapidly darkening countryside about them as if trying to fix their exact location in his mind. "I am not certain, but I believe it is not far from here that the Comanches have a meeting place. It is a place they gather after raiding. It is where they go to meet the Comanchero traders."

Comancheros! Nick's mouth tightened into a grim line. For rustled cattle, horses or captives, they traded guns, ammunition and whiskey to the Indians. He knew many a Texas longhorn had ended up in the hands of the Comancheros, who in turn sold the cattle to a New Mexican market. The same destiny awaited any stolen horses. But the captives . . .

They were either ransomed or sold, depending on their worth. He'd seen more than one white woman in a Mexican whorehouse because her family had not been rich enough to buy her back or because the Comancheros had not even given the family an opportunity to try.

"I think we will catch them before they get there, however," Diego stated confidently. "I believe it is yet another day's ride to this meeting place." He looked up at Nick. "Let us hope so anyway."

Nick did not answer. His eyes were following the tracks going south. "We better wait here for awhile," he told Diego after a moment. "Let them get settled in camp before we push on. If they light a fire, it'll be easier to see exactly where they are. I don't want to stumble on them and have a running fight."

Diego kicked at the dirt absently, nodding in reply. If they could catch the raiding party when they were sleeping, it would better their chances. But, Indians were deadly no matter when attacked. They'd fight to the death for what they believed was theirs, and any captive was considered their property. He swung himself back up into the saddle.

So far they had been lucky. With continued luck they would be able to get into the Indian camp and release the hostage. But as for getting out, a few silent prayers might be the only hope of escaping from the camp with their lives.

Chapter 7

The firelight danced brightly across the camp from Jessica as she sat huddled and tied beside a rock. Her body ached. Her head throbbed. This was the first time the Indians had stopped to make camp since leaving the stage. The only other halts they had made had been short. No food had been prepared, little water had been passed around, and no mercy had been shown.

She had been held relentlessly in the saddle for hours, days, she didn't know. Time had ceased to exist. One minute to the next everything remained the same. Jolting horses, burning sun, heavy dust. On and on, day and night.

She tried to move into a more comfortable position, and every muscle cried out in protest. She didn't know why they even bothered to tie her. She couldn't run away even if she had the energy to try. Hours of endless riding had left her stiff and sore, and the steady glare from the sun had burned her fair skin to scorching pink. Even now with the sun no longer shining, she could feel the heat radiating from her arms.

Nonetheless, Jessica shuddered as the first of the cool night breezes whispered across the sand to touch her. It got so cold at night, but she knew there was no hope of a blanket being offered to her. She looked down at her blouse and skirt—such as was left of them. They were torn and ragged. With ripped out seams and continued wear, she wondered that they hadn't fallen off her body completely. What a sight she must be! And she was so hungry . . .

She squeezed her eyes shut and tried to force her mind to think coherently. Feeling sorry for herself would solve nothing. She had to think of a way to escape or of how she could convince her captors to let her go. Was that possible? Did Indians let captives go? She pushed the thought aside. It didn't matter.

Somewhere in this territory there had to be people—white people. Surely when the stage didn't come in, someone would go out in search of it. And, when they found it had been raided, a search party would be sent after her. Wouldn't it?

She furrowed her brow harshly. With all the others lying there dead, would everyone assume all the passengers had been killed? How would they know she alone had survived? There was no one to tell them she was still alive. But surely, the coach line kept records. If they checked the list of travelers, they would realize she was missing. But would the records even be checked?

She felt like crying, but no tears would come. She was too tired. She couldn't think now. Later she would. Later she would think about escape. Somehow she'd get away.

Jessica laid down on the hard ground and closed her eyes to the camp around her, to the Indians kneeling by the fire, to their words which meant nothing to her except sound. They had stopped for now. That was all that mattered. That and the chance for sleep.

Above in the rocks around the camp site, Nick and Diego watched silently. Neither spoke as they continued to observe the camp though both men now knew who the only captive was. The only thing they could do was wait. Wait and see if any opportunities presented themselves. Or, they would have to make their own opportunities.

The camp was small, the Indian number fewer perhaps than was usual. The warriors were all young, more than likely braves eager to go out and make names for themselves, to prove themselves and to impress the elders of their tribe. Evidently the stage had been the only thing worth attacking on their raid. They had taken it rather than return to their camp with nothing to show for their prowess.

The night wore on, and Nick and Diego patiently waited above the camp watching as the Comanches reluctantly, one by one, retired to their respective bedrolls to sleep. They were resisting rest because there were more important things on their minds. They were feeling good. They had made a successful raid. There would be much talk and storytelling on their return. They would be important men. But finally, the last brave lay down.

It was the better part of an hour, though, before Nick motioned briefly to Diego. He had to be sure there was no further movement from the camp. Diego nodded, immediate understanding and slipped silently away

toward the horses tethered together in a group to the
side of the encampment. Nick moved in the opposite
direction, circling the area to where Jessica lay.

Sliding quietly into position, Nick waited and
watched the horses from across the silent camp. He
could not see Diego yet. He should be there . . .
Suddenly one horse's head jerked up in alarm. Nick
held his breath. The animal was staring intently into the
night. One skittish movement from the pony could
rouse the Comanches.

A tense moment passed. The horse continued to
watch. Then, its curiosity satisfied and assured there
was no danger, the mustang's head dropped once more.

Nick let out his breath slowly. It had been close. He
watched a shadow detach itself from the rocks to mingle
with the grazing ponies. Slowly, the ropes holding the
horses in place went limp.

With studied movements, the shadow continued to
walk among the horses, encouraging them gently to
wander leisurely away from the edge of the camp.
Agonizing minutes crept past. The Indians rested on,
and crickets continued to chirp undisturbed. But, at
last, his mission accomplished, the shadow separated
himself from the animals and slid back into the rocks
and disappeared.

Nick counted slowly to himself, scanning every
bedroll where a Comanche warrior lay before moving
forward. With practiced stealth, he eventually crept
from his hiding place. Each foot was carefully placed in
the dirt as he advanced into the camp. He stopped
counting as he halted beside a sleeping Jessica and
glanced up at the rocks above. Diego should be in place
by now.

He stooped down and covered Jessica's mouth with his hand. She did not move. She only slept heavily on. He gritted his teeth grimly. Exhaustion. He might never be able to wake her. Then he'd have to carry her out. He began to lift her from the ground. Instantly some subconscious reflex within her reacted. She jerked into a panic-stricken consciousness.

Nick tightened his grip harshly and clamped a hard hand over her mouth. He had to hold her still at all costs. He couldn't let her cry out. He trapped her against him and managed to force her face toward his.

Jessica fought the arms that bound her. She had to get away! They were going to kill her at last! Her neck strained under the twist of hard fingers, and she was suddenly staring up into the dark face of a stranger. This was no Indian! It was a white man! Her breath caught in her throat. Not just a white man. She knew him!

Nick watched her eyes widen in surprised recognition and slowly eased his grip.

Jessica remained rigid as he removed his hand from her mouth. Her heart was hammering madly with fear and disbelief. It was Nick. It really was Nick! With his jaw now covered by a few day's growth of beard, he had frightened her. She hadn't recognized him immediately. But the eyes . . . the eyes were the same.

Suppressing the flood of relief and joy which rose in her, Jessica responded obediently to his touch and sat up. She leaned against him as he cut the rawhide binding her wrists together behind her and watched as with the same cautious movements, he sliced the strips of leather around her ankles.

Nick brushed the broken restraints aside and

grasped her hands. He rose without sound to his feet and firmly pulled her up to stand in front of him.

She swayed weakly for a moment but stubbornly refused to give in to her own human frailty. Renewed hope had ignited within her. It gave her strength. This was a chance to get away.

He put a stern finger against her lips to insure her continued silence and watched as she quickly gathered her tattered skirts in one hand before sliding the other, trembling with fear, into his.

Nick led the way from the camp and into the rocks. Step by careful step, he showed her where to go. Her footprints had to echo his. There could be no loosened rocks. No noise. Cold sweat broke out on his back and his face at the effort. So close and yet so far, but he couldn't hurry. Though every muscle in his body was tensed to move and move rapidly, he had to remember Jessica. She was frightened and weak from days of endless riding. He couldn't take the chance. He had to go slow. He had to be patient while the minutes dragged past.

Following behind him, Jessica clung tightly to his hand. She was suddenly foolishly afraid he would pull away and leave her alone to face the Comanches. It was terrifying. All this quiet. The blackness of night. The danger. The fear. She wanted to cry out at her helplessness. She was so frightened and her body felt so shaky. Every movement was a supreme concentrated effort. What if she fell? She couldn't see in the dark. Where was Nick taking her? What if the Indians followed?

She had to bite her lip to stop the panic threatening to overwhelm her. They were getting away. They *had* to get away. She couldn't falter now. If she did, it would

mean going back to her captors, going back to an
unknown future, and it would mean taking Nick with
her. She remembered the men from the stage and
shuddered. If the Indians caught them now, they might
spare her, but they'd kill Nick.

At last the rocks disappeared behind them, and
they reached a stretch of soft sand. Nick immediately
pulled Jessica into a stumbling run, dragging her
roughly back up when her steps faltered under the
power of stiff and uncooperative muscles.

Her body cried out in protest as she was jerked
forward, and a beaten sob threatened to overwhelm her.
Would the punishment never end? She couldn't take
any more . . . They rounded a grouping of dry brush,
and Diego and two horses stood before them. In a flurry
of movement Nick lifted Jessica into the saddle and
leapt up behind her. Diego mounted the other horse,
and the eyes of the two men locked.

Nick nodded wordlessly. Diego repeated the
gesture and urged his horse away from them and into
the night. Nick wrapped his arm firmly around Jessica
and turned his horse's head in the opposite direction.

Jessica sat stiffly in front of him as the horse
walked rapidly from the still silent camp. To her ears,
each step the animal took thundered through the dark.
She held her breath and prayed. Now was the moment.
They either escaped or . . .

The blast of a rifle shattered the silence, and Nick
dug his heels into the horse's sides. The animal lunged
forward into a driving run, and Jessica was thrown back
against Nick. She gritted her teeth to stem the fear
welling up inside her and listened in petrified silence to
the gunfire and shouting behind them.

Abruptly, though, the firing stopped, leaving only the sound of a rapidly moving animal coming on after them. In a moment Diego appeared out of the night, and the two horses charged on in reckless unison into the black cover of the desert plains.

When enough distance was put between the Comanche camp and themselves, the two men began to lessen the pace. But, they didn't stop as the hours waned on. They rode through the blackness of the early hours, passing eerie shadows of cactus and rock, and continued to push their mounts as much as they dared. Holes couldn't be seen in the darkness, and a broken leg would mean a lost horse. And, a lost horse meant they would be put afoot where the Comanches were certain to catch them. Only putting many miles between the warriors and themselves could insure their safety because the Comanches would try to follow. They would try to avenge themselves on the white men who had robbed them of their prize.

Fear alone kept Jessica conscious during the passage of time. Fear of being caught again. Fear of being a victim of the Indians once more. Images of the dead men from the stage haunted her. It could be Nick and Diego this time. It could be her.

The sliver of moon in the night sky robbed her of clear vision, but her ears strained continually for the telltale sound of pursuit, for the echo of hoofbeats. How far would they have to go to be sure they would not follow? How long would they have to ride?

At last light began to glow from the eastern horizon. It fingered its way over the rocky ridges to touch the land. But still they did not stop. Beneath them the sides of the horses were lathered with sweat. Their breathing was hard. Jessica feared the sturdy animals might collapse and realized they must stop soon in order to save them. But in saving their mounts, would they lose the freedom they had come so far to keep?

Ahead a cluster of rocks and brush thrust itself out of the rolling plains. The men swerved the weary horses towards it. It was a possible haven. It could offer shelter from the day's coming heat and serve as a fortress of protection should the Comanches track them this far.

The horses were pulled to a halt, and Diego jumped to the ground. Immediately he slipped into the rocks, climbing until he was at the highest vantage point.

Below in tense silence, Nick and Jessica waited. The sun was now clearly above the eastern horizon. The land was fully awake and ready for another day of bombardment from the orb's strong rays. As the minutes stretched on, Jessica stirred anxiously in the saddle in front of Nick and felt his arm tighten unconsciously around her. She raised her eyes again to where Diego sat stone still watching. What did he see?

Several more moments passed until Diego finally moved. He scampered lightly from his lookout point and joined them once more. "There is nothing moving. I think, perhaps, we have lost them."

"At least temporarily," Nick agreed tersely. It did not pay to take the Comanche for granted. They were proud people. It was dangerous to underestimate them.

Diego nodded and, storing the rifle he had been clutching in his hand back in his saddle boot, reached up to take Jessica from Nick's grasp. However, when her feet touched the ground, he found she could barely stand. He held her gently to him and helped her over to a portion of shade the rocks offered and sat her down against their formidable walls. He stayed with her, offering silent support, until Nick came with a canteen.

"I will look around the area. There might be a small spring among the rocks," Diego told Nick. "Then I had best see to the horses."

Nick did not reply but bent down to kneel beside Jessica. He handed her the canteen and watched her trembling hands put the container to her lips. She swallowed convulsively and choked. He pulled the canteen away. "Take it easy. Not too much too fast. You'll only make yourself sick."

She nodded, accepting the canteen once more, and forced herself to drink more slowly. Done, she relinquished the container to Nick and leaned back against the face of the rock. She closed her eyes and felt chills of relief rush through her body. She couldn't believe she was free! The nightmare was over. The Indians were gone. And, she was free!

Unexpectedly something touched her face, and she jumped violently. With terrified eyes she stared at the harmless cloth Nick had moistened to wash some of the dust from her face. She might be free from the physical bonds of the Comanches, but the fear they had instilled lingered on. Ashamed of her reaction and afraid once more, emotions overwhelmed her and she began to cry.

Nick's jaw hardened, and he pulled her to him. She shook against him in uncontrollable agony, and he felt an aching helplessness he'd never known before. There was nothing he could do for her, nothing he could say. He could only offer his presence and his understanding. Somehow, though, it just didn't seem to be enough. "It's all right," he murmured softly as sobs wracked her body. "You're safe now. You're safe."

In only a few moments she was gasping for breath between broken sobs and was trembling violently. She was too exhausted to cry more. It was all too much to comprehend, to reason out. Everything had happened so fast! She didn't know where it had all begun or where it was all going to end. There was no certainty anymore.

Nick's hands gently rubbed her arms against the chills shaking her, stopping only briefly to shrug out of his jacket and drape it over her shoulders for warmth against the shock. Then he pulled her to him again and rocked slowly back and forth. Gradually the trembling began to subside, and the tight grip of her fingers on his shirt loosened.

Carefully he eased her back so she lay on the ground. He stroked the hair away from her tear-streaked face. "You stay here," he told her quietly. "Get some rest while you can. We'll have to ride on again in a few hours."

He made a move to leave her side, but she quickly put a hand out to stop him.

He took it in gentle reassurance. "Don't worry. We won't leave you. We'll be right over there seeing to the horses."

He watched her eyes seek out the animals, touching them briefly before she turned hastily back to look up at him again. He smiled warmly and squeezed her hand. Then, rising slowly, he moved away, knowing her eyes were on him as he went. It took more determination than he had imagined to keep on walking.

Diego looked up at Nick's approach, a silent question in his expression.

"She'll be all right," Nick told him tightly, his voice gruff with unspent emotion. "She's scared and plenty tired, but she'll be all right.''

Diego nodded thankfully. "I found a small spring between the rocks just behind us. It will provide enough water to refresh ourselves, the horses, and to refill our canteens.''

"Good.'' Nick stripped the saddle from his lathered mount and took to rubbing the horse with dried grass. "I'll go up to watch our trail for a while. It wouldn't pay to be too trusting of our Comanche friends.''

"No, this is true, but I do not think they will be coming after us very quickly,'' Diego replied. "I made certain their horses were runing as swiftly as possible in the opposite direction when we escaped. I do not think they will catch them very soon—at least not all of them.''

"Maybe not all, but one could be bad enough.''

A few hours later Nick knelt down to gently shake Jessica. She moaned and moved stiffly, fighting off consciousness.

"Jess,'' he called to her softly. "Jess. You have to wake up.''

She moaned again as if in protest and turned her face away from him.

He sighed regretfully. He would have liked to let her sleep, but they couldn't take the risk. Grasping her beneath the shoulders, he lifted her bodily from the ground. He stood her in front of him and held her firmly upright until she woke fully enough to stand on her own.

Jessica blinked against the bright glare from the sun and brought a tired hand up to rub the sleep from her eyes before managing to meet Nick's observant gaze. "Are we leaving?" she mumbled groggily.

He nodded. "In a few minutes. But first, come with me."

Her hand in his, she followed his lead between the rocks to a bubbling spring no more than a foot wide.

"As soon as you freshen up, we can move on," he told her, handing her a shirt. She took it in questioning silence. "You'd best get rid of the one you've got on and wear this instead. It won't fit as well, but it will offer better protection than yours."

Jessica looked down at her ragged blouse. The sleeves had been all but ripped away, and one shoulder was left completely bare. She touched the expanse of skin self-consciously and felt a warm flush fan her cheeks. "Thank you."

Staring down at the slightly bowed head, Nick was filled with a mixture of outrage and pity. He had to knot his hands into fists to stop himself from pulling her into his arms. She looked too small and vulnerable to be here in this harsh country. She belonged in a safe house somewhere back East with someone to look after her.

He thought of the father she had been going to meet. Some father. What man would allow his own flesh and blood to wander helplessly through this Godforsaken territory? He spun away from her abruptly to put an end to his thoughts and strode rapidly away.

She watched him go with a suddenly worried expression. What had made him so angry? What had she done? She sank to her knees beside the pool. She didn't understand him. But the rhythmic gurgling of the small spring soon diverted her attention, and she reached thankfully into it to splash the cool water on her face. It felt so good!

She dipped her hands in again to bury her face once more. Then she quickly stripped the remnants of her blouse away and used it as a washcloth to rinse the layers of dirt from the rest of her body.

When she emerged from behind the rocks several minutes later wearing the shirt Nick had given her, her face had been scrubbed until it glowed and she had managed to untangle the long length of her hair enough to wind it into a single thick strand that hung down her back to her waist.

Nick watched her come toward him, not missing the deepening of the color in her cheeks as she stopped before him. She wouldn't meet his eyes. "Sleeves are a bit long, aren't they?" he observed and reached out to take the material covering one of her arms.

Jessica found it unexpectedly difficult to speak. She felt so defenseless, so reliant on this stranger who had saved her. She seemed so small and insignificant next to him. He was so tall and broad. She didn't even come to his shoulder.

Not used to feeling so helpless, she quickly sought refuge from the motions of the long fingers that occasionally brushed her skin as they rolled up her sleeves by looking up to where Diego sat on the rocks. "The Indians. Are they . . . ?"

Nick dropped her arms. "No. There's no sign of them, but we're not taking any chances." Turning from her, he put his hands to his mouth to issue a call not unlike a bird native to the desert.

Diego waved acknowledgement, but he stopped to

glance once more across the plains before sliding down the rock face to the ground. "Still no sign," he told them with a grin. "Luck is with us."

"Let's hope it stays that way," Nick answered and without another word led Jessica to his horse and lifted her into the saddle.

With a few hours rest and her fill of water, Jessica found herself better able to absorb her surroundings. Some of the fear had ebbed, and with the solid wall of Nick's chest behind her, she felt secure. It might be a temporary security, but she didn't want to be afraid any more. Instead she turned her attention to the land around them. "Where are we?"

Diego flashed her a bright smile. "New Mexico."

"Santa Fe?" she asked hopefully.

He shook his head. "Several days away, *chiquita*."

Hope quickly died, but not completely. She was close. It was only a matter of time. She looked out at the land around her. This territory had kept her apart from her father for years and now, somehow, it was still managing to do so. It wasn't fair. But she wouldn't let it defeat her. Not this time.

As they rode, except for the sun, there seemed no way of telling which direction they were heading. There were no roads, no towns, no people. However, after riding for some distance, Jessica realized the two men with her knew exactly where they were going. She might be lost and uncomfortable in this new territory, but not so for Nick and Diego. Diego had probably been raised here. But what of Nick?

"Hungry?" Nick asked, interrupting her thoughts.

She nodded, feeling almost guilty at her human needs. These men had already risked their lives for her.

She didn't want to become a complete burden to them. "Yes, but it's all right. I can wait until we stop."

"No need." Rummaging in his saddlebags, he pulled out a piece of jerky and handed it to her. "It's dried beef. It's not the best food in the world, but it will take the edge off your appetite."

Jessica accepted the hard meat gingerly. "The Indians," she stammered, wanting to explain her hunger. "They didn't stop to eat."

"They usually don't. They sometimes go for three or four days after a raid without stopping to eat or rest. You should consider yourself lucky."

Lucky. She thought of her rescue, of the stage, the other passengers. There would be no rescue for those who had traveled with her. "They killed the others."

Nick heard the break in her voice. "Forget it. It's over."

Jessica thought of Aggie. Her companion. Her friend. She had been so eager to see Santa Fe. "Aggie . . ."

"Forget it." Nick's voice was necessarily harsh. It would do her no good to dwell on the death of her friend. It would only prolong the grief.

She flinched at his tone and fell silent. She bent her head to chew feebly at the jerky while blinking back the tears burning her eyes. Why should Aggie die and she live? She thought again of how unfair it was. Life wasn't fair . . .

Nightfall found them still moving on, the horses continuing to plod steadily across the hard earth, their hoofbeats the only constant sound in the mysterious desert air.

Tired and hungry, Jessica wondered when they

would be stopping again. She hoped it was soon. She was getting cold, and she was so sleepy. It was hard to stay awake. If only she could lie down . . .

Seeing her sway in the saddle, Nick wrapped his arm around her waist and drew her gently back so she leaned against him. She didn't move once there, and he knew it wouldn't be long before the constant motion of the horse beneath them eased her into a sound sleep. He was amazed she'd lasted this long. She was exhausted, and when they finally stopped to make camp, she only stirred briefly when Nick lifted her from the saddle and laid her on the ground.

But the night cold immediately enveloped her, brushing at her weary senses. She murmured incoherently and tried to curl herself into a ball, but before she could shake away the cold alone to fall back into the heavy cloud of slumber, someone lay down beside her.

Feeling the new and welcome warmth, she huddled closer, snuggling against the body next to hers. The warmth comforted her, chasing away the shivers running through her, and her mind slid willingly into the black depths of sleep once more and remained there until after morning had dawned.

Jessica moved slightly, unexpectedly finding herself trapped. There was an unfamiliar weight holding her where she lay. She frowned and reluctantly opened her eyes. She stared in puzzled amazement at the arm wrapped possessively around her and then up at her captor.

She gasped. How had she gotten herself into such a position? She couldn't remember. Only vague memories reminded her of a stop and the laying down to sleep.

She moved again, hoping to free herself from Nick's embrace and abruptly found herself gazing into his now open eyes.

"In a hurry to go somewhere?" he asked, his voice husky.

"No, I . . . it's just . . ."

Nick's grin was crooked as he squeezed her waist and pulled her closer. "You're not used to sleeping with men."

The flush flooding her cheeks deepened. "Nick Driscoll!"

He arched an unconcerned eyebrow and watched her color brighten. "Better than sleeping alone on a cold night."

"Better alone than with strangers," she retorted, trying vainly to quench the fire of embarrassment burning her face.

"You didn't think so last night."

"Last night . . . I don't remember last night."

He clucked his tongue. "What a pity."

Stammering for words, too conscious of the hard length of his body and the face only a hand's distance from hers, she blurted, "What do you mean 'what a pity'?"

Nick shrugged, the casual movement sending chills down her spine. "Just that you were more than glad to share my bed last night."

Jessica sputtered.

"Lost for words?" He grunted. "A rare occasion. It's the first time that's happened since I met you."

"I . . . you . . . I'm not lost for words. I'm . . . will you let me go?"

"If I do, where will you go?"

Jessica gasped. "That's none of your business!"

This time both eyebrows arched. "Do you know anything about the Chinese?"

"Ch . . . Chinese?!"

"Yes. There's quite a few of them in San Francisco, you know," he told her casually. "They have a saying."

"Saying . . . Will you let me go?"

"The saying . . . I can't remember the exact words, but it's something to do with saving someone's life," he continued as if she hadn't spoken. "They believe if someone saves their life, from that moment on, they become their rescuer's property."

"Property! Are you insinuating that I'm your property?!" she hissed hotly, trying futilely to push herself away from him.

"No. Just thought you'd be interested in knowing how the Chinese feel."

"Interested . . ." Finally, realizing struggling would get her nowhere, she relaxed. "Mr. Driscoll . . ."

"Nick."

She stopped to take a deep breath. "Nick. Will you please let me go?"

"Hello! Are you two up over there?" Diego's voice suddenly interrupted.

Jessica froze, color draining from, then flooding back into her face. She turned back hurriedly to Nick. "Nick . . ."

"It's all right. Diego knows you're sleeping with me."

"Oh! You . . . you . . ."

"Yes?"

"Let me go!"

Smiling mirthlessly, he chuckled and abruptly rolled away, leaving her free. "All right. Seeing as you insist. I'd rather have a willing bed warmer anyway."

Struck silent once more, Jessica scrambled madly from under the blanket to make the most dignified escape she could under the circumstances. However, she didn't leave until she sent a well-aimed glare in his direction which he received with an unchastised grin.

Chapter 8

"How much farther?" Nick asked, pulling his horse to a stop and raising his hand to take off his hat and wipe the sweat from his forehead.

"A night's ride," Diego answered, turning in his saddle to face his friend. His glance touched Jessica doubtfully before his eyes met Nick's.

"I can make it," Jessica protested quickly, intercepting the look the two men shared. Despite the steadily growing ache in her body from the long day's ride, she was determined not to make them wait for her.

Since breaking camp in the morning, they had stopped only briefly for a quick lunch of jerky and water. Now it was almost sundown, and the desert sand around them was rapidly taking on an orangish glow as the sun began its descent. She was determined not to slow them down.

Nick met Diego's eyes over her head and nodded slowly. They would continue. It would be better to have one long rest rather than sporadic hours of fretful sleep caught here and there.

Time marched on, keeping a steady pace with them, and darkness eventually wrapped itself around them as the last rays of daylight left the sky to make room for the stars and the silver sliver of moon. With the evening came the desert night sounds.

Crickets began to sing, and nocturnal rustlings whispered to Jessica who stared out into the blackness in a futile effort to find the sources of the strange chorus. She was alternately alarmed and fascinated by the distant howls, nearby whistles and other calls she couldn't decipher. It was like a foreign land at night. All the creatures who slept the day away came out now to hunt and scavenge for food during the cool of twilight.

Some animals padded from their daytime hideaways. Others took to the air to scout their territory from above. They were all mysterious to Jessica, but try as she might, there was nothing to be seen through the blackness. The dark was a wall she couldn't see through, and soon she grew tired of staring into vacant space and attempted instead to keep her mind alert by thinking ahead to Santa Fe. Santa Fe and her father.

During the brief break for lunch earlier in the day, Diego had sensed her worry about the man she had been going to meet and had tried to console her while Nick was seeing to the horses.

"Do not worry, *chiquita*. It will not be so long before you are with him."

"But what about the stage, Diego? If he hears what happened, he might think I'm . . . that I died, too."

"If by some chance this happens, it will only make him that much happier to see you when you arrive."

Jessica had smiled at his kind words, wishing she could feel as confident as he, but she could not. Doubts lingered, and she wondered if her supposed death would come as a relief to her father. Maybe he would be glad. Maybe he . . . She shook her head. No! She mustn't think like this!

"Something wrong?" Nick asked from behind her.

Startled by his voice, she half-turned in the saddle to look up at him. Hard as it was for her to believe, for a moment she had forgotten she wasn't alone. Nick was still riding behind her. "No. No, I . . . I was just thinking."

A smile touched his mouth in the dark at what he thought to be a lame excuse. "If you're tired, you can lay back against me."

"No!" she objected too quickly. "I mean, no thank you. I'm not tired."

"Suit yourself."

Biting back the retort burning on her lips, Jessica turned forward again to stare into the night. She wouldn't give him the pleasure of arguing. It was not her fault he was impossible to get along with, and she would not let him annoy her. She wasn't going to become an object for his amusement again. This morning had been bad enough. She wouldn't let him catch her off guard any more.

Not completely unaware of the train of thought she was following, Nick could not help the smile that remained on his lips as she sat rigidly before him in the saddle. Her backbone was stiff, and her hands were firmly clutching the saddle horn to stop her from swaying either against him or into the sleep that was waiting to claim her. She was stubborn.

However, time was her enemy. It wore away at her resistance, and no amount of concentration could keep the steady rocking motion of the horse from making her drowsy. At first she dozed off lightly, waking with a start when her head dropped wearily and her grip slackened. But, eventually, a heavier sleep touched her, and she slid limply in the saddle.

Nick, ready for the final sign of her giving in, quickly wrapped his arm around her and pulled her back against him.

Waking to the feel of his arm propping her securely against him, she protested weakly. "No. I'm not tired."

"Sure you're not," he murmured in agreement and remained silent and motionless until the last defiant attempt to stay awake slipped from her. He shook his head in the dark. She had again held out much longer than he had expected. Though small and weak in stature, she had proven over and over that her spirit was bigger than her body.

"She is a stubborn one, this little woman," Diego said from beside him.

Nick nodded solemnly, his arm tightening gently around her. "Very."

The door to the darkened room opened, but Nick hesitated briefly before stepping inside. He stood silent for a moment watching instead, but the figure in the bed did not stir. He walked forward slowly. There was still no movement. The young woman sleeping in the bed remained completely unaware of his presence and of the sunshine beating steadily at the curtained window.

It was mid-afternoon, and while everyone else in the house had been awake for hours—including himself and Diego—Jessica had slept on. Even when they had arrived just past dawn and he had carried her into the bedroom, she had not stirred. The trauma and shock of the last few days had finally caught up with her.

He sat down on the side of the bed, reluctant to wake her. He preferred for the moment to watch her sleep. Her golden hair was loose, spread out over the pillow and the brightly sewn quilt in an arc of color. The quilt covered all but one slender bare arm and shoulder.

Her face was serene, the marks of fatigue now erased by sleep. She looked peaceful and innocent, too delicate to be in such a rugged country as this unwatched and uncared for. What was the mystery behind her and her father? He frowned thoughtfully but realized for the moment it didn't matter.

Reaching out he brushed the long hair from her face and touched her shoulder gently. She stirred, but did not wake. He touched her again, his hard fingers lingering on the soft feel of her skin. She moved and her eyes opened slowly.

For a moment Jessica was only aware of a warm feeling of security as her much-needed rest came to an end. Memories and fears were far away in the recesses of her mind. She didn't want to think right now anyway. She only wanted to enjoy the warm cloud of sleepiness still enveloping her. She stretched restlessly under the quilt and shifted, unwilling yet to completely give in to waking. But, there was a weight on the bed next to her. She turned her head and looked up to see Nick watching her.

"Welcome back, little one."

She smiled dreamily. "Where are we?"

"At a friend's house."

She moved, preparing to sit up, but her hand unexpectedly brushed bare skin. Her clothes . . . Sudden realization shot through her with lightning force. Her clothes had been removed! She was completely naked. The only thing separating her from Nick was the thin quilt covering her. "What happened to my clothes?" she demanded in alarm.

Nick smothered a smile as her face burned under his lazy scrutiny and she struggled to sit up while clutching the quilt tightly to her. "I wish I could say it was me. But, unfortunately, the pleasure was not mine."

Reacting without thinking, she raised her hand to lash out at him but stopped abruptly to regrasp the quilt as it began to slip. But it was too late to draw back. Nick had recognized the intent of her movement and grabbed her by the arms to drag her roughly to him.

"That's no way to say good morning."

Before she could protest, his mouth was on hers. She tried to twist her head away, but it was useless. His lips were as strong and relentless as the grip of his fingers on her arms, and every motion she made in an attempt to free herself only seemed to draw her more securely to him.

Helplessly she whimpered as she felt herself weakening to his insistent demands. She couldn't get away. He was too strong. And she really didn't mind, did she? Finally her lips softened, and her resistance melted to acceptance. She began to return his caress.

Feeling her submission Nick pulled her closer to him, and his mouth became more coaxing and gentle on hers in seeking the response he wanted. His hands moved from her arms to slide over the soft flesh of her back. She shuddered under his touch and moaned in trembling protest. This was not what she wanted. This wasn't supposed to happen.

Sliding his hands back to grasp her arms once more, he bent his head to kiss her neck and whisper provocatively, "Don't worry, little one. I won't seduce you . . . unless, of course, that's what you want."

Jessica gasped sharply and began to struggle for release once more, trying desperately to get away while keeping her hold on the quilt. "You . . . !"

"Me what?" he asked casually, keeping her firmly in place. The reaction he'd received had been exactly what he'd expected, but he wasn't through. He baited her further because he was finding more and more that he liked to torment her. "Does that mean you want more?"

"Never!"

His eyebrows shot up in mock surprise as he looked down into her sparking eyes. "So vehement? And here for a moment I thought you were actually enjoying yourself. Was I wrong?"

Struck silent she stammered, sputtering for words. He was impossible! "I . . . I hate you!"

"Do you? Should I show you how much?"

Stiffening as he began to draw her toward him once more, she quickly bit back her retort as the door opened and a young Mexican girl looked in. "*Señor* Nick! why did you not tell us she is awake?"

"She just now woke up," Nick assured the girl without looking away from Jessica. He met her flashing green eyes with a careless shrug and released her. "Looks like we'll have to continue this conversation later," he murmured softly so only Jessica could hear.

"I've nothing more to say to you," she snapped back hoarsely.

"We'll see."

Their eyes locked. His a calm, unreflective blue. Hers a stormy and turbulent green.

He nodded and rose slowly to walk unperturbed to the door where the young girl stood. "Teresa, perhaps you will be so kind as to fix Miss Wescott up with some more clothes. She's a bit upset over the loss of her other ones."

"I will do this, of course," Teresa quickly agreed, smiling brightly at Jessica. She did not hear the sharp intake of breath from Jessica or see the amusement dancing in Nick's eyes. "But first I think she might like to wash. You have been riding many days, no?"

Jessica managed a tight smile as the girl approached, tearing eyes that spit fire away from Nick. "Yes. Many. And a wash sounds wonderful."

Nick acknowledged her last murderous glare with a mocking bow before slipping quietly out the door to let Teresa's chatter divert Jessica's thoughts to more pleasant things.

Leading the way outside some time later, Teresa had Jessica sit on a bench while she took a brush to Jessica's freshly washed and still-damp hair. "You have beautiful hair, *señorita*. It is so thick and golden."

"Now," Jessica agreed with a wry smile. "A few minutes ago . . ."

"It is always the same here," the young girl answered, stopping to flick her own long black braids over her shoulders. "So much dust. It is because we have so little rain."

"Do you like living here?" Jessica asked, looking

out from where they sat behind the small adobe house to the land beyond.

Teresa shrugged expressively. "It looks lonely, no? But it is not so bad. We have fiestas and also good neighbors."

"Neighbors?"

"*Sí*. There is the Morales family. They are the only ones very near, but . . ."

Jessica smiled at the soft glow in Teresa's eyes. "There is a young man there?"

Teresa lowered her face shyly as she colored lightly and smiled. "His name is Esteban."

"And are you going to marry him?"

"Oh no! We are too young to marry . . . but we have talked, you understand?"

"Yes, I understand."

"Teresa!" came a call from the house.

"Mi madre," Teresa said jumping to her feet. "She will need my help preparing the supper. You will be all right until then?"

"Of course," Jessica assured her, accepting the brush from her. "You go ahead. I'll stay here and enjoy the sunset."

Teresa flashed her a bright smile and hurried off, her long braids flying after her. She was a lovely young girl with large almond-colored eyes, and she'd been trying so hard to please her guest.

Jessica smiled and turned to look out at the New Mexican grasslands. Everything was blazing with the brilliant colors of the fading light of day. It was so beautiful here at times, and yet . . .

Biting her lip thoughtfully, she rose. Even from the short time she had spent here, she could see it was a land of contrasts. Temperatures rose and fell, water was abundant or there was none at all, and then there was the ever-present threat of Indians to threaten the peace of any given day.

She sighed heavily. What other dangers were there she didn't even know of? Was it really possible for someone to love such a hard place? Did her father love living here? She stopped to stand beside a small adobe wall and searched the horizons. Which way was Santa Fe and how far was it from here? Diego had told her the Comanches had carried her south for almost two days. Since then Nick and Diego had been taking her west. Did that make Santa Fe north and east of where she stood?

She frowned. Did her father know the stage had been attacked? Did he think she was dead? Did he even care? She suddenly felt very alone. No one knew where she was, and anyone who cared probably believed she had been killed by the Indians.

Tears welled up unexpectedly in her eyes and slid down her cheeks before she was fully aware of them. She had never been so alone before. Alone and in the middle of nowhere. What was she going to do?

"Tears?"

Jessica jumped as the hand touched her face, and she quickly backed away from Nick, wiping vigorously at her eyes to remove the tears. "No. I'm not crying."

Nick crossed his arms over his chest and cocked his head speculatively as he leaned against the wall to watch her. "It's not raining and you're not crying, so . . . your bath? No, you finished your bath quite some time ago."

"How would you know when I finished my bath?" she demanded, her fists clenching as anger overtook her feeling of sudden loss.

"I'm very observant."

"Observant! You weren't even there!"

He shrugged, putting his head to one side as he looked down at her. With her long hair streaming over her shoulders and dressed in the light cotton peasant blouse and skirt which left her shoulders, arms and ankles bare, she looked small and vulnerable. "Is something worrying you?" he inquired, bringing the conversation back to his original question.

"No."

His eyes narrowed, but momentarily he was determined not to let her stubbornness and pride anger him. She had received a shock when the Comanches had carried her off, and she was probably just now beginning to realize how far away she was from anything or anyone she knew. She was undoubtedly frightened. He had to try to remember that. Even if he was not always known to be a patient man . . .

"If you're wondering when you're going to get to Santa Fe," he told her, "I'm afraid it won't be for a while. Diego and I will take you there as soon as we can, but for now you'll have to stay here with us until we get some business taken care of."

"I didn't expect you to make any special arrangements for me," she countered, unreasonably angry at him for finding her crying and, because it was him she must depend on for protection and care. She would almost rather be left to fend for herself.

Putting his hands on his hips, his eyes hardened at

the tone of her voice. His patience was evaporating. "There are times when you ought to be glad you're not a man."

She blinked at his sudden change in subject. "What?"

"Because if you were," he continued, "you'd be sitting in the sand on that delicate little bottom of yours more often than you'd be standing on your own two feet."

"How dare you talk to me that way!"

"It's about time somebody did."

"And what's that supposed to mean?"

"It means you're spoiled. You're so used to getting your own way, you can't be bothered with being polite to others even when they're trying to help you. All you can think of is yourself."

"You're a fine one to be lecturing people on manners!" Jessica stormed, stamping a sandaled foot. "You don't even have the pretense of being a gentleman. It's a small wonder to me how you managed to avoid jail when you were back East. They usually lock uncivilized people like you up. Or, perhaps, is that the reason you're out here? To blend in with the rest of the misfits of society who have no place else to go?"

Nick eyed her narrowly, anger passing slowly to amazement as he stared down at her. "You have more fire than sense," he finally announced with an exasperated sigh. "I'm beginning to wonder if those Comanches would have ended up being the captives and you the captor."

At the mention of the warriors who had carried her away, Jessica's fire immediately dimmed as a pang of fear stabbed through her. ''They won't follow us here, will they?''

Nick pushed himself away from the fence, a perplexed frown creasing his forehead at her abrupt change in mood. One minute she was spitting at him like an angry cat. The next she was cowering like a frightened kitten. He didn't know whether to slap her or hold her and wondered if he'd get away with either approach. ''Not likely.''

Left suddenly with no words to say and with the darkness steadily deepening around them as they stood alone in the yard, Jessica fidgeted nervously. ''We better go in. Supper should be ready shortly.''

''We'll be leaving tomorrow morning,'' he told her as she turned to leave.

''For where?''

''A town. It's not far from here. About a day's ride.''

Curiosity got the better of her, and Jessica reluctantly moved back to face him. ''This . . . business. Will it take long?''

''Depends.''

Something in the way he answered told Jessica he would say no more, and she suddenly realized how little she knew about this man. Boarding a stage over a week ago, they had met, and fate had continually thrown them together since.

He was like no other man she had ever met. Strong and silent, he frightened and yet reassured her. When he was with her, she felt safe and then again, he made her feel confused and rebellious, weak and strong, inferior and equal. No other man had done that to her before.

No man had ever been able to rob her of her self-confidence.

Until now the men she had known had treated her with respect and courtesy. They had courted her, pampered her, done everything in their power to impress her. Often she had felt more superior to them than was expected of a young lady and had been more exasperated than flattered at the attention they gave her.

But Nick. He was different. He didn't try to flatter or impress her. He didn't even seem to like her. But, he had still kissed her. No, she didn't understand him and she was afraid to try.

Looking up she found him beside her, the clear blue of his eyes watching her above the beard that had grown to mask his face.

"Do you feel strong enough to travel again? If you don't . . ."

"I feel fine," she assured him quickly, unexpectedly afraid he would leave her behind. "I was just tired before. I'll be all right tomorrow. I won't slow you down."

He nodded, studying her face as if trying to find an answer to an unasked question. "We better go in," he said after a moment. "Try to eat a good meal and get some more sleep. We'll be up and moving early."

Jessica nodded agreement, her usual rebellion in taking orders, even when framed as suggestions, remaining dormant. With this man she somehow knew there were times when disobedience would not be tolerated, and punishment, whatever the form, would be handed out freely.

Chapter 9

Jessica looked down doubtfully at the pair of white cotton pants covering her slim legs. Teresa had brought them and the matching shirt to her under Nick's orders not an hour before when the young girl had awakened Jessica for a pre-dawn breakfast.

It wasn't that the pants didn't fit. They did, or at least they seemed to. It was hard to tell when she had never worn pants before. It was, rather, she wasn't quite sure she liked them. They gave her more freedom than the bulky skirts she usually wore, but . . .

She suppressed an outrageous giggle as she thought of Mrs. Abbott. What would her guardian say if she could see her ward now? And her grandparents!

Jessica suddenly remembered the men waiting for her outside and quickly smothered her imagination. She had to hurry. Nick and Diego had been up hours before her, Teresa had told her, preparing for their departure this morning.

She wound her hair into a knot on the top of her head and wrapped it securely in the bandana Teresa had also provided before completing her native peasant outfit by donning a small straw sombrero. Putting the hat firmly on her head, she was glad for once there was no mirror to tell her how she looked. She wasn't sure she would have the courage to leave the room if she could see herself first.

And, what little confidence she had in her appearance was quickly wiped away when she stepped outside into the gray of early morning.

Nick turned from his horse to watch her approach. His eyes ran slowly over her, taking in the shirt and pants which clung loosely but undeceptively on the soft curves of her body. "You're not flat-chested enough to pass for a boy," he observed aloud.

"Probably because I'm not one," she retorted coolly, realizing now why he had wanted her to dress this way.

"Obviously," he granted, unable to stop his eyes from sliding down to linger on the material covering her breasts as she moved toward him.

"Will you stop staring at me as if I was some . . . saloon girl," she stormed angrily, trying ineffectively to stop the hot blush from flooding her cheeks and resisting the urge to cross her arms over the feminine flesh.

Nick looked over at a grinning but silent Diego who was standing nearby. "The lady doesn't appreciate being admired, *amigo*."

"I think, perhaps, it is not the admiration she minds, but maybe the man who is doing the admiring?"

Jessica was startled by Diego's words and watched

as Nick turned a thoughtful eye on her. What would he say? Or, rather, what would she say if he asked her if what Diego said was true?

She had always enjoyed being admired by men. She liked the way men would silently compliment her by following her wherever she went with their eyes. But Nick. Nick. Did she like being admired by him? Did she want to be? What was it about him that disturbed her so? What he said, what he did. He often made her angry—as he had only moments ago merely by looking at her as if she was a desirable woman. Didn't she want to be desired?

Her hesitant footsteps brought her to a halt before him. Why should she be angry with him for showing her honestly what he felt toward her? Would she prefer him to hide his interest behind the affected manners and protocol the men followed back in Boston?

"You'll ride behind me today," he said abruptly, breaking the silence between them and swinging himself easily up onto his horse. Once seated he put a hand down to her and pulled her up into the saddle in back of him. "You can hold onto me if you like," he told her over his shoulder, lowering his voice so only she could hear his words. "You're safe enough there, but don't forget what happened yesterday when we met face to face."

Jessica opened her mouth to retort hotly, but her protest was lost as the horse started off with a jerk and she was forced to wrap her arms around Nick's waist in order to stop herself from falling off. She could feel the laughter rumble inside his chest, but as Diego pulled up beside them, she realized she'd have to wait to tell Nick exactly what she thought of him.

It was late afternoon when the town Nick had told her of came into view. It was a small Mexican village, built around a series of narrow dirt streets which ran between a few rows of sun-baked adobe buildings.

There were more people on the streets than would be expected for a village of its size, and Nick was quick to notice more than one man who wore American dress. The gray and brown pants and colorful cotton shirts contrasted sharply with the white peasant clothing the men native to the village wore.

Nick and Diego stopped the horses beside a low, wide-set building that served as the village stable, and Nick reached back an arm to let Jessica down to the ground before sliding from the saddle himself.

"The village has visitors," Diego said as he dismounted and came to stand beside them.

"I noticed," Nick agreed, his eyes following two men down the street.

"*Señor* Nick! Diego!"

At the shout Nick, Jessica and Diego turned to watch a young and lanky Mexican boy race from the stables. Keeping a hand on his sombrero to hold it firmly in place as he ran, he sped across the yard and skidded to a halt before Nick.

The boy's black eyes were shining as he tilted his head back to look up at Nick. "You came back!"

"As I said I would," Nick acknowledged, reaching out playfully to tug the sombrero down over the boy's eyes.

"All of the *gringos* say they will come back, but not many keep their word."

Nick nodded and glanced down the street before looking back at the boy. "Is the stable empty?"

"Except for the horses, *sí*. You wish to talk?" And without waiting for an answer, he quickly gathered up the reins to both horses and led the way inside.

Jessica followed the men in, wearily sliding to a seat on the soft hay in an empty stall. She was beginning to wonder what it would be like to spend some time out of the saddle. She felt as if she'd been living her life on a horse. She sighed and pulled the sombrero and bandana she wore from her head. It had been another long day in the sun. They had stopped occasionally, resting the horses and taking a moment to stretch before moving on, but it had been so hot!

At the same moment she pulled the bandana from her head and her hair cascaded down over her shoulders in a golden shower, the young boy turned back to face them after securing the horses. His expression changed from one of elation to one of total disbelief. "She's a girl!"

Nick turned to look at Jessica, a smile playing across his mouth. "Yes, she is."

"But I don't trust girls."

"You can trust this one, Rito."

A strange undercurrent in Nick's voice made Jessica look up. He was watching her. Puzzled, she stared into the fathomless depths of his eyes, but before she could put a meaning behind his intense gaze, he turned away.

"We need your help, Rito," Nick told the young boy, taking him by the shoulders and diverting Rito's attention from Jessica.

"You know I will help if I can," Rito hurriedly agreed.

"We are looking for a man, *chico*," Diego told

him, moving to stand beside Nick. "He is average size and a *gringo*. He would have arrived here two, maybe three days ago."

"He wears a shirt like the Confederate soldiers used to wear," Nick added.

Rito furrowed his brow thoughtfully. "There have been many *gringos* here lately," he said hesitantly. "They come and go. They are many faces and they cause no trouble, but the people do not like them here. There are rumors about why they have come."

Nick and Diego exchanged a quick look.

"I think I remember this *gringo* you speak of, though," Rito told them with an emphatic nod. "He came in late one night. I was sleeping outside because it was so hot, and he came riding to the edge of the village very quickly. There he slowed down and went to the cantina. His horse had run far."

"And is he still here?" Nick inquired.

"*Si*. I saw him just this morning at the café."

"Good," Nick sighed, a note of relief in his voice.

"He stays alone?" Diego asked.

"No. He stays with some other *gringos*. Two or three of them. These are the ones who have been here the longest."

"You said the people do not like them here," Nick commented. "Why?"

"Because of Juarez. They believe these men are against him and are trying to help Maximilian win the revolution," Rito answered in youthful exasperation, certain everyone must know of Juarez and the war to the south.

"Have you seen these men with any wagons or perhaps some pack mules?" Nick questioned.

"Once or twice. Mostly no." The boy shrugged. "It is very strange how these men come and go. They come during the day and leave at night."

Nick nodded and smiled, putting his hand on the boy's head to ruffle the black hair that laid so thickly upon it. "You've been a big help, *muchacho*." He looked up, and his eyes abruptly locked with Jessica's.

She had not listened very closely to the conversation when it had begun, but now at its end, she was very much aware of every word.

She had read quite a bit about both men they had mentioned, Juarez and Maximilian, in the papers back East. Even while the Union and Confederacy had continued to fight before the war between the States had ended, there had been editorials and articles on the plight of the Mexicans under a French rule. Many editors had clamored for the United States to intervene in the Mexican cause, claiming it was necessary, a requirement of the Monroe Doctrine.

And now here she sat in a stable listening to two men and a young boy she hardly knew discussing these important men, talking about them as if there was a conspiracy of some type taking place. And, they were following someone . . . someone who wore Confederate gray. What did the Confederacy have to do with the rebellion in Mexico? And how were Nick and Diego involved in the conflict?

"And I think you can be a bigger help," Nick added, his eyes not leaving Jessica's.

"How?" Rito rejoined anxiously.

Nick motioned toward Jessica. "You can take care of the *chiquita* for us." And as the young boy's face fell, "It is very important to us that she remains safe.

You see, she has been kidnapped and after we finish here, we must try to return her to her father.''

"Kidnapped?" Rito echoed, his eyes widening.

"*Sí, amigo*," Diego gravely agreed. "By very desperate men. This is why she is dressed in men's clothes. We hope to keep her identity a secret."

Rito pointed an accusing finger at her. "She will not remain very secret with her golden hair down like that."

Nick smothered a grin and agreed. "Do you have a place we can hide her until we're done?"

Rito frowned. "There is only one place I know of where no one will go. The hayloft." He looked up at the hay-covered boards above them. "No one ever goes there but me. It is usually where I sleep and is very safe."

Nick tilted his head back to look at the loft, too, and a wistful smile curved his lips. If memory served him correctly, he seemed to recall one or two haylofts that had not proved to be too safe for virtuous young ladies. But, under the circumstances and considering the company she would be keeping . . . "All right. Here she'll stay. Can you get her something to eat?"

"*Sí*. This is easy. You need not worry, *Señor* Nick. I will make sure no one finds her."

Nick smiled warmly. "You do that, *chico*."

Rito followed Nick's eyes to where Jessica sat. He jerked on Nick's sleeve, and Nick stooped down to allow Rito to whisper in his ear. "What is her name? This *gringa*?"

"Jess."

"Jess? It is a funny name for a girl."

"It's short for Jessica, *chico*," Nick responded

with forced sobriety. "You see even with her hair tied up, if we called her Jessica, people would know she was a woman."

Rito nodded immediately as if he'd known all along. "Of course. I understand."

Nick rose and ruffled the thick black hair once more before moving toward Jessica, watching her rise gracefully to her feet at his approach. "You'll have to stay here with Rito. It's safe, and he'll see you get plenty to eat."

"But what about you?" she asked, her eyes filling with uncertain concern. She did not understand why Nick and Diego had come to this small village, but she sensed that no matter what their reasons, what they were about to do was dangerous. She could feel a tension in the two men now that had not been present before.

"Where we'll be going, you can't come," he replied lightly, his eyes flashing their amusement.

Jessica sighed in exasperation and put her hands on her hips angrily. "That's not what I meant and you know it."

His eyebrows arched slowly at her fiery response, but he only shook his head slowly. "It's better you don't know what we're doing. Not yet. When we're through here, maybe I'll tell you."

About to protest, she fell silent at the hard look that suddenly gleamed in his eyes. He would say no more. It was useless to ask.

"Stay here and keep out of sight. We'll be back as soon as we can." He hesitated, about to go, and found himself again cursing the fates that had put Jessica in his hands. Something could go wrong here. If it did, she'd be on her own. She wasn't the type to panic, she had proven that. But left alone in a strange territory, in a village far from anyone or anything she knew and one occupied by men of questionable morals, she would be helpless. "If something should happen," he began, pausing as her eyes widened. "Take Rito and the horses and go. He knows the way well enough to get you to the next village, and from there the two of you should be able to arrange for some sort of transportation to Santa Fe."

She watched him reach into his pocket and pull out a pouch of coins. She backed away mutely as he held it out to her, but he forced it into her suddenly cold hands.

"Use it, if you have to."

She looked up from the pouch to meet his steady gaze. Her heart was thudding heavily against her ribs. "I won't have to," she told him confidently, her voice much stronger than she felt. "You'll be back."

For a moment Nick did not reply, did not move, but remained still to stare down at her. What was it about her that mesmerized him so? Was it only that it had been so long since he'd been able to spend some time with a woman? Or, was it her? Jessica Wescott? Was it her beauty? The fragility she tried to hide with defiance? Why couldn't he ignore the temptation she supplied? Damn it anyway! Abruptly he leaned forward to catch her chin with his hand and planted his mouth firmly over hers.

She fell against him in surprise, but he didn't return the embrace. He released her as quickly as he had taken her, and before she could react, turned away to join Diego at the door.

In stunned silence Jessica followed his steps with

her eyes, fighting to understand the chaotic emotions he always released within her. Rito came to stand beside her, and they watched the two men go. Rito watched with admiration, Jessica with fear, but both watched with the hope that Nick and Diego would return again soon.

"You know *Señor* Nick well?" Rito inquired hours later as with the stable doors bolted below them, he and Jessica sat eating in the hayloft.

"Not very," she answered. "But you do?"

"He has come here many times before."

"Has he lived here then?"

"No, of course not," he told her with a look which seemed to her to confirm his belief that women knew nothing. "He does not live anywhere. He . . ."

"Drifts?"

"*Sí.*"

"It must be a lonely life."

"I do not think so. I think it would be very much fun, and besides, he cannot be very lonely when he has so many friends. Why, he has friends everywhere," Rito exclaimed enthusiastically. "He told me once he has friends as far away as the place called Oregon."

"Yes, he mentioned he'd been to San Francisco."

"*Sí*, he has told me many tales from there."

Jessica smiled as she watched the young boy who defended and continually proclaimed his friend's qualities between swallows. "He has no family?"

"No. He is like me now, but up to a few years ago there was his father."

"What did his father do?"

"He was a hunter and trapper. He spent much time in the mountains and traveled many places with *Señor*

Nick. He killed many buffalo and other game and took them to the traders to sell. He made much money this way.''

"And Nick does the same thing?''

"Oh no, he traveled much with his father, but he likes ranching much better than hunting," Rito explained importantly. "His father went many places to make his living, but *Señor* Nick, he prefers it here where the weather is hot almost all year. He told me once he will some day build himself a big ranch and raise many cows and horses there. Then he will be a very important man.''

Jessica smiled at the boy's confidence in the man he had so obviously come to adore, and again she found herself wondering at the different sides of Nick Driscoll. He had done so many things, been so many places. Who was he really? What was he? What was he doing here? She frowned at her thoughts and immediately steered them to another subject. "You said you have no family, Rito?''

"No, they are all dead. For a long time now.''

Jessica was surprised at first by the indifference in his young voice but quickly realized the indifference was only a defense against his inner feelings of loss and loneliness. "You live all alone then?''

"*Sí*, except for the animals, of course," he answered solemnly. "*Señor* Ojeda who owns the stable pays me to stay here and keep watch. It is a good job.''

"*Señor* Ojeda has a family?''

"*Sí*, a wife and two daughters," Rito said with a grimace as he mentioned the two girls.

Smiling briefly at the face he made, Jessica wondered why the man would not allow such a young boy as Rito to share his family life when Rito had none of his own. "How old are you, Rito?"

"Ten," he declared loftily. "Soon I wll be able to go out and be my own man."

Jessica nodded solemn agreement. "Yes, soon."

Silence fell around them as they finished their meal of chili and enchiladas. When they were through and Rito went below to check on the animals, Jessica lay back against the soft hay.

What was Nick doing now? Why was he here? For what purpose? He and Diego were following somebody. Why? Did it have something to do with the revolution in Mexico? But how could they be involved in another country's war? They were Americans. But why else would they be interested in Maximilian and Juarez? She sighed. There were so many things she did not know about this man, Nick Driscoll, and suddenly she found herself wanting to know more.

Chapter 10

Nick and Diego left the small café where they had eaten and walked slowly toward the cantina Rito had pointed out to them earlier.

"You think this man we followed will recognize you if he sees you?" Diego asked as they went. "If he does, it might not go so well for you if he has friends."

Nick rubbed the now thick stubble of beard covering his chin. "Hopefully, this will help, *amigo*. If not, we better be ready for anything."

"I think, perhaps, we should be ready for this anyway."

Nick nodded and fell silent, his eyes fastening on the cantina ahead. There was no way of knowing what would happen now. If things went well, they would be able to discover why the Confederates were here and discover Franklin's whereabouts. It was possible this village was only a supply point for the Confederate arms and men, or it mightly simply serve as a meeting place.

The frequent comings and goings of so many men seemed to confirm the latter.

Both Diego's friends and Rito had assured them no wagons or large numbers of men had passed through this area. There were only small groups of three or four men traveling together, and there had been no sign of any heavily laden wagons which would point to the transportation of arms.

If this was only a meeting place, a place where further instructions were received—instructions which would take the men and arms to Franklin and Mexico—Nick and Diego had a difficult obstacle to overcome. How did they, two strangers, convince the men in this village to trust them? How could they convince them to reveal Franklin's location?

Nick frowned. Where was Thomas Franklin? Where would he hide and be able to keep a camp that would be safe from exposure to local people and from searching authorities? Mexico? The territories? Where would he feel safest?

The territories were big, endless in that few settlements existed and communication was slow. Only to the north and toward Santa Fe did the population of the New Mexico Territory increase and also to the West near Tucson in the Arizona Territory. If a man was willing to search long enough, he could find a place to hide not only himself but others. He could hide for a long time without fear of discovery.

It was doubtful the hideout was in Mexico. It would be too exposed there, too vulnerable. If the Juaristas found it, no quarter would be shown. They would kill everyone in the camp and confiscate any supplies without so much as one question being asked.

No, it had to be in the territories, in the United States. But where? And how close was this village to it?

Several horses were hitched to the posts outside the cantina door, and from within laughter and the strumming of a guitar could be heard.

Pushing the swinging doors aside, Nick led the way into the room, making his way to the bar without looking either to the left or right. He ordered whiskey, and he and Diego stood silent at the bar until the drinks came. They leaned heavily on the counter as if resting after a long day's ride.

Downing the first glass of burning liquid in one toss, Nick refilled his glass before finally allowing his gaze to travel with an air of mild interest to his surroundings.

There were not many people in the cantina. Two women, the guitar player, a group of men playing cards at a table, two men sharing a table and a bottle, and a gathering of three at the other end of the bar. It was there Nick's eyes locked with the man in the Confederate gray shirt.

The man was staring at him as if trying to place where he had seen Nick before, but he hurriedly looked away when Nick returned his stare.

Diego had seen the man just before Nick, and he had not missed the searching look his friend had received. Now, picking up the bottle, he lightly nudged Nick's arm and motioned silently to a table in the corner.

Nick followed him and slid into one of the old wooden chairs to stretch his long legs beneath the table. He left his back partially to the bar, leaving only a rough profile for the man they'd followed to examine.

"He sees you, *amigo*, but I do not think he knows you."

"Let's hope it stays that way," Nick murmured.

Time passed and the two men standing with the man in gray cast several curious glances at Nick and Diego. However, Nick and Diego seemed not to return their interest and continued to remain at the table, drinking and lounging with apparent indifference. But, silently, Nick was cursing his ignorance of the Confederate movement. If only he knew how they made contact with one another . . .

"We are about to have company, *amigo*," Diego said suddenly, and Nick raised his eyes to watch the two men approach their table. The man in gray remained behind to fidget nervously at the bar.

"Mind if we join you?" one of the men asked, his deeply tanned and lined face framed in a smile.

Diego shrugged. "The chairs are there."

"Name's Cab," the man introduced himself once they were seated. And nodding his head toward his companion, "This here is Jeremiah."

Nick's eyes narrowed as he met Cab's across the table. "Driscoll," he acknowledged briefly, his tone curt.

"Diego Terez."

Cab nodded, his eyes switching from one man to the other thoughtfully. "Looks like you boys have been moving around for awhile."

Diego nodded absently. Nick remained silent.

Jeremiah, a young, light-haired boy of perhaps twenty, cast an anxious glance at Cab and moved uneasily in his chair.

Undaunted by their cool reception, Cab merely

sipped his whiskey and asked, "You boys from Texas way? I ask because I just came from there myself not long ago."

Diego grinned lazily. "Texas. *Sí*, we have come from there. It is not such a good place to be right now."

Cab nodded. "Yeah, it's bad all over."

Nick silently refilled his glass, aware of the soft Southern drawl blending with the man's words.

"We think perhaps California might be a better place," Diego ventured after a long pause.

Cab shrugged. "Depends on what you're looking for. People there aren't too friendly to some."

"He means the War," Jeremiah added nervously. "They don't take too kindly to those who fought on the wrong side."

"Which side is the wrong side?" Nick demanded abruptly, his deep voice cutting through the air with open hostility.

"You fought in the War?" Cab offered soothingly while Jeremiah recoiled visibly at Nick's verbal assault.

"I did," Nick agreed, his eyes hard and cold as they met Cab's across the table.

Cab leaned back in his chair and nodded sadly. "So did we." And after a moment, "Damn long war. Some people lost a lot."

"Some lost more than a lot," Nick retorted and threw back the last of his whiskey into his mouth sullenly.

"You must excuse my friend," Diego said with an anxious smile. "He lost everything in your war. His home, his only brother . . . As you said," he explained with an expressive spread of his hands, "it was a long war."

Cab smiled sympathetically at Diego and cast a curious, yet not unfriendly glance at Nick. His question had been answered. "Well, we'll just let you two gentlemen enjoy your drinks. I've never been one to intrude on a man's thoughts."

Diego watched them go, aware that Nick was, too, even though he appeared to be looking down. "What do you think, *amigo*?" he asked softly when they were gone.

"I think we may still have trouble."

Diego glanced quickly at Nick before returning his attention to his drink. "How is this so?"

"Their friend is still watching me."

"So I see," Diego agreed, putting the glass to his lips. "You think he recognizes you?"

"I think if he keeps staring at me long enough he's going to."

Cab and Jeremiah returned to the bar, and the man in gray looked away to listen to what words Cab had to offer.

"Perhaps he has given up?"

Nick didn't answer but leaned back in his chair to covertly watch the men. The talk was mild, Cab appearing to do most of the speaking. Jeremiah ventured a comment and a negative shake of his head. The man in gray repeated several studious glances in Nick's direction but spoke little. If they were making a decision, they were in no hurry to come to a definite conclusion.

"I think it's time we left. If they want us, they'll find us," Nick said and stood. Diego led the way, and Nick ambled in arrogant silence out the swinging doors behind him. He was not unaware of the pair of eyes that followed him as he went, but he had no way of seeing the sudden recognition that dawned in them when they fell on the gun hanging snugly on his hip.

"Where to?" Diego asked outside.

Nick glanced casually up and down the now quiet street. Daylight was fading. Dusk would fall soon. "Let's have a look around. Maybe we can find something."

Diego nodded and they moved off to wander along the narrow lanes and alleys in search of some clue, some sign that would tell them where to go next. But there was nothing to see. Only a quiet, little Mexican town.

Diego heaved a sigh as they came to a stop on a dimly lit corner not far from the cantina. "What do you think, *amigo*?"

"I think the both of you ought to stand real still," a voice replied from behind them. The speaker was hidden in the shadows of the alley, and the cocking of his revolver provided the incentive to obey his command.

Nick stood tense and silent as a figure detached itself from the shadows to step behind him and Diego on the walk.

"Now raise your arms nice and easy."

Left with no other choice, Nick and Diego did as they were told, remaining silent as their guns were taken from their holsters.

"Keep your hands where I can see them and start walking down the street. We're going to that poor old jail that hasn't been used in so long," the voice drawled.

Nick shared a meaningful look with Diego as he stepped off the boardwalk holding his hands above his head. He knew what had caused this. The man in gray had recognized him at last. But, what would these men do now? How would they connect his being here after killing Jessop in Fort Dodge? They would have to decide if Nick had followed their friend to this village or had just happened to be in the same place he was twice in a span of a week. Somehow Nick didn't think coincidence was a strong word to defend himself with.

Two more men were waiting in the small jail with rifles held firmly in their grip. Without speaking they waved Nick and Diego into a cell and locked them in.

Looking around the tiny block woefully, Diego pushed back his hat and sighed. "Something tells me it was not such a good idea to stop in this nice little village."

Nick grunted in reply, conscious of the guards who remained standing a short distance from the cell, and turned in apparent unconcern to lower himself onto one of the bunks.

"I do not suppose you gentlemen might tell us why you brought us here?" Diego ventured through the iron bars. The only answer he received came in the form of a cold stare. He shrugged and sat down beside Nick.

Nick met Diego's eyes and grinned sheepishly before murmuring quietly, "Guess my beard wasn't good enough, huh *amigo*?"

Diego snorted. "My friend, a face like yours is hard to forget no matter what you wear on it."

Nick's grin broadened but he remained silent, wondering what the Confederate's next move would be. And, as if in reply to his unspoken question, the door to the jail house opened.

Cab entered the main room and approached the cell

slowly. Jeremiah and the man in Confederate gray followed behind him.

"We meet again," Diego greeted brightly. "You will excuse us if we do not get up?"

Cab smiled and nodded. "Might as well make yourselves at home because it looks like you might be staying for the night."

Diego threw his hands up and shrugged. "It is better than the stable so I shall not complain, *señor*."

Cab turned his eyes on the silent Nick. "You don't talk much, stranger."

"I suppose it's because I don't have much to say," Nick returned levelly.

"Even when you've been thrown in jail for no apparent reason?"

Nick moved his shoulders noncommittally.

Cab indicated the man in the gray shirt. "Our friend here thinks he recognizes you. Thinks you were in Fort Dodge a few days back."

"Could be," Nick agreed.

"He also thinks you may have killed someone we knew."

"Possible."

Cab pointed to the man in gray who was shifting restlessly from foot to foot. "You recognize him?"

Nick put his head to one side and stared at the man until he was squirming in his boots. "Think so."

"You're not denying you shot the man he was with?"

Again Nick shrugged. "What's to deny? He drew on me first."

"So Bobby here tells us." Cab paced away to look

out one of the two jail house windows. "What side did you boys fight for in the War?"

"I did not fight," Diego answered. "I was in Mexico."

"Then where, may I ask, did you meet him?"

"My friend? I found him in Texas. He had been shot very badly, *señor*. You will remember I told you he lost everything in your war?"

"I remember," Cab agreed and met Nick's eyes which were now hard and cold on him. "If you were in Texas during the War and if you lost everything in the War, you wore Confederate gray. No man in the Union lost all he owned."

Nick remained silent, watching Cab pace away once more.

"But there's this coincidence of you being here in this village after you happen to kill a friend of ours and after another friend of ours who was at the killing arrived." Cab swung to stare at Nick. "What are you doing here?"

"I told you, *señor*, we are going to . . ." Diego began.

"California," Cab retorted harshly. "Why are you so far south to go to California? Why not go north through Santa Fe?"

Diego shrugged. "It is the way our horses took us and a way I know. There is no purpose to the direction we go."

Cab continued to watch Nick whose expression did not change with any words that were passed. "Don't you have anything to say?"

"Seems to me my friend answered your question."

"Seems to me, friend, that you don't realize what's

happening here. If you don't justify your being in this particular town on this particular night, these men behind me might just decide to kill you."

Jessica stirred in the hay, vaguely aware of the murmur of voices. Still sleepy, she opened her eyes slowly, trying to remember where she was. Her fingers trailed through some hay, and memory returned. The hayloft. It was dark now. She didn't remember falling asleep, but she must have after eating. There was a blanket draped around her. She smiled. Rito must have covered her.

The muffled sound of low talking came to her now conscious mind, and her smile abruptly broadened. Nick and Diego. They were back! An unexpected elation flooded through her at the thought of their return, and she moved to throw the blanket aside. But, a small hand suddenly clamped itself on her arm to still her.

In the dim light of the loft she was able to make out the thin form of Rito in the dark. He was holding a finger to his lips.

Obeying his warning reluctantly, Jessica strained to hear what was going on below them. If it was Nick and Diego, why was Rito worried? She frowned. Was it possible the voices she heard weren't the men they were expecting but someone else instead? But how could it be? The stable doors had been bolted . . .

"These must be their horses," a man's voice said quietly, barely audible in the loft above. "You take that bag over there."

Noises followed, rustling sounds, indistinct movements that pounded on Jessica's eardrums in the tense silence. Someone was searching through someone's belongings. Could it be Nick and Diego's? What were these men looking for? And, where were Nick and Diego? Did they know these men were here? Had something gone wrong? Jessica remembered her parting with Nick, and her hand moved silently to touch the pocket where the bag of coins he'd given her rested. What had happened to him?

"Nothing. You?" came a voice from below.

"Naw. Ain't nothing here. Cab is jumping at anything. I say kill them."

"Yeah," the second man agreed. "They killed Hennings."

The voices faded away until they could no longer be heard. The men were moving across the stable to the door. The door creaked and then closed.

Expectant moments passed with neither Jessica or Rito moving. They had to be sure they were gone. Then, Rito scrambled off. With long-practiced ease, he found his way through the dark to the ladder and down to the stable floor.

Feeling her way more slowly, Jessica groped blindly after him, reaching the bottom of the ladder to hear him race across the stable to rebolt the doors. "How did they get in?" she asked in a hoarse whisper.

"The bolt," Rito whispered in return. "They lifted it out with a stick through the crack. It is what woke me."

Jessica followed him with eyes that were rapidly adjusting to the darkness. He was coming back towards her. "What were they looking for?"

Rito stopped to pat a horse's nose in reassurance. "They were going through *Señor* Nick's and Diego's saddlebags, but I do not know what they looked for.''

Jessica's stomach turned over. They had him. Him and Diego. They had them and they wanted to kill them! She spun to look at the bolted door.

Rito touched her arm. "I must go. I will find out where they are. They must be warned that someone is looking for them. You will wait here and bolt the door after me."

"Rito . . ."

"I will be back, *señorita*. Do not worry."

Stammering uselessly for words, knowing even as she wanted to stop him, she wanted him to go, Jessica followed him to the door. "Be careful, Rito."

He nodded silently and slid outside, disappearing quickly into the night and leaving Jessica alone.

Closing the door after him, she bolted it with trembling hands. What had happened? She stilled her scrambled thoughts. She'd know soon enough. She leaned back against the door and stared into the black shadows of the stable. Her breathing seemed overly loud in the quiet, and the walls seemed to be much closer in the dark. She squeezed her eyes shut. She had to stay calm.

Minutes dragged by, and she bit her lip apprehensively and rubbed her arms to stop the chills running over her. The worst had happened. Nick had not come back. Why? Fear shook her, and she ran a frantic hand through her hair and forced herself to keep still to listen for Rito's return. How long had Rito been gone? What had he found? Was Nick still alive?

She blinked back sudden tears and put a hand up to her mouth to stop the cry lingering there, but the touch of her fingers only served to remind her of the quick pressure of Nick's lips on hers before he'd left. He had suspected something might happen. He had felt it.

She shook her head in denial of the thought. She had to stop thinking like this. No one had known anything. He had only been exercising caution when he gave her the money. And the kiss, it had merely been to . . . reassure her?

A sound outside the stable startled her, and she pressed herself against the door to listen.

"*Señorita*! It is me, Rito."

She slid the bolt up and he hurried in. "What is it?" she asked anxiously, barely getting the bolt back into place before spinning to question him. "What's happened?"

"They are in jail. There are many men and they are asking them questions. I could not hear all they said, but I could tell all is not well. I think they mean to kill them tomorrow."

Jessica's heart lurched against her ribs. "No! They can't! We can't let them. We have to stop them," she said stupidly, words pouring out before she had given herself time to think.

Rito nodded slowly but then shook his head. "The money *Señor* Nick gave you. He said . . ."

"I don't care what he said. We can't just let them kill him."

Rito was frowning fiercely. But, suddenly, he smiled. "You are not so bad for a girl. You have fight."

Unable to help herself, Jessica gave a short if somewhat hysterical laugh before falling to her knees to take Rito by the shoulders. "Is there anything we can do, Rito? If there is, we have to try."

"I must think," Rito answered solemnly. "It is an

old jail. We could try to break them out, but," he shrugged, "there are many men."

Jessica watched his expressive young face, realizing helplessly that Rito's knowledge was the only chance Nick and Diego had for survival. Because alone, she knew she could do nothing.

"I must go out again," Rito abruptly stated and turned back toward the door. "I have an idea. You wait here. I shall be right back."

Without waiting for her permission or agreement, he hurried to the door, lifted the bolt and was gone. Chills ran down Jessica's spine as she huddled close to the door, her thoughts anxiously chasing themselves around in circles. Nick in jail, about to be killed. Why? How had it happened? What had he done? Was he hurt? Who was holding him there? The man he and Diego had followed? The man they had said wore Confederate gray?

Running her hand through the thickness of her hair, she shook her head in puzzlement. She didn't understand the whys or wherefores, but it didn't really matter. The only thing that did matter was what was going to happen if she and Rito couldn't get Nick and Diego free.

If they couldn't get in the jail to release them . . . Hopeless tears burned her eyes. What could she and a small boy do against so many men?

Anger surged to life, and she clenched her teeth in grim determination. She would not give up. She blinked back her tears. Lives were at stake, the lives of two men who had risked death to save her. Could she do any less for them? No, there had to be a way. And she and Rito would find it.

Taking a deep breath, she forced herself to think
calmly and logically. Sooner or later the men holding
Nick and Diego would have to move them from the jail.
Surely they couldn't chance killing them there in the
middle of the village. No, they would have to take Nick
and Diego away, and when they did, when they were out
in the open, that was when she and Rito must do what
they could.

The door slid open and Rito hurried in, his arms
filled with a barrel.

She followed him to an empty stall and watched
him set it down. "Rito what's this?"

"Blasting powder, *señorita*. We will blast them
out!" he exclaimed enthusiastically.

Jessica smiled at his eager response but sobered
quickly as she knelt to finger the small barrel he had
brought back. It was an idea, but . . . maybe there was
another way. "Rito, can you get more of this?"

"More? We need more?"

Jessica nodded, trying to remember. She had heard
her grandfather talk with his military friends. They had
discussed blasting powder one night, even explained it
to her when she had asked. She wasn't certain exactly
how much they needed. But she did know too much was
better than too little.

"Yes," she told Rito. "We need as much as we can
get, and right away. We're going to blast them out, but
not the way you mean." And gathering the barrel in her
arms, she said, "Let's go."

Chapter 11

Nick stared out the cell window at the alley behind the jail. The early light of dawn was slowly creeping into its dark width. He frowned. It wouldn't be long now before Diego and he would be taken away to be killed.

Last night after a search of their saddlebags in the stable had proven nothing, Cab's protests had gotten weaker and weaker under the persistent demands of the other men. They wanted blood.

Three of them wanted Nick's life in exchange for the life of a man named Hennings. Hennings, Nick reasoned, must have been the real name of the man he had killed in Fort Dodge.

He sighed. He hadn't been as cautious as he should have been. The gunfight, the meeting of the man in gray last night in the cantina. He shook his head. He was no good at this any more.

Shortly after the Confederate invasion of New Mexico and the resulting Union victory that had driven the Rebels back to Texas, Evans had stepped into his life. Evans had enlisted Diego, himself and a few others to ferret out facts for the Union Government. In essence, they had become spies, men who risked their lives to get and bring back necessary information, at all costs. Some of them had been killed for their efforts—shot, hung by vigilantes, or worse.

He and Diego had survived, easily skimming the countrysides undetected from a lifetime of practice. They had both been drifters when the War had begun, living a free life with no ties anywhere. But, war had spread into the territories, and they had joined in. Neither of them had formed any strong opinions on slavery, but they had resented the threat the Confederate invasion of the New Mexico Territory had made on their way of life.

They began to fight, standing beside men like themselves who were willing to die for a land they claimed as home. Both had savored the adventure, the danger, the suspense, the risks, and the killing. There had been times when he had even enjoyed the killing . . .

But now. Now it was different. The feeling of suspense had waned, the risks had become too great, and the odds of winning were almost too heavy to beat. And, the fighting, the killing, the blood. Peace of mind was too high a price to pay. The War was over, the need for subterfuge had passed. There was no reason to take risks any more. It was time to quit.

Diego felt the same. They both wanted to return to a life they knew, a life they enjoyed. No longer did they want the cumbersome weight of being responsible to someone else's demands. They wanted to go home. They wanted to be free.

They had been reluctant to go to meet Evans this last time. They had been thinking of returning to the territories, of starting out anew, of starting on dreams. The past held too many deaths, too much hate. They wanted the nightmare to end.

But it was too late to refuse Evans. It was too late to turn back. They had started a job they might not finish. However, if they didn't finish it, someone else would. Franklin had to be stopped. If he wasn't, innocent people would suffer. Innocent people like Jessica.

Jessica. Warmth flooded his limbs as he thought of her, and he stared hard down the alley. He could not see the stable from the window, but she must still be there. When the men had gone to the stable hours before, Nick had feared the worst. But they had not found her, and he thanked God for her safety.

Southern gentlemen or no, she was a beautiful woman, and they were men, surrounded by dark-haired, Spanish-speaking women. Jessica, golden-haired and white. If they had discovered her . . .

His mouth thinned. For him there was a chance yet. He and Diego might still get away. Only time would tell what fate had in store for them. This was not the first time he had been close to death. He had been in similar situations in the past. None of them had been pleasant, but none of them had killed him either. He had survived. But, Jessica.

Jessica and Rito. Could they make it across the desert and plains to Santa Fe? Indians. Bandits. The desert itself. There was no end to the dangers which lay hidden in the land. They stayed dormant, waiting for unsuspecting victims to fall into their traps.

Abruptly a slow smile touched his lips. Whatever the danger was, that woman, she'd meet it head on. She had a mind of her own and a will to match. But she was still only a woman and was weak in a woman's way. No amount of courage could make up for that.

His mind flashed back to the corral and the man with the whip. She had stood there unflinching, ready to take what the man had been willing to give simply because she had felt she was right. Crazy woman. She could have been hurt, badly hurt, maimed . . .

A movement in the alley distracted him, and he watched in hopeful yet angered surprise as Rito scampered away, stopping only to glance hastily back at the jail building before disappearing around the corner.

"What the hell?"

Diego came to stand beside Nick, quickly looking at the men who sat unmoving beyond the bars before speaking. "What is it, *amigo*?"

"I wish I knew," Nick mumbled, turning from the window to eye the guards anxiously before motioning Diego away to a seat. He, too, sat down, forcing his tensed body to a position where he could calmly recline on a bunk. What the hell was Jessica up to? What was she doing with Rito?

Jessica was asking herself the same question as she stood clutching Nick's rifle beside a building. The weapon felt big and cold in her hands, awkward and heavy. She didn't know how to use it. She hoped she wouldn't have to try. If they were lucky and things went according to her plan, there would be no shooting and no need for guns. If . . .

She bit her lip and glanced anxiously at the horse tied to a post behind her. It was saddled and bridled and ready to ride. Somewhere by the jail, she knew, Rito was waiting, too. He was standing by Diego's horse, perhaps holding Diego's rifle in his small hands.

She turned back to look up and down the street. There was no one about yet. Dawn was just beginning to lighten the sky. Surely they'd try to move Nick and Diego soon. They'd try to do it before the local people became aware of their intentions.

A door across the street suddenly opened, and Jessica jumped back to press herself against the building. They mustn't see her. They mustn't know Nick and Diego weren't alone, that someone was planning on helping them. She held her breath. She had to stay perfectly still.

Seconds slipped past. Cautiously, she moved to look around the corner of the building wall. Two men were walking down the boardwalk on the other side of the street. They were headed toward the jail.

"Get ready, Rito. Get ready," she whispered and knew it was going to happen soon.

Inside the jail Nick remained seated as Cab approached the cell. There was no change in the man's expression as he turned the key in the lock and held the door open.

"I wish I could say I'm sorry, but I'm not sure I am," Cab told Nick as the imprisoned men were waved to their feet and out of the cell at gun point.

Nick said nothing but paused to look into Cab's unblinking eyes until a prod in the back with a rifle urged him on out the door. Diego followed him onto the porch, and the guards came behind Diego.

Nick stopped on the boardwalk and casually looked around the silent village, searching for some sign of Jessica or Rito. There was none. There was no one on the street except him, Diego and the guards. His jaw tightened slightly. Where were they? What were they planning?

Diego saw the seemingly indifferent expression on his friend's face but was not fooled by the pretended calm. Nick was tense. Diego could feel it. Something was going to happen.

The door closed and Nick turned his head to see the three men who had been so anxious to see him dead standing behind him. Cab and the man in gray weren't among them. They had stayed inside. Nick wasn't surprised. They weren't the type of men who lived on violence. They only gave orders to men like these and accepted orders from men like Franklin.

One man motioned them to move on, pointing in the direction of the stable. "To the stable, Driscoll. Real nice and peaceful. Wouldn't want to have to shoot you accidentally."

Nick looked down at the rifle the man held. "No, I don't imagine you'd like that at all." The man grinned maliciously and Nick turned away with a shrug. It didn't matter. Not yet. Soon one of them would die. But for now, nothing was certain.

Suddenly two horses burst into the street. Coming from opposite sides of the road to their immediate left, the animals were a blur of unexpected motion and sound in the silent village. The startled guards swung toward the charging mounts, and Nick and Diego reacted.

Nick grabbed the rifle one man held. He jerked it from his grasp and swung it back and down. The cold

metal connected viciously with the man's ribs as Diego
sent his fist into the second man's jaw.

Fighting to get his gun up for a clear shot, the third
man found himself trapped behind the other two. He
was forced backward and tripped, careening wildly into
the building when one of the men reeled into him from a
blow struck by Diego. The man's gun erupted harmlessly into the porch boardwalk.

Nick jabbed his fist into his opponent's face. The
man staggered and fell to his knees. Nick turned to see
Diego leap from the walk into the street. He followed,
and they ran to meet the oncoming horses.

Bracing himself for the coming lunge, Nick
watched the struggling men on the porch and waved the
rider charging toward him on. Any minute now those
men would regain their feet and start shooting.

Then the horse was there and he was hanging on,
throwing himself into the saddle behind Jessica as a rifle
barked. A burning sensation tore through his arm, but
the pain was lost as the village abruptly exploded with
sound.

The street shook and the jail house quaked under a
thundering roar. Powder ignited behind the building to
rip at the foundation, and the back wall collapsed as
another keg of the explosive lit. Adobe and timber rent
the air. The roof caved in, and men screamed.

Nick glanced back over his shoulder. As he
watched, the windows to the jail exploded outward onto
the porch. The glass showered the men there as they
were thrown to their knees. He didn't need to see any
more. Escape was in sight. He turned forward and
whipped the horse beneath him on to race neck and neck

Kim Hansen

with Diego and Rito towards the desert beyond the village and the safety it would afford.

Hurled back in time, Jessica felt herself being held in the saddle once again. A horse was carrying her and a man onward, plunging them across the endless terrain to an unknown destination. Only this time she wanted to run away. She wanted to escape. She wanted to go with the man who held her in the saddle. Elation filled her. He was safe! They had done it! They had really done it!

Relief and joy, however, faded rapidly as hard miles were pounded away behind them, their mad run only slowing to an easier loping gallop for the sake of the horses. They were far from safe. They could be followed. It would take precious time for those left behind in the village to organize and get mounted—if they mounted at all. It was possible they'd done enough damage, caused enough confusion and killed the right men. If they had, they would be safe. No one would come after them.

When the sun reached its noon summit and the horses were lathered with sweat, Nick and Diego swung the animals into a rocky gorge. Nick urged his horse deeper into the protection of the small, cliffed walls, motioning briefly for Diego to remain behind. He scouted ahead to the other end, surveying the land beyond the gorge and the walls around them before returning to Diego to dismount.

"We'll be safe enough here for a few hours," Nick told them, helping Jessica down. "Even if they try to come up on us by surprise, we should be able to get out the other end."

Standing beside the weary animal she had dismounted. Jessica listened to him, flexing stiff muscles and examining the high cliffs crowding around them. It was over for now. For the moment, they could rest. She turned to look up at Nick, ready to do his bidding, and immediately gasped. "Nick! You're hurt!"

Nick followed her concerned gaze down to his arm and shrugged carelessly. His sleeve was now clotted with dry blood. "It's only a scratch."

"Scratch!" she exclaimed, grasping his arm gingerly. "Diego, do you have any medicine?"

"But of course," he agreed happily, reaching for his saddlebags.

"You don't have to be so helpful," Nick protested.

Diego grinned his response, words lost as Jessica took control.

"Be quiet and sit down," she ordered. "That wound has to be cleaned."

Amazed and amused at her tone, Nick made a brief ceremony of handing his horse's reins to Rito. "Do you feel up to rubbing him down, Rito?"

"*Sí, Señor* Nick. I can do it," Rito agreed with a weary but willing smile. A night without sleep and all the excitement of the escape had left his youthful energy nearly exhausted.

"As soon as you're done, Rito, you'd best lie down for awhile. We'll be riding again soon," Jessica scolded him lightly as the young boy turned away.

"*Sí, señorita*," Rito obediently answered, leading Nick's horse away after Diego.

"You're ordering everyone around, aren't you?" Nick asked as he eased himself down against the wall face to sit. His only answer was a determined glare. He shrugged and removed his hat, watching as Jessica knelt beside him.

Carefully she tore the bloodstained material away from the wound until it was completely free of the sticky garment.

Nick watched the color drain from her cheeks. "Have you ever cleaned a bullet wound before?"

"No," she replied, fighting down a sudden wave of nausea as she stared at the raw flesh. She tore her gaze away and swallowed tightly, reaching for a cloth Diego had given her with water from a canteen. "But if it's only a scratch . . ."

"Ouch!" he yelped as the cloth connected with his arm.

"Serves you right," she snapped irritably.

"Serves me right! Right for what?"

"For scaring me half to death," she retorted hotly, dabbing gently but firmly at the wound and ignoring his grimaces. "Rito and I were up all night trying to . . ."

"That reminds me," he interrupted. "What the hell do you think you were doing back there?"

"Saving your life."

"It didn't need saving. I could've done it myself."

"How?"

Nick narrowed his eyes on her. "I told you to leave if anything happened."

"Yes, you did, but I didn't say I'd go."

He stared hard at her. "You don't take orders very well."

"Maybe it's because of the way you give them."

Abruptly Nick smiled, remembering their last brief parting. It had ended with his kiss. "Which part of the giving didn't you like? The words or what came after?''

Without replying she applied the ointment and put a crudely ripped piece of clean cloth over the wound with a decisive tug.

He yipped in protest and grabbed her by the arm when she tried to get up to leave. "You little vixen!" He pulled her down so she fell beside him and grasped her by the shoulders. "Just what the hell are you so mad about?"

"I'm not mad."

"Then why are you scowling?"

She opened her mouth to retort sharply but the words died on her lips when she met his eyes. How could she tell him how frightened she had been? How could she tell him the thought of his dying had been enough to make her want to die, too? How did she tell this man, this man she barely knew, she was in love with him? How could she tell him, when she found it so difficult to accept herself?

"Were you really worried about me?" he asked softly, a gentle smile touching his mouth.

Jessica watched the smile for a moment before quickly looking away to lick her lips nervously. "No. I was worried about myself. Remember, you're the one who told me I was selfish. I was afraid I wouldn't be able to get to Santa Fe without . . ."

He stopped her with a motion, putting his hand to her head to bury his fingers in the thickness of her hair. "Liar."

She felt the pressure of his hand on the back of her neck pulling her forward and immediately tried to break away. "Nick, I . . ."

But his mouth was on hers, and he was drawing her

closer. At first, determined to resist, she planted her hands firmly against his chest. Her resistance was halfhearted, however, and she quickly weakened to his demands, melting against him to feel his hard body next to hers.

The kiss was long and draining, and it was with some difficulty that Nick managed to pull away to hold her head gently between his hands. "I knew you were trouble when I first saw you."

She looked baffled at his words, and he pulled her to him again to press the softness of her to his chest. She shuddered as he ran his hands down the length of her back and buried his face in her hair.

"I better get you to Santa Fe soon," he whispered in her ear. "Or your father's going to be coming after me with a shotgun."

Jessica felt her cheeks burn at his meaning, and she avoided his eyes when he looked down into her face once more. "What's . . . what's going to happen now?" she stammered, her voice trembling and her limbs weak.

"That's a very leading question for a woman to ask a man."

Burning hotter, Jessica stuttered, "I didn't mean . . . I meant . . . it has . . ."

Nick laughed softly and pushed her away. "You're right. It's time to change the subject." Rising to his feet, he put a hand down to help her rise. "Seeing as I kept you up all night, you'd best take your advice to Rito and get some rest while you can."

She nodded silently, still avoiding the intentness of his eyes. She felt as if her bones were made of water. It was hard to stand. Why did he have the power to do this to her? Why him? She didn't even like him! She trembled. It was as if she were being drawn by a magnet. She couldn't stay away. Even now she wanted to lean against him once more, to feel his arms around her.

He kissed her forehead lightly and moved away, leaving her to sway weakly against the rock face. "Go get some rest, Rito," Nick told the young boy as he reached the horses. "And see that Jess gets some, too."

The boy smiled sleepily and walked away, and Nick bent to hurriedly finish rubbing his horse down. When he completed the task Rito had begun, he looked up to find Diego watching him, a wide grin spread across his face.

"What are you smiling at?"

Diego shrugged. "Nothing. Nothing, *amigo*."

"Nothing," Nick echoed aggressively. "I've never seen you smile at nothing before."

Diego shrugged innocently but was unable to stop his glance from wandering to where Jessica sat preparing to stretch out for a short rest beside Rito.

Nick saw the gaze and cursed to himself.

"What did you say?" Diego inquired.

"I said too much sun."

Diego grinned broadly. "I think it is because it is reflecting off something very white and golden. She is very beautiful, *amigo*."

Nick threw a sidelong look across the narrow gorge, now sure Diego had seen him kiss Jessica. "Too beautiful."

Diego smiled to himself and continued to brush his horse's coat. He had seen Nick with many women, but this one, she made him act differently. Like the others she made him feel like a man, strong and masculine and protective, but also, also she held back. She resisted where others had too willingly given in, and it baffled and yet fascinated Nick.

Diego smiled again. He had seen the results of such symptoms before.

Chapter 12

"There is no one following us, *amigo*," Diego told Nick as he slipped down to sit by the fire the next night. "No one yesterday. No one today."

Nick swallowed the rest of his coffee and nodded. "I was hoping there wouldn't be after the way that jail blew up."

Silence held them for a long moment, the fire between them crackling brightly and causing shadows to dance on the walls of the wind-carved cave they had found. Two days of riding had taken them far from the village, and from whatever leads they had on finding Thomas Franklin.

"So what now, my friend? *Señor* Evans will not be so happy we made our escape, I think—at least not before finding where we should go next."

Nick cast a scornful glance at Diego but nonetheless ended up scowling into his empty coffee cup. He had accepted the job. He should finish it. He wasn't one to let things go undone. "I don't know, Diego. We've nothing to go on."

A movement from the back of the cave made both men look up, and they watched as Jessica came forward from the shadows to kneel beside the fire.

"Rito's asleep," she told them quietly. "He's exhausted. Is there any way we can stop for a day to let him rest?"

"No reason why not," Nick answered, an inquisitive eye on her as she spoke. No complaints for herself, she who had sat determinedly in the saddle with him every step of the way, her shoulders hunching in fatigue, her green eyes underlined with shadows. "We're sure no one's following us, so there's no need to push on right away."

"Good," she responded with a heartfelt sigh and stared into the fire for awhile before glancing first at one man and then the other. Neither of them had spoken much since their escape. They spent the days in silence, each wrapped in their own thoughts. It was as if they were uncertain of where to go and what to do. Nick's eyes lifted to meet hers, but there were no answers to her questions in their blue depths. She wondered again, about the man in gray. Where would these two men go now he was gone? What would they do? She looked away from him and into the flames. "When we leave, where will we be going?"

Nick shook his head and looked across the fire to Diego. "We were just discussing that. Suggestions, *amigo*?"

Diego grinned widely, his teeth flashing in the dancing light. "Why not Santa Fe? We could take our *chiquita* home and perhaps do well for ourselves, too. It is a big town. Many people with many ears.''

Nick nodded, now avoiding Jessica's eyes though he knew she was watching him. ''Good a place as any. Unless, of course, you want to go back to Texas.''

Diego groaned and pushed his hat down to hide his face. ''Please, *amigo*, I cherish my life. Let us not go back there until we have tried everywhere else.''

Nick smiled but Jessica looked baffled.

'',What's wrong with Texas?'' she questioned.

''It can get a little wild next to the territories,'' Nick explained. ''Colorado to the north, New Mexico and Arizona to the west. There's a lot of outlaws who run along the territorial boundaries looking for an easy way to make some money.''

''What about the law?'' she asked.

''There's not enough lawmen to be everywhere, especially not now with the War cleanup going on. Even the local people resist the law.''

''But why?''

''Because they see it as Union law. Texas was a Confederate state.''

''But the War is over. There is no more Confederacy.''

Nick exchanged a quick glance with Diego. ''For some. For others, the South will never die.''

Jessica caught the brief look of understanding between the men. ''Like the men back in the village? The man you followed was wearing a Confederate army shirt.''

Both men remained silent. Neither of them had offered any explanation for what had happened in the village. Neither had tried to help her understand even though Nick had said he might do so when they'd been at the stable.

Finally Nick shook his head. "It's not important any more."

"But why were they there? Why were you following that man?"

Nick stared into the bottom of his cup. "Forget it. It's over."

"But why won't you tell me?" she demanded, angry at being left out. What was the big secret? If it was over, why couldn't they tell her what it had all been about?

Diego huddled down where he sat, his hat hiding his face. Nick turned his head to meet her fiery glare with cool indifference. "It's over," he repeated. "Let it go."

She glared at both men for a moment. They were impossible! Then she jumped to her feet and stormed away.

"Now see what you have done," Diego admonished Nick with a crooked grin. "You have made her angry."

Nick shook his head in denial, not taking his eyes from her retreating figure. "It's her own ignorance that makes her angry."

Diego snorted. "Such words of love, *compadre*. You shall never win her heart that way."

Nick shot him a burning stare and stood up.

Diego watched him step away from the fire to begin walking in the direction Jessica had gone. "Do not get too close, *amigo*. Wild cats scratch."

Nick stopped to glare back at Diego silently, his eyes narrowing.

Diego immediately held his hands up in surrender. "I was only concerned for your safety."

"Keep it up and you're going to have to start worrying about your own."

Outside the mouth of the cave, Jessica wandered slowly into the night to stand looking out at the expanse of the moonlit New Mexican plains. The silver planet was shining brightly in a black sky filled with stars. It looked so peaceful. It didn't reflect the turmoil of emotions within her at all. She sighed heavily. Why wouldn't Nick share with her? Why did he always lock her out?

She hated not understanding him, his motives, this land he lived in—this land she had come to live in. How had everything changed so much in such a short time? Her life had always been so orderly and predictable. Now it was completely the opposite, completely foreign. It was frustrating and, at times, frightening.

She wanted to know and learn and understand, but there was so much! And everything was so unlike anything she'd ever known. How could she possibly have believed she could just move from Boston to Santa Fe and fit right in? How naive she had been! She should have planned better. She should have prepared herself more.

She shook her head in denial. Prepared herself. How could she possibly have prepared herself for all of this? The stage, the Indians, the flight from the village, Nick . . .

She leaned her head back to stare up at the sky.

Nick. What an enigma he was to her! And he was the catalyst that had gotten her into this mess! Why did she always let him get the better of her? Why was he always proven right? She gritted her teeth. She hated him for it. He was always so sure of himself—sure of her! Oh, yes, how she hated him!

"Are you still trying to take walks by yourself at night?" Nick asked, silently coming up from behind her. "I thought you'd have learned by now that it isn't safe out here for a woman to walk alone."

Jessica opened her mouth to retort but suddenly stopped. What had he said? She spun to face him. Independence, Missouri. How would he know about that night? She'd never told him. Could it have been . . . "It was you! It was you back in Missouri!"

Nick sighed and pushed his hat back on his head to look down at her. "It was."

"Why didn't you say anything when we met again?"

"What was the point?"

She started to reply but stopped immediately. She turned away sharply. "Oh, what's the use. You never make any sense."

Behind her Nick frowned in gentle surprise. She was still angry. He reached out and buried his hand in her hair, grasping her neck to turn her toward him. "I make sense to me."

"Well, not to me!" she answered hotly and tried to pull away.

"Not so fast, little one," he told her, holding her more firmly.

"Let me go!" She lashed out at him. "I don't want to be manhandled by you!" But his grip only tightened.

She struggled for release, trying to break free, but instead found herself imprisoned against him. She beat vainly at his chest. "I hate you!" she spit up at him.

"Do you?"

She gasped when she saw his head start to lower towards her, but when she tried to twist away, he forced her face back by grabbing a handful of hair.

His lips found hers. He felt her push against his chest, but he didn't give in to her wishes. He merely held her fast and waited while his mouth coaxed hers for a response. Her struggles soon began to weaken, and slowly she melted to him and reached up to entwine her fingers behind his neck. He raised his head to look down into her face, brushing his fingers lightly across her cheek. "You don't hate me."

Jessica moved in protest, but her denial was lodged in her throat. She watched helplessly as his lips descended to hers once more. She couldn't resist him. She didn't want to. She was crushed weakly against the hard length of him and shuddered as his hands traveled over her back. His touch was hot. It burned her through the thin material of the peasant shirt she wore.

The embrace deepened. Their breathing became ragged. Jessica moaned in confused ecstasy. He was doing it again. He was taking control, and she couldn't stop him. But then, she didn't want to, did she? Something inside her told her she had to, and when he released her to bury his face against her neck, she tried feebly to push him away. "Nick . . ."

He raised his head to cover her lips once more before tracing a path of caresses across her cheek to her ear. "It wasn't fair of Rito to take my bed partner away from me, you know."

Jessica gasped and tried harder to push him away. "Nick. Stop. Please stop."

Straightening but keeping her firmly against him, he looked down at her. "Why do you want me to stop?" he asked her quietly, his voice deep and vibrant in the darkness around them.

"Because . . . I . . . Nick . . ."

Nick smiled gently and lowered his head to kiss her again, running his tongue along her ear instead when she turned her face away. "Why do you fight me, little one? Don't you want me to kiss you?"

She moved against him, trying to look up into his eyes and fighting to control the breath coming rapidly from between her lips. "Nick."

"What?"

"Please. I can't."

"Can't what?"

"I can't . . . talk to you when you're holding me like this."

He laughed softly. "So don't talk."

She stiffened against him as he lowered his head once more. "Nick!"

He sighed and straightened again. "What?"

"Please let me go," she pleaded. And when he did not answer, "Please!"

Nick stared down at her, seeing the rapid rise and fall of her breasts and feeling the weak submission in her limbs. How could he let her go now? She wanted him as much as he did her. He was sure of that. But the soft plea in her voice . . . She wasn't sure—not of herself. He could make her give in. But, did he want her only when her body was on fire and her mind remained frosted with doubt? He could persuade her to love him now, but what about tomorrow? What would he see when he looked into her green eyes tomorrow? "All right," he finally agreed softly. "But first. Kiss me."

Startled, she threw her head back to stare up at him, her eyes wide. "What?"

"Kiss me."

She ran her tongue over her lips in nervous agitation. His grip on her was relentless. Gentle yet merciless. She didn't have a choice. But would it really matter if she did?

Still locked within the circle of his arms, she raised herself on her toes to reach him. She hesitated for a moment, her heart pounding harshly inside her. Then, quickly, she pressed her mouth to his and rapidly retreated back against his locked arms to wait release.

Nick sighed, shaking his head in disappointment. "Jess. Can't you do better than that?"

Shocked and hurt, afraid and yet willing, she bit her lip anxiously.

His arms tightened slightly to draw her closer to him. "Come on, Jess. I know you can do better and so do you."

"Nick," she began in protest but stopped when she met his eyes. Dark, unreadable, they dared her and damned her. She took a deep breath and raised herself on her toes once more, putting hesitant hands on his shoulders before pressing her mouth to his.

He responded this time, lifting his hands to press the softness of her body against his before, with trembling awareness, she slipped back away from him.

He stared down at her for a long moment. The moonlight was turning her hair white just as it had on the first night he had seen her. He dropped his hands to his sides and clenched his fists in the dark against his own desire. "Go then . . . if you want to."

Looking up at him with eyes filled with uncertainty, Jessica stood hesitating. She wanted to go. She wanted to stay. She didn't know what she wanted. She stumbled back a step. Her heart was thudding in harsh, single beats in her chest. She continued to watch him, but he didn't move, didn't speak. She took several more faltering steps around him and stopped. She was near the entrance to the cave. She was free to go. She looked back. He still hadn't moved. Was she wrong? Abruptly her control broke in a wave of confusion, and she spun to hurry into the cave and the safety of her bedroll.

Thankfully Diego had already retired to his blankets. Rito was sleeping. She was alone with her thoughts, and Nick was outside. A chill shook her, and she wrapped her blanket tightly around her. Here, for now, she could lie securely next to little Rito. She could temporarily block out thoughts of Nick.

But tomorrow she would have to face him again and sit with him in the saddle. She would have to sit with him and feel his strong body against hers. A shudder ran through her, and her heart quickened its pace in anticipation and fear of the new-found weakness within her.

Chapter 13

After breakfast the next morning, Jessica made her way to the front of the cave. Everyone had slept later than usual, and Rito was still sleeping. At the fire Nick and Diego were still lingering groggily over their coffee, and despite the tension of the night before, she felt more relaxed than she had in days. Once she had fallen asleep, after hearing Nick re-enter the cave a long time after she had, it had been to fall into a deep blackness of heavy slumber. It had refreshed her.

She stretched her arms out from her sides as she reached the cavern entrance. It was so good to be able to wake slowly, not to have to leap on a horse immediately and run from someone you couldn't see.

She stepped out into the sunlight with a contented sigh and put a hand up to shade her eyes from the glare. A hiss of disbelief slid through her lips. She stared, staggered back a step. It couldn't be! Her heart faltered and lurched suddenly against her ribs. It was! She spun, and a scream tore from her throat. "Nick!"

Nick was on his feet and running before her cry had ended. It had been filled with terror and made his blood run cold. What had happened? Where was Jessica? He raced toward the entrance with Diego on his heels. But his progress was unexpectedly interrupted as he collided with Jessica as she ran into the cave. She collapsed against him with a frightened sob, and his arms automatically wrapped around her. "What is it, Jess? What's wrong?"

Stuttering and stammering, she couldn't form any words. She could only point to the cave entrance in petrified fear.

Frowning, he stepped back from her. "Stay here," he ordered, giving her shoulders a stern shake. Then nodding to Diego, he drew his gun.

Hugging the wall, he crept forward, conscious of Diego against the opposite wall echoing his movements. He didn't know what was waiting for them outside, but whatever it was had severely shaken Jessica. The entrance loomed ahead, and he slouched down, holding his gun tightly in his fist.

Cautiously he edged closer until he reached the rock edge. Cocking his head, he looked out. His breath drew in sharply, and he pulled hastily back inside. Apaches! And they were sitting right outside. No wonder Jessica had screamed. For her it was the return of a nightmare. For him, it was the beginning of one.

Abruptly the air split with a whooping yell, and Nick jerked around in stunned surprise to see Diego race outside. He swallowed the cry that rose in his throat and spun forward, leveling his gun on the nearest warrior. But, he never fired. It wasn't necessary.

Watching from where he stood, Nick watched Diego and one of the Apaches embrace while talking loudly, smiling and laughing. Nick let out a heavy sigh of relief and sank back against the wall with a shake of his head as the two men outside gestured emphatically and clasped each other in friendship once more. He remembered now. Diego had told him about the Apaches in this area.

Jessica appeared beside Nick. She'd heard the yell, seen Diego run outside, but no shots had been fired. She looked up in fearful anticipation at Nick, but he wasn't showing any sign of anxiety. In fact, he was smiling! And, his gun was holstered! She glanced cautiously past him, and her jaw dropped open in shock. Diego and one of the Indians were talking and laughing.

Diego pointed their way, and Nick and Jessica watched as he spoke more incoherent words. The brave beside him nodded agreeably in reply and turned to his companions to speak before nodding again to Diego. A few more words were exchanged, and then Diego was bounding back toward them.

"We're in luck, *compadres!* My friend, Running Wolf. His scouts saw us yesterday and recognized me. He would be honored if we would go with him to his camp."

"To his camp!" Jessica exclaimed in horror.

Nick nodded understanding. "He's your blood brother?"

"*Sí,*" Diego agreed with a wide grin. "The one I told you of."

Nick nodded again as he recalled earlier conversations with Diego. Diego had lived with his parents in this region of the New Mexico Territory, having moved north from Mexico when he was merely a baby.

Peasants and farmers, the Terez family had lived off the land in addition to raising a few head of cattle and some chickens. The Apaches never bothered them for they were little enough of a threat, but the Indians' disinterest in them turned to friendship when Diego reached the age of long-limbed boyhood.

Already fond of wandering, Diego took one of the family mules one day to go riding. He'd been gone most of the day when he came upon an Apache youth. Lying beneath the blazing New Mexican sun, the boy was unconscious and bleeding. A large gash split across his skull.

From the amount of blood, Diego realized the boy was badly hurt, and from the amount of dried blood, he also realized the boy had been lying there for some time.

It was obvious what had happened. Not far from the young Indian lay a lathered pony, one that had stepped in a hole, broke its leg and thrown its rider. The boy had been knocked unconscious when his head struck a rock. The pony was still alive and suffering.

Diego did the only thing he could—shot the pony with the rifle he'd brought along for hunting and took the Apache boy home to be cared for. Ultimately, the young Indian turned out to be Running Wolf, and after Running Wolf regained his health, he made Diego his blood brother.

The two youths became close friends and shared many a day together, hunting, tracking, dreaming and enjoying all the activities most boys will when exploring life together.

"Better get packed," Nick told Jessica. "They won't wait forever."

"Packed!" she echoed in disbelief. "You can't mean we're going with them!"

"Exactly," Nick agreed. "Now, get going. Get Rito up and let's go."

Still horrified beyond belief, Jessica shook her head. "But . . . but they're Indians!"

"Good Indians. Friendly Indians. These are Apache not Comanche, and Running Wolf is Diego's blood brother," Nick told her patiently.

She looked wildly at Diego who pulled up his sleeve to show her a hairline scar on his wrist.

"Blood brothers," Diego assured her. "I promise they will not hurt you. I am their friend and yours, so you are their friend, too."

Jessica was far from convinced.

Nick smiled at her confusion and fear and put an arm around her shoulders. He gave her a reassuring hug. "Don't think about it. Just get ready."

Still unsure and unwilling, moments later Jessica was tightly clutching Nick's hand as they walked from the cave to join men whom she considered to be fearsome warriors. To her inexperienced eyes, they looked exactly like the Comanches, and she expected them to treat her no differently. But, they did.

Instead of trying to kidnap her, they ignored her. It was as if she wasn't there. They were only concerned with Diego, and as she accepted Nick's hand to be pulled up into the saddle behind him, the braves gave a sudden cry of glee and turned their ponies around to thunder off. They were going to lead the way to the Apache camp.

Nick smiled as Jessica slid into place on the back of his horse and immediately wrapped her arms around him. She trusted him, but she wasn't ready or willing to trust any Indian. He lifted his head to nod to Diego who had Rito in the saddle with him, and they turned their horses to follow the Apaches.

Rito was as appalled and amazed as Jessica to find himself suddenly surrounded by Indians, but in quite a different way. Completely confident that Nick and Diego knew exactly what they were doing, he was all eyes and smiles during a short ride that took them straight into Running Wolf's camp. Rito wasn't worried at all.

Jessica was. In wide-eyed silence, she stared about her as Nick and Diego brought their mounts to a halt in the midst of the village. Tepees stood erected beside a small running creek, and buffalo meat and skins hung drying in the sun. Naked red-skinned children darted around the horses calling and waving, and women in buckskin dresses with long black braids stopped their various chores to watch them arrive. Her attention was drawn quickly to one brave, however. An old warrior, his face wore the lines of years, and his hair was iron gray.

"The chief," Nick told Jessica quietly, speaking over her shoulder in hushed tones. "Running Wolf's father."

Jessica watched as the older and younger Apache came together to talk. She wondered what they were saying, what would the chief feel about having four unexpected visitors—white men at that—come to his camp. And, her uneasiness at being in a potentially hostile environment heightened when slowly but surely she became increasingly aware that more eyes were on her than were on Running Wolf and the Chief.

Cautiously she rolled her eyes sideways, not wanting to turn her head. Her vision collided with one observer. Then another. And yet another. Her heart began to pound with slow, heavy beats. People were watching her! Why? She rapidly scanned the faces around her.

Most of those watching her were women and children. They were staring at her intently. Their gazes seemed to linger, probe and caress. Jessica fidgeted apprehensively. What were they all thinking? What did they want from her?

"Nick," she whispered anxiously.

He turned his head to look over his shoulder.

"Why is everyone staring at me?"

Nick quickly surveyed those standing nearest to them before answering. "I'm just guessing, but I'd say it's your hair, little one. It's gold, and your eyes are green. They're not used to seeing white women—at least not with white men. Usually the only time they see them is when their warriors bring them to camp as captives."

"Captives!"

He put a reassuring hand over one of hers as her arms remained firmly locked around his waist. "You're safe. Don't worry."

Before Jessica could retort, Nick turned away again, and she was forced to resume an unwilling silence. She wasn't quite sure she believed him—or trusted the Apaches. She continued to look warily around her, but fear was replaced by curiosity when Diego abruptly dismounted to approach the elderly chief. She frowned. The chief actually appeared to be pleased Diego had come.

"What does it mean when you say Diego is Running Wolf's blood brother? They couldn't have had the same parents."

Nick shook his head negatively. "Being blood brothers has nothing to do with coming from the same family. Diego became Running Wolf's blood brother through a special ceremony. When both of them were boys, Diego saved Running Wolf's life. The chief made Diego a member of the tribe, and Running Wolf accepted him as his blood brother." Lifting his hand, Nick indicated his wrist. "They become brothers by mixing their blood. They cut their wrists and put them together. The Apaches believe this allows their blood to mingle, and the two men become one."

Jessica nodded thoughtfully, continuing to watch the chief and Diego. She began to relax a little, and her fear began to slip away as she realized they were indeed welcome in the camp. The eyes following them were not angry, merely curious, even friendly.

Abruptly everyone's attention was drawn to where Diego stood beside the chief as the leader of the Apache tribe called to his people to listen.

The tribal members gathered swiftly to hear the strange words he spoke, and Jessica could feel excitement spreading through the people as the chief's voice echoed around them. They seemed pleased. However, Diego suddenly did not. Shifting nervously, he looked uncomfortable, if not distressed.

"What's wrong with Diego? What's the chief saying?"

Nick shrugged helplessly. "I can only understand a few words."

The chief finished speaking, and the Apache people dispersed, chattering happily. Diego returned to his friends slowly, though, dragging his feet and avoiding looking directly at them.

"What is it, Diego? What's wrong?" Jessica asked anxiously, her heart beginning to pound with fear once more.

"Nothing is really wrong, *chiquita*," he assured her, smiling meekly. "It is just . . . well, you see . . ."

Nick was beginning to get an uneasy feeling about all of the movement around him. He leaned low over his mount's neck and smiled. The threat of his voice, however, did not match the expression on his face. "Diego, if you don't tell us what's going on right now, I'm going to shock your Indian friends by getting down off this horse and knocking it out of you."

Diego put up his hands in submission and laughed hollowly. "All right, *amigo*. I will tell you. But I do not think you are going to like it." He swallowed with difficulty. "There is going to be a ceremony tonight."

Nick and Jessica exchanged looks. "So?" Nick asked. "What's this ceremony got to do with us?"

"Not so much us," Diego answered, pulling at his ear as his color deepened beneath his bronze skin. "More with you and Jess."

"Are they going to be in the ceremony?" Rito asked from astride Diego's horse, obviously eager and willing to see such an event.

"*Sí, chico*, they are. They are going to *be* the ceremony."

"Diego, what the hell are you talking about?" Nick demanded through gritted teeth. His temper was rising rapidly at his friend's ramblings.

Diego pulled off his hat and beat some dust from his pants. "You see, *amigo*, you and Jess are getting . . . are going to be married tonight."

"Married!" they cried in unison.

"*Sí*," Diego agreed with a grin. "You like the idea?"

"Idea . . ." Nick jumped from his horse to the ground. "You have some fast talking to do, *compadre*, and it better be good."

Diego took a hesitant step backward at Nick's aggressive approach. "It is quite simple really. You see, when I met Running Wolf this morning, he asked who you were. The Apaches, they do not understand our ways so well. They see a man and a woman together and assume they are married because Apache women do not travel with men alone unless they are married."

"Get to the point."

"I told them you were not married . . . yet. I thought they might understand better if I told them I was taking you to Santa Fe so that you might be married because you wanted to be."

"Because we wanted to be." Nick sighed heavily and rolled his eyes to the sky, mentally trying to tick off degrees of his temper. "Diego. *Amigo*."

"*Sí?*"

"Why couldn't you just tell them the truth? Why couldn't you tell them she was carried off by the Comanches and we're returning her to her father? They don't like the Comanches. They would have thought it was a great coup—their blood brother taking a woman from their enemies.''

"I did not think of that at the time," Diego answered honestly with a resigned shrug. "Besides, it was so complicated with the stage and then the village and . . .''

"You wouldn't have had to tell them everything!" Nick snapped, and gesturing in futile frustration, turned away to lean against his horse. A tense moment of silence passed. Finally he raised his eyes to look up at Jess. "You haven't said anything yet."

"I don't know what to say," she responded bleakly.

"Neither do I." He turned back to Diego. "There's no way of explaining . . .''

"No.''

"I didn't think so." He glanced at Rito who was grinning from ear to ear.

"I think it is good, Señor Nick. After all it does not really matter. I mean, you like one another anyway. You would not kiss each other if you did not."

Jessica gasped sharply and Nick, despite himself, began to laugh.

"What's so funny?" Jessica demanded from atop the horse.

"His logic," Nick said with a sigh. "I wish it was that simple."

Jessica looked down at Nick. Married! By Indians! But what choice did she have? None. "Diego, this ceremony . . . what do we have to do?"

"Not much really," Diego answered eagerly, hoping they would accept the idea. "Usually the celebration is three days long, but seeing as we are strangers and new and will have to move on quickly, they will do it in one night.''

"That way we don't have too long to think about it, is that it?" Nick inquired sarcastically.

Diego merely grinned sheepishly.

"But the ceremony, Diego," Jessica pressed. "What are we supposed to do?"

He gestured graphically. "Just be there. The chief will marry you."

"But we can't even understand him!" she protested.

"You do not have to. He will understand. This is all that matters," Diego replied.

"Oh, Diego . . ." She stopped as some women approached and spoke urgently to Diego, gesturing frequently toward Jessica. Jessica shifted restlessly and reached down to touch Nick's shoulder. "What are they saying?"

He shook his head. "I don't know."

"Nick!" she pleaded in exasperation.

He shrugged and turned to face her, raising his arms to lift her down from the horse. "Just hold tight for now. Everything will work itself out . . . .I hope."

"You hope!"

Diego turned to them, nodding to the Apache squaws. "They want you to go with them," he told Jessica. "They will take you to the creek and . . . so you can wash and then give you a dress to wear."

She looked from the giggling, smiling women to Nick and back to Diego. "But I can't understand anything they say."

"And they cannot understand you. They will not

hurt you. They only want to prepare you for the ceremony.''

"Prepare her," Nick scoffed. "It sounds like a sheep being readied for the slaughter.''

"Nick!" Jessica exclaimed in alarm.

"Sorry," he mumbled, pushing his hat back on his head. He looked at the waiting women. "I guess you'd better go.''

"Alone?"

"Unless you want me to come along and help them give you a bath.''

"Nick!"

He took her by the shoulders. "Listen. Whatever the ceremony, that's all it is. An act. And, it's only for a little while. Diego said they won't hurt you. So, go with them for now. We won't go anywhere without you.''

Jessica looked anxiously at the eagerly waiting Apache squaws and then at Nick again. "Promise?"

"Promise."

She licked her lips compulsively and turned to look up at Rito who was still on the other horse. "You'll take care of Rito?"

"Don't worry about us. Just go now. They're waiting.''

Staring up at him, she nodded slowly. "All right. Where do they want me to go?"

"Just follow them," Diego told her, and as she moved away after one last long look over her shoulder, "Oh and Jess, I forgot to tell you. In the ceremony you will have to have your wrist cut. Your blood must be mixed with Nick's.''

She didn't have time to respond. She was hustled off by the giggling women. They hurried her along, pushing and pulling her until they reached the creek. There, they rapidly stripped her of her clothing, pushed her in the cold water and noisily assisted her in taking a bath.

Chapter 14

Jessica sat alone in the tepee staring into the warm glow of the fire in its center. She now wore a soft buckskin dress and beaded moccasins. Her long hair had been washed and combed and then partially braided with beaded leather strips. Two long braids hung down either side of her face to rest on her shoulders while the remainder of the golden mass hung freely down her back.

What a day it had been! Stripped and scrubbed raw by a group of giggling Apache women, she had then had her skin rubbed with a sweet-smelling liquid. Throughout the passing hours she had been fussed over, poked and prodded, dressed and finally blessed by the tribal medicine man. When all had been said and done, she had then been deposited in this tepee to sit alone. She didn't know how long she'd been waiting and was afraid to think about whatever might come next.

She glanced away from the fire to scan the spacious

interior of the tepee in nervous anticipation. Outside she could hear chanting and talking and the steady rhythm of pounding drums. She could only guess at what was happening beyond her temporary sanctuary.

A chill slid down her spine, and she raised her hands to massage the goose flesh from her arms. How had all of this come about? She squeezed her eyes shut. Where was Nick? Was he outside? What was he doing? Thinking? Did he mind what was going on? Did he care that she was about to become his wife?

Wife! She shied away from her thoughts and fingered the intricate bead work of the dress and the fringes hanging on its seams. Marrying Nick. She had come out west to find her father and instead was about to gain a husband!

Her stomach turned over. To be Nick's wife. She'd never thought about it. Never wished for it. That she was attracted to him could hardly be denied, but to contemplate becoming his wife . . . She didn't understand him, and at times, she wasn't even sure she liked him! He was so infuriating!

Yet, she wondered, how would it feel to have him always at her side? How would it feel to know he would always be there when she wanted or needed him? Did she want him to be hers? Did she want to be his? She clasped her fingers tightly together to stop their trembling. Yes. She did. She loved him, or at least she thought she did. She stared at the fire once more. How did someone know when they were in love?

Did being in love mean having your heart beat faster when someone approached? Did it mean pain whenever you were apart? What about the pain when you were together? Jessica sighed. She didn't know what being in love meant. She'd never been in love before, never felt the way she did before. Wasn't that enough? To feel the way she did?

Her mind wandered back over the past weeks to when she'd met Nick. How much they'd been through in such a short time! They'd saved each other's lives, risked everything to insure the safety and future of one another. Yet, in spite of this, they seldom got along.

It seemed they couldn't talk for more than a few minutes at a time before they were snarling like two stray dogs fighting over a bone. The only time they were able to endure one another's company was when he touched her . . .

Another chill tickled Jessica's body, and her face burned hotly. She was about to become his wife—to have and to hold from this day . . . When he touched her, everything else ceased to exist. There was only the two of them, together.

A worried frown creased Jessica's forehead. That was the way she felt about him, but what did he feel about her? He desired her, yes. But was his desire only for her body, or for her? Did he love her just a little? Didn't the way he held her, the gentleness underlying the hard strength, testify to something more inside him for her than mere physical want?

The music outside the tepee abruptly stopped, and the night filled with a black vacuum of quiet. Jessica's heart began to beat heavily. What now? One of the women who had spent the day with her entered the tepee. She smiled and motioned for Jessica to rise and follow her. It was time.

Jessica took a deep breath and stood slowly. Mindlessly she brushed at the buckskin dress and stared at the tepee entrance. How could she go through with this? How could she give herself to a man she knew so little about and yet cared so much for? A tremor passed through her. It was too late to run away. She must face whatever was about to happen. She must face it with Nick.

Sudden reassurance flooded into her. She wouldn't be alone in this. Nick would be there, too. He wouldn't let her be hurt, and he wouldn't hurt her. Of this, she was certain.

The flap of the tepee was held aside, and she emerged into the night. All around the camp bonfires were burning brightly. They held back the darkness with their dancing light and reflected off the sea of faces before her. There seemed to be people everywhere, their features alternately revealed and shadowed by the flickering flames. All eyes were on her.

Her chin lifted fractionally even as her knees began to tremble. She would not show her fear. She wouldn't let them know how afraid she was, and with grim determination, she began walking to where the chief stood. He was watching her, too, waiting for her.

She passed between the waiting people. They were all around her, and she could feel the warm black of their eyes following her every step. It was unnerving. She had to force herself to keep walking.

Her eyes darted ahead to the chief uncertainty, and his gaze locked with hers. A strength and wisdom earned from a lifetime of gladness and sorrow was etched deeply into the weather-beaten face of this aged warrior. He looked so proud, so commanding. And, in him, the echo of a once young and limber warrior, Jessica found the confidence she needed to put her fear aside. He did not expect her to falter, and she would not.

The distance closed between them, and Jessica's gaze dropped momentarily from the chief's only to raise again and encounter Nick's. Her heart skipped a beat as she was enveloped in the warm blue of his stare.

Dressed in buckskin also, Nick stood beside the Indian leader. His face had been shaved, and his eyes reflected the firelight as he watched Jessica approach. The soft, fringed dress she wore clung alluringly to her slender form, and the light glistened off the bead work woven to the leather and on the golden length of her hair.

Yet again he was struck by her beauty, by the fragility and the strength of her, and pride swelled within him. Though she must be afraid, surrounded by Apache Indians, caught up in events beyond her control, her head was held high. She wouldn't show her fear. She stopped before him, and together they turned to face the chief who began to speak.

The gray-haired Apache warrior's tongue played over strange new words in a melodic speech. He raised his hands and eyes to the sky and chanted praises to his gods. His people echoed his words, and when he lowered his arms again, it was to accept a long-bladed knife from the tribal medicine man.

Jessica forced her lips together to silence the gasp in her throat and determinedly offered her arm as the chief reached out toward her. Nick did the same, his expression unreadable.

Pain burned them both briefly as the knife gleamed brightly in the light, and then their wrists were pressed one to the other. Jessica felt suddenly dizzy and squeezed her eyes shut, opening them again when more words were uttered and a song was begun.

Chanting filled the air as their wrists were parted, and they turned to see the people gather in a dance. Drums beat out the rhythm and large shadows danced across the tepees as the Apaches moved in a circle around a roaring fire.

Jessica watched in trembling silence. It was over. It was really over. She glanced hesitantly up at Nick. He was watching the dancers. He seemed so calm! Her strength was renewed by his solid presence, and she willed the giddiness that had taken hold of her away. She returned her attention to the ceremony and watched it continue. It couldn't last much longer. Soon everyone would go back to their tepees, and she would sit down before her quaking knees collapsed.

Nick moved slightly, and she saw him lean towards Diego who was standing nearby. Nick listened intently to whispered words. Vaguely she was aware of Diego motioning across the camp, but her attention was caught by the dancing and chanting of the people around them and by the chief who was smiling down at her.

At last the music stopped. Jessica let out a silent sigh. Maybe now they could leave. But her hope died instantly as the drums began to beat again. The ceremony was not over. She swallowed tightly. How much longer?

Someone touched her arm, and Jessica looked up into Nick's face. Silently he encouraged her to move away, his firm hand on her arm guiding her carefully through the crowd of singing people and laughing children. She hoped no one would stop their departure.

She didn't want to stay any more. No one seemed to notice their leaving, however, and eventually they reached a tepee isolated from the rest.

Nick lifted the flap aside, and she stepped in with a sigh of relief. At last no one was watching them, no one was waiting. They were alone.

Nick followed her in, stopping to pull the flap shut behind them. It was finally over. He turned to speak, but stopped when Jessica unexpectedly threw herself against him. He smiled and gathered her to him gently to hold her for a long moment. He could feel the wild beating of her heart and the trembling in her limbs. Her fear was still a living thing. He drew her closer and stroked her hair softly, waiting patiently until the tension drained away and she lifted her head to look at him. "All right now?"

She nodded silently, her safety reassured, and turned without releasing herself from his embrace to look around the darkened tepee.

There was only a small fire illuminating the enclosure. It cast soft shadows on the blankets and fur rugs that had been lain out on the floor. There was also an assembly of clay containers with food and beverages for their consumption. All the comforts an Apache home could offer were here.

"In case you haven't guessed, this is the wedding tepee," Nick told her, his voice vibrating in her ear as it rested against his chest. "It's ours for as long as we stay."

Nick waited for her response, expecting a fiery retort, but none came. He frowned and realized she had suddenly become very still in his arms. He looked down to find her gazing up at him, and his throat tightened at the naked emotion he saw reflected in her eyes. His own yearning rose in response, and he dropped his head to roughly cover her mouth with his.

Jessica yielded willingly to his demands, molding her body against his. Her mind closed to all thoughts except him. The waiting was over. He was hers. She his. She wanted no more than this, having him touch her, hold her, set her on fire and crush her to him until she felt she could no longer breathe.

But Nick unexpectedly pulled away, pushing her back from him with suddenly stiffened arms. "You're too beautiful, Jess. You go to a man's head."

But still she didn't speak. She couldn't. She didn't want to. She only watched him, her eyes asking questions, saying words she had never been moved to speak before.

"Jess." The word sounded like a groan. "I won't touch you if you don't want me to."

Hesitantly her hands came to rest on the arms that held her away. "I . . . I want . . . I do want you to touch me."

Her words were barely audible, but Nick heard them. His blood began to pound, and his hands itched for the feel of her body under them. "Jess," he whispered hoarsely. "You've got to be sure. Because if I, if I touch you now, I don't know if I can stop."

She shook her head, her eyes still staring into his, green pools of open emotion. "I don't want you to stop."

They fell together, and Jessica clung to him as his hands buried themselves in her hair and pulled her head back. His lips covered hers with passionate fire and then moved to ignite the sensitive skin of her face and neck.

She pressed closer. She wanted more, and he was willing to give.

His hands dropped to caress her body. His fingers stroked and teased, and she gasped at the sensations he was creating. But she didn't pull away. This was what she wanted. All of him having all of her. Her fingers wound into the thickness of his hair and brought him down to her.

He met her quickly but then pulled back. He took her hands from him, and in one swift movement stripped the buckskin shirt from his chest. He tossed it aside and reached for her once more.

Her fingers contacted his warm skin. Hard muscle and bone moved beneath her trembling fingers, and she was crushed to the warm expanse of his flesh. His hands rushed over her body. His mouth was bruising, and his touch was hot. He couldn't get enough of her. Desire roared through his body, and his mouth harshly claimed hers again.

Her body arched back over his arm, and she whimpered at the massive assault on her senses. It was too much! She stirred fearfully against him. She felt dizzy and weak. He was overwhelming her. Her mind was reeling with the attempt to keep up with the erratic signals charging through her flaming limbs. She didn't want to stop, but she was afraid to go on.

Nick heard the helpless cry. It caught at the saner part of him. He was hurting her. He immediately loosened his hold and cursed himself. She wasn't used to this. She wasn't used to men. What was wrong with him? He was frightening her. He forced himself to stillness and folded her writhing body against his. She clung to him blindly, trusting even through her fear. He felt a shudder shake her and struggled to control his broken breathing. "I'm sorry, Jess. I'm sorry." He turned her face up to kiss her lightly. "I shouldn't rush you." He stroked her hair. "I'm going too fast."

She pressed her face against his bared chest and waited while the waves of chaotic sensations within her ebbed to a gentler tide. There was nothing to be afraid of. He understood. She became conscious of a trembling and thought it was she who shook. But it wasn't. It wasn't her. It was Nick. She moved hesitantly, unwilling and unable to release her hold on him. She lifted her head to look up at him and was immediately consumed by the blue fire of his gaze. His eyes were alive with desire, a desire waiting to devour her, but he wasn't moving. He was waiting. For what?

Sudden understanding dawned within her, and she wondered at her discovery. He was uncertain. He was afraid of his own power and of her power over him! And now he was waiting for some sign from her, waiting to see if she still wanted him or if he had destroyed her desire by the ferocity of his.

She murmured incoherently and reached a gentle hand up to touch his face. He caught it and kissed her palm. His eyes met hers for a long moment. Then his head slowly descended. She met the feather-light touch of his lips. It teased her, and the taunt drew her closer. She wanted more than this.

He groaned and gathered her to him, but not with the crushing intensity she had experienced before. No, this time it was with a tenderness that was more devastating than his earlier passion. She melted against him and trembled as the embrace deepened warmly.

His fingers lowered to the leather thongs fastening

the buckskin dress together. A tug here. There. The garment slipped from her. Cool air fanned her body, and she shivered against him. Their flesh brushed together, and his hands framed her face. His hands were lost in the thickness of her golden hair. His mouth coaxed, and he moved slightly, guiding her. Then, without a word, he eased them both down to the waiting bed.

Camp sounds echoed outside the tepee as Nick laid next to Jessica, holding her against him. During the past night he had possessed her and she him. Never before had a woman touched him the way she had. Shrouded in innocence and yet yearning to please him, she had made him show more patience than he knew he had.

His arm tightened instinctively around her. She moved closer in response, seeking his warmth unconsciously, but she continued to sleep on. Her arm was draped over him in naive possession. She looked so vulnerable, so beautiful.

The sounds outside the tepee drew his attention once more, and Nick frowned. He did not want her to wake up alone, but there were things to be arranged. He had to see Diego. As much as he wanted to stay, he knew he had to go.

With careful reluctance, he extracted himself from her hold and stood to dress. It took only moments to slip into the buckskin clothing he had discarded the evening before, but he didn't leave until he knelt to cover Jessica with a woven blanket and listened to the deep and steady rhythm of her breathing. It assured him that it would be a while yet before she woke.

He stepped out into the sun and blinked against the

sudden glare of light. He hadn't realized it was so late. He shaded his eyes momentarily to get his bearings and then continued on.

The camp was alive with sound and movement. Children played, women cleaned skins, cooked and carried out other numerous chores. He passed one old woman who nodded to him with a knowing grin playing over her almost toothless jaws.

Embarrassed heat surged into his face and burned beneath his tanned skin. He jerked away immediately, angry at his own foolish reaction. Then Rito suddenly appeared, running across the camp to halt beside him.

"*Señor* Nick, where have you been? You and Jess have slept a long time."

Nick shifted on his feet uneasily, looking away from the suspicious eyes. He was not willing to feed the ears he was certain had heard more than Rito would willingly admit. "We were tired, *chico*. Where's Diego?"

"Over there."

Nick followed the direction of Rito's pointed finger and saw Diego wave and begin to move toward him. Diego had been talking with Running Wolf and some of the young braves of the Apache camp. Nick walked to meet him.

Diego's habitual grin was spread across his face as he approached, but with studied care he said nothing of the night before. "I have been speaking with Running Wolf, *amigo*, and we may have improved on our luck."

"How so?"

"There have been wagons and mule trains through here recently. The men who run the wagons have given the Apaches traded goods to insure safe passage through the territory, but Running Wolf and his people are growing suspicious of their many passings."

"Does Running Wolf know what these men are carrying?"

"No. But he says the wagon tracks are heavy in sand."

"Guns."

Diego nodded. "I think yes."

"Does he know where they're going or where they're coming from?"

"Only directions. They usually come from the northeast and go south," Diego replied. "Running Wolf has sent scouts to try to give us a more accurate direction."

Nick frowned thoughtfully. "I can't believe they're coming from Santa Fe. Going south, yes." He shook his head. "If they're south of here, that means we've been searching too far west because since leaving that village, we've been going northeast."

"This is what I was thinking also. Perhaps they are only a day's ride into the territory but are sending their men further to serve as decoys and to insure their own safety. By having the men travel so far and so long, their loyalty would be proven before they were allowed to meet Franklin."

Nick nodded. "But north and east. Where from, Diego?"

"It cannot be Santa Fe. Oklahoma perhaps?"

"Through the Strip?" Nick frowned again. "Hard territory to get through. There's been a lot of Indian trouble there."

"But, if they could do it . . ."

Nick slowly nodded. "If they could do it, it would

be perfect. Going north out of the Confederate states, they'd avoid all the Union scouts and within days be inside the Texas Panhandle. Not many people are settled there, but what few there are, it's pretty certain they'd be southern sympathizers.''

"From there it would be a short journey into the territory and safety. I think this is what is happening, *amigo*.''

"We'll have to split up.''

Diego shrugged. "There should be no problem for this. But whoever goes north could see to it that our *chiquita* gets home and Rito with her.''

Nick frowned. "I don't like taking them with us again. It's too dangerous. We've already run into trouble. We're bound to meet it again.'' He paused thoughtfully. "Running Wolf. Could his people see they get to Santa Fe? They can move easier through this territory than we can and can go undetected.''

Diego nodded. "It is possible. I will speak with him.''

"Good.'' Nick glanced back toward the tepee where Jessica lay. Sending her away. It wasn't going to be easy, and for more reasons than one. He turned back to watch Diego approach Running Wolf. They exchanged rapid words and motions. In moments Diego returned.

"He tells me he will see to it himself,'' Diego told Nick with a satisfied smile. "They will be seen there safely.''

Nick nodded thankfully to Running Wolf who remained standing a short distance away and turned again to Diego. "I'll go tell Jess. You take care of Rito?''

"I will do this. You wish to leave tomorrow?"

"First thing. I'll head north."

"And I south."

Nick moved off, his jaw setting grimly. Leaving Jessica behind. She'd fight him. There was no doubt in his mind that she would. But he would win. He had to. And, he had to make her understand. After last night . . . His frown deepened. He wouldn't risk her life again.

Slipping the tepee flap aside, he entered, standing a moment to allow his eyes to adjust to the darkness. Jessica was still sleeping, curled peacefully beneath the warmth of the blanket.

Nick fell silently to his knees beside her and reached out to brush her face gently with his hand. She moved drowsily. He ran his fingers over her bared shoulder, and she stirred again, stretching under the blanket and blinking her eyes open. He smiled. "Welcome back."

She returned the smile but colored brightly as memory returned. Self-consciously she cradled the blanket over her nakedness and glanced around the tepee. "What time is it?"

He shrugged. "Late. Near noon I expect."

"Noon!" she exclaimed sitting up, clutching the blanket to her.

He smiled and sank back on his heels to watch her, the heat in her face was deepening. "Don't worry. People are used to newlyweds sleeping late the morning after."

"Nick!"

He raised an inquiring eyebrow. "Would you rather we'd have slept all night so we could be up early?"

She shifted uncomfortably under his steady gaze and held the blanket tighter to her. Last night. How could she wish it hadn't happened?

Reaching out he pushed her down until she lay on her back looking up at him. "Should I answer my own question?"

She shook her head mutely but did not resist when he took possession of her mouth with his.

Raising his head slowly, he stared down into her eyes. "We're leaving tomorrow."

"Where to?" she asked, watching as he sat up and turned away. Warning bells went off in her head immediately. There was something wrong. He wouldn't look at her.

"I'm going north, Diego south, and you and Rito are going with Running Wolf to Santa Fe, or at least to a white settlement near there."

"What?"

"You heard me and no arguments."

She struggled to a sitting position as he poked harshly at the ashes of the dead fire with a stick. "I won't go."

"You will."

"I won't. I'm going with you."

"You can't."

"Why not?"

"It's too dangerous."

"I don't care."

"I do."

She glared at his back, scowling darkly before spinning away to bury her face in the rug.

Nick turned to look down at her. Her backbone was stiff with anger and frustration. "Jess . . ."

"Leave me alone."

Sighing in exasperation, he moved to touch her shoulder, but she jerked away. "Jess, stop it!" he snapped, his intended patience evaporating.

"I told you to leave me alone," she retorted bitterly, trying to stop the tears from sliding down her cheeks. He was leaving. He had used her and now he was leaving. It hadn't been real . . .

Eyeing her back in frustration, Nick felt his temper rise at her illogical reasoning and at his own inability to explain. Angrily he stood to leave. He was more than willing to accept her wishes. But, he couldn't go. Even as he spun to leave, he turned back and fell to his knees at her side. He grasped her shoulders and jerked her around.

"Let me go!" she cried, lashing out at him. "You got what you came for. Isn't that enough?"

Gritting his teeth, he blocked her blows until he was able to grab her wrists. "I told you to stop it!" he said giving her a vicious shake. "And stop saying things you know aren't true."

"How do I know they're not true?" she demanded tearfully, her eyes pleading for an answer.

"Because," he stammered helplessly. "Because we're man and wife."

"According to the Apaches. You told me last night it wouldn't mean anything in a white man's court."

"I said I didn't know."

"You said it wasn't likely."

"Damn it, Jess! I'm not a lawyer," he snapped. "Now stop fighting and listen to me."

"I'm not going to listen," she shot back hotly and clamped her hands over her ears.

Nick pulled her hands away and shook her again. "Will you stop acting like a child?"

"No!"

His eyes narrowed, and he glared down at her. "If I have to take you over my knee and warm that bare bottom of yours to get you to listen, I will."

"You wouldn't dare," she seethed.

"Wouldn't I?" he demanded. "If you want to act like a child, I'm going to treat you like one."

Returning his glare, she felt her determination waver under the hard gray of his eyes. But not soon enough. His hand moved. She tried to jump away, but fell flat on her face when he grabbed her ankle and pulled it from under her.

The protecting blanket was forgotten. It fell aside as she rolled, bit, kicked and scratched in an attempt to get away from him. But it was no use. Within tortured seconds she lay gasping for breath beneath him while he pinned her arms above her head.

"Now. You're going to listen to me," he told her through clenched teeth. "Last night has nothing to do with why I'm leaving. Diego and I have something to do. We started it before we even met you, and we're going to finish it."

He released her and sat back looking down at her.

"You can believe me or not. It's up to you. But your opinion won't change our leaving tomorrow." He rolled away. "I never expected last night to happen. It wasn't something I'd planned."

Jessica studied his back and chewed apprehensively at her lip. He was right. It wasn't his fault. But she didn't want him to leave. What if he never came back?

"Does that mean you're sorry it did?"

"I didn't say . . ." He turned his head to look at her. "No. I've wanted that for a long time."

Forcing herself to meet the angry glitter in his eyes, she sat up, trying to rearrange the blanket so it covered her nakedness. "Can't I come with you?"

"No."

"I could help."

"No. You saw what happened back in that village."

"But that's why I want to come with you."

He gestured impatiently. "No, Jess. I mean it. I've told you why and I won't say it again." He rose quickly to his feet, avoiding her eyes. Damn her! Didn't she know he wanted to take her with him? Why couldn't she understand? "I've got things to do." He moved to the tepee entrance.

"Nick! Please don't go," she pleaded. "I mean, not now. Not yet."

He stopped and slowly turned back to face her. Her hair was tumbling over her shoulders, and she was clutching the brightly woven blanket to her. His throat tightened and he clenched his fists against the rising heat of desire.

"Won't you stay with me? Can't you? For a little while?"

Sighing and running his eyes over her, he watched the color begin to glow in her cheeks. "Are you sure you want me to?"

She rose and walked to him.

He stared down at her for a long, silent moment, not moving. One minute he wanted to wring her neck, and the next . . . He put a hand out to brush the hair from her face. "Woman, what am I going to do with you?"

She smiled tremulously and moved forward into his embrace. He did not object when she wrapped her arms around his neck, and the blanket fell away.

Chapter 15

Darkness crept upon the Apache camp, and with it came the approaching sound of running horses. Sitting outside the tepee with Diego and Running Wolf, Nick rose with the two men to watch a band of braves thunder into their midst whooping wildly and calling out in excitement.

Several young men in the camp answered the new-comers' words with echoing shouts and turned eagerly to watch Running Wolf as he stepped forward to speak rapidly with one of the newly arrived bucks.

"What's happening?" Nick whispered to Diego as Jessica hurriedly crossed the camp with Rito to join them.

Diego's expression was grim. "Comanches. They have invaded the Apache territory."

A dark frown settled on Nick's face at Diego's response, but Jessica didn't understand why. "What does that mean?"

"War," Nick answered bluntly. The word sent a cold chill down her back. "The Apaches will have to go out and meet the Comanches and try to drive them back."

"It is a war they do not always win," Diego added softly. "The Comanche warrior is the only enemy the Apache fears."

Rito moved closer to her, and Jessica put a comforting arm around the boy's slim shoulders. War between two rival tribes. It meant conflict and death for the braves who would come together on the battlefield, but what did it mean to those left behind? What did it mean to them, white men in an Indian camp? "What are we going to do?"

Diego shook his head, his eyes locked on his blood brother who stood talking to the braves who had brought back the news. "We will have to wait and see, *chiquita*."

They watched Running Wolf turn away and hurry to his father's tepee. The other elders of the tribe were quick to follow, joining their chief and his son in council, and as the flap to the single tepee closed, the braves left outside huddled together around the other rawhide structures in animated and angry talk.

The peaceful atmosphere of the camp was abruptly gone. It had been replaced by the tension of hostile emotion, and the village began to hum with activity.

The young men were ready to fight to defend their territory and were quick to gather weapons and discuss plans of battle while solemn-faced women hurried about preparing food for the camp supper. The squaws knew it was a meal which could prove to be the last they would share with some of their men, but any personal worry was not expressed. The enemy had come and had to be stopped and, it was for the men of the tribe to see it done.

Twilight faded into the darkness of night with no sign of movement from the chief's tepee. The sky filled with stars, and fires were lit to illuminate the camp site while the evening meal was consumed. After eating, the bustle of activity gradually dwindled to expectant silence. Warriors and their women sat waiting by their lodge doors. A decision would be reached by the council soon. It was only a matter of time.

Jessica sat outside, too, quietly observing all the sober faces around her. Even Rito was affected by the solemnity that had descended on the camp. He sat without speaking, close to her, but with an eye for Nick and Diego.

Jessica was watching the men, too. It was obvious they were concerned, but neither voiced any opinions. It wasn't a time for guessing. What would happen, would happen soon enough without any speculation. However, she knew the worry between the two was greatest for Diego. As the chief's son, Running Wolf would no doubt hold a position of responsibility in driving the Comanches from Apache land. That would place him in the thick of any fighting. Jessica was sure Diego's fears were centered on his blood brother's safety.

At long last, with firelight dancing across his aged face, the chief emerged into the night. The elders of the tribe followed him out of the tepee and stood with unreadable expressions as the old warrior prepared himself to speak to his people.

The Apache tribe gathered swiftly and quietly to

listen, moving into a semicircle surrounding their leader, and when he began to speak, no other sound could be heard as an intense quiet covered the camp.

Jessica sat very still as the chief's voice filled the air, tension holding every muscle in her body rigidly in place. Each face she could see, whether man, woman or child, was blank. Each revealed no thought. Emotions were hidden as everyone listened to and accepted the word of the chief and as everyone waited willingly to do his bidding.

But suddenly, as the chief stopped speaking, the silence broke, and the night was rent by the chilling cries of the young men. Their voices blended together into one united battle cry. It was war! They were going to meet their enemy!

Across from her Diego sighed, and his head bent slightly as he looked away from the scene of jubilantly yelling warriors. "Diego?" she ventured anxiously.

"At dawn tomorrow the braves will leave to meet the Comanche to drive them away." Diego spoke the words slowly, sadly.

"All the men will go?" Jessica asked, watching the braves break from the crowd to make their way to their separate tepees.

"All who are physically able. Only the old, crippled and very young will remain behind," Diego replied and stood.

Nick stayed seated and silent as Diego left them to make his way to where Running Wolf stood by his chieftain father. Nick knew what this raid would mean to the Apaches. He knew what it would mean to Diego to see his blood brother go off into a battle from which he might not return. And, he knew what it would do to their own departure plans. Slowly he rose, too, his eyes never straying from the trio of men who stood talking across the camp.

Jessica got to her feet as well, and Rito quickly followed their example and slipped his hand into Nick's.

"*Señor* Nick, does this mean we will not leave tomorrow?"

Nick looked down and ruffled the thick black hair on Rito's head. "No, *amigo*. We'll leave. We just won't be going like we expected."

Jessica tried to make Nick meet her eyes, to make him answer the question beating hopefully in her throat, but he would not. He was intent on watching Diego, not her, and so forced to keep an unwilling silence, she turned to watch as well, looking in time to see Diego clasp Running Wolf tightly before moving away to return to them.

It did not take long for Diego to cover the distance, but when he arrived, many unbroken moments passed before he was able to speak. Emotions had locked his throat tight. "There will be horses and supplies for us tomorrow."

Nick nodded at the short explanation. It was what he had expected. "We'll leave first thing in the morning."

Diego, his dark eyes avoiding those of the others, held a hand out to Rito. "Come on, *chico*. We must get some sleep."

Jessica opened her mouth to speak as Diego and Rito turned away, but a firm hand on her arm silenced her. She looked up at Nick with uncomprehending eyes. What did Diego mean they would be provided with horses and supplies? Did that mean they were leaving together? That they weren't going to split up, go separate ways?

But there were no answers for her as Nick abruptly left her to enter their tepee. She followed hastily but once inside hesitated to speak. Nick was squatting by the fire, poking at the flames with a smoldering stick. His face was closed, his eyes blank as he stared unseeing into the dancing light.

Silently she knelt beside him. She wished she understood more. She wished she knew exactly what it was that Nick and Diego were doing in the New Mexico Territory and why they were following people who seemed to be Confederates. She had tried to make Nick tell her, asked him to explain, but he would never say. Her questions had been evaded, her curious looks ignored, and when she had become too persistent, she had been stilled by the weight of his body on hers, his lips holding hers.

"You better get some rest," he finally said, his eyes still held by the flames. "We'll be leaving early tomorrow."

"I know," she answered, holding back the flood of words threatening to pour out. "I'd rather wait for you."

His head turned, and he met her steady gaze. "That's likely to be awhile."

"I'll wait."

A small smile touched his mouth. "You're ready to fight me yet, aren't you?"

She didn't return his smile. "If I have to."

He nodded slowly. "You'll still have to wait." And so saying, he stood to leave.

"Don't make me wait too long?"

Without answering Nick stooped and went from the tepee, the flap falling into place behind him. For a moment he stopped to listen in the dark. The camp was filled with sound. He began walking through it. A combination of private preparations was coming from each individual tepee. Women gathering food, men readying weapons. He reached Diego's tepee. It was quiet there, and as he had suspected, Diego was not inside. He was standing next to the tepee staring up at the sky.

Diego turned at Nick's approach, and a companionable and understanding silence enveloped them for a moment before Diego finally spoke. "You will go with Jessica tomorrow?"

"I don't see any other way," Nick answered, watching a single gray cloud drift slowly across the stars. "Maybe on the way I can find some means of getting her back to Santa Fe. Let's hope so anyway."

"There are friends two or three day's ride south of here who will keep Rito for a time. He will be safe there until we have finished."

"Did the scouts bring back any more information?"

"Only more of what Running Wolf has already told us, *amigo*. The men come from the north and east and go south."

Silence returned to linger over them.

"How long do you think it will take you to get the answers down south?"

Diego shrugged. "Three weeks?"

"Where should we meet?"

Diego paused thoughtfully. "There is a village near

the Pecos called Piedra. It is not so far from Santa Fe. South and west maybe two day's hard ride and close to where I think our answers might be.''

"I know it. You're sure you can make it in only three weeks? You've a lot of ground to cover.''

Diego looked off to the south. ''I do not think this will take so long where I am going. It is only a matter of discovering in which direction they go and a look at the land. I know the area south of here well. Once close, I will not need to see exactly where they go to know where they are.''

"I wish I could say the same. I may be in for a long ride.''

Diego grinned. "Maybe you will not be back in three weeks, eh? Perhaps I will have a chance to entertain the *señoritas* of Piedra.''

"Perhaps,'' Nick agreed with a reflective grin. "Ride carefully, *amigo*.''

"And you also. I do not think our *chiquita* would take kindly to you being shot.''

Nick rolled his eyes at the wide grin Diego sent him and moved away. The plan was laid. With the arrangements at least partially settled, he felt somewhat better. But, he hadn't counted on having Jessica with him.

It was going to be a hard ride over even harder land, and he couldn't guarantee safety for himself much less her. If he was lucky, he would be able to find someone in a small village he could trust to take her to Santa Fe. She'd be safer with her father than with him.

But as he stepped inside the tepee and saw her sitting beside the fire waiting for him, combing out the golden hair she had braided only hours before, he couldn't suppress the hope that such a village might not be found any more than he could suppress his sudden desire.

She turned as he entered, looking up at him from where she sat, and was suddenly reminded again of that night so long ago in Independence when she had sat on the ground gazing up at him. He seemed taller, broader, and she felt her heart start to beat in anticipation as he stopped to stand above her.

A strong hand reached down to help her rise.

Wordlessly she came to her feet before him. Where would they be tomorrow? Together or apart?

His fingers caught her chin, and he stared down into her green eyes now wide with unasked and unanswered questions. "We're leaving together tomorrow."

Jessica's heart leapt in excitement, but she managed to keep her voice steady. "We. You mean . . . ?"

"Us," he answered and stopped further discussion by closing his mouth over hers and holding her to him until her body melted against his in complete submission.

The next night Jessica sat huddled inside the warmth of a blanket listening to the sounds Nick made while checking on the horses hobbled a short distance away.

At dawn she and Nick, along with Diego and Rito, had stood in silence as the Apache braves of the camp had ridden off into the gray morning. Running Wolf had been with them, war paint lined across his face and torso. All of the young men had similarly decorated their lean bodies, and all of them had carried bows and arrows. Some of them also had stolen rifles.

The women, children and elders of the camp had also watched as the young men of their tribe had raced off to war. None of them had spoken, however, and none of them had shed tears or given way to fears of their own never returning. Instead they had only waited to see their warriors go before turning to do daily chores. This day was to be treated no differently than any other. War, for them, was an accepted way of life.

With the young men of the village gone, the chief came to say his farewell to Diego, smiling warmly at him and nodding approvingly at Jessica.

Jessica smiled back as he spoke to her but had to look to Diego for the meaning of the chief's words. "What did he say?"

Diego grinned, but a soft flush of embrassassed heat rose to shine beneath his skin. "He says he hopes you will have many fine sons for my friend."

Jessica felt her own face flame hotly in response and heard Nick grunt before he managed to smother a smile. She shot him a meangingful glare and struggled to recover her voice. "Please thank him for his best wishes, Diego, and for allowing us to stay."

Diego, fighting down a grin of his own, translated her words for the chief.

The Apache leader soberly accepted what she said, spoke once more, clasped Diego to him and walked away, his gray head held proudly erect as he returned to his tepee. It was the last time Jessica saw him, for the four of them left the camp together then, following in the wake of the departing braves but at a much slower pace and in a different direction. They'd traveled only a short distance, however, before drawing to a halt. It was time for them to separate.

"You make sure he does not lead you both into trouble, *chiquita*," Diego cautioned her with a lopsided grin. "Sometimes my *amigo* does not think before he acts."

Jessica smiled and ignored Nick's sour look. "I'll do my best, Diego, but considering your friend's disposition, it will not be an easy task."

Diego laughed merrily at her emphatic shrug. "I think, perhaps, it will not be easy for either of you."

"Amen," Nick had agreed with a reflective eye on Jessica.

Now Jessica smiled as she looked into the night, but the smile had a touch of sadness to it as she remembered the parting. Little Rito had been so excited, looking forward to whatever adventure lay ahead. For him there was no thought of danger. Only for fun. She sighed. Oh, to be so young and eager! How she wished she could share his high spirits and enthusiasm! But how could she?

Sitting in a dark camp where no fire burned to reveal their location to any other travelers who might be about, it was difficult to feel anything more than apprehension toward an uncertain future. She wondered again at the rapid turn of events that had placed her in this place and time. It had all started so simply . . .

She shook her head at her thoughts. The best laid plans, or so her grandmother had often said. Her smile returned in happy reflection. What would that aged and graceful lady say if she could see her granddaughter at this moment? Back in her peasant shirt and pants, riding astride a horse like a man . . . and sharing a bed with a man.

Jessica looked up as the sound of Nick's footsteps carried him to her, and defiance flared up to counter her inquiring thoughts. She didn't care how anyone else felt toward her actions. She didn't regret anything she'd done. Circumstances had brought her together with a man she'd come to love. She wouldn't change anything leading up to that.

Nick stooped down to sit beside her. "Tired?"

"A little."

He smiled in the dark, a small private expression for the woman beside him. She was as stubborn as ever, unwilling to admit her own weaknesses. "We'd better get some rest. We'll be up and moving before dawn."

Jessica listened to and watched his vague shadow as he spread a blanket out on the ground and then guided her to it. She lay down next to him and snuggled close to the hard length of him as he pulled another blanket over them. For a moment she could feel desire for her in him, but he remained silent and unmoving beside her, apparently wanting only to hold her for now. But, tired though she was, sleep would not come. Her body wanted to rest. Her mind did not.

Silence hung heavily around them, and for her the darkness was almost oppressing. It hid everything. Kept it from view.

A cricket chirped, and its song echoed hollowly through the air. This land seemed so endless, and more so in the black of night. Endless and unknown. Unconsciously she shivered and moved closer to Nick.

Nick felt her stir and tightened his arm around her in gentle reassurance. "Frightened, little one?"

"Yes," she murmured quietly and was glad for the lean strength of him beside her. But, despite the comfort of his presence and the need for sleep, she found nagging questions hanging persistently in her mind. "Nick?" she ventured after a moment.

He grunted in response.

"Are you and Diego chasing somebody?"

Silence. "I thought you were tired."

"I am, but . . . I want to know." Another moment of silence followed her curious retort, and disappointment burned her. It seemed he was going to deny her an answer again. But she was wrong.

"Yes."

"Is he doing something wrong?"

"He is."

It was her turn to fall silent, but she couldn't remain still. There was more she wanted to know. "What are you going to do when you find him?" She felt him shrug in response.

"Stop him if we can."

"How? What's he doing?"

Unexpectedly Nick squeezed her, making her expel the breath in her lungs. "I'm tired. Go to sleep. We'll talk tomorrow."

Resentful of his tactics and his ability to control her, Jessica pushed back from him slightly. "Why do you always get your way?"

"Because I'm bigger."

"Nick . . ."

"Go to sleep."

Something in his tone warned her not to persist, but it made her mad. Why did he always win? Irritably she flopped on her side and put her back to him. It wasn't fair. He never told her anything.

A well-muscled arm snaked out and wrapped around her. Before she could protest, it tightened and pulled and brought her back to Nick with a jerk. "You're mad."

She didn't answer but remained stiff and silent.

"Why?"

Still no answer.

"Because I'm bigger than you?"

She could hear the laughter in his voice and had to smile herself. It was silly to argue. Silly because it kept her from him instead of near him. She rolled onto her other side so they lay face to face. "No, because I care about you. Because I want to know everything about you."

His fingers reached out to stroke her face in the night. "You already know everything that's important."

Jessica felt his lips brush hers, and she asked no more.

Chapter 16

Two days came and went as time dragged slowly on through the scorching New Mexican heat. Resting only occasionally, Jessica and Nick spent most of the long hours in the saddle with Nick stopping often to dismount and examine tracks in the sand.

The tracks showed wagons had been through the area, wagons that left deep ruts in the dust-ridden plains. Jessica wondered at his interest in the wagon tracks, asking herself countless times why he should be when he was after one man, but she maintained her silence.

The talk he had promised the next morning had never come, and somehow she knew better than to pursue the subject. He didn't want to talk about it and wasn't going to. And, left with too much time to think, she tried to ignore any plaguing questions by turning her thoughts to other things.

"Are we far from Santa Fe?" she asked the third

night as they sat once again in a dark camp chewing on jerky and drinking water from a canteen.

"Not very. A few days' ride." He looked at her in the moon's soft light. "Thinking about your father?"

She sighed. She was getting used to the way Nick could seemingly read her mind. The past long hours had allowed her ample opportunity to wonder about the man she had come west to see. "I wish I knew what he was doing, what he feels about me. I was supposed to be there by now." Had her not reaching Santa Fe upset him in any way? By now he would have had to have heard about the attack on the stage. Had the news caused distress or had it come as a relief? And what of the others in her life? Those she had left behind in Boston? "I wonder if he's written Grandfather about me yet."

"And if he has?"

She shook her head with a small smile. "I hate to think. Grandfather will yell, and Grandmom will cry. Mrs. Abbott will probably say she was right all along and that it was all my father's fault."

"What will your father say when he gets that response?"

She shrugged uncertainly. "I wish I knew."

Nick felt the curiosity he had experienced while traveling on the stage with her stir again. She had mentioned her father rarely over the last several days, but he'd often seen her lost in thought. Was it Nathan Wescott who was on her mind? She didn't say, and he hesitated to ask. There was a reluctance on her part to discuss the parent she'd come so far to see. Why? "You said once you hadn't been out here since you were born. Haven't you seen your father since then?"

"No. He sent me back East to be raised when I was very young."

"He never went to Boston to see you?"

"Never."

He heard the bitterness and hurt in her voice, but there was confusion in her moonlit expression as well. "Why did he send you away? Where was your mother?"

"She died from a fever shortly after my birth."

"I can understand why he sent you away," Nick said quietly after a long moment had passed. "This territory isn't easy to live in now. It was worse twenty years ago. More Indians, more bandits, the aftermath of our fight with Mexico for Texas." He watched her closely. She wouldn't meet his eyes. "The first settlers out here didn't have it easy. My mother died out here, too."

"Your mother?" she asked, abruptly forgetting her own loss. Nick had never spoken to her about his family.

"Yes, she died when I was about six. She was thrown from her horse."

"I'm sorry."

He shook his head. He barely remembered the woman who had borne him. Over the years, she'd become little more than a distant image. "It was a long time ago." He glanced at her. "Your father never wrote?"

She started out of her reverie. She had been imagining Nick as a young boy. "Not very often."

"Men don't generally find letter writing easy."

"Just because it isn't easy doesn't mean he shouldn't do it," she retorted sharply.

"Did you write him?"

"When I was old enough."

"And before then? Did your grandparents write?"

"I don't know. I suppose so." She fell silent. "They don't like him very much."

"Maybe that's why he didn't write more often. Maybe your grandparents discouraged him, or maybe he just didn't know what to say. After all, he didn't know you—still doesn't."

"That's his fault!"

Nick sighed. "Could be he has a perfectly good reason, Jess. I wouldn't condemn him before meeting him."

She shifted uneasily. "I don't, not really. It's just . . ." She looked up at him, her uncertainty reflected in the depths of her eyes. Did her father care about her? Did she matter at all to him?

"I know," he whispered softly. "I know." And lowering his head to hers, he kissed her and pushed her back against the waiting blanket.

Before dawn had tinted the eastern horizon with its rays, they were in the saddle again, once more following wagon wheel tracks. It was mid-afternoon when Nick stopped to dismount to study the tracks for several minutes. Raising his head, he stood with his hands on his hips staring off to the east.

Until now he'd been backtracking wagons. But recently, the tracks had become fresher. When he'd left Diego, it had been to follow the Confederate's trail north until he was able to determine where the tracks originated. Diego, on the other hand, was to follow the tracks south until he found where the trail ended.

Nick frowned. In the process of going backwards up the trail, he'd come to a separation point—where old tracks continued south and where new ones, coming from the northeast and going south, joined in. It could only mean one thing. A new shipment was in the area.

There was a loop in the trail where he stood now. A loop that circled away from the main trail before coming back to it. Nick's frown deepened. There was a village he knew of not too far beyond this point. Was it where the loop led to? Was that where the Confederates were at this moment—with a new shipment of weapons?

"Nick? What is it?"

He glanced back at Jessica and then to the tracks once more. "There's a village a few hours' ride from here."

Jessica's brow furrowed at his response. Though spoken in answer, the answer sounded like a question. "Do you think the man you're looking for is there?"

"No," he replied decisively, turning back to swing himself up onto his horse. "He's not there, but some explanations might be." Nick started off, leaving Jessica no option but to follow on behind. He wanted to take a look in that village. He wanted to see how the Confederates were transporting the weapons. If there was a shipment in the village, there was even the possibility of being able to disrupt delivery. If he could do so, he would. Then he would have to return to backtracking the trail to continue his search to discover exactly where the guns were coming from—even though he had a good idea already. Once he was sure, he could meet Diego in Piedra, compare findings, and they could meet Evans and turn all they knew over to him.

The village, Jessica observed wearily hours later,

even under the cover of darkness looked much like the one they had been in before. Adobe buildings huddled together along dirt streets.

Nick pulled up in the shadow of a building and scanned the quiet, empty walks carefully. It was past midnight, and there were few lights glittering from the windows along the street. There was no sound or movement he could detect either, or at least none that was human.

The wheel tracks led right through this town. Down the main street. He wondered. Was this part of a chain? A chain of isolated villages which served as stopovers for the Confederate drivers, a place where they could eat and sleep before continuing on their way to their final destination?

Jessica moved restlessly beside Nick on her horse, and he turned to look at her. A few days of continuous travel had already taken their toll on her. Though she was rapidly becoming used to the weather and the riding, the two elements combined were more wearing on her because she was not as used to this kind of travel as he was. He'd have to find her some place safe to rest and stay. She'd have to be out of the way tomorrow. He wanted the people in this town to believe he'd arrived alone.

Moving slowly into the sleeping village, he led the way to the back streets in search of a sanctuary. Thankfully, it didn't take long to find and came in the form of an apparently empty house. He stopped his horse in front of it and dismounted. Carefully he stepped around the door which had half fallen from its broken hinges. He had to make certain there was no one inside. He drew his gun.

Jessica watched him disappear into the building in silent alarm. She'd known Nick long enough to realize he never took out his gun unless he was planning on using it. But what could he use it on here? She strained to hear what was happening inside the dark and deserted structure. But, there was no sound. Only silence. What was he doing? Why were they stopping here? What was he looking for? Fear gnawed at her stomach and made her skin crawl. Where was he? She moved to slip from her horse to join him but stopped when he emerged unharmed and hurried toward her.

He lifted her down from the saddle. "Go on inside. It's dirty but empty and safe."

"Why . . . ?"

"Just do as you're told," he snapped harshly.

Hurt and surprised at his tone, she stumbled away into the building, turning to watch as he led her horse inside after her.

Nick quickly went outside again, though, and Jessica moved to a broken window to watch him. Why were they staying here? Why not the stable? And why bring the horses inside? Or rather, why only her horse? She shook her head uncertainly as he led his horse around the side of the house before returning to her.

"Nick, what . . . ?"

"Be quiet and listen," he told her firmly but more gently as he came to her, drawing her from the window. "I haven't got much time."

Guiding her cautiously through the darkness of the rooms, he found an unbroken chair and sat her down. He knelt in front of her and grasped her shoulders.

"I want no arguments now, Jess. I'm going to tell you this once. You've got to listen and do as I say. I'm going to leave you here . . ."

She moved to object, but his fingers tightened on her shoulders.

"You stay here with your horse, and no matter what happens, don't go outside. Stay hidden. You've got food and water, and you'll be safe enough here for a day. I'll get back to you as soon as I can."

"But what about you?" she blurted.

"I'm going to go back out and down to the stable. I want the people here to think I've come alone. It'll be better that way."

"But why? What are you going to do?"

"I'm going to wander around and ask a few questions."

"But . . ."

"No buts, Jess. I mean it." His voice was hard. "If something happens, if I don't come back within two days, you go. Understand? You get on that horse and ride."

"Nick . . ."

"No! You don't come looking for me, and you don't ask any questions. You just wait until it's dark and ride out. You get on that road and keep riding, understand? It will take you north to Santa Fe."

"But what about you? What if you're hurt and can't get back to me? I could help . . ."

"No, Jess, no!" He shook his head angrily, impatiently. This time she could not interfere. It was too risky. He was too close to the source of supply. The men in the village would be wary, and they'd be ready to kill to protect what they carried. "If I don't come back, under no condition are you to come looking for me. It'll be too dangerous."

"But why?"

He sighed. "Jess, I can't explain. There's no time now, and it's best you don't know. The less you know, the better. Just do as I say. All right?"

"I . . . all right."

"Good girl." He gave her a quick hug and looked around the room. "There's a bedroom over there. The bed may not be in the best condition, but it'll be softer than lying on the floor." He turned back to her. "You'll be fine here."

She nodded at the statement, more than a little confused at this rapid and unexpected turn of events. "I'll wait for you."

"Seems to me you're always waiting," he told her softly.

"I don't mind."

He smiled and pulled her to her feet. She wrapped her arms around him tightly, and he squeezed her in response. "I've left you the rifle. Use it if you have to." He felt her shiver against him and hugged her in firm reassurance. "I've got to go."

Reluctantly she released her grip and leaned back from him. He took hard and quick possession of her mouth, stepped away from her, and was gone.

For a bemused moment Jessica stood staring into the darkness of the room. What had happened? Tired and bone weary, she put a trembling hand to her head. First he was there, then he wasn't. Why all the secrecy? What was going on? What had the man Nick and Diego were chasing done?

She shook her head to try to clear her muddled thoughts. He must be dangerous. His men had tried to kill Nick and Diego once. She felt her stomach turn over

convulsively and stared anxiously at the door Nick had
passed through. She wished she understood. She wished
she could help. She felt tears burn her eyes. She wished
he was here.

The following afternoon, having eaten a meal in
the small but busy, spice-scented café, Nick lounged
back in a chair on one of the few boardwalks and
propped his feet unceremoniously on the rail in front of
him.

The booming business of the café was only one of
the interesting contrasts he'd found in the sleepy-
looking village. The customers hadn't all been local
peasants. No, most of them had been Americans
wearing rough and dirty clothes with faces burned from
long hours in the sun and wind. A man could get like
that driving a wagon.

The streets were filled with such men, filled to the
point of it being more than a little unusual. The village
was out of the way, surrounded by a few Mexican-
owned farms and ranches. There were no Americans
who lived in the area. This was a strictly Mexican town.
That knowledge made it obvious that these men didn't
belong. They stood out.

But where were the wagons? Last night after
leaving Jessica, Nick had tried to look around the
village but had been wary of watching eyes. If this
movement of arms and men was as well organized as he
had come to believe, there would be lookouts on the
alert for intruders.

He had not had a chance to explore during the day
either, but he was certain there were wagons hidden
somewhere. There were too many men present, too

many for one shipment, and he doubted two trains of wagons would be sent out at the same time. Again he considered how well the movement seemed to be planned. Was it possible the large number of men represented not only the drivers who had brought the wagons in but their relief as well?

Nick speculated at the sequence of actions the Confederates would set up. A group of wagons would arrive in a village. The horses would be changed and, so would the men. The drivers would be replaced by those from a prior shipment. In this way, the men would get a few days' rest before moving on again, and the wagons would roll on within an hour. This would prevent any loss of delivery time. All of this, of course, would be done at night to minimize observation from the villagers.

But, what if some delay occurred on the road? What if a train of wagons came in late, too late to leave again before dawn, before the people of the village awoke to see exactly what these *gringos* were doing?

Could some of these men be part of a layover from a late arrival last night? The wagon tracks Nick had followed in yesterday had not been more than a few hours old. He frowned under the brim of the hat covering his face. Guessing. It was all he could do. If only he'd had a chance to check the road outside of town in the daylight. A short inspection would have told him if what he suspected was true. But it was out of the question now.

His presence had aroused curious stares already. He didn't want to add to any suspicions by wandering about. By remaining aloof and openly indifferent to everyone and to everything around him, he hoped to be looked on as a drifter stopping for a rest on the way to some unknown destination. However, even accepted as a passing stranger, he knew he couldn't stay long. At least not stay and live.

The men driving the wagons were no youngsters. They were hard-bitten soldiers, bitter with memories of the fallen South and lost ideals. There would be little mercy in their hearts for a Yankee spy.

Slow hours passed by as the temperature rose to its peak and then began to fall with the setting sun, but still Nick sat watching, feigning sleep or dozing disinterest. It wasn't hard to do. There wasn't much of anything happening.

Men walked to and fro, their numbers decreasing as the afternoon wore on, but there was still no sign of any wagons. Could the gradual lack of activity be caused by men retiring to catch a few hours' rest before they left this sanctuary to take the wagons out in the dark of night?

As for the peasants of the village, they showed complete acceptance of the Confederate's presence. The Americans were obviously careful to avoid trouble, and a few pesos deposited in the right pockets would insure unwelcome questions were not asked. But even if they were, where would the villagers go to report strange weapons coming and going? Where and why?

The only reason the Mexicans might take an interest in the wagon movements would be if they backed Juarez, but strong support was doubtful in a village so far to the north. Further south it would be a different story. Further south they'd be closer to the border. But, here, the Rebels were safe from question because this local population would not care about their actions.

Sunset arrived to find a small canteen fairly crowded with pleasure-seeking customers, and pushing aside the battered swinging doors, Nick joined them. He ambled to the wooden plank set up on big-bellied barrels which served as the bar.

Covert gazes were sent his way as he approached, but he ignored them all. He greeted the man behind the planks and then ordered a bottle of tequila in American-accented Spanish.

"*Gracias*," he told the heavily paunched bartender and turned from the bar to look for a table. Pushing his hat back on his head, he scanned the room with weary indifference until he located a vacant table near the cantina windows. He made his way slowly toward it, passing between two tables seating several Confederate men. He reached the vacant table and sat down.

He threw his hat onto the dust-ridden table top and poured a glass of the burning liquid noisily into his glass. The tequila seared its way down his dry throat but warmed his belly with familiarity.

Stretching his legs out under him, Nick poured a second glass and turned his eyes to the street outside. Fleetingly his thoughts lingered on Jessica. He'd been conscious of her often during the day and had found himself wondering what she was doing.

He frowned slightly. If only those damn Comanches hadn't entered Apache territory. If they'd stayed in their own hunting grounds, he wouldn't have had to worry about her. He would have known she was safely on her way to Santa Fe instead of sitting in a deserted house on the other side of town.

He shook away his thoughts and emptied his glass once more. She was safe for now. Alone maybe, but for the moment safety was the only thing he could offer.

Glancing back into the room, he startled one of the men at the other tables who was staring at him. The man looked quickly away. Nick showed no reaction at all.

Absently he wondered where Diego was and what success he was having. Nick hoped it was immediate. He was rapidly tiring of this game of hide-and-seek he and Diego had been playing for three years now. He'd had enough of Evans . . .

A chair scraped the floor and footsteps echoed on the board planks, but Nick didn't turn to look until he knew the steps had stopped at his table. He looked up to meet the openly curious eyes of a lean and graying man.

"Mind if I sit a spell?" the man asked, his voice carrying the obvious Southern drawl.

Nick silently indicated one of the vacant chairs.

"Noticed you in town today," the man offered politely. "Thought maybe you might have come up from the south, Mexico."

Nick twirled the tequila in his glass and shrugged. "In a roundabout way. I came from the west, the Arizona Territory. I was near the border once or twice, but it isn't the safest place to be right now."

"Reckon not, with the revolution and all. You know much about the fighting down there?"

Nick shook his head negatively. "Nope. Don't pay much attention to things that don't concern me and, besides, this is the farthest east and south I've been in some time."

"You're not from around here then?"

"No, been north for the past few years, into the Oregon and Wyoming territories."

"You own property there?"

Nick eyed the man slowly as if the questions were beginning to annoy him. "No. I don't own property. I prefer drifting to staying."

The man grinned in a friendly manner. "Probably been roaming all over this country then. Wish I could say the same." He shook his head. "I'm afraid most of my traveling's been in the South. Last few years I've been moving with the War."

Nick swallowed a glassful of tequila. "Yeah, I heard about that. People up north of here been listening to the talk coming their way about the fighting. Yankees finally won, so they say."

The man's face suddenly hardened and he nodded curtly. "They did."

Nick raised a curious eyebrow at the man's reaction, but he said nothing.

Overcoming greater emotions, the man forced a grin. "Sorry to be so sour, but family and friends of mine lost a lot in that war."

Nick nodded. "Imagine so. You going west now to find yourself a new place?"

The man shifted slightly in his chair. "Was thinking on it."

Again Nick nodded, staring speculatively at the half-empty bottle of tequila. "Not much farm country west of here. North the lands are better. More green. Awful dry here."

The man relaxed. "Thanks for the advice."

Nick corked the bottle and stood. "Think I'll take a walk now and retire to the stable," he told the man with a grin at the tequila. "Warms a man's bed as well as his belly."

"Pleasure to have met you, mister. You'll be moving on in the morning, north I suspect?"

Nick shrugged carelessly. "North, east, doesn't really matter." He walked away, swaying slightly, and left the cantina. As he made his way past the cantina window to wander farther down the nearly deserted street, he was aware of curious and wary eyes on him.

Chapter 17

Jessica stared out the window at the darkness. The long day had finally passed and night had come, yet there was still no sign of Nick.

She turned from the dusty and broken panes of glass and walked cautiously through the room. Having nothing better to do for most of the day, she had spent the endless hours clearing the broken furniture out of the way so she could walk through the house without falling over the deserted belongings. The dust still hung heavily in the confined air, though, for there had been little she could do about it except blow it around.

Stopping beside her horse, she stroked the velvet of its nose. Where was Nick? What was he doing? Was he in trouble? There had been no shots during the day. No shouting. Only quiet. Was that a good sign?

She wrapped her arms around the animal's neck and gave it a lingering hug, praying as she did that Nick would soon return. She wanted to be with him. She wanted to know he was safe.

It would have been small comfort for her to know that only a short distance from the building where she stayed hidden, Nick had stopped on a corner to survey the street around him. He leaned heavily against the side of the small shop and put his head back, pressing the bottle of tequila to his lips. But he drank none of the fiery liquid.

The motion was only for effect. Nobody was watching him as far as he knew. He could see no one. However, he could not be sure.

Vague noises kept him headed in the direction he was going. The noises sounded very much like harness jingling and animals moving restlessly. Was the wagon train of guns up ahead?

He crossed the street and turned into a narrow alley. He disappeared into its black protection and immediately regained a sober stance in the darkness. He stopped to listen. The gentle stirrings were coming from somewhere ahead of him. He crept stealthily along the length of the alley. Not far beyond its end, he could see the faint glow of a circle of light? From a lamp?

He stopped and listened once more. An animal shook its head, and the sound of wagon harnessing echoed through the night. Another animal blew noisily through its nose. The low murmur of hushed voices blended in with these sounds. There were men with the wagons. Was he too late?

Nick crouched in the alley, waiting patiently for further movements, but those reaching him remained unchanged. There were no wagons starting out. Not yet. What were they doing? The loading should be done. All hat was needed once the horses were harnessed was the drivers.

He watched the end of the circle of light carefully, looking for shadows. None came. Surely there were men here. He'd heard them. Hadn't he? Abruptly, the light was put out.

Nick stiffened. Were they getting ready to go? No, the wagons weren't moving. He strained his ears to listen. Were those footfalls he heard moving off? Had someone merely come and prepared the wagons, leaving when their job was done?

Edging to the other side of the alley and removing his hat, he stared cautiously around the corner into the dark recesses beyond. Dark movements were shadowed in the night, and muffled steps carried the dim figures of two men down another alley and out to the street from where Nick had just come.

Nick stayed perfectly still. The steps reached the street, crossed the boardwalk and came to the end of his alley. He held his breath. The steps moved on. Now was his chance. But, he'd have to hurry. The drivers were sure to arrive soon.

He slid from alley to alley, shadow to shadow as he sought out the wagons and their cargo. They couldn't be much farther, and suddenly, they weren't. He rounded a corner, and there they were—not twenty feet from him. Startled, he leapt back into the alley. How had he stumbled onto them so quickly?

With his heart pounding loudly in his ears, Nick stared cautiously around the corner and into the dimly starlit night. Immediately he was able to see why he had come upon the wagons so abruptly. They weren't where he thought they were.

No, he had been expecting to find them outside the village, beyond the adobe buildings. But, they weren't that far away. Instead, they were in the midst of the village, standing where an old home once had been.

All that remained of the home now was a blackened wall, the black scars from a fire that had probably gutted the structure. The Confederates had taken advantage of the deserted homestead and cleared out its remains to make a space wide enough to allow several wagons to stand. It was a perfect hideaway. In between two buildings, the yard stood in the center of the village instead of on its edge. No one looking for a train of wagons would think of searching here.

Nick moved cautiously forward. There were long-eared mules and horses standing harnessed to five wagons, but there was no sign of any men. Nick was suspicious of such good luck. He wasn't willing to take the chance of blundering onto someone when he least expected it.

He stooped down, putting his head near the ground. Slowly he scanned the area, looking under the wagons and between the legs of the animals for a guard or guards. But, there were none.

A chill shuddered down Nick's spine, and he straightened to a crouch. He didn't like it. Either the Confederates were very confident of their plans, or they were going to be moving out soon and didn't feel a guard was necessary.

He rose slowly to his feet. Like it or not, he was here and they weren't, and time was slipping away. He cast one more wary look around the yard and edged his way to stand beside the nearest wagon. He listened tensely, but there was still no human sound reaching his ears. He shrugged uneasily and moved to silently peer over the tailgate of the wagon.

His eyes wandered over sacks of grain, a trunk, bundles of food, a big barrel of water, but no boxes. He frowned. There was nothing resembling a container loaded with arms inside the wagon. It didn't make sense.

Stepping back, he critically examined the wagon and then slid to his knees to look more closely at the bottom. Tapping softly but clearly, he listened to the echo within the wagon. Hollow, except for whatever was inside.

Standing again, he strode without sound to the front of the wagon. He stopped to glance around, reassuring himself he was still alone. Then, stepping on the front wheel, he hoisted himself up and reached under the seat to examine the floor of the wagon.

Planks moved under his probing fingers, and with a decisive jerk, one slid away. Quietly Nick reached inside and traced the outline of a box he could not clearly see. Long and square. He knew what it held. Rifles. He nodded to himself. So it was true. They were running guns, and right under the Union's nose!

"You! Stop! What are you doing?"

Nick froze where he was. His heart thudded to a halt. His breathing stopped. They'd found him! An eternal second passed. His muscles bunched. Then, he moved.

Leaping clear and backwards from the wagon, he hit the dirt and rolled. A gun roared in response, and as he came to his knees, the dirt beside him rose in a small cloud of dust where a bullet slammed into it.

Nick didn't wait for more. He jumped to his feet

and dove for the alley, the gun barking again as he charged into the dark byway. He had to get away. There was only one man chasing him now, but there would be more soon—the shots would bring them.

He raced blindly on, hugging the walls. But it made for slow going. He kept ramming into boxes and barrels. He had to move faster! He abandoned the walls. The guard might be able to hear him, but the man wouldn't be able to see him. The black of night would provide protection from view. He could use it as a cover. But, the blackness was a deceptive curtain.

The man behind him halted at the alley's entrance and emptied his gun into the unlit corridor. Ricocheting off walls and discarded boxes, the bullets whistled and whined harmlessly into space until finally one of the tiny lead missiles found its mark.

The bullet caught Nick squarely behind the right shoulder blade. Its impact threw him forward. He tripped, stumbled, lost his balance and fell to the ground with a thud.

The breath hissed from his lips. His head reeled with shock. What had happened? It took a moment for grim realization to dawn. He'd been hit. Where? There was no pain. Not yet. He shook his head to try to clear it. He had to keep moving. He had to get up.

He shifted slightly, and his body reacted with a throb. It became an undefined ache. The ache began to spread, slowly. He groaned. It was his shoulder. The bullet was lodged in his shoulder.

A shout came from somewhere nearby. Running steps answered. The Confederates! He couldn't stay here. He had to keep going, and Nick struggled to gain his feet. The fight to stand brought immediate pain. It shot down his right arm and was followed by a sharp, tingling wave of sensation. Grim lines of agony marked Nick's face as slowly his shoulder began to stiffen, then numb. His arm was useless, paralyzed.

Nick took a step and grimaced. His limp limb swung of its own accord. He grabbed it, wincing again when its unresponsive fingers brushed the holstered gun on his hip. He couldn't fight back now. He wouldn't be able to shoot and shoot accurately. His gun arm was gone.

Yells and light echoed and shone to his right. He gritted his teeth and dodged as quickly and quietly as possible between buildings as alerted men raced down the street toward the wagon yard. They'd start searching right away. No place would be safe.

A stick reached out in the dark, invisible to the naked eye. Nick's foot hit it. He stumbled and fell to his knees. Pain was instantaneous. It lanced through his body with devastating force, threatening to black out his mind. Oblivion was trying to claim him. He shook his head forcefully. He had to fight it! He couldn't stop now. He had to get away. And, clutching his arm, he suddenly remembered Jessica.

When the Confederates began searching for him, they'd go through every building. She wouldn't know what was happening. She wouldn't understand. She wouldn't know what to do. She wouldn't know she should run until it was too late.

He lurched unsteadily to his feet once more and banged harshly against the wall. He winced but staggered blindly on. He had to reach her! He couldn't let them find her!

The shots brought Jessica from the deserted home

into the street just outside its door. She stood in petrified silence as her ears strained to find the source of the sound. Where had it come from? Who was shooting? An indecipherable shout was her only answer. What was going on?

She couldn't see from where she was. She had to get closer. She crept cautiously to the edge of the main street of the village and clung to the building beside it for cover. A glance around its edge, and she could see men running and gathering in the glow of lamps some distance away.

She pulled back and leaned against the hard wall. Nick! Was that who they were shooting at? Had he gotten away? Was he hurt? She hesitated, common sense and fear waging an open battle in her head. What should she do? She retreated toward the deserted house. If Nick was in trouble . . .

Suddenly a figure burst from a nearby alley. Jessica stifled a scream and jumped out of the man's path. But he wasn't so easily avoided. He saw her and staggered in her direction. Jessica spun and ran. She had to get back to the house—back to the house and the rifle Nick had left her! She raced through the door and grabbed the weapon, swinging immediately toward the entrance. But it was too late. The man had followed her! He was coming inside! Fear gripped her throat. What was she going to do? If he didn't stop, she'd have to shoot him!

The horse at the opposite end of the room snorted in fright as the stranger stumbled into the dark interior of the house. Jessica raised the barrel of the rifle to aim, but her finger froze on the trigger. She couldn't just shoot someone!

"I'm warning you, if you don't stop, I'll fire!"

The man didn't answer. He only put a hand out toward her.

She watched as he swayed just beyond the doorway. He tried to take a step, tripped, and fell to the floor face first.

She stared at the still figure, and uncertainty raged wildly within her. Who was he? What was he doing here? What did he want? Jessica let her trembling aim slowly drop. He hadn't moved since falling. Maybe he was hurt. Or, the way he was moving, in uncoordinated jerks, perhaps he was drunk and had passed out.

Jessica hesitated but gradually overcame her wariness and moved to stand fearfully over him. It was so dark. She could barely see the outline of his body as it lay sprawled across the flor. She bit her lip doubtfully. If only she had a light . . . Carefully she knelt down and put a shaking hand out to him.

The man jumped at her touch, and she hastily pulled back.

"Jess . . ."

The rifle dropped from her hands. "Nick!" She grasped him by the shoulders. "Nick! Nick, what is it?" Something warm and sticky ran hot on her hand, and she sobbed as she recognized it for what it was. Blood! He'd been shot!

She helped to roll him over onto his back, and tears burned her eyes as she tried to cradle him. But he would have none of her.

With one hand he angrily tried to brush her away. "Get out! Get on your horse and go!"

She shook her head in adamant denial. "No, not without you."

He grabbed one of her wrists with a vicious twist.

"Go, damn you!" An equally ferocious shove sent her careening backwards onto the floor, and she gasped in pain as her back impacted sharply on the hard wood.

Stunned, she sat staring at him in disbelief, unable to understand why he would hurt her so. She only wanted to help him! How could he expect her to leave when he needed her?

A sharp shout abruptly stabbed through the night outside, and Jessica sucked in her breath. The commotion down the street. She'd forgotten! There had been angry men looking for something or someone. Her eyes flew to Nick. Nick. It was Nick they were after! She jumped to her feet. She had to find out what the men were doing.

Jessica hurried to the door and looked out. She frowned. She couldn't see anything, not from the house. She'd have to leave the building to find out what this new burst of shouting was about and to find out just where the men seeking Nick were.

She darted outside and went around the house. Whatever was happening, Nick had caused it, and by following the direction he had come from, she would probably be better able to see what was going on. And, she had to know that if she was going to keep Nick safe. No matter what, she couldn't let these strangers catch him!

She stumbled in the dark and almost collided with a two-wheeled ox cart. She stepped hastily back to look at the vehicle. It had two huge wheels that stood almost as high as she stood tall, and it was filled with sacks and various pieces of merchandise.

A man and woman's hushed voices reached her ears, and she paused to listen. The two were standing in front of the building beside the cart. They were talking rapidly in alarmed Spanish.

Trying to get some meaning from their words, Jessica moved closer. Down the street, beyond the couple, she could make out the shadows of men searching alleys and doorways. Her heart faltered. There were searching for Nick in earnest.

Jessica glanced at the couple, being careful to remain hidden around the corner of their home. They were watching the activity, too, and Jessica saw the man gesture emphatically toward where she stood as they continued speaking, shaking his head and saying two words she knew—Santa Fe.

Surprised, she looked back at the waiting cart. Santa Fe. Could the man be taking these goods to Santa Fe? He must be! Jessica didn't wait to think more but sprinted quickly back to the deserted house where Nick lay.

Rushing into the room, she fell on her knees beside him and touched his face. He murmured incoherently. He was only half conscious.

Jessica scurried over to kneel by his head. She hurriedly slipped her arms beneath his shoulders and grasped him beneath the arm pits. She lifted, pushing and pulling him into a sitting position. But where could she go from there? She couldn't carry him.

"Nick," she whispered hoarsely, her breathing ragged from the effort of sitting him up. "Nick, stand up. You have to stand up."

Nick groaned at the relentless tugging of her hands but semi-consciously struggled to do as she asked.

He was dead weight against her, but she managed to help him to stand before guiding his staggering steps to the door. She paused there and transferred his weight to the doorjamb.

"Stand here, Nick. Just for a minute."

Silently, he obeyed, and she fell to the floor once more with searching hands. It didn't take long to find what she was looking for. Her fingers touched cold metal, and she grabbed the rifle. She stood again and moved back to Nick.

"Nick, you've got to walk. Not far. But you've got to walk."

Stumbling and leaning heavily on her, Nick forced one foot in front of the other, his mind blocked by pain and a threatening blackness. He couldn't think. It was too much of an effort. He could only do as he was told and tap his remaining strength to continue moving.

Jessica urged him on until they reached the home of the man and woman she had seen. There she supported him against the structure's back wall and quickly scanned the open yard. The cart was still standing where she had first seen it, and the man and woman were exactly where she had left them, standing in front of the house talking. If they would only stay there for a few more minutes, she'd have Nick safe.

"Up here, Nick," she murmured, starting to help him forward. "Up here by the cart." But their progress suddenly halted when Nick managed to pull away from her and knocked her aside with a savagely intent arm. The momentum of the blow carried her to the dirt with a startled gasp. What was he doing? She twisted to look up at the angry man she was desperately trying to save.

"I told you to go," he ground out harshly. The pain was helping to clear his mind. He remembered now. Jessica. He thought she'd gone, but she hadn't.

She was still here. Still here and trying to save him instead of herself.

Hopeless rage surged through her as she continued to stare at him, and Jessica jumped to her feet. "Nick, stop it! We don't have time!"

"Damn right we don't. Now get out of here." He glanced around wildly. "Where's your horse?"

She swung away from him and towards the house, anxiously searching for some indication that the man was about to depart in his cart. There was no sign of him yet, but he could arrive at any minute! She turned back to Nick, her temper flaring. "Damn you, Nick! Listen to me for once. We're leaving together." She reached forward and grasped his left arm. "Now hurry."

Nick tried to pull back, jerking hard, but the action brought immediate and obliterating pain, and he staggered forward instead under Jessica's insistent demands.

Jessica heard him gasp as he stumbled towards her, and it took all her strength to catch him and keep him from falling. But stubborn determination and desperation were firm supports, and she fought to help him reach the waiting cart.

Once there she propped him against one of the big wheels and whirled to attack the contents of the cart. She clambered into it and began tearing madly at the bundles and blankets strewn around her. Pushing and shoving, she rapidly rearranged the goods until she was sure Nick could fit inbetween them. Then she turned to get him.

She scrambled out of the cart and hurried to his side. She looked up to speak, and her heart caught in her throat. The reflection of his face in the dim moon-light was strained and pale. "Nick, please. Just a little longer. You've got to get into the cart. I can't lift you."

Unable to fight her, Nick gritted his teeth and, with what strength he had left, tried to do her bidding.

Alternately pushing and pulling, Jessica helped him crawl into the cart. She followed behind to help him squeeze his long frame between the various articles. Once he was lying safe, she again jumped out of the cart and ran to retrieve the rifle she had lost when he had knocked her down.

She reached the discarded weapon and stopped to listen. There were men calling down the way, and lantern lights were bobbing steadily nearer. She swallowed tightly. She hoped the Mexican left soon!

Panting heavily, she returned to the cart and climbed in next to Nick. She quickly and quietly began piling things on top of them, spreading blankets and lighter items over their bodies to keep them from being seen.

In her haste, it seemed she'd never finish but, at last, she was done. She lay back carefully. In the confined space of the cart, she was almost lying on top of Nick. "Nick?" she whispered hopefully, but there was no answer.

Her heart thudded loudly in her ears, and fear chilled her spine. He couldn't be . . . She strained to listen for his breathing but quickly gave up. It was impossible. She couldn't hear him over her own gasping breaths.

She put out a trembling hand to search for his heart. The hardness of his chest met her fingers, and they traced his rib cage to where his heart lay. She held her breath as her fingers lingered in hope.

For a fleeting moment, there was nothing. The warmth of his skin but no other indication of life. Then it came. A beat! Strong and steady. The air she had captured in her lungs whispered past her lips in relief. He was alive. He had only passed out.

Beyond the cart voices suddenly echoed, and Jessica huddled into stillness with her arms wrapped protectively around Nick. She prayed and listened. Foreign words were spoken. There were murmured responses, a creaking as someone climbed on top of the cart. More words were exchanged. Then, the cart jerked, and the wheels began turning forward. They were moving.

Jessica squeezed her eyes shut. They had to make it!

Minutes passed like hours as the cart rolled slowly out of the village behind a lumbering team of oxen. Hiding beneath a blanket, Jessica waited for the shouts, for the calls that would stop them, but none came. Only the distant calling from the continuing search by unknown men reached her. And, slowly, that noise faded until only the sound of the cart and the oxen's hooves could be heard. But would there be pursuit? Would anyone from the village come after them? Had anyone seen the cart leave? It was a dark night, the moon was shrouded by clouds, but someone might have seen them . . .

More time saw the journey continue without pause and without any indications of a chase, and Jessica began to relax. They had made it. They had gotten away. But, there was no time for rest. The wounded man beside her needed her help. She had to try to stop the bleeding.

As silently as she could, she searched for the source of the blood. She found it and fumbled for the kerchief knotted around Nick's throat. Forcing the cloth against the flow of life-giving fluid, she kept one hand firmly on the kerchief and the other against Nick's chest to assure herself by the beat of his heart that he was still alive.

She didn't know where they were heading. She hoped it was Santa Fe but, at the moment, she didn't really care. For now they were safe. She'd have to deal with arriving at their destination when they got there. Her only worry at present was to keep Nick alive and to get him away from the village and whatever it was there that had almost, and still could, take his life.

Chapter 18

Jessica woke with a start and momentarily stared up in numb confusion at the blanket hanging over her. Where was she? She had been in a deserted house in a village. Groggily she attempted to straighten an achingly stiff leg and jammed her foot into an unseen obstacle. She mumbled grumpily against the stuffy and cramped confines she had been left in and put out a hand to push herself up. Her fingers hit hard flesh, and she frowned as complete wakefulness prodded her mind. Nick? Had he come back?

Come back! Yes, Nick had come back! Jessica's mind cleared with a snap. The cart. They were still in the cart. She must have dozed off.

Cursing her weakness, she put an anxious and trembling hand to Nick's face. She frowned immediately. In the veiled darkness of their hiding place, it was difficult to see his skin color, but he was hot to the touch. Fever had invaded his body. He was burning up.

Her teeth clamped over her bottom lip, and Jessica stroked his hair back from his damp forehead. What was she going to do?

Light was squeezing through the goods stacked around them. That meant morning had come, and that the terror of the previous night was behind them. But, with the coming day, a new assault would begin. Heat. As the sun rose in the sky, so would the temperature beneath the blankets they were under.

Unexpectedly Nick moaned under her touch, and Jessica quickly pressed her fingers to his lips. What if he became delirious and started thrashing about? How would she be able to keep him hidden then?

Wildly chaotic thoughts raced through her head. She had to do something for him. She had to have water, fresh air . . . She glanced up at the blanket hanging over them and wondered futilely about the man driving the cart. Would he help them? Her fingers touched Nick's rifle. She could force the man to help, but how long would that work? Trying to soothe and care for Nick, she couldn't watch the driver, too.

She chewed at her lip apprehensively. If only she could reach her father's ranch. She searched her memory. Where did it lie? Near Santa Fe—south of Santa Fe on the Pecos River.

Nick had said Santa Fe was only a few day's ride away two nights ago. They must be closer now, and if this man was traveling to Santa Fe with these goods he obviously hoped to sell, wouldn't it be likely he had traveled this route before? And wouldn't it be possible he had heard of Nathan Wescott? Her father had said his ranch was large, one of the largest in the territory at present.

She looked down at Nick's pale, sweat-covered face in the dimness of the cart. She didn't really have a choice. For Nick's sake, she had to try to talk to the driver. She had to try to get the man to help them. And, reaching up, she threw the blanket covering them aside . . .

Jessica wiped the perspiration first from Nick's face and then from her own. He couldn't make it much further, and she was beginning to doubt she could.

She glanced up to look at the road ahead and met the eyes of the Mexican peasant who called himself Enrique. Seeing her worried expression, he hurriedly attempted to assure her with words she did not understand.

She smiled despite her ignorance of the language he spoke and nodded agreeably. She wished she could make him hurry, wished the two oxen pulling the cart would pull harder, and as if he understood her feelings, Enrique turned to urge the plodding oxen on. The smile on her lips trembled weakly at his efforts. He seemed like a nice man. She shook her head. How she had surprised him when she had emerged from the back of his cart!

Sighing, she looked down at Nick once more. It hadn't been easy trying to explain what she wanted to Enrique, but by repeating Santa Fe and her father's name several times, she had finally made herself understood. And, in an attempt to insure speedy compliance, she had taken what money Nick had on him and given it to the kindly Mexican, repeating her father's name once more and motioning to Nick's still form to impress urgency.

Enrique had responded immediately. Nodding fervently and chattering in Spanish, he had hurriedly turned to urge the oxen on and in the next minute had handed over what water and food he had for his journey.

That had been two long days and nights ago. Now the food was gone, and the water had to be rationed carefully. If the water ran out . . . she didn't even want to think about it.

Jessica lifted weary eyes to look out at the expanse of plains around her. The third day had begun. How much farther could Santa Fe be? She knew Enrique was doing his best to get them to their destination in a hurry. He had kept the cart rolling on through most of the hours, only stopping during the hottest part of the days to save the oxen and at night for meals and rest, but to Jessica, Santa Fe and her father's ranch seemed as far away as ever, and Nick was getting worse.

Frustration screamed through her, and her fists clenched in impotent rage. Their pace was so slow! If only there were horses, not oxen, pulling them on! If only there was some way to comfort Nick. If only there were more water to do it with. If only, if only, if only!

Helpless tears burned her eyes, and she wiped blindly at Nick's face. How much longer could he hold on? Last night delirium and chills had shaken his body, and she had been forced to continually fight to keep him covered and still.

Pushing her hands away, Nick had tried repeatedly to break free from the confinement of the blankets wrapped securely around him and had murmured unintelligibly at her attempts to sooth his restlessness.

Now he was sleeping calmly, but the fever burned

relentlessly in him, draining his strength. Jessica knew her own strength was fading, too. She looked away to the brightly lit eastern sky. Dawn was passing into day. She shuddered. Another day of heat and sun and dust and sweat. More bouncing over a rutted road. More agony of watching Nick slip away from her. A sob locked in her throat. Had they come this far only so she could see Nick die?

Suddenly Enrique exclaimed loudly and pointed with a wide grin to the north.

Jessica strained to see what it was he was motioning to, but her tear-blurred vision prevented her from recognizing what it was immediately. But she finally saw it. A gleam in the distance. A silver streak across the land. A river?

She struggled to a straighter sitting position beside Nick. Was it the Pecos? She stared harder. Were those cattle she saw, too? She shaded the sun from her eyes with her hand, and hope surged through her in a powerful wave. Yes, they were cattle! A large herd of cattle. The grazing animals spread out for as far as she could see.

Her fingers convulsed around the rag she held. The cattle meant they were near a ranch, and the size of the herd meant it was probably a large ranch. Maybe it was her father's. Maybe they were almost there! They had to be! And looking at Enrique's smiling face, Jessica realized he certainly thought they were. She smiled back at him, hysterical laughter bubbling on her lips.

"Not much longer, Nick, not much longer," she murmured to the feverishly sleeping man. She touched his face gently and looked north again to confirm the ranch's presence. It was there. She wasn't hallucinating. It couldn't be much longer before they met someone who worked on the ranch or before they came to the ranch house.

But the minutes dragged by with agonizing slowness, and there was no sign of the ranch houses she so desperately wanted to reach or of the men who worked the ranch. Anxiety twisted her stomach, and more frustrated tears burned her eyes. How much longer? Nick moaned, and she put a trembling hand to his hot forehead. She couldn't lose him now. Not when they were so close!

For a moment everything swam before her in dizzying waves. She put a hand to her own head. What was wrong with her? Suddenly someone shook her, and she raised foggy eyes to Enrique. He was grinning, pointing ahead again. She forced her fading vision to focus and fought off the tingling in her limbs.

There was a fence post and a gate to the side of the road up ahead. A sign was on one of the fence posts. She strained to read it, but it was too far away. But steadily, the cart drew closer, and the letters became clear. Wescott. It said Wescott! They'd made it!

Jessica almost collapsed with relief, but one look at Nick warned her that it wasn't over yet. There was still a distance to go. They hadn't reached the ranch house. They were only within the ranch's boundaries. Until they reached the heart of the property, there would be no help. Help still lay beyond them.

They passed through the gate, climbed slowly up a rise, and her father's home came into view. The main house was set to one side and stood two floors high. Its tall, white adobe walls were majestic in their simplicity, and from them ran a low adobe enclosure which served as a patio and offered the meager efforts of a garden.

The stable was off to the right surrounded by a series of corrals, and there were several smaller structures nearby that housed the ranch hands and their families. All in all, it was a huge complex, and in her exhaustion, Jessica thought she'd never seen a more beautiful sight.

Activity was high in the yard as the ox cart rolled into it, and men stopped what they were doing to watch the strange vehicle's progress into their midst. But Jessica wasn't interested in ranch hands. She was interested in a single man, the man she had come so far to see, the one who was in charge of this ranch, and the one who could help Nick.

The cart came to a halt in front of the white-walled, adobe house, and Jessica slid from her perch to stand on the ground. Absently she brushed her rumpled shirt into place and abruptly became aware of her ragged appearance. She was full of dirt, covered with sweat, and her clothes were wrinkled and foul from the days of travel. Her hair was uncombed as well, and her face was probably red from exposure to the sun. But with the same abruptness, she realized she didn't care. Nick needed help. Appearances be damned.

She turned toward the house and watched a man come forward from the structure's veranda. He tipped his hat to her, and she found she had to look up at him as he greeted her.

"Ma'm," he said politely. "Is there something we might help you with?" He was tall and solidly built with a face burned by the sun, but his face was a mask at the moment, disguising any reaction he might be feeling toward her unexpected appearance.

"Yes. I want to see Nathan Wescott."

"Mr. Wescott? He . . ."

"What is it, Tom?" a deep voice asked, and Jessica turned to see an even taller man round the oxen to come to stand beside the first. He wore the standard western dress with a broad-brimmed hat sitting securely on his head, but there was no gun strapped to his hip.

"I'm looking for Nathan Wescott," she repeated firmly, her chin raising defiantly as she glared up at him.

He nodded and touched the brim of his hat with his fingers. "I'm Nathan Wescott."

Jessica felt relief wash through her, a flood so strong she had to lean against the cart to continue standing. But stubborn pride and Nick's fevered presence gave her renewed strength, and she straightened again to meet his gaze with blazing eyes. "Nathan Wescott, I'm your daughter."

The big man's mouth dropped open, his eyes reflecting first shock but quickly sharpening to a scrutinizing stare. He rapidly took in the tousled blonde hair, the green eyes, and the face streaked with dirt and tracks of dried tears. Something about her seemed vaguely familiar, but Jessica? How could she be Jessica? The stage had never arrived. Comanches had killed everyone. But still, there was something. A resemblance to the woman he had lost so many years ago?

"Are you just going to stand there and stare or are you going to help me?" Jessica demanded, finding the energy to stamp her foot angrily. "I've got a man with me, and he's been shot. He needs help."

"Shot!" Wescott didn't waste time on more questions. He galvanized everyone into action. Calling orders and snapping out reprimands, he alternately praised and cursed the actions of his men as they hurried to do his bidding.

Jessica watched in fearful anxiety as the ranch hands carefully lifted Nick from the wagon and began carrying him toward the house. It was all right now. Nick could get the care he needed here. The men bearing Nick's limp form disappeared through the door, and she realized she wanted to follow. But, somehow, she didn't seem able to.

Nathan Wescott came to stand beside her. "You all right?"

She nodded wearily, wondering absently why she suddenly felt so dizzy and why the ground didn't seem to be as level as it had before. "I promised the man, Enrique . . . I promised him more money."

"He'll get it," Wescott answered decisively. "Can you make it into the house?"

"Of course I can," she retorted sharply, but her first step forward was her last. The earth tilted, the sun dimmed, and she collapsed.

Chapter 19

Jessica lay in the big bed totally unaware of the diligent watch being kept by the man in the room with her. She didn't know he was there. She didn't know that when she'd collapsed, he'd caught and carried her up the stairs of the house to the bed she rested in. She didn't know any of this because she hadn't stirred since she had fainted. She was asleep, her mind and body claimed by the deep clutches of exhaustion.

Nathan Wescott shifted quietly in the chair. It had been hours since the doctor had passed on a diagnosis, and the bright hours of the day that had seen the medical man first arrive and then depart had turned into the gray hours of dusk beyond the windows of the spacious bedroom. Wescott had been within the confines of the room for most of that time. Since he'd caught his collapsing daughter mere feet from the porch of his home, he'd had little desire to be anywhere else.

He stared at her sleeping face and felt again the stir

of long buried emotions. Jessica. His daughter. Here
With him. He closed his eyes silently and shook his
head. He'd waited years for her to come, wondering
through the passing of time if, indeed, he would ever see
his daughter again. He had hoped he would, and his
hopes had been realized when he'd received Jessica's
letter telling him she was coming.

Wescott had gone into Santa Fe a day before the
stagecoach was due to arrive. There was a regular
schedule for the stage line, but any number of natural or
man-made occurrences could throw that schedule off,
and the stage could arrive either early or late. Whatever
the timing turned out to be for this particular stage, he'd
wanted to be ready. He'd wanted to be there to meet the
daughter he had once sent away.

Therefore, being prepared and used to the unpre-
dictable time schedules the Territory could create,
Wescott hadn't been unduly worried—only disappointed—when the stage didn't come in the next day as
planned. His wait wasn't over yet, he'd realized, and
he'd returned to his hotel, assuming the stage would
come the next day. But, the following day, the stage
again didn't pull in. No, a telegram came in its stead. A
yellow piece of paper bearing nothing but bad news.
The stage had been attacked by Comanches. All on
board were dead. The message had also listed names.
Jessica's name had been among them.

Wescott had been stunned. His only child dead.
But fate had played a cruel trick on him. She hadn't
really been killed. She wasn't really dead. She was here
in this room with him, in his house on his ranch. How
she'd gotten there, he had no idea. He could only guess
that she'd either gotten off the stage before it had been

attacked or that she had somehow managed to escape the Comanches when they'd ambushed the coach. And, that was where the man lying in the bed in the room at the end of the hall might have come into her life.

Wescott frowned as he thought of the man. There wasn't something right there. As a matter of fact, there was something very wrong. The man was in bed because he'd been shot—in the back. The bullet had still been buried in the man's flesh. The same doctor who had examined Jessica had operated to remove the lead from the back of the stranger's shoulder.

Despite the man's critical condition, Wescott had hoped the stranger would gain consciousness at some point while the doctor was present. There were questions he wanted to ask. However, it had been too much to hope for. The man was in bad shape, delirious and extremely weak. The doctor wasn't at all sure whether the man would live or not. He'd lost a lot of blood and was suffering from shock. But who was the man? And why was he with Jessica?

He was no Easterner, that was certain. One look at the rugged western clothing the man wore along with the well-oiled six gun tucked in his holster was enough to tell Wescott that. But this only added to Wescott's confusion. Jessica had been coming straight from Boston to Santa Fe. How could she have gotten involved with a man who obviously knew and had lived in the West? Especially one who had managed to get himself shot in the back?

Wescott watched his peacefully sleeping daughter, concern evident in the blue of his eyes. She would be all right even if the man didn't recover. A few day's rest and some good food were all she needed. Too much

exposure to the blazing New Mexican sun and no
enough rest and food had drained her. But she wa:
young. As young as her mother had been when Wescot
had decided to marry and make a life out in the New
Mexican Territory.

Time wavered for him as in his mind he saw
another woman with golden hair and deep green eyes
Jessica had grown to be the image of her mother—a
mother she'd never known. Wescott felt the pain o:
doubt and guilt nudge him as it had frequently during
the passage of years. Had he been wrong? Had he been
wrong to send Jessica back East to be raised by her
grandparents as Jessica's mother had before her? By
doing so he had robbed Jessica of the opportunity o:
ever knowing either of her parents. But had there really
been any alternative under the circumstances?

Wescott sighed deeply and ran a patient but restless
hand through the thickness of his dark but gray-tinged
hair. There were no easy answers. Not to whether he
had made the right decision long ago and not to why or
how Jessica had managed to return to the place of her
birth with a gun-shot stranger in tow.

A dark frown returned to Wescott's square face.
The Mexican with the ox cart had been of little help.
Enrique had spoken no English, and Jessica had spoken
no Spanish. The only information Enrique had been
able to pass on to Wescott was how Jessica and the
stranger had come to be in his ox cart—or, rather, when
he'd come to know they were in his ox cart.

When Enrique'd left his home in a village a few
days' ride from the ranch, he'd thought he was alone. It
wasn't until hours into his journey that Jessica had

appeared from beneath a blanket in his cart with a wounded man at her side.

Wescott sighed again. No, there were no easy answers, but there were answers—and he'd have them once Jessica was awake, once she was feeling stronger and could talk. The big man's expression suddenly darkened with uncertainty as he looked at the young woman lying on the bed. He imagined she'd have some questions she'd want answered, too. Wescott had the feeling he wasn't going to enjoy listening to her ask them.

But, when Jessica woke some time after the sun had gone down and the sky had darkened into the black of night, her questions were not centered on herself.

She woke slowly, stirring groggily beneath the warmth of the blankets covering her, and it took a moment before she opened her eyes to look at the strange walls around her in blurry confusion. Where was she?

She turned her head on the pillow, and her gaze immediately collided with that of the big man seated in a chair near the bed. In a rush, memory washed over her. This man was her father. She was on his ranch, in his house. She had arrived there—how long before?—with a gravely wounded Nick.

Abruptly she struggled to a sitting position. "Nick. Where's Nick?"

"The young man you arrived with?" Wescott asked, and at her decisive and anxious nod, "He's sleeping in another room. The doctor's seen him, and the bullet's been removed."

"He'll be all right then?"

Wescott rose slowly to his feet, his expression carefully guarded. "He's lost a lot of blood. We can only wait and see."

"I've got to go to him." Jessica tossed the covers aside and jumped to her feet, but before she could take a step in any direction, she was struck by a dizzy spell that buckled her knees and forced her to sink back down onto the bed.

Wescott hurried to her side and knelt down on one knee next to her. He watched her lift a hand to her head and told her gently, "I don't think you'll be going anywhere for a little while."

Jessica removed the hand from her reeling head. "But . . ."

"There are no buts," Wescott told her with quiet firmness. It wasn't hard to recognize the distress on her face. This man might be a stranger to him, but the man obviously meant something to Jessica. "There's nothing you can do for him. He's resting, and that's the best thing for him." He paused, not wanting to strip her of hope. "He looks strong enough. He should heal given a little time."

"You think so?"

Wescott managed an encouraging smile. "I think so." He watched Jessica nod in reluctant resignation. Weariness was still etched clearly across her face. "But I also think you better get back in bed. Your Nick isn't the only one who's got some recovering to do."

Jessica allowed herself to be guided back into the bed and covered up once more. She wanted to see Nick, but she knew this man with her was right. Nick would have to do his own fighting now. He would have to heal himself, his body supplying all the strength he would need. There was little she or anyone else could do to help him beyond what this man, her father, had already done. A strange sense of unreality touched her, and she looked up to stare at the raw-boned, large-framed man hovering beside her. This man, her father . . .

"The doctor says you've had too much sun, too little food and water, and not enough rest," Wescott told her, continuing to stand beside the bed. "You've already caught up on some of your rest, but you'll no doubt need some more." He met the green of her questioning gaze and saw the conflicting emotions reflected there. She was remembering who he was, who she was, and where they were. Her worry for the stranger had robbed her of total memory for a few moments, but total memory was beginning to return.

He realized she was only starting to absorb the abruptness of their meeting, the reality of her being here. He'd already had time to sort through most of that in the last few hours. She'd have to catch up with him.

"I expect you're hungry, too. I'll have some food brought up." He continued to watch her for a moment, waiting for her to speak, but it was too soon. The speaking would come later when both of them had had time to examine their emotions and thoughts. This meeting had been a long while in arriving. No good would come from rushing into it now.

Jessica watched him move to the bedroom door and pause there, a large man with graying hair and weather-lined features and deeply browned skin. Her father.

"If you need anything, just call."

She managed a nod and watched him leave, the door closing quietly behind him. Her father. She sank back against the pillows and tried to organize her rebelliously rampaging thoughts. There was so much to think about. There was so much that had happened, and in the whirl of events she had almost forgotten why she was here, why she had come to the New Mexican Territory to begin with.

She'd been so concerned about Nick that she'd forgotten where she was and who she was, and she'd almost forgotten who she was with. Yet now, even with the full realization upon her, she didn't know what to say to the man she'd come so far to see.

She raised a tired hand to her head. What had happened to her carefully rehearsed speech? Where were the words she'd prepared for this moment? She couldn't have lost them. She sighed. All the thoughts she could possibly have seemed to be colliding with one another, and every question she'd planned to ask and demand an answer to had been swept up in a mental cloud of confusion.

Her hand dropped limply to her side. Everything would straighten out. It had to. There were too many things she wanted and needed to know to simply forget.

Jessica closed her eyes. She couldn't remember what they were just now. But, she would. She was just too tired to put anything in order. That would have to come later . . .

Jessica was sound asleep when the young Mexican girl arrived with a tray of food. Hunger was suppressed by the need to sleep, and it wasn't until early the next morning that that need had finally been fulfilled.

When she woke again, it was to find sunshine streaming past the cracks in the curtains and dancing across the bedroom floor. She smiled at the warm sight

nd sat up in bed with a long and luxurious stretch. The
obwebs were gone. Her mind was clear. She knew who
he was and where she was. And that thought sobered
her.

Less impulsively this time, she threw the covers
rom her and rose slowly to her feet. She still felt a little
ight-headed, but a good meal would cure that and
vould silence the angry grumbling of her suddenly
gurgling stomach. She moved to one of the windows
nd drew one of the curtains aside.

The bright glare of the New Mexico morning
greeted her, and she squinted against it. It took a
noment to get used to. Then she could look beyond the
pane at the activity in the ranch yard. It appeared to be
he same as it had the day before. Though, admittedly,
her memory was somewhat blurry. What with Nick . . .

The door behind her opened quietly, and a black-
haired Mexican woman looked in. A bright smile
immediately slipped across her lips when she saw Jessica
by the window. "Ah, you are up!" The woman entered
he room, her hands firmly holding a tray of food. "I
hought you might be up so I brought you some break-
ast. You have not eaten since you arrived." She put the
ray down on the stand beside the bed and turned to face
Jessica. "I am Anita, your father's housekeeper. It has
been many years since I have seen you." She nodded
approvingly. "You have grown to look much like your
mother."

Jessica dropped the curtain in surprise and moved
back across the room towards the other woman. "You
knew my mother?"

"*Sí*, I knew her," Anita nodded with a gentle
smile. "She was a very beautiful woman and very good

to me and my family. Our family and yours, they have been together since *Señor* Wescott came to this ranch. But, here, you must sit down and eat while the food i. warm. There will be plenty of time to talk later.''

Jessica obediently sat down on the bed and wa: quickly surrounded by the tray and the aroma of fresh warm food. Her stomach reacted with greedy rumbles

"You must eat and regain your strength. You father would never forgive me if I let you do otherwise.''

Her father. When would she meet him again' Jessica pushed some food across her plate. "Is my father here?''

"But, of course, *señorita*!'' Anita exclaimed. "H has been a big bother since you have come. Always in the way. Always asking questions, following me every where.'' She waved her hands expressively. "But it i: right he is concerned, no? He is very glad you are back But you eat now. Then I will see you have a hot bath and then you can ask your father your questions and no me. He is who you have come so far to see after all yes?''

Jessica could only nod agreement to the en thusiastic chatter of this woman. Obviously Anita thought Jessica should get any answers she needed from Nathan Wescott and not from anyone else. Jessica could hardly argue with that, but all the answers she wanted were not about herself. Anita returned to the door and opened it. "Wait!'' Jessica called. "The man came with, Nick. How is he?''

Anita shook her head gravely. "As well as can be expected, *señorita*. He is alive and resting which is the best one can hope for after having been so badly injured.'' She watched Jessica's face darken with fear. "Do not worry, *señorita*. I have seen many men suffer from wounds such as his, and if a man makes it past the first night as this one has, it is a good sign. But, the doctor will return again today to see if there is anything else that we can do." She smiled reassuringly. "You must believe he will be well again, and you will help to make it so."

The door closed behind Anita, and the next couple of hours forced Jessica to shove her worries aside as she quickly devoured her breakfast and enjoyed a long soak in a hot tub. The food gave her strength and the bath, along with a fresh change of clothing from the suitcases she had shipped to Santa Fe before leaving Boston, gave her confidence as she finished dressing.

However, once ready to leave the room, Jessica's newly found confidence nearly deserted her. But, there could be no more delaying. Too much time had passed already. The moment had come for her to finally meet her father.

She took a deep, steadying breath and went to the door. It opened onto a corridor which had several doors leading off of it. She hesitated, wondering in which room Nick lay. She wanted to find him—see him and assure herself he was all right, but there was someone else she wanted to see as well. And, that someone was waiting for her.

She straightened her shoulders in an attempt to bolster her flagging confidence. No, Nick was only an excuse. He was in good hands. She could do no more for him than had been done already, and with that resolving thought she turned determinedly toward the nearby stairs and descended to the first floor.

On the bottom step she stopped to look at the white-washed adobe walls around her. The corridor immediately in front of her led in two directions, to the back of the house and most likely the kitchen and forward to what appeared to be the front door of the home. On the way to that exit were other doorways.

She moved hesitantly forward, advancing until she saw a door standing ajar just ahead. A study perhaps? Was this where her father waited?

Jessica walked to it quietly, but halted in the hall outside it when she saw the man sitting behind a desk within. It was her father.

Her heart skipped a beat, and she silently watched him from across the room. His head was bent over some papers. He was unaware of her presence.

Again her confidence faltered. This was the perfect opportunity to escape, to retreat back to her room or to find Nick's, but Jessica shook off the fear of discovery—the fear of finally finding out why her father had sent her away—and stepped into the room.

Chapter 20

Nathan Wescott looked up from his writing, prodded by an instinct he'd come to rely on while living in an untamed land. The instinct was one that told him he was being watched. He looked up and found Jessica standing silently not five feet from his desk.

"I'm sorry," Jessica said awkwardly. "I didn't mean to disturb you."

"You're not." Wescott dropped his pen and stood, shoving his chair back and moving around his desk to approach her. "How do you feel?"

"Better, thank you," Jessica told him with a tight smile. This was her father she was talking to, and it felt as if she was speaking with a complete stranger. She chided herself. He was a complete stranger. She didn't know him. She looked away from the strength of his gaze and moved to one of the floor-length windows within the room. "The sleep helped."

Wescott smiled, feeling the same awkwardness his

daughter was feeling at speaking to someone he felt he
should be close to, but who in reality, he didn't know.

"I thought it would."

A difficult silence fell between them, and both
struggled to find the words they wanted to say. But how
to begin?

"I was surprised to see you," Wescott started after
a moment. "To say the least," he added with a grin
when she turned to face him once more. But the smile
quickly faded. "When news of the stage reached Santa
Fe, I thought the worst. They sent a telegram from the
nearest station. It confirmed you'd been riding the
stage."

Jessica saw the dark pain in his eyes, and her heart
went out to him. "I'm sorry. I never meant . . ."

He silenced her with a sober shake of his head.
"You could hardly be prepared for an attack by
Comanches but, thank God, it worked out all right.
You're safe." He gestured to his desk. "I've been trying
to write a letter to your grandparents to tell them what
happened."

"You haven't written them yet, have you?" she
asked anxiously.

"No. I started to, but I was never able to finish it."

Jessica let out a sigh of relief, and he laughed. It
was a rich sound, and it broke the tension between
them.

"I agree. Your grandfather can be an almighty
terror when he's angry."

She nodded regretfully. She remembered her
grandfather's temper all too well. "Yes, he can." She
hesitated to continue but somehow knew she must. "He
doesn't like you very much."

Nathan Wescott rubbed his jaw self-consciously, and Jessica found herself studying his movements and features. Her father had a strong, honest face. Browned and lined from hours of sun and wind and from the passage of time, she decided she definitely liked it.

"No," her father answered. "He never did."

Jessica continued to study him. Was it regret she saw reflected in his eyes. "Why?"

He started at the question. He hadn't expected such bluntness, and confronted with it, he wasn't certain how to answer.

His mind flashed back through the range of twenty some years to Boston. Time had passed quickly, and yet, there had been days, even years, when the hours had seemed to drag by. "I don't think there's any one reason." He met her steady gaze. There was no condemnation there, only open curiosity, genuine interest. "Partly, I think it's because I took his daughter away. And, because he blames me for her death." His expression darkened in memory. "But mostly, mostly I think it's because he doesn't understand me. He doesn't understand why I or anyone else would want to live out here."

"In New Mexico?"

He shrugged. "Anywhere out here—'out west,' as they say back East. And he's not alone."

"I don't understand."

Wescott frowned as he attempted to explain. "Some men just can't reach beyond what they can see, beyond what is already there and proven. They trust and rely only on those things that are tested and true. They can't imagine going beyond that, can't see why someone would want to reach for what has not already been had.

They don't want to start anything new, don't want to go where no one's ever been."

"Is that what you wanted to do by coming here?"

He stopped to look at her in surprise. "I guess I never thought of it quite like that before. But, yes, I suppose it is." He smiled slowly. "It all began as an adventure. A bunch of us boys left Boston after graduating from school. Everything we were reading in the papers sure made this sound like the place to be. So, out we came."

He shook his head. "From the start, when I first saw New Mexico and the other territories, I fell in love with it. And, the more I saw, the more I wanted to stay. But, by the time I'd decided I wanted to settle here, I didn't have any more money, and neither did any of my friends. So, we figured on going home and borrowing some from our folks.

"We cut back across Texas—it wasn't a state back then but it was trying to be. And, on our way through, we got involved in Texas' fight with Mexico. By the time I got out of that and back to Boston, some years had passed, and when I arrived, I discovered I didn't need to ask for a loan. My folks had died and left me all they had."

Jessica could see him in her mind's eye. A young man out for an adventure, returning with high hopes and big dreams. What a shock it must have been to find his family gone. "I'm sorry."

He shrugged and smiled gently. "It was a long time ago, but it was then I met your mother. I was getting ready to come back. I was out about town settling what was left of my folk's affairs and was disposing of those things of theirs I didn't want to keep.'' His smile turned sheepish. "Your mother and I sort of swept each other off our feet." He looked at her. "You're a lot like her."

"That's what Grandmom always says."

"Your grandmother," he repeated warmly. "Now there's a good woman. If it hadn't been for her, I don't think your mother and I would ever have made it out of Boston."

"But why?"

"Your grandfather didn't want to let us go. He thought I was a no-good wanderer out to steal his little girl. Your grandmother convinced him otherwise."

Jessica was startled. She knew her grandmother. She knew how hard it must have been to stand up to Grandfather and convince him to let their only child go with a man to a land far, far away. It would have been something Grandmom, in her heart, wouldn't have wanted to do, but as was so typical of her, she had put her own feelings aside for those of her daughter. "And mother?"

"She didn't like going off with a cloud over us as it was, so she stood right up to your grandfather." He chuckled at a picture Jessica could not see, one stored away lovingly in his memory. "Shocked him a bit, I think."

Jessica smiled. She could imagine. "Grandfather's used to getting his own way."

"I don't imagine he was too happy when you decided to go?"

"No. I guess I shocked him, too." She didn't even want to think about the scene she had created when she'd announced her plans to go. Grandfather had hit the roof. It was Grandmom who had soothed the troubled waters for her, too, and it was Grandmom, Jessica knew, whom she would miss the most.

Wescott laughed, his imagination providing a graphic vision of the wrath Jessica must have incurred in order to get her way. But, he quickly sobered. "I'm glad you came."

Her breath caught in her throat at his unexpected confession. "Are you?"

His eyes met hers with conviction. "Yes."

She looked away, uncertainty and confusion waging a war within her. She wanted to believe him! "Why did you send me away?" Her gaze met his once more. "Why did you send me away and then never come to see me?"

A guilty flush darkened the color in his face, and Wescott's eyes dropped from hers. He turned away to walk to a window, pushing his big, calloused hands into his pants' pockets as he went. Moments passed. "After your mother died, I didn't know what to do. I only knew I couldn't keep you here. The ranch was new. We were struggling to survive. There were Indians, and the issue with Mexico and Texas was still unsettled. The only place I knew you'd be safe was back East, and the only people I knew back there were your grandparents. My family was gone."

"But when I was older, why didn't you bring me back?"

He turned to face her. "Because I wasn't sure I should. I'd already lost your mother." He shook his head. "When I married her, it was against your grandparents' wishes and against her better judgment. I knew what the land was like. I knew how hard it would be to live here, especially for a city-bred woman like her."

"But she wanted to come. Grandmom told me she did."

"Yes, she did." He smiled gently. "And when she made up her mind to something, that woman was worse than a horse with a burr under its saddle. She wouldn't take no for an answer."

"You loved her very much," Jessica observed softly, recognizing the pride and love in his words and on his sun-browned face.

Nathan Wescott nodded emphatically but looked quickly away to hide the loss reflected in the sudden moistness of his eyes. "We came out here to make a place of our own, and we were doing well enough, I suspect, until the Apaches went on a rampage."

"The Apaches?"

"Yes," he ground out harshly. "We'd been living with them peacefully. We didn't bother one another. We had a few skirmishes during the first couple of years we were here, but after that we came to kind of an under-standing. They left us alone and we left them alone—or at least it was that way until some men came through over the Santa Fe Trail and brought trouble with them. They killed some Apaches, and the Apaches killed in return. The Apaches didn't care who they killed. They only wanted revenge for the death of their people."

Jessica stared at him in puzzlement. What did the Apaches have to do with her mother?

"Some of the men and I were out on the range, away from the house when the raiding party came." His voice thickened with emotion. "Your mother managed to hide you but not herself. They killed her."

"No!" Jessica exclaimed and grasped the chair beside her in stricken disbelief. "That's not true! She died of a fever."

He turned to face her grimly. "They told you that?"

"Yes," she agreed, tears filling her eyes at the thought of the lovely young woman she had always dreamed about being killed by Indians.

"So that's the way it was," Wescott said slowly, anger rising in him. "I'd wondered."

"You mean it's true. She . . ."

"Yes," he answered, unable to keep the harshness out of his voice. "Yes, your grandparents lied to you."

Jessica sank into the chair she had been holding on to. "But why?"

"To keep you away from me." He ran a hand through his hair. "When I first took you back and then returned here, I tried to write. You were way too young to read or understand what had happened, but I'd hoped as you grew older, your grandparents would explain so you'd understand. I guess I was wrong to trust them."

Jessica watched him pace the floor.

"It was obvious from the start that they weren't happy with my writing. They only answered sporadically, or rather, your grandfather did. He was always short and gruff. I thought it was his dislike for me, his unhappiness at losing his daughter, but I thought eventually he'd come around. Time can soften things." He stopped his pacing. "But as you got older and didn't write, I wondered sometimes. I wondered if somehow he'd used his hate to turn you against me."

Jessica watched him with a furrowed brow. "If you

suspected him, then why didn't you come to see me, bring me back?"

"Like I said, I'd already lost your mother. The letters I got from your grandfather—and occasionally from your grandmother when she sent a letter from you along—seemed to say you were happy, and your happiness was what I wanted. So I let it ride. I decided I'd wait. I wrote once in awhile to stay in touch and to let you know I was here. I thought it best to leave the future up to you. You'd been raised proper like your mother, and I figured when you were old enough to go your own way, you could make your own choice instead of my forcing mine on you. I thought if I brought you out here, you might not feel free to leave again. But, if you came on your own . . ." He shrugged.

Jessica felt a smile tremble on her lips, and she rose slowly to walk to him. "I wish I'd known, understood . . . I would have come sooner." Her eyes fell from his. "But I was afraid. I was afraid you didn't want me."

He laughed, the booming sound filling the room. "That is a statement far from the truth." And the wide grin on his face told her how ridiculous the idea was.

She laughed, too, and then, they were hugging each other. The years slipped away, and all the questions and uncertainties time had wrought slipped away with them.

The moment passed, and Wescott put her gently from him. "But, enough about me. What about you? And what about that young man upstairs?"

"Nick," she said automatically. "Nick Driscoll."

Wescott nodded in response. "Well, at least now I know his name."

Jessica echoed the smile he sent her, but when she

realized he was waiting for her to speak again, she gestured futilely. "I don't know where to begin. So much has happened."

He motioned to the couch beside them. "Seems to me we should make the time for catching up, and as for where to start, the beginning's usually best. What happened after you left Boston?"

It wasn't easy, but Jessica began to speak, stumbling over her words at times and stammering with emotion at others, she told her father about the events that had caught her by surprise and pitched her into the middle of a conflict she was still trying to understand. It made it hard to explain to her father when she didn't totally understand herself, but she tried to put meaning behind the search Nick and Diego were involved in.

Wescott listened intently to her telling, finding it difficult to maintain his silence on more than one occasion. Hers was a startling story, and it soon became obvious to him that while she might have left Boston only a matter of months before, her journey had brought about changes. Circumstances had forced his daughter to do a lot of growing up in a short period of time. She'd been exposed to some of the harshest sides of life and had seen many of the dangers that living in a new territory could afford.

Jessica didn't finish speaking until a good part of the afternoon had crept by. Then she concluded by explaining how she and Nick had come to be in the ox cart that had brought them to the Wescott ranch. There was more she could say. There were a few things she'd left out, but . . . she'd covered all the major points leading to her arrival. The rest, well, the rest she'd have to explain later.

Wescott let out a heavy breath when he realized she was done. There were things he wanted to ask, but something told him he'd better watch his words—especially when it came to this Nick Driscoll. His daughter seemed to be fairly interested in this stranger. "This young man seems to mean a lot to you," he ventured carefully.

"He does mean a lot to me," Jessica agreed hastily and then flushed under her father's direct gaze. She looked away. One of the "things" she'd left out of her tale had been the ceremony in the Apache camp that made her and Nick man and wife, at least under Indian law. But, how could she tell her father about that? However, at the same time she realized he'd have to find out sooner or later. She took a deep breath. "You see, we're married."

"Married!"

As quickly as she could, Jessica told him of the Apache ceremony.

"And he went along with this ceremony?" Wescott demanded.

"There wasn't much else we could do."

His eyes narrowed. "You said we, not he."

Jessica stiffened defensively. "I could have objected."

Wescott caught his temper and rose slowly to his feet to pace away from her. He recognized the glitter in her eyes. Her mother had gotten the same rebellious gleam when she'd gotten riled. But, married!

He frowned fiercely. Marriage itself wasn't so bad, but look who she was married to—a man who'd been shot, in the back, because he was chasing somebody. Who and why?

Who was Nick Driscoll, and exactly what was he involved in? The little Jessica knew and related, he guessed, was part supposition—based on her wanting to defend this Driscoll. That in itself spoke ill of the man to Wescott. If a man married a woman, he trusted her enough to tell her what he was doing and why. Driscoll hadn't trusted Jessica enough—or, could it be he was afraid to trust her, afraid that by trusting her with the entire truth that he'd put her in some type of danger? Could Jessica be in any danger now? Would someone be searching for this Driscoll and, therefore, Jess?

Wescott turned back slowly to face Jessica, his worries hidden behind a composed expression. She had enough to think about and had been through enough without his adding to her concerns. He decided to change the subject. "That's quite a tale you've told, young lady. I only wish I'd known you were out there. That way I could have come after you, helped somehow."

Jessica smiled, relaxing. She didn't want to fight with him. "At least I'm finally here."

Wescott nodded agreement. "At least."

She stared up at him searchingly. She sensed there was something he wasn't saying. She took a guess at its source. "You're not angry about me and Nick being married, are you?"

Wescott forced a congenial smile to his mouth. "Let's just say I have some questions I'd like to ask him. It's hardly fair to judge a man without knowing all the facts."

Jessica smiled brightly. Once Nick was better, he and her father would talk, and her father would see

Nick was not a bad man, that he could be trusted, and Nick . . . And Nick.

Jessica remembered Anita's words. If a wounded man made it through the first night, it was a good sign. A good sign. It had to be a good sign that he'd come so far and suffered so much and was still alive. It had to be. And suddenly, the happiness she felt at having finally discovered her father faded, overshadowed by her fears for Nick.

Chapter 21

"You're sure you won't come with me?" Jessica asked her father, looking down at him from where she sat astride her horse. "It's your ranch after all. You should be the one to show it to me."

"It's *our* ranch," Nathan Wescott reminded her with a smile. "And maybe tomorrow I'll go. But right now, I've got to . . ."

"You've got to do the books. You haven't done them in weeks," she interrupted him with an exasperated sigh. But, nonetheless, she smiled, too. It was hard to believe she had only known this man for a few short days. It felt as if she'd known him for much longer.

They'd had many conversations since that first one in his study, and the result was a bond that was strengthening daily. It amazed Jessica that they'd become so close so quickly, for she realized it could have been very different. They liked each other. Regardless of the blood link that made them father and daughter, they genuinely enjoyed one another's company. She shuddered to think of what it would have been like if there had been any animosity or an instant dislike between them.

It had been a concern for her—wondering what her father would be like and if they'd get along—on leaving Boston. As a young girl she had fantasized about her father, about what he looked like and what they would do together when they met, but as an adult venturing out to meet him for the first time, she'd realized childhood dreams did not always develop into reality. Reality could be much harsher and all too honest. She'd known there was every possibility that she and her father would not get along. However, regardless of the possibilities, she had come, bringing the wishes she'd harbored as a child along for they had never quite died. Her hopes had kept them alive. And, she was glad those hopes had proven true.

Granted, Nathan Wescott was not exactly what she had imagined or expected, Jessica thought watching him now. She had been lucky. He had turned out to be something much more.

Big and strong in stature with skin burned dark from the sun and with hands roughened from hard work, he appeared formidable, and his thundering voice could strike terror into any of his men with a single word. Yet, it was a terror laced with respect. The ranch hands dreaded his anger, but they were also fond of the man who paid their wages. Yes, inside Nathan Wescott was a gentle man, and she could understand why her mother had been willing to leave all she'd known to go west with him.

However, as glad as she was to be united with her father at last, all of her thoughts during the last four days had been far from entirely happy. Nick had been a constant worry. The delirium and fever had clung to him tenaciously until, on the second night, it had finally broken, leaving Nick exhausted and weak.

Jessica spent every moment she could with him, but Anita closely monitored Jessica's time in his room and refused to allow Jessica to remain for more than an hour per visit. She insisted Nick needed sleep more than he needed Jessica's company.

Jessica had protested against Anita's treatment at first, but she quickly realized Anita was right. As much as she wanted to be with Nick constantly, she knew part of his recovery would depend on him getting a lot of rest. In fact, though his condition had much improved, Nick was still bedridden and slept most of the days away, but each day she could see his strength gradually returning. Nick had proved the doctor and her father wrong. He had lived.

Yes, her father had doubted Nick would pull through, and Jessica suspected Nathan Wescott doubted a lot more about Nick. Even with Nick's regaining consciousness, Nathan Wescott had still not met Nick. He had avoided his sick guest's room, telling Jessica there was plenty of time for him to get acquainted with Nick, that it would be better to wait until Nick was feeling stronger. But her father's procrastination worried Jessica.

She wondered how the two men would react to each other, how they would get along. There was a wariness on her father's part towards Nick which Jessica thought might come from their marriage. Perhaps it was the thing Nathan Wescott found so hard to accept. She wondered belatedly if it would have been better to spring the news of the wedding ceremony on her father later. After all, as much as she didn't want to admit it, she had her doubts about the ceremony, too. Was Apache law the same as white man's law in this instance? Were she and Nick really man and wife? It was a question she badly wanted to ask someone but didn't dare. If her father thought she had any fears about Nick's intentions towards her . . .

"All right," she told her father reluctantly as her horse chomped enthusiastically at its bit. "I'll be back in a little while then." She hesitated. This uncertainty between her father and Nick. It was time for it to stop. They had to meet. And, as far as she was concerned, the sooner the better. "After I get back maybe I can introduce you to Nick. He's feeling much better now."

Nodding slowly, Nathan Wescott agreed. "I suppose it's about time I met this young man you talk about so much."

Jessica felt warm color brush her cheeks at the intentness of his gaze, but she didn't look away. "I think so."

Nathan Wescott stepped back and watched his daughter ride away with his foreman, Tom Barnett. Tom was the only person he'd allow Jessica to go out alone with. It wasn't that he didn't trust his other ranch hands, it was only that he and Tom had been through years of trial and triumph together. As well as being boss and foreman, they were friends. Wescott knew with Tom, there was little chance of anything unexpected happening while riding the range. Tom was levelheaded and would blunt any impulsive urge that might strike Jessica.

Wescott smiled as he watched the two canter up the rise from the ranch yard. Impulsive and stubborn. She was a lot like her mother—painfully so sometimes, but he was glad Jessica was with him and proud of the way she'd turned out. Her mother would have been proud, too.

But this Nick Driscoll. Wescott glanced toward the house and to the windows of the room where this stranger lay. If it wasn't for the man's presence, Wescott would have willingly shown Jessica around the ranch he had built over the years. As it was, he'd only been able to take her around the area close to the ranch house, something he'd enjoyed because she was so eager to learn. She was constantly asking questions. There were times when he was hard put to answer them all, but it pleased him all the same.

However, it was for her sake that he wasn't showing her the rest of the ranch on this day. It was for her sake that he'd decided to stay behind. There were many unanswered questions about this man, Nick Driscoll. Too many. He'd saved his daughter's life, granted, but it seemed to Wescott that Driscoll had been well rewarded for his efforts—too well rewarded.

Jessica was willing to trust the man without question, had done so up to now. Her feelings for him blinded her to everything she didn't know or understand about Driscoll. Wescott had no such problem. There were things he wanted to know. Things Jessica had too willingly ignored.

Wescott straightened to his full height as he stared

at the house. He was Jessica's father. It was about time
he started acting as such, and he started off toward the
house.

The books had merely been an excuse for Jessica.
He had wanted her out of the way. She was right. He
should meet Nick Driscoll. And, he intended to. Alone
and now. Not when Jessica was there to interfere. He
wanted no protection for this man and no defense
except for what the man could provide himself.

Nick was awake when the knock came, and when a
tall stranger entered, he didn't need to ask to know who
this visitor was. Nick had been expecting Nathan
Wescott. He'd known it was only a matter of time before Jessica's father came.

Through the blur of the last few days, Jessica had
been in to see Nick often, as often as the stout little
Mexican woman named Anita would permit, and each
visit had brought more news of her father and the
ranch.

Nick had been glad to let her ramble on excitedly
about her father, the ranch, and the other people who
lived and worked on the huge spread. Glad because the
chatter took his mind away from the pain still burning
in his back and glad because he knew she was happy. It
made it easier for him to turn his thoughts to the
meeting with Diego which was to take place in less than
two short weeks.

But, when not thinking of the meeting and the
results it would hopefully bring, Nick had found himself
expectantly waiting for the appearance of this man.
Nathan Wescott. Jessica had painted nothing but
glowing pictures of her father so far, though she did

dmit he could be stubborn. However, while good to his daughter, Nick had no delusions of what Nathan Wescott's thoughts would be toward him.

The questions about Diego and himself that Nick hadn't answered for Jessica would be more prominent in the mind of Nathan Wescott. Wescott would want to know everything about the man who had saved his daughter and who had, in turn, ended up in her bed.

Nick grimaced whenever he thought of that crossing her father's mind. Being a man himself, Nick could appreciate what a father would feel toward that subject.

"You'd be Nick Driscoll, I suspect," Nathan Wescott stated, coming to a halt just inside the door.

"I am," Nick answered evenly, not flinching from the steady intent of the man's eyes on him. "And you'd be Nathan Wescott, Jessica's father."

"I would be," Wescott agreed, stepping forward to pull a chair to the side of the bed to straddle it with his arms resting on its back. "She's told me most everything that's happened since she met you. I say most now because I've noticed a protective streak in her when it comes to you. A woman will cover up for a man she cares for if there's covering up to be done."

Nick's lips twisted into a wry smile, and he nodded. "She would," he conceded, pausing to meet the determined gaze of the man before him. Their eyes locked and held. "I don't usually make excuses for myself, Mr. Wescott, and I don't usually give any man explanations for why I do things, but I think I owe you one."

Wescott nodded. Honest and direct. He was

beginning to like this man already, grudgingly. H
motioned for Nick to continue and remained silen
while Nick talked.

Nick sketched briefly over the way he'd lived ove
the years before diving straight into how he became
involved in the War and the events that had put him int
Jessica's life.

Diego and Evans became real people to Natha
Wescott as he listened to Nick speak, and slowly
Thomas Franklin began to take form, too, a man deter
mined to meet the demands of his cause.

Nick finished by telling what he remembered of th
escape from the small village days ago. "I don'
remember much after her getting me into the damn cart
All I know is it was a hell of a long ride."

Wescott nodded soberly. "Riding's longest when
man's hurting."

Nick didn't answer but watched as the big ma
silently digested all he had been told, mulling over th
implications of each word before clearing his throat t
speak his mind.

"Sounds to me as if you've got yourself a big job ir
catching this man, Franklin's his name?"

"Thomas Franklin, and you're right. We do. Bu
we're close now. If Diego can find out where the arm
are going, I've got a fair idea of where they're coming
from."

"You think you can stop him then?"

"With a little help from Evans. If we can break the
chain, Franklin will have to move on. He'll have no
choice. When we stop the source, he'll have no place to
get guns from. And, if he decides then to go to Mexico,
he'll have Juarez to deal with."

Wescott grunted. "From what I've heard, *Señor*

Juarez is not a man to be taken lightly. I don't think he'd much care for your Mr. Franklin marching to Mexico City to deliver men and guns to his enemies.''

"No, I don't believe he would.''

Wescott rubbed his square jaw thoughtfully. "If you need any help in getting wherever you've got to go to get this thing done, you can have what you need. After being involved in the fight to win Texas from Mexico, I'd like to see New Mexico become part of the States, too. I'd hate to have your Franklin preventing that from happening by running guns through the Territory.''

Nick nodded. "I'd appreciate the help, but I think all I'll need is a good horse to get me where I've got to go.''

"You've got it,'' Wescott stated flatly. He met Nick's gaze once more. "But what of Jess?''

"I'll be honest, Mr. Wescott. I love your daughter and I'd like to take care of her, but the truth is, I've got nothing to offer her—at least not yet and especially not now with Franklin still on the loose.'' Nick shook his head grimly. "I told a man I'd do the job. I'm going to have to see it through. Then, when it's over, I'd like to talk to her about a spread of our own.''

Wescott nodded slowly. Sometimes a man had to do things he'd rather not. But, if a man didn't have any honor in his word, what did he have? "I understand. I'll keep Jess with me.''

Nick smiled. "You've got a lot of catching up to do.''

Wescott nodded again. "There's been a lot of years pass since I saw her last.''

"From what she's been telling me, I'd say you

won't have to worry about that happening again.''

Wescott cocked his head. ''She know you're planning on leaving to meet this Diego fellow?''

Nick grimaced. ''No, not yet. I thought I'd wait until I'm more up to a fight before I tell her. I prefer to be able to protect myself when a wildcat gets loose.''

Wescott snorted and grinned appreciatively. ''I seem to recall collecting a few of those scratches myself.''

Chapter 22

The front door banged shut, and Nathan Wescott looked up from his writing to watch Jessica enter the room. Dressed in a durable tan riding skirt and a cream-colored blouse, her hair was windblown, and her cheeks were flushed from her usual early morning ride.

"I hope you weren't out by yourself," he stated, a definite ring of parental authority in his voice. He still insisted someone accompany her whenever she went out riding.

Jessica rolled her eyes to the ceiling in exasperation at his repetition of the daily warning and threw herself gracefully into a chair. "No, I wasn't. I had Tom with me," she answered with a wave of her hand at the study door where Tom now stood.

Wescott nodded to his foreman and friend. "Morning, Tom."

"Morning, Nathan."

"This daughter of mine behaving herself on these rides?"

Tom grinned quietly, his teeth bright white against the dark tan of his skin. "As well as any Wescott might be expected to, I suppose."

Jessica laughed at her father's stunned expression. "He's been telling me all about you, you know," she teased, taking advantage of his momentary lack of words. "Seeing as he's been with you since you started this ranch, I guess he knows just as much about you as you do."

The big man shifted uneasily behind his desk and eyed his old friend with a set jaw. "Tom, if you've been telling her . . ."

"All about the things you won't tell me," Jessica interrupted firmly. "You should thank him, not berate him with that thundering voice of yours. Lord only knows how the rafters of this house have stayed in place as long as they have with the way you yell."

Tom smothered another grin as Nathan Wescott stammered for words. "I think she's got you pegged already, Nathan."

Jessica flashed a bright smile at Tom. Big-boned and shy, standing nearly as tall as her father, Tom was a quiet man but one who bore the responsibility of his position as foreman well. Unlike her father, however, Tom's authority wasn't readily discernible from his carriage or manner.

No, he didn't look or act the part. He was totally unassuming. He didn't issue orders or yell at or berate the men he supervised. His way was more subtle. When things went wrong, he'd look whoever was in trouble in the eye, scratch his head in a type of bewilderment and suggest whatever problem had arisen had better never come up again.

Tom's easygoing manner was not taken for granted, though. His word was law on the Wescott range, and the men knew that crossing Tom would mean losing their jobs. They also knew that Tom understood more about ranching than any three of them combined, and they readily respected and looked to his knowledge and experience for answers and advice.

Tom returned Jessica's smile with one of his own, but he shifted restlessly with a touch of uneasiness, too. He knew a lot about running a ranch, but he knew nothing of women—and Nathan Wescott's daughter was no exception.

When Nathan had first asked him to look out for Jessica when she was out on the range, Tom had been unsure and suspicious. Unsure because most women he'd known were nothing but trouble once they got on a horse and suspicious because he was worried about his longtime friend and boss. Nathan Wescott had held out hopes for his daughter for many years, and Tom had seen the pain when news of the Indian raid had left everyone believing Jessica was dead. But then suddenly and miraculously she'd reappeared and was trying to take a place on the ranch.

Tom hadn't been as willing to accept Jessica as Nathan had. He'd been wary of her—leery of what she really wanted because his experience with women had left him believing they all had ulterior motives. Granted that belief was partially due to his being too open and trusting of all people. Tom just naturally liked everyone, and not everyone was good enough not to take advantage of that side of his nature.

However, Jessica hadn't coaxed or bullied her way into his confidence. She had won it instead as every day Tom had watched her and Nathan Wescott growing closer. She had a genuine interest in the ranch and in her father, and so the guard Tom had been prepared to hold up against any charm she might exert had soon been broken.

Only trouble was, she had this way of making him say the dangedest things. The two of them had taken to riding together every day, and on most of those occasions, in some way or another, she'd get him talking about himself and ultimately Nathan. Once someone got him going, he'd forget who he was talking to and tell tales not fit for a lady to hear—not that she ever seemed to mind. But looking at Nathan, Tom wasn't so sure how his friend felt about the subject . . .

"Have you been up to see Nick this morning?" Jessica abruptly inquired, changing the subject. It was a habit her father was discovering she was very good at when she didn't want to discuss something.

"No, he hasn't. So I've come down to see him."

Jessica spun around in the chair to see Nick standing in the doorway. His face was pale, and he was leaning against the door frame. "Nick!" she exclaimed jumping to her feet and running to him. "What are you doing out of bed?"

He didn't answer as she wrapped a supporting arm around him. He saved his strength to make his way with her to the couch. He wasn't about to tell her how much the effort of coming downstairs had cost him. He hadn't realized himself how weak he was until now, and that wasn't good. If he was to meet Diego in Piedra, he would have to leave the ranch within the next few days.

"You shouldn't be out of bed yet," Jessica
admonished him in a worried voice. "The doctor
said . . ."

"The doctor said he could get up when he felt
strong enough," her father interrupted, shoving back
from his desk and rising to his feet. Though coming to
Nick's defense, he had seen too many men suffering
from wounds such as Nick's to not recognize how much
determination it had taken for Nick to get this far. And,
the young man's face showed it.

"But . . ." she objected.

"No buts," Nick interjected, smiling with an
effort. "He's right. That's what the doctor said."

Jessica scowled at Nick and then at her father.
"You two are very much alike, do you know that? Pig-
headed and stubborn."

Tom snorted at Jessica's usual blunt honesty but
quickly clammed up again at Nathan Wescott's sour
look.

"Didn't your grandfather ever teach you not to
speak like that in front of guests?" Wescott repri-
manded, finding it more than difficult to discipline his
daughter. At times it seemed she'd inherited the worst
of both his and her mother's temperaments.

"Nick is not a guest," she retorted. "He's . . . oh,
never mind. Who he is is not the point. The point is, he
shouldn't be out of bed."

Nick felt a grin tug at his lips but refrained from
smiling. For Jessica he wasn't a guest, but she wasn't
certain he was family either. Even though married under
Apache law, she wasn't sure if, under white man's law,
they were considered man and wife.

He knew the subject had crossed her mind more

than once over the past few days, but she never broug
it up. Instead she was waiting for him to. Stubborn
the end, while any doubts remained as to what he rea
felt for her, she wouldn't ask him to commit himself
her.

Nick reached out to her now and, with a supren
effort, pulled her back against the couch to sit next
him. "Woman. Shut up."

Jessica began a stammered retort but clamped h
mouth shut as his eyes narrowed. She had seen that lo
before.

Nathan Wescott smiled to himself as with a r
luctant pout, Jessica relaxed beside Nick. He hadn
misjudged this young man. He was exactly what Jessi
needed. "Tom, seeing as Nick has the situation und
control, how about you and I going out to the w
range to have a look at the stock?"

Tom nodded amiably. "Sounds good."

Jessica waited until the two men had left, closi
the door behind them, before turning concerned eyes
Nick. "Are you sure you feel strong enough to be up?
she asked, noting his lack of color with silent alarm.

"I'm sure," he told her, tightening his left ar
around her shoulders. It still pained him to use his rig

She sighed and cautiously rested her head again
his left shoulder. She didn't really believe him. She ha
seen him wince in pain too often when moving sudden
to believe the pain had abruptly disappeared. But
least he was safe. They both were. Here on this ranc
she couldn't believe anything could harm them. "I'
glad you and my father like each other."

"Were you afraid we wouldn't?"

"For awhile," she admitted looking up at him.

He smiled and, bending his neck, pressed his lips against her forehead. She returned his smile happily and nuggled closer, wrapping her arm around his waist. Gazing down at her golden head, Nick tightened his arm protectively. He had almost forgotten how good it felt o hold her.

He relaxed and sat back to look around the room, aking in the books on the shelves, the curtains at the windows, the flowers in a vase on a table. A man could get used to this, and a sudden feeling of contentment illed him. It was comfortable here. It felt ike . . . home.

He frowned thoughtfully. He and Nathan Wescott had spoken often since that first meeting in his room when both of them had been on guard. The conversation's subjects had varied and had taken place both with and without Jessica, but whatever the discussion and no matter who was present, Nick had come to like Wescott. He was a man who didn't pull punches. He was straightforward and honest and, he'd given Nick food for thought. Wescott had asked Nick to consider returning here to the ranch to settle when his business was over with Franklin and Evans.

Nick had always thought he'd start from scratch, begin slowly and build, but there was Jessica to consider now. Nick didn't doubt that if he asked Jessica to go, she would, but such a request would be far from fair. She'd grown close to her father in the short time she'd known him—and he to her. It would hurt them both to pull them apart, and there was no real reason to demand t. Nick had no family, no place to call his own. Jessica did, and Wescott had invited Nick to share it. Wescott had made a good and generous offer. A man could definitely do worse. However.

Nick frowned. He had work to do first. He had a job to finish before he could look to his future. Before he could do any planning, he had to go to meet Diego.

Alone in his room upstairs, many empty hours had given him time to think, to think about Diego and Piedra and Thomas Franklin. He vehemently wished it was over. But it wasn't. Not yet. But it soon would be.

Nick glanced down again at Jessica who sat in comfortable silence beside him. Now was as good a time as any to tell her he had to leave. She knew the rest of the story on Thomas Franklin. Both he and her father had discussed him with her. The only thing they hadn't told her was of the coming meeting in Piedra. She would have to know sometime, though, sometime soon.

"I'm going to have to leave in a day or two, Jess."

Jessica didn't move. She wasn't sure she had heard correctly. Surely she was imagining things? She pulled away to look up at him, her eyes filled with disbelief.

"I have to go," he repeated and watched as her face darkened.

"Why?"

"Thomas Franklin."

Her small brow furrowed. "Thomas Franklin?"

"Yes. I'm not done with him yet."

She got to her feet and walked away from the couch, leaving her back to Nick. The peace of the day had just been shattered. Fear had come to destroy it.

"What do you mean you're not done with him?"

"We haven't stopped him yet."

"We?"

"Diego and I," he answered, his eyes never leaving
er. "When I explained Thomas Franklin to you
efore, I didn't tell you that I'm supposed to meet
iego soon in a small village south of here called
iedra."

She spun around to stare at him. "You're in no
ondition to ride."

He gestured impatiently, angry at himself because
e knew she was right and angry at her for recognizing
s weakness. "I'm going to meet Diego in Piedra in
ur days, Jess."

"No!"

"Yes."

"Then I'm going with you."

"The hell you are. You're staying right here where
ou belong—with your father. I'm not going to let you
et involved in this again."

"You're not going to let me . . . I'll do what I
ant," she declared with an angry stamp of her foot.

Nick's eyes narrowed dangerously. "You're
aying here."

"And who's going to make me?"

"I will and so will your father. He knows the risks
nvolved as well as I do. It's dangerous work I'm doing.
ou, of all people, should know how dangerous it can
e."

"That's exactly why you shouldn't go alone."

"That's exactly why I am going alone."

They glared at each other across the room, neither
f them hearing the door open and Anita enter.

For the past few days the older woman had
vatched these two young people. They loved each other.
he was sure of this. But they were both stubborn! She

shook her head as she watched them now. They we
fighting. A disagreement brought about, no doub
because they cared for each other. Anita smiled to he
self. For the young, the road to *amor* was never
smooth one. "*Señor* Driscoll. Why did you not tell m
you were getting out of bed this morning?"

Both Nick and Jessica started at the words an
turned in surprise to look at the rotund Mexican woma
who had been caring so diligently for Nick.

Nick opened his mouth to answer but stopped whe
Jessica moved.

The interruption and appearance of Anita in th
room had closed the discussion about Nick's leavin
but it had not dispersed Jessica's anger. With one la
burning glare at Nick, she turned on her heel and spu
away, marching around Anita to disappear out th
study door with a decisive slam.

"Did you know he was planning on leaving?"
Jessica demanded of her father shortly before dinn
that night. For most of the day she had wrestled with t
idea of Nick's going. She couldn't come to terms with i
She couldn't—wouldn't—believe it was true.

"I did."

"And you didn't tell me?"

Nathan Wescott watched his daughter whirl awa
to walk to the window. Her back was stiff with ange
"He asked me not to, and I agreed."

She swung to face him once more. "You know he
not strong enough."

"I don't know that at all," he countered firml
"He's a man. He knows his own strength and his ow
mind. He's got something that needs doing, and he
going to do it."

"Even if it costs him his life?"

Wescott sighed and looked away from the fear in her eyes. "Even if it costs him his life."

Jessica stamped her foot. "I won't let him do it."

"You can't stop him, honey." And walking quickly to her, he took her shoulders in his hands. "Listen, he's given himself more than enough time to get to Piedra. He's got at least one more day than he would usually need if he were riding at an easy pace. That'll give him plenty of time to rest along the way."

"Rest or no, he shouldn't go, and he especially shouldn't go alone," she protested. "What if the fever comes back? What if his wound opens up again?"

Wescott shook his head. "It's his decision."

"It's mine, too!" she declared and pulled away to walk to the door. "He's not going," she repeated loudly with her hand on the doorknob.

Nathan Wescott heaved a sigh as the door closed behind her. If he'd been twenty years younger and standing in a room of the small ranch house that had once been built on the same site this one now occupied, he would have sworn he had just had a fight with his wife.

"How is he, doctor?" Jessica asked the graying but lean-muscled man as he descended the stairs. She had been waiting there for his departure since leaving her father in the study. She wasn't at all happy about Nick's plans to leave. She knew he was getting stronger, knew it was only a matter of time before he would be back to all his normal activities, but she also knew what his leaving meant.

Selfishly she admitted she wanted him to stay and stay for good, and she realized some of the selfishness

was fear—fear he wouldn't come back, and not because
he couldn't but because he didn't want to. He'd never
told her he loved her or wanted to stay with her. He'd
never made any commitment to her—except at the
Apache wedding ceremony, and that hadn't been of his
own free will.

No, he might not want to stay with her, but she
couldn't stop her feelings for him. She wanted him to be
safe, healthy and happy, and going to Piedra would
assure him none of those things. The Confederates were
desperate, and desperate men did desperate things. They
killed men. They'd almost killed Nick. She couldn't let
him put himself in that position again—particularly not
while he was weak and hurt. But how could she stop
him? What could she do?

"Still weaker than he'd like to admit, but the
danger's passed," the doctor replied, coming to a halt
beside her. He was used to seeing her and answering her
questions. Whenever he came to the ranch to see Nick
Driscoll, Jessica was sure to be somewhere nearby. The
doctor recognized the symptoms of her regular
appearances and assumed he'd be attending a wedding
soon. "He's a strong man, and the worst is over. He's
been up and moving around already. In a couple of days
it'll be even easier for him to do so, but it'll take some
time to build his endurance back up to where it was."

Jessica nodded thoughtfully. "Is he still having
much pain?"

"Not that he'll admit."

She smiled understanding, but the smile suddenly
deepened. She had a plan! "It's what I thought. You
wouldn't have anything for the pain, I mean, something
he wouldn't know he was taking?"

The doctor smiled down at her. He was familiar with male pride, and he knew she cared a lot for this young man. "That I do. I can give you something to put in his drinks. Maybe you can slip it to him with his supper. It'll let him get a good night's rest."

Jessica nodded emphatically. "That's exactly what he needs. A good rest."

The doctor pulled a small bottle from his case and quickly explained how to use it. "A tablespoon will let him sleep for a solid night, possibly up to ten hours."

She turned the bottle over in her hands carefully. "It's not possible to give him too much, is it?"

"I wouldn't advise giving it to him too often," he replied. "No more than two tablespoons at a time and twice a day should be enough. If he has pain during the day, it'll make him drowsy enough to sleep for several hours."

"I'll be careful then," she assured him. "And thank you."

"My pleasure."

Jessica smiled as she saw him to the door. Closing it behind him, she merrily eyed the bottle. "No, doctor, the pleasure is all mine."

Chapter 23

Two days later Jessica was up early, rushing to get dressed. She had continued to try to convince Nick not to go, but he refused to listen. And her father, he was no help at all. It was up to her to do what must be done.

She stopped in front of the vanity mirror to quickly survey herself. She'd tied and braided her hair into a long strand that lay down her back. Doing it now would save time later, and the clothes she wore, they would do for what came later, too. She brushed at her skirt and then turned to hurry downstairs toward the kitchen. Anita would be fixing breakfast for Nick there. The oider woman always took Nick's morning meal up to his room. Lately Nick had been joining Jessica and her father in the dining room for lunch and dinner, but the morning ritual had remained the same.

However, this particular morning, Jessica planned to take his breakfast to him. It was an essential part of her plan, as what she carried in her pocket was. She reached the kitchen door and stopped to pat the pocket to insure the bottle of medicine was safely tucked away and ready for use. It was ready, and so was she.

She walked into the kitchen to find Anita putting the final touches to Nick's tray. Jessica breathed a silent sigh of relief. She was just in time. "Would it be all right if I took Nick's breakfast up to him today, Anita?" Jessica asked with just the right tone of melancholy in her voice.

"But of course," Anita agreed with a sympathetic smile. "After all, this will be the last morning you will see him for a while, yes?"

Jessica nodded.

Anita took the look in Jessica's eyes for sadness instead of regret and clucked her tongue in understanding. "Do not worry, *señorita*. He will hurry back to you. A man who looks at you the way he does cannot stay away too long."

Jessica smiled appreciatively and accepted the tray from Anita's steady hands. She wished she could be as sure of Nick's affection as Anita was, and she hoped her hands would remain as steady as hers when she saw Nick. If he knew what she was planning . . .

Slipping out the kitchen door, Jessica quickly crossed the hall to the stairs. She stopped at the bottom step to look anxiously down toward the study. No one was in sight. She looked back down the hall to the kitchen. She could hear Anita puttering with the pots and pans and singing. It was safe.

Balancing the tray on the railing, Jessica pulled the bottle from her pocket. She smiled to herself, but the smile quickly vanished. She didn't have a spoon! Her heart sank. She'd forgotten to get one. She cursed her-elf and looked at the one on the tray. She couldn't very well use it. She shrugged. There was nothing for it. She'd have to guess and hope.

She tipped the bottle and dribbled some into the glass of milk. She eyed it speculatively. Was it enough? She shook her head. She wasn't taking any chances. She tipped the bottle again and allowed a few more drops to fall in. Then she mixed it with her finger, wiped the finger on her skirt, capped the bottle and continued up the stairs with the medicine tucked out of sight in her pocket once more.

She reached his door and knocked. "Nick, it's me."

Footsteps crossed the room, and then Nick was standing before her.

She smiled up at him hopefully. He was completely dressed already. "Still leaving?"

"Jess . . ."

"I only asked," she protested and hurried past him to set the tray on his table. "I thought I'd bring you your breakfast today." She glanced over her shoulder at him but quickly looked away again. "After all, this will be the last time I'll see you—at least for a few days?"

He smiled at her hesitation and followed her into the room. She was still baiting him for a direct answer on his intentions toward her. "For a few days," he confirmed and opened his arms to her when she turned from setting down the tray.

She entered eagerly and hugged him tightly as his embrace closed around her. He *had* planned on coming back! She squeezed her eyes shut. Knowing that made it that much harder to do what she had to.

Nick held her close and swore to himself. He was

going to miss her, damn it. He was going to miss her a
lot. Since he'd first told her he was leaving, she'd
continued to try to make him stay, but with each day he
felt stronger and more sure of himself. The pain in his
shoulder was minimal, the wound well on its way to
healing. He was ready. He was going.

She pulled away reluctantly, a guilty flush adding a
touch of color to her cheeks. It wasn't going to be easy
to do this to him. "You better eat your breakfast while
it's warm. It'll probably be the last good meal you'll
have until you get back."

Puzzled but thankful for her sudden change of
attitude, Nick obediently sat down at the table and
began to eat. She was a little more willing to let him go
than he'd expected. He had been ready for another
fight, but evidently she had finally accepted his going.
Or had she?

She met his questioning stare with a tight smile. He
was drinking the milk. Now if it would just work—without him tasting it! "Is something wrong?"

"No. You seem awfully calm is all."

She shrugged and looked away toward the window.
"Father told me I couldn't stop you. He said I should
get used to the idea of your going."

"And have you?"

"No."

His eyes narrowed on her, but when she turned to
face him again, he was surprised to see she was smiling.
She really wasn't going to fight him after all. A frown
settled on his face. If he didn't know better, he'd think
she was up to something. However, there was nothing
she could do. There was no way she could prevent him
from leaving.

"Anita's packing some saddlebags for you. Should I go get them?"

"You're being very helpful this morning."

"Maybe I'm trying to convince you to take me along."

Nick grunted. "Jess . . ."

"I know, I know." She watched him swallow a forkful of eggs. "I'll go get the bags."

Walking to the door, she hesitated, looking back at him once more. He had the glass in his hand. But he was watching her, too. She smiled quickly and ran down the stairs. He couldn't suspect. He just couldn't! But, even if he did, it was too late—she hoped.

With the leather bags firmly in her hands moments later, Jessica reentered the room to find Nick draining the glass of milk. She had to bite her lip to keep from smiling. "Here they are."

Nick nodded and pushed back his chair. "I'll be going then."

Jessica watched him rise and suddenly sway. Her heart lurched against her ribs. "Nick, what is it? What's wrong?"

Nick put a hand to his spinning head. What was the matter with him? He felt so dizzy. "Nothing. Nothing's wrong." He took a staggering step forward, and the room began to reel. He groped wildly for something to catch his balance with, and Jessica rushed to his side.

With her arm firmly around him, she helped him over to the waiting bed. "You better lie down, Nick. You're going to sleep for a while."

"Sleep . . . no . . ."

"Yes," she insisted, meeting his rapidly glazing eyes. "The doctor gave me some medicine to help you sleep, and now you're going to rest while I go to Piedra.''

"No!"

The exclamation was vehement but mumbled. Jessica was sure now he wouldn't be able to fight it. The medicine was already taking hold. "Please, Nick, understand," she pleaded as shaking his head, he tried to sit up. "It'll be better this way. You've gotten so much stronger in the past two days. I don't want you to hurt yourself again by making this trip."

He groaned and felt waves of blackness wash over him. Her words were a distant echo rumbling softly through his head. He tried to understand, tried to fight. He couldn't let her do this. It was too dangerous. She didn't realize what she was getting into!

"I'm sorry," she told him. His movements were becoming weaker. "I'm sorry." She felt tears burn her eyes. She didn't like doing this to him. She didn't want to trick him, but she had to. She couldn't let him risk his life to meet Diego. They were only going to exchange information and then contact this man called Evans to do the rest. She could do that for him. There was no need for him to take the chance of having a relapse.

His struggles finally ended, and she reached out to brush the dark hair from his forehead. She leaned forward to press her mouth lightly to his before getting to her feet. Looking down at him, her fingers twisted together anxiously. He was going to be so angry when he woke up! She grimaced. She was glad she wasn't going to be here. She turned away and looked around the room.

First she had to take the tray back to Anita who was still busy in the kitchen. By doing so, Anita wouldn't come up here looking for it later and find Nick still here. Jessica hurried to the tray and hustled it down the stairs, slowing only long enough to smile in a forlorn manner at Anita before rushing back to the room to collect Nick's saddlebags.

Jessica stopped by the bed. Nick was sleeping soundly. She bit her lip. If only there'd been another way. She shook her head. There hadn't been. She'd done the only thing she could, and now she had to finish what she had started. She turned away and went out the door, locking it behind her.

Moments later she was walking toward the stable where Tom was waiting for her by the horses. As usual he was expecting her for their morning ride.

"Those Nick's saddlebags?" he asked at her approach.

"No. They're mine."

Tom blinked and shook his head as if uncertain he'd heard correctly. "Yours?"

"Yes. I'm going to Piedra. Not Nick."

"But . . ."

"No buts, Tom. I'm going. Where's my father?"

Stammering for a moment, he finally found his voice. "Out on the north range."

"Good."

Tom watched in amazement as she tied the bags in place behind her saddle. "Nathan knows you're going?"

"No."

"And you're not going to tell him?"

"No."

Tom grimaced, attempted to speak, but Jessica interrupted him.

"And you aren't either. At least not until tonight.

He opened his mouth again but was silenced by wave of her hand.

"Tom, Nick can't go. He's not strong enough. In few more days he would be, but he wants to go now an I'm not going to let him take that chance. I can go an meet Diego just as well as he. All they have to do exchange information so they can tell this Evans wh̲ they've found."

"And Nick agreed to this?"

She blanched. "Well, no, not exactly."

Tom lifted a suspicious eyebrow. She wouldn̲ meet his eyes. "Where is he?"

"Sleeping."

"Sleeping?"

She bit her lip. "I gave him some medicine."

Tom let out a low whistle. "Your father doesn̲ know. Nick doesn't know." He lifted his hat with on̲ hand to scratch his head uneasily. This was a fin̲ howdy-do, and a hell of a way to start the morning. H̲ looked down at her as she stood by her horse. By he̲ expression, he could see she was determined to go, bu̲ how could he let her? "What if you get lost?" h̲ suggested.

"I won't get lost because you're going to ride wit̲ me until we reach the edge of the ranch and point me i̲ the right direction."

"I am?"

"You are."

Tom met her steady gaze. "Look, Jess, if you're s̲ fired sure Nick shouldn't go, couldn't I go instead? Yo̲ shouldn't be out riding around alone."

"You can't go because you don't know Diego," he responded simply, climbing into the saddle. "You may understand what it is Nick and Diego are looking for and you may be able to tell Diego everything Nick knows, but how will you recognize him? How will you know who Diego is? And, how will he know who you are? Even if you did find him, why should he trust you? He doesn't know you."

Tom shifted restlessly. "That makes sense, Jess, but your father. Nathan's not going to like this."

"I don't care if he does." She swung her horse around to face the gate. "Now. Are you coming or not?"

Tom swallowed convulsively. He had to talk her out of this somehow, but he couldn't think of anything to say. Maybe after they'd ridden for a while he could think of some way to dissuade her. He swung into his saddle and followed her lead, but some time later he was still minus a good reason to stop her and, having listened to her reasoning some more, his arguments were waning. She wasn't going too awfully far, and she'd be going on a well-traveled road. Nick was still ailing, and he was worried for him. It all made perfect sense somehow that she should go, didn't it? But what about Nathan? Tom shied from the thought. He'd face Nathan soon enough.

He stopped his horse and scanned the land ahead of them thoroughly before turning to Jessica who had pulled her mount to a halt beside his. "You're sure about this?"

"I'm sure." And recognizing his distress, Jessica stretched out a hand to touch his arm. "This has to be

done, Tom, you know that. You've heard Nick and m[
father discussing Franklin. The man has to b[
stopped.''

Tom nodded readily. "I know, but couldn't I com[
along, Jess?''

She shook her head. "No. You're going to be i[
enough trouble as it is, and someone has to explain thi[
to Nick and my father.''

Tom winced. "That ain't going to be easy.''

"But please try,'' she pleaded. "Nick's going to b[
so angry . . .''

"Not to mention Nathan.'' Tom grimaced agai[
but nevertheless smiled winningly. "Don't worry non[
about them. I'll handle it. You just take care of your[
self.'' He pointed south. "It's safe enough in this are[
to travel alone. Not many Indians come through her[
and not many bandits. It's too settled here for them t[
cause much trouble.''

"There's more than one village then?''

"And plenty of small *haciendas*, but you won'[
have any trouble finding Piedra. There's woode[
markers along the road.'' He met her eyes and saw th[
fear and uncertainty shining in them. "You going to b[
all right?''

She nodded decisively and flashed him a smile. Sh[
couldn't lose her resolve now. "Don't worry. Diego wil[
look after me. And as soon as we see this Evans, he'[
bring me back safe and sound. It should only take [
couple days.''

"Probably more like a week.''

Jessica nodded soberly. "Probably.'' She met hi[
steady gaze for a long moment. "You take care of your[
self.''

"You, too," Tom agreed.

She started out then, and Tom watched her go. He watched her until she became no more than a small speck on the horizon and until she disappeared into the rolling plains beyond him. As she went, though, he couldn't decide which way *he* should go—after her or back to the ranch.

He really didn't believe she'd come to any harm on the road. The area was safe enough, and this Diego fellow would look out for her when she reached Piedra, but he still didn't like it. He wanted to follow her. Stay at a distance until they were well away from the ranch and then join her. However, there was Nathan to consider. How would he know what had happened and why unless someone told him?

Either way he went, Tom thought with a loud sigh, he figured there'd be hell to pay. There was a Wescott waiting on either end, and those Wescotts, he knew from experience, they had terrible tempers.

Nick awoke well after noon, his head still clogged with the drug's effects, his mouth dry and foul. But he had to get up. He had to stop Jessica. Staggering and swaying blindly against the remnants of the sleep that had captured him, it was some time until he was able to make it to the door.

It was longer still until he made enough noise for Anita to come upstairs to find out who had been locked in a room. By the time the key was found and Nathan Wescott got home, it was almost evening. And, by the time Tom confessed, it was too late to try to go after Jessica. The next day would have to do.

But Jessica wasn't waiting for the next day. She

was pushing her horse on through the night at a slow pace, her white-knuckled hands firmly holding the rifle from the saddle boot. She couldn't afford to tire the animal out. She had rested it during the heat of the day, but she didn't want to give anyone who might follow time to catch up either. The further she got ahead, the better. If she could get the mission done before seeing Nick again, it might help alleviate some of his anger. But if he caught her first, before she was able to arrive and meet Diego, she didn't even want to think about the consequences.

However, think about them she did—all the way to Piedra, a small village she reached a long two-and-a-half days later. Having ridden day and night, except for resting during the midday heat, she thought she'd fall from the saddle before she managed to climb down, but stubborn determination held her in good stead and she made it to the stable and handed her horse's reins over to the boy in charge.

Waiting by the door while the young Mexican settled the horse in, Jessica stared out at the village streets. She had made it, but now what? Where did she meet Diego? How did she know he was even there?

There had been no set meeting place except for this village. She chewed on her lip anxiously. The one place he might be, she couldn't go—the cantina.

She turned to look at the boy and her horse. But the boy could, if Diego was here. She remembered Rito and smiled. Nothing had gone on in his little village he hadn't known about. Was it the same with this one? And, could he be trusted?

She had money with her. But she should be sure Diego was here before sending the boy on such an errand. The question was, how could she be sure? Her eyes wandered to the other horses. If Diego had indeed made it to Piedra, he would have stabled his horse. Maybe she could identify it.

Starting on one side of the stable, she began walking slowly down the aisle. She examined each horse carefully and the saddle beside it as she went. If there was one thing she could recognize of Diego's, it was his saddle blanket. Made of brightly woven colors, she would know it was his anywhere.

She reached the end of the aisle, and her hopes fell. There was no sign of such a blanket. What would she do if he wasn't here? She turned to make her way back up the other side of the stable, and her teeth caught at her lip. It just had to be here. *He* had to be here.

She continued to walk slowly, hesitating by each stall. One horse after another. One blanket after another. Her eyes searched, and her fists clenched. She was beginning to lose all hope, but then she saw it. About halfway to the door, it was slung across a stall wall. Her heart stopped and her gaze fastened on the bright square of woven color.

She hurried forward to touch the blanket, and a smile broke across her face. It was Diego's! It was! He was here!

The stable boy suddenly appeared at her side. He had been watching her travel the aisle. Now she had stopped. Had she found what she was searching for? He looked up at her with huge and deeply curious black eyes. "*Señorita*?"

Jessica turned to answer him. She would have to trust him. She would have to let him try to locate and bring Diego to her. She reached for her money, and within moments the young boy was gone and she was alone.

Nervously, she paced the stable floor as she waited. She hoped the boy could find Diego. She hoped Diego would come. She brushed at her dusty riding skirt. It would be such a relief when all of this was finally over. She sighed and continued to pace. Minutes crept past. Where was the boy? Had he been able to find Diego? What if he couldn't?

Footfalls sounded outside the stable. Jessica spun toward the door. It had to be him. It had to. The door slid open. Bright sunshine streamed in and illuminated the face of a man. She didn't even wait until he got inside before moving. She just ran and, with a squeal of glee, threw her arms around his neck.

Diego staggered under the unexpected embrace but began to laugh when he realized who it was who was clinging to his neck. "*Chiquita*, take it easy! You will have my head off if you squeeze any harder."

Jessica laughed and stepped back, releasing him. "I'm so glad to see you!"

"I could not tell," he answered with a smile and looked past her for the man he was expecting to meet.

"Nick's not here."

Diego's eyes sobered and his smile faded instantly. "He is safe?"

"Safe but hurt."

"It is bad?"

She smiled in reassurance. "Not any more, but he's still not well. He was shot almost two weeks ago in a village we'd traced the wagons to, but we managed to escape and get to my father's ranch. That's where he is now."

"And he sent you to meet me?" Diego asked in disbelief.

She wrinkled her nose and bit her lip. "He didn't actually send me . . ."

Diego rolled his eyes to the loft above, his smile returning. "I think we had better find ourselves a seat and let you explain." He turned to the boy who had brought him. "*Muchas gracias, muchacho.*"

The boy who had stood watching the two of them greet each other grinned widely as Diego slipped a coin into his hand. "*Gracias, señor!*" he responded and flashed Jessica a bright smile. Two payments for one service! Errand running was a profitable business! He scampered off into the shadows, leaving Diego to lead Jessica to a stack of crates near the door.

There, sitting with Diego beside her, Jessica hurriedly told him what had happened since they had parted by the Apache camp. He listened intently to every word, waiting until she was done to let out a long sigh.

"So, at least he is well and what needed to be done is done. We now know where Franklin is and where his guns are coming from."

"You know where he is?" she exclaimed.

"*Sí.* I know where he is. I was waiting for Nick to arrive before sending word to Evans. It will be up to him now to have the Army stop him."

"He'll send soldiers?"

"You did not expect us to do it ourselves, did you?" he inquired with a grin.

Jessica laughed. "No."

Diego got to his feet and extended a hand to help her rise also. "But, before we send a message to our

Señor Evans in Santa Fe, I think we shall find you a
good meal, yes?"

"I am hungry," she admitted. And as they moved
to the door, "Rito's not still with you, is he?"

"No, he is safe with friends for the moment.
Perhaps after we see to Thomas Franklin, we could
bring him to your father's ranch?"

Jessica smiled. "Of course, and you'll have to
come to stay for a while, too."

Diego grinned. "I can hardly wait, *chiquita*. It has
been a long time since I have put my feet up and
watched the sun pass from one horizon to the next."

"It's going to be longer yet, friend. Because before
you go anywhere, Mr. Franklin would like to see you."

Jessica's blood turned to ice at the sound of the
voice, and Diego froze beside her. Coming in from
behind the stable door, two men entered with drawn
guns. From where they had been waiting, they could
have heard every word Diego and she had exchanged.
Jessica glanced anxiously up at Diego, but he was
watching the men.

"You've led us a merry chase," one man told
Diego with a soft Southern drawl while leveling a rifle at
him. "Spotted you down Mexico way some days back.
Mr. Franklin figured on what you were up to and sent
us to stop you and whoever you met. But we didn't
expect you to be meeting with a lady."

Diego stepped in front of Jessica. "She has nothing
to do with this. She is my friend's wife. Your men
succeeded in wounding him badly. She only came to tell
me he is safe."

"That's not the way we heard it."

The second man waved his rifle in Jessica's

rection. "What are we going to do now? Franklin
idn't count on us meeting up with a woman."

The first nodded doubtfully. "We better take them
oth back to camp. Killing a man's one thing, but I
on't want any part in killing a woman. And, I don't
think Franklin does either."

"He's not going to like our bringing them back."

"We don't have a choice."

Chapter 24

At noon the following day Nick rode into Piedra along with Nathan Wescott and Tom. Leaving before dawn the day after Jessica, the three men had trailed her to the village. She had ridden slowly, following the roads with uncertainty. But they had known where they were going and had made much better time than her. With any luck, they'd catch her here.

For the first part of the journey Nick had found it difficult to stay in the saddle. Stubborn pride had been the only thing that kept him seated. But, as the hours had worn on, the sharpness of the pain in his shoulder had become an accustomed ache, more of a nuisance than an actual hindrance. He had ridden with wounds before, and he was determined to do it again now.

"Where were you supposed to meet him?" Wescott asked as they rode down the village streets towards the stable.

"We usually met at the cantina," Nick replied

gesturing to a doorway where guitar music echoed softly.

"Jess wouldn't go there," Tom objected, immediately flinching under the glare Wescott turned on him. His ears were still burning from the lecture he'd received on helping Jessica go. Somehow all her explanations hadn't stood up to her father's and Nick's objections.

"No," Nick agreed, irritable at the mention of the woman they'd followed. "She'd probably go to the stable and try to find out if Diego's come in." Silently Nick hoped Diego hadn't arrived yet. He wanted Jessica alone. His palm was itching to make contact with her backside.

They reached the stable and dismounted, glancing around the small yard for some sign of Jessica or Diego. There was none. The stable door swung open, and a young boy came out to greet them, his eyes round with curiosity.

Nick handed the boy the reins to his horse along with a silver dollar. "*Chico*, have you seen a woman riding through here? One with golden hair?"

"*Sí, señor*," he replied readily.

"Is she still here now?" Nick asked with a tight smile. He was going to enjoy turning her over his knee.

Unexpectedly the boy's eyes fell, and he kicked the dirt at his sandaled feet restlessly. Back in the shadows where he could not be seen, he had watched two men come into the stable to confront the young woman these men sought and the man she had sent him to get. The men had forced the golden-haired woman and her friend on horses and ridden off with them. He raised his eyes to look at Nick. "No, *señor*, she is gone."

"Gone?" Nick echoed incredulously. "Where?"

The boy shrugged his thin shoulders and kicked at the dirt again, hesitating before responding. "She and her *amigo*, they were taken away."

Nick felt his heart falter and his spine stiffen. A glance at Nathan Wescott showed the older man shared his distress. His face had suddenly paled beneath the weatherbeaten brown of his skin. Nick turned back to the boy. "*Chico*, can we go inside? We want you to tell us everything you know."

As the boy's words tumbled out, Nick's worst fears were realized. His stomach knotted with frustration and anger. Jessica had walked right into a trap. From what the boy had heard, the men had followed Diego from Franklin's camp in the south. They had been waiting for him to meet with someone, someone they would assume to be his partner.

By now Franklin would be aware of Diego's and his past presence in the village where they had followed the man in gray and his presence in the other village where he had discovered the guns. Franklin would know someone was on his trail and getting closer all the time. He would have sent the two men to silence whomever was following him. The only thing that had saved Diego's life was that he had met a woman instead of another man.

Nick slammed his fist against a stall wall as the boy finished speaking. "They've taken them to their camp."

"Do you know where it is?" Wescott asked. "Can we go after them?"

Nick shook his head. "I have a rough idea where it is, but I don't know for certain. And as for catching them." He shrugged helplessly. "I don't know. They've

got at least a good day's lead on us. It'll depend on how
fast they're traveling.''

"We could try," Tom suggested earnestly. "If we
can catch them before they reach the camp . . .''

"That's a big if," Nick stated flatly. "We could
walk into a trap ourselves, then all we've learned will be
worthless.'' He stared hard at nothing for a moment
and then turned to Tom once more. "We're going to
have to try to get them out, but I don't know if we can
do it alone. You'll have to go back to the ranch. Get
word to Evans in Santa Fe. He'll notify the commander
at Fort Union. They'll send help."

"Much as I like the Army," Wescott put in. "They
can be all fired slow. Seeing as Tom's going to the
ranch, why not have him bring some men back? In the
meantime, you and I can start out, leave Tom a clear
trail, and get the lay of the land."

Nick hesitated.

"If you and I fail, if we can't get Jess and your
friend out by ourselves," Wescott went on. "I'd rather
do it with men I know. If the Army has to go in
shooting, they're not going to have time to worry about
my little girl."

Nick nodded reluctant agreement. "All right."
And to Tom, "Franklin's camp is straight south of
here. I'm betting it's not more than three or four day's
ride."

"Don't worry. We'll find you," Tom responded
and looking to Wescott, "with a fresh horse, I should
be able to make it back to the ranch in a little more than
a day riding hard."

"Take one that looks solid," Wescott answered
with a wave to the stabled horses. "I'll pay whoever he

longs to. If he doesn't want the money, I'll shoot him
stead.'' Neither Nick nor Tom doubted that he meant

Miles to the south Jessica swayed in the saddle, but
e was in no danger of falling off her horse. Her hands
d been securely tied to the saddle horn as had Diego's
a his horse. They'd been riding constantly since leaving
edra. Plodding along at a slow but steady pace, they
opped only twice a day. Once during the midday heat
d once during the night to give the horses a rest.

"Try to sleep, Jessica," Diego murmured seeing
r lean forward heavily with fatigue. "Lay on your
arse's neck. Do not fight to stay awake."

Too tired to answer, she merely attempted to do as
e was told. She hadn't slept since leaving the ranch.
e had found it impossible to sleep while alone on the
ains, and she was sure it would be impossible to sleep
w, tied to a horse. But, she was wrong. Pushed to the
int of exhaustion, she fell into a blackness that ended
ly when, in the middle of the night, she was pulled
om her horse. It was time for their second rest of the
y.

She slumped beside Diego on the ground. "You'd
ink I'd be used to this by now."

Diego grinned at her feeble smile. She was as
abborn as he remembered. "You should be. We have
agged you around enough, eh?"

She shook her head in denial as much as to clear it of
e last of the sleep. "No, not enough. Otherwise I
ouldn't be so tired."

Diego watched as one of the men began rubbing the
imals down. "It is not much farther. Another day's
le, perhaps a little more. It is hard to say traveling as

we are. They will know shortcuts and perhaps have another entrance to the canyon they are in.''

"You haven't seen the canyon?" Jessica asked surprise. She had expected him to know everything about the location of Thomas Franklin.

"No. I only know where they are," Diego replied "I could not risk getting too close." And, with a sour look, "But evidently I got close enough."

"You mustn't blame yourself for my being here Diego," she protested at his expression of disgust. "It my fault. I'm the one who drugged Nick."

"And perhaps it is a good thing you did, *chiquita* If he had come instead of you, we would both probab be dead."

A cold chill shook Jessica. "What do you thin Franklin will do with us?"

Diego shrugged. "I do not know what he will do but I know what Nick will." He lowered his voice as I watched the men who still lingered near the horse "They do not expect you to be followed, but you wi be. Nick will come after you, *chiquita*. Do not think I will not."

"But I told Tom not to let him," Jessica proteste in a harsh whisper.

Diego grinned down at her. "You think that wi stop Nick? No, you have made him angry. And, whi perhaps you did not think of this, he would have. Ther was a chance I might not have made it to Piedra. I coul have been caught as he almost was, and then you woul have been waiting in a strange village by yourself." H shook his head. "No, he will come."

"My father will probably come then, too," sh agreed in a distressed voice. "They could be killed."

Diego scoffed and grinned again. "Do not tell Nick
ou ever said this," he objected. "He would not take it
a compliment."

"They have a chance of getting to us?"

Diego looked down into her hope-filled eyes. "*Sí,
iquita*. They have a chance, and so do we. Nick is a
nart *hombre*. He has been in many bad situations and
otten out alive. Franklin is not the first man we have
llowed for Evans, nor is he the most dangerous."

Jessica unexpectedly found herself looking far into
e future. "Diego, when this is over, if we get out, are
ou and Nick going to work for Evans again?"

"No, *chiquita*. We will not," he answered, and
ere was no smile on his lips this time. "Nick and I
ve had enough. The War was one thing. We fought to
lp the Union win, and in a way I think we only let
vans give us this job of finding Franklin because this is
ill part of the war. But after this, there will be no more
vans."

"Thank God," Jessica whispered and turned to
atch the men who were now rummaging in their
ddlebags for jerky to eat. She hoped she might see the
ay when Nick worked for no one but himself and had
e ranch he had told Rito he wanted. Perhaps, if she
as lucky, she, too, would be part of his future.

Time proved Diego was right in his expectation of
riving at the canyon within the next two days. Follow-
g still another full day and night of riding, the next
wn showed them a rougher terrain, covered by large
cks and stone walls.

"We are getting close," Diego told Jessica in a low
urmur so the two men could not hear. "We will be
ere before noon."

Jessica turned anxious eyes on him. Fear w
beginning to gnaw at her. What would the Confederat
do with them? Question them, surely. But what then

Diego saw the question in her eyes and smiled
reassurance. "Do not worry, *chiquita*. I do not thir
they will harm you."

"But you, Diego, what about you?"

"You are not to worry about me," he told h
firmly but with a smile. "I have strong luck. It h
carried me through many unpleasant situations in tł
past years. It will not desert me now."

Jessica had no time to reply because rounding
curve in the rocky trail, a huge wall loomed befo
them, and on top of it stood two men.

At a signal from their captors, the men on tł
canyon wall waved and disappeared. Soon the hors
were going single file, passing through a ragged crevas
which ran through the rock face from top to bottom.
was a crude trail, but it took them inside, into a canyo
with adobe huts, corrals and a wagon yard comple
with wagons and a warehouse. This would be the pla
they stored the arms they brought in until they we
ready to ship them to Mexico.

Jessica looked around her in surprise. It w
organized and settled, almost like a small town, b
everything was in transit. Nothing was made to last. Tł
huts were not well constructed. They were on
temporary shelters. The whole place had an atmosphe
of constant motion, one of people moving in ar
moving out, and indeed there were people—me
women and children.

Nick had told her whole families were moving
Mexico, but she hadn't believed women would take pa

such a thing as gunrunning. But then, she hadn't
ally thought about it. Under different circumstances,
it was Nick heading this movement, wouldn't she be
re with him? She had risked her life for him. These
omen were doing no less for their men.

When she looked at Diego to see his reaction to the
nyon camp, he was frowning. Glancing nervously at
e guards who still rode beside them, she ventured to
eak, "What is it, Diego?"

He shook his head as if in disbelief. "There is so
tle here. Not so many men as I had suspected. We did
ot think Franklin would be holding the guns for one
g shipment to Mexico—it would be too risky—but he
ust be sending his men in regularly with the guns. I
ad heard Maximilian had granted the Confederates
acts of land to settle, to make into colonies, but I had
ought it was only a rumor. But it is evidently true. The
onfederates have moved to Mexico."

Jessica let her eyes roam once more, trying to grasp
hat had happened to cause this movement. The South
ated the North for its prosperity in industry and for its
olitionist beliefs. They wanted to be independent of
e states above the Mason-Dixon line. But did they
ate the Union so much that they were willing to leave
eir own country to go into someone else's? It seemed
ch an enormous step.

The horses stopped, and the men who had brought
em untied their hands to allow them to dismount
hile being kept under armed guard.

Jessica moved around her horse to stand beside
iego to wait, rubbing her sore wrists. Now they were
ere, she didn't know what to expect, and she was
fraid to guess. These people had fought for their

beliefs and lost. But, they had not given up. They were
determined group. They were continuing their battle i
another, more subtle way, and Jessica was sure the
wouldn't welcome anyone who interfered with the
efforts.

The front door to what seemed to be the ma
house opened, and a tall, long-limbed man stroc
rapidly toward the men who had found them in Piedr
He was wearing a Confederate uniform. "What's goir
on here? The lookouts told us you were bringing i
two . . ." He stopped when he got close enough to se
Jessica and Diego standing beside the horses.

"This is the man we followed," one of the
captors was quick to explain. "We followed him t
Piedra. He met her there. We heard them talking abou
Franklin . . ."

The man waved him to silence and walked slowl
forward to stop before Jessica and Diego.

Jessica met his stare evenly when he turned shar
but curious hazel eyes on her and Diego. She wa
surprised by his age and the respect he got with it. H
couldn't be much older than she was but obviously ha
a rank of authority in the camp. His uniform was i
better repair than some of the others she could se
around her, too. It fit snugly over his lean but muscula
form.

"A woman, huh?" he queried with a lopsided grir
not flinching from the fiery green glare being fastene
on him from the female in question. "The Union mus
be getting desperate." He spun back to the two me
who had caught Diego and Jessica. "Go inside an
report to Colonel Franklin. He'll want to know what th
devil you've gotten him into this time."

The two exchanged a fretful look and reluctantly moved off toward the house as two others came forward to take their place as guards.

The tall man watched them go before turning again to Jessica and Diego. "I don't suppose you'd be interested in telling us your names?"

Diego shrugged carelessly and grinned. "It hardly matters, *señor*. My name is Diego Terez. This is Miss Jessica Wescott. You may have heard of her father."

Jessica threw Diego a look of surprise. Why had he mentioned her father?

"Wescott," the man repeated. "It sounds familiar. Rancher?"

"Yes, he is," Jessica answered sharply.

The man smiled at the defiant tilt of her chin. "So be it. If it's of any interest to you, my name's Dawson. I serve under Colonel Franklin, and unless I miss my guess, if what those men say is true, you'll be meeting the Colonel soon." And, "You know Colonel Franklin?"

"Fortunately, I haven't had the dubious honor," Jessica retorted scathingly, untouched by Dawson's amiable manner. He was the enemy. She didn't care if he was good-looking and had an easy Southern charm.

Diego laughed and tilted his hat back on his head. "You must excuse the *señorita*. She does not take so kindly to your Colonel Franklin since some of his men tried to kill her *novio*."

Dawson grinned, the smile crooked on his handsome face. "I suppose that would tend to make a woman sort of mad." He looked away from them to motion to the two men standing nearby. "See that these two get put in a hut until the Colonel's ready to see them. Give them some food and water. They'll want to clean up some, and I imagine they're hungry.''

Jessica was so surprised by the unexpected attempt at hospitality that she was struck silent and was unable to do little more than stare at Dawson when he tipped his hat to her before turning away. She didn't understand these people. Why were they being nice to her and Diego? Even the men who had brought them here had treated them kindly—and had shown her nothing but courtesy and respect. Why? They knew she was involved with others who were trying to stop them. It didn't make sense.

"They aren't what I thought they'd be at all," she told Diego in confusion when they were alone in a small one-room adobe hut that held little more than two bunks, two chairs and a table within its walls. "They're . . . nice."

Diego grinned and threw his hat down on the table. "*Sí*, they are. They are not bad people, Jess, you must not think this. They are only people who do not believe in the same things we do. They are people who have lost their homes, members of their families."

"But they weren't the only ones to lose homes and family in the War," she protested. "People from the North did, too."

"*Sí*, both sides lost much, but sometimes it is easier only to see the hurt on your side. So they are running away to a new start, a new South, and they are willing to kill anyone who tries to stop them."

A chill shook Jessica. She knew from experience that what Diego said was true. These people would kill. Nick and Diego had been marked for death when they had followed the man in gray, and the Confederates had almost succeeded in killing Nick when he'd discovered a train of their wagons loaded with guns. Now, they had her and Diego.

Jessica moved to look out the one small window of the hut. Outside she could see a guard standing watch by the door. A hollow feeling filled her stomach as her eyes locked on the gun the man held. How desperate were these people? How far would they go for their cause? How many people had they killed to come so far? Were she and Diego next?

Chapter 25

Diego woke with a start as someone slid the bolt away on the outside of the door. He'd fallen asleep! Alarmed and irritated at himself, he jumped off the bunk to meet whomever was coming in. How could he have been so foolish as to have let himself doze off? He cursed himself silently, but under the circumstances, he had to admit it had been bound to happen.

When he and Jessica had arrived in the hut hours before, they had barely gotten a chance to look over their prison when food had been brought for them. The meal had been far from lavish, but after days of jerky and water, any type of solid food was a delicious luxury. Both of them had eaten heartily and greedily. However, once their hunger had been satisfied, the uncertainty of their situation had returned to torment them.

Diego had tried to appear calm for Jessica's sake. He had nonchalantly stood at the window observing the Confederate's movements outside or lounged at the table, but the tension wasn't so easily ignored. He had watched as Jessica had paced the room, trying occasionally to sit as he did but unable to remain still for long

She was waiting for the summons. She was anticipating what it would be like to meet Franklin and what would happen during that meeting. But time slipped steadily by, and no summons came. Diego had recognized the tactic Franklin was trying to use. Franklin was attempting to play on their nerves by making them wait. He was hoping to make them anxious, to break their confidence, by drawing out the time indefinitely.

Under other conditions, his ploy probably would have worked, too. But he had not anticipated several factors going against him—the biggest one being fatigue.

Jessica was worried about the meeting, about what would happen, but after days of riding without adequate rest, after a full meal and with the midday heat upon them, anxiety had quickly begun to succumb to the need for sleep. Her pacing had gradually slowed, and Diego had watched her fight to stay awake.

Eventually, realizing Franklin was in no hurry to put the meeting with his two prisoners behind him, Diego had tactfully observed that it appeared as if they were going to have a long wait and that he was going to lie down and rest. So saying, he had stretched out on one of the bunks hoping Jessica would do the same.

Jessica had been reluctant to follow his example, though. Questions and worry had plagued her. What if Franklin came while they slept? She had decided to resist sleep, but it was a battle she had been doomed to lose. When still more time passed and no one came and

Diego remained apparently resting comfortably while he played sentinel, Jessica had finally given in and decided Diego was right. She had laid down, too.

A quick glance across the room now told Diego she was still sleeping soundly. He had never meant to sleep himself, only to convince her to. He had expected only to wait until he was sure sleep had claimed her before getting up again, but instead, he had fallen asleep, too, and now it was too late for regrets. The time for the meeting had come. If nothing else, the rest would give him a clear mind when he met the man he and Nick had been tracking for so long.

Dawson entered the hut holding a kerosene lamp up against the encroaching night. Behind him over the canyon walls outside the last bright colors of sunset were fading from the sky. He nodded to Diego before his eyes fell on the sleeping Jessica. He smiled when he saw her. Laying on her back, oblivious to those watching her, her hair was fanned out on the worn pillow and the feminine fragility of her slender form was easy to see. "Looks like some of the fire faded out of her."

Diego followed Dawson's gaze and nodded agreement. "She has been through much and shown more courage than some of her kind I have known."

"I'm glad to hear that because I reckon she's going to need all the courage she can muster," Dawson acknowledged casually. "Colonel Franklin wants to see her."

"Alone?"

"Alone."

Diego frowned. He did not like the idea of being separated from Jessica. He looked past Dawson to the

two guards standing just inside the door. There wa
little he would be able to do about it with two rifle
being held on him. She would have to go. He walked to
the bunk where she lay and shook her shoulder gently
"Jess. Wake up."

Jessica stirred groggily, opening her eyes slowly
When she saw Dawson standing in the middle of the
room, however, she quickly slid off the bed with an
assisting hand from Diego and stood to face him.

"Colonel Franklin would like to see you now, Miss
Wescott," Dawson announced formally with a sligh
but perceptible bow and touching his fingers briefly to
his hat.

Jessica looked immediately up at Diego. "Wha
about Diego?"

"He wasn't included in the invitation, ma'm."

"I won't leave him," she declared stoutly.

Diego smiled. "Jess, I do not think you will have
much choice. They are much stronger than you, and
with their guns on me, I will not be able to help you
fight."

"I won't go without you," she insisted, glaring
defiantly at Dawson.

Dawson sighed and shook his head. Her reaction
was exactly what he had expected it would be. "I was
afraid of this." And over his shoulder, "Boys, you want
to escort the lady out?"

The two men behind Dawson stepped further into
the room, and Jessica stamped her foot angrily. "You
wouldn't dare!"

"They'll carry you out if they have to," Dawson
replied calmly, admiring her spirit but remaining

unmoved by her determination. Orders were orders, and he'd been given some for her to be brought to the Colonel's house. After following Franklin's instructions for more than three years, Dawson had no intention of stopping—even to champion the cause of a pretty woman.

Diego touched her arm lightly. "Go with them, *chiquita*. It is a fight you cannot win."

"But . . ."

He shook his head.

With a sinking feeling Jessica realized Diego was right. There was no way she could win. She looked back at Dawson, her jaw set grimly. "All right, Mr. Dawson. Have it your way—this time."

Dawson stood aside as she swept past, smiling silently as he turned to follow her out. Something told him the Colonel was going to have his hands full tonight . . .

"How close do you think we are?" Wescott asked Nick as they saddled their horses in the gray of evening. The sun had just set, leaving the plains shadowed and quiet before night fully descended and the nocturnal creatures of the desert woke to roam and hunt.

Nick shrugged. "It's hard to say. We've been making better time than they have by pushing harder, so I'd say we're down to a half day's ride behind them."

"You think we'll catch them before they reach their camp?"

"No. I don't think so. Franklin can't have gone too much farther south than this. He wouldn't be able to risk it. If he put himself too much closer to the border, he'd take the chance of being continually raided by Juarez's men, but if he stays this far away, he'd be just out of striking distance."

"Then we might run across their camp tonight," Wescott speculated.

"If we don't come across it, we should at least be able to see it from where we stop." Nick mounted his horse and indicated the heavy overhang of clouds above. "Those clouds will help isolate any light coming from the ground, and a big camp ought to put out quite a bit of it."

"Let's hope so," Wescott stated and swung his large frame on top of his horse.

Nick led the way out, kicking his horse into a fast trot along the trail they were following. Neither he nor Wescott mentioned Jessica or Tom. Neither man wanted to put their fears or hopes into words. It wouldn't help. It would only make things worse. They could do little more than guess as to where Tom might be. They could only hope he was on his way back with the men and was close to catching them. But, as for Jessica, they didn't know Franklin well enough to even venture a guess.

Outside, walking through the silent camp Nick and her father sought, Jessica was only too aware of her armed escort. It was unnerving as well as irritating. What did they think she was capable of doing alone and unarmed?

Dawson's hand touched her elbow as he tried to guide her toward the house. He was only trying to be polite, act the role of a Southern gentleman, but unreasonably, she didn't want him to be nice to her. She jerked away.

The abrupt and unexpected movement caught the guards by surprise. They were young, and they were edgy. They weren't used to having prisoners. Especially a woman. But it suddenly appeared as if this prisoner was trying to escape! They grabbed her instantly.

Jessica squealed in protest at the uncalled-for attack. She was caught and jerked backwards. Fingers dug into the flesh of her arms, and for her it was the last straw. Fear and anger ignited in a scalding cry, and she swung blindly. Her elbow connected with soft flesh. A grunt accompanied by the whistle of expelled breath followed. She gritted her teeth in satisfaction and struck out again. Her booted foot smashed someone's toes. The hold on her arms was released with a howl of pain.

She staggered under her new-found freedom, but she'd barely caught her balance when the second guard grabbed her again.

Trying to stop the wildly infuriated struggles of the woman alone, the guard yelped as her teeth sank into the back of his hand. But somehow he managed to hang on to her even as he yanked his bleeding fist from her mouth.

Dawson stood by and watched in stunned silence as Jessica continued her attack. He couldn't believe what was happening! And he couldn't understand how it had happened! He stammered for words. What the hell had caused this? Why were his men manhandling this woman? He'd merely touched her elbow, and she'd pulled away. It was no reason to attack her!

Jessica's foot connected with one of the guard's shins, and a muttered oath broke the air.

Dawson took an angry step forward. He didn't know if he should help her or hit her. His men seemed to be getting the worst end of the battle. "For Pete's sake let her go!"

But struggling to regain control of the situation, the men refrained from answering until, dodging well-aimed kicks and raking nails, one managed to pin her arms while the other got hold of her feet.

Looking at the absurd spectacle being played out in front of him, Dawson ground his teeth and repeated more loudly, "Will you let her go?"

"Let her go?" the two echoed in disbelieving unison. The one's hand was smeared with fresh blood. The other, if asked, would have sworn his toes were broken. Neither was willing to release their captive again. It had been too hard to catch her the first time!

Abruptly the front door to the house opened, and light flooded the yard. A man stepped out into the night and paused to stare at the scene before him. It didn't take long to absorb the sight of one young woman being held by two men while a third looked on. "Release her," he snapped. "She's a woman, not an animal."

Each man flinched at the words, and both guards hastily obeyed the command. They let Jessica go and backed away swiftly, putting as much distance as was reasonably possible between their bodies and the teeth and nails of their glaring prisoner.

At an awkward disadvantage, Dawson searched for the right words of explanation. "A misunderstanding, sir. The men thought she was trying to escape."

"A mere slip of a woman escaping from three strapping men?" the man inquired with a scoffing laugh. "It would be some woman who could do so successfully."

Dawson grinned sheepishly as he met Jessica's ashing green eyes. Her temper was still hot. "It ouldn't be so hard, sir, if the men in question were ying not to hurt her."

The newcomer nodded silently at the response. Perhaps." He waved a hand at the two men standing hind Jessica. "You can wait outside." But, turning to r, "Miss Wescott, if you would be so kind?"

Jessica watched him bow slightly and gesture wards the door. He wanted her to go inside. She lked at the idea as she suddenly forgot her fury and alized who this man standing before her must be. Fear mediately flooded through her, proving itself to be a rong coolant on her flaming temper. This was Thomas anklin, and the time for the meeting had come at last. e wasn't at all sure she was ready for it.

What would he say? What did he want from her? hy had he sent for her alone instead of with Diego? hy did he want them apart? What was he planning on ing to them? Fervently, she wished Diego was with r. She didn't want to face Franklin by herself. What uld she possibly say to him?

A long moment crept by as only the chirping of the ickets broke the silence between the two people facing ch other. At last, the man shrugged. With the light ming from the building behind him, he could see her ce and sense her distrust. "Very well," he com- omised. "You may follow me. I'll go in first."

He disappeared through the doorway, but Jessica mained where she was, silently considering the tuation. There wasn't much to consider really. She ew she had to go after him. She had no choice. But her feet were no longer willing to carry her forward.

Watching her uncertainty, Dawson quietly cleare
his throat to remind her of his presence.

Jessica's head jerked around at the sound. She
forgotten Dawson was still with her. Immediately s
swallowed tightly and tilted her chin defiantly. S
could not see his expression. It was veiled from her
the shadow being cast from the brim of his hat, but s
knew what he must be thinking. He was thinking s
was afraid, and she wasn't about to let him know ho
right he was. She threw him one last burning glare a
stepped foward to enter the house.

She followed the retreating figure of the man wh
had entered the building before her down a short h
and into a small room. It was furnished meagerly.
held only several wooden chairs and a large table whic
he obviously used as a desk. Other than that, the wa
were barren and so was the floor. There were
curtains at the windows, no paintings or decorations
any kind. Not even a rug. She frowned. There we
definitely no comforts of home for him here.

"Tell me, Miss Wescott," he said turning to gre
her as she edged nervously into the room. "Do yo
know who I am?"

Trying to exhibit more confidence than she felt, s
faced the bearded man squarely. He had unwaverin
brown eyes and a strong stature. Yet, he wasn't a b
man. He stood only inches over her own height, b
there was an air of authority about him. It was exhibite
in the way he stood, in the way he spoke. It made hi
larger than he really was. He was sure of himself,
control, but she was determined not to be intimidate
by him. "Thomas Franklin."

"And?"

"And you're an ex-Confederate officer who's smuggling guns over the Mexican border to the French."

"And how do you know all of this?"

"Because N . . ." She stopped abruptly and clamped her mouth shut. She had walked right into his trap! He had set her up, and she'd fallen in. She glared angrily at him. She would tell him nothing.

Franklin smiled warmly and gestured to Dawson who had followed her in and who now stood quietly beside the door. "She's too honest to be a Yankee spy, too trusting." He turned his attention back to Jessica. "You were about to say because someone told you, am I correct?" And when she didn't answer, "You're doing this for someone. You're trying to help this person, aren't you?"

Jessica chose not to answer, knowing too late that by saying so little, she had said too much.

"Your silence confirms this. Will you tell me who it is?" He smiled again when still she didn't answer. "You're loyal. That's good. It's good to be loyal to your leaders. But, is your leader right?"

"What do you mean?" she demanded shortly, angry at herself for speaking so easily and at him for tricking her into doing so. She'd have to be careful she didn't slip again.

"How do you know what I am doing is wrong? How can you be so sure whoever you're following is right and I'm wrong? Is it only because this person says so?"

"No, of course not."

"Then why are you helping him? Why are you

trying to stop me?"

"Because I want to."

Another smile touched his mouth, a quiet slash through the dark beard trimmed neatly around his jaw. "That's no answer." He walked toward the window and gestured beyond it. "Do you know what's going on here? Can you understand?"

"You're trying to help the French defeat Mexico."

He laughed heartily. "You see, wrong already. The French are not trying to defeat Mexico. They are trying to help Mexico. By themselves and under their own rule, the Mexican republic has come to nothing. They have no management, no goal, no aim. The French can provide all of that and more. The French want to help Mexico prosper."

"And you want to help the French."

"Yes. Because by helping the French, we can find a new home, a new South if you like. Already Maximilian has granted us permission to settle in several places throughout Mexico."

"Why won't he let you settle there without your bringing in guns?"

"Oh, but he will."

"I don't understand," she said confused. "Why are you doing this then?"

"Because by helping them, we're fighting the United States. The Union. Because the Union is helping Mexico."

"But the people of Mexico have the right to choose their own government and their own leader."

"That's the Union's opinion. Not ours. I've already explained how we feel about the French helping Mexico."

"But you can't you oppose the Union!"

He shook his head and looked at Dawson with an xpressive spread of his hands. "I don't think she nderstands." He turned back to Jessica. "My dear oung woman, you are operating under a misconeption. You think the War is over, but it's not. We ever stopped opposing the Union."

"But the Union won," she protested.

"The Union got General Lee to sign a piece of aper saying they had won," Franklin corrected. "One nan saying so does not necessarily make it so."

"Does that mean you're planning on fighting the Jnion again?"

"I wish we could but, alas, we are too few. We annot fight openly with any hope of winning."

"So you're fighting them by helping the French nstead?"

"Exactly," he agreed enthusiastically. "This is nerely another issue that we and the Union do not agree n and so we are working against them the only way we an—subtly. We don't have enough men to confront hem, but we can irritate them. We can help those who hey do not want to help."

He paused and watched her digest what he had aid.

"Of course, if we have to fight, we will. If someone ries to stop us or follow us into Mexico, we will have no :hoice. And that is what they're attempting to do, isn't t?"

Jessica opened her mouth to answer but mmediately closed it again. Another trick. He had almost gotten her to speak again with another trick.

Franklin sighed and sank into the chair behind the

table. "You must love this young man very much."

Jessica's eyes widened in astonished silence. How could he know about Nick?

"You're surprised I know about him? You shouldn't be. The men who brought you here told me of your conversation with *Señor* Terez in the stable. They heard my name mentioned several times but they also heard that of another man. They told me you were very concerned about him, that he'd been wounded. In fact, the only reason you were even in Piedra was because this other man could not be."

Jessica kept her tongue in check.

"Yes, you told *Señor* Terez that my men had wounded him. So, it must have been him who was discovered looking into the wagons of one of my trains about two weeks ago. Am I correct?" She looked down and he smiled. "Tell me, how did he escape?"

"In a cart," she answered victoriously, raising flashing eyes to his.

"You helped him?"

"Yes."

He nodded. "You must love him if you're willing to risk your life for him." He waved his hand when she didn't answer. "No matter. It is not important, but this man—this Evans is. He's waiting in Santa Fe for your friend in the hut to come and tell him where I am."

Jessica's stomach knotted at the mention of Diego standing helplessly in the hut. What was Franklin going to do with him? And Evans. If Franklin knew where Evans was . . .

Franklin did not miss the recognition and response in Jessica's eyes to this new name. She could remain silent, but her eyes spoke for her. "Evans will be the one

o has had men following me since I left Missouri.''
sighed heavily. ''That was my mistake. I never
uld have gone.''

''What are you going to do with us?'' Jessica de-
nded when he did not speak again immediately but
tead fell silent as he became absorbed in his own
ughts.

Franklin smiled congenially and shrugged. ''For
w, hold you here. You'll be my guests, for a time.''

''Hold . . . for what reason? Why don't you just
us go? By the time we could reach any help, you and
ur men could be across the border to Mexico.''

''But our work here is not yet finished,'' Franklin
d her patiently, as if explaining something to a child.
here is one more shipment of guns to come and, now
ere's you. If someone was foolish enough to let you
t this far, someone will be foolish enough to come
ter you.''

''How could someone come after me if they don't
ow where I am?'' she bluffed hopefully. She couldn't
him believe someone was following her.

''You are the daughter of a local rancher and the
ancé of a man my men wounded. Won't they care
out you? Won't they worry when you don't return
mediately?'' He shook his head. ''Of course they will
d, of course, they will try to find you. Granted, they
ay not arrive until well after the shipment has come
d we are gone, but we cannot take that chance. So,
u will keep us company until we are ready to leave.
nyone who is thinking of rescuing you will not try to
sturb us while we have you.''

Nick and Wescott pulled their horses up to listen to

the night. There was something different. There wa
sound that didn't belong. They strained their ears. W
was it? A quiet but steady rumble. Was it wago
Could it be wagons?

Nick stared through the black night towards
sound. He couldn't see anything, but if what
suspected was out there . . . He motioned Wescott
his horse. It was dangerous to speak unless necessa
Sound carried well over the desert plains.

Wescott quickly slid off his mount and came
stand beside Nick, his rifle firmly held in his hand.

"We're going in on foot," Nick whispered low
"If those are wagons we hear, it's probably anoth
shipment. They could be our answer to getting inside
camp."

Wescott nodded understanding and quietly fell in
step behind Nick to make his way through the darkne
toward the echo of rolling wheels.

Nick felt a spark of admiration once again for t
big man behind him. Time and again Nathan Wesco
had proven he was equal to any situation, this ti
belying his large size and expected awkwardness
slipping through the night as silently as an Indian migh

As they drew closer, the sounds grew louder, a
Nick crouched beside some rocks to study the blackne
around them. Clouds were blocking out the light of t
stars and moon, leaving only a dim glow to illumina
the landscape. It was impossible to see for any gre
distance.

Moments passed. They waited. Crickets sang,
soft breeze blew, and the wagons came on. Yet, the
continued to be heard but not seen.

Nick frowned as he listened. It couldn't be much
~ger. They'd have to be able to see them soon.

Wescott touched Nick's shoulder.

Nick followed the point of the older man's finger
~o the night and nodded. There they were. Little more
~n moving shadows in the black of night, there were
~gons. A train of them, and they were heading south.

Nick motioned to Wescott and they moved off once
~re, crouching low and running from cover to cover.
~ally Nick stopped again, and both men stooped low
~ hide themselves behind some rocks and brush the
~mbering wagons would soon reach.

Steadily the train came on. The first team of mules
~ssed the rocks. The second. One by one they plodded
~ as the two men remained motionless and watched the
~ogress of the wagons until the last one came into view.
~rattled quietly past, and both men moved.

Darting out quickly, they scrambled to get them-
~ves behind the wagon and out of the driver's view.
~ey fell into step behind it. The only thing left for
~em to do was to get inside without being detected and
~main there until they reached the camp.

Wordlessly Nick handed his rifle to Wescott and
~ached forward to grasp the wagon's tailgate. He
~ung himself up cautiously, gritting his teeth and
~noring the pain that shot angrily through his shoulder.
~e slipped quietly inside.

Without a sound he edged forward and let out a
~othered sigh of relief when he saw the panel of canvas
~vering the wagon was pulled firmly shut behind the
~iver. Unless the man riding in the front seat untied the
~p to look inside, they would be safe from discovery.

Bending back out over the gate, Nick took the ri
from Wescott whose long strides had kept him right
with the untrying pace of the wagon train. The big n
hoisted himself inside next to Nick and looked arou

There wasn't much to see. Sacks, barrels
blankets lay scattered throughout the dim storage a
Wescott motioned to the blankets, lifting one up
indicate climbing underneath.

Nick shook his head negatively and indicated
night outside. He moved his hands in imitation o
clock and again shook his head. They would wait
they were lucky, they would reach their destinat
during the night. He hoped so. That way they'd be a
to slip out of the wagon and use the darkness as cov
Once inside the camp, they'd need some type
protection until they could find another place to hide
would have to be somewhere safe. Somewhere t
could wait. Somewhere they could plan fr
and—with continued good fortune—somewhere cl
to Jessica and Diego.

Chapter 26

Inside the adobe hut Diego drew a blanket over a sleeping Jessica. She had returned late the night before. Very late. Franklin had kept her for such a long time, in fact, that Diego had begun to fear the Confederate leader was planning on keeping them separated indefinitely. However, thankfully, Diego's fears had been ungrounded. Jessica had come back, but she had been unusually subdued.

Jessica had sat down at the table with an unnatural calm knowing Diego was anxious to hear what had happened, and had begun to tell him of her meeting with Thomas Franklin. The words had come easily enough at first, but not far into the telling, they became jumbled, she lost control, and she began to cry. Her nerves couldn't take the strain any more. Her composure could no longer be maintained, and the rest of the evening's events were relayed between broken sobs.

Diego had quickly realized that Franklin had manipulated Jessica with subtle agility during the course the meeting. He had plied her with questions, gently an politely, taking her by surprise with his congeni manner and attempting to break down her guard wi quiet concern. It hadn't been what Jessica had expecte She had been ready to face someone hard and dete mined and had been braced for the worst. Franklin well-practiced cordiality was the opposite of what she been prepared for, and it had robbed her of her ange taking away a vital defense.

Yes, Franklin had planned his attack well. He ha wanted her to tell him all she knew about the g movement and about those who were attempting to sto the movement, and he had known less aggressive tacti combined with quiet persistence would play on h nerves and on her willpower. It had been a clever plo and he had used it with a genteel persuasion, but h efforts had gained him little. Despite his planning an despite asking the same questions over and over again different ways during the long evening, he knew n more now about his pursuit by Evans than he ha before seeing Jessica. However, that hadn't stoppe him from frightening her.

Without missing a chance in his attempt to mak Jessica talk, Franklin had passed on a veiled threat. On he knew would haunt her. He had assured her that h realized she would be followed and that his men woul be watching and waiting for those who were comin after her.

Jessica had pretended cool indifference at th warning. She hadn't wanted to acknowledge hi educated guess. She had wanted to dissuade him instea

d so had tried to act as if there was no possibility of
nyone searching for her, but she knew Nick and her
ther were coming. She knew the two men who meant
e most to her would try to get to the Confederate
mp, and the tears she had shed were not for herself
it for them.

Dawn was a long time coming as Diego had tried to
omfort her. He had tried to console her and wipe the
lent question reflected in her eyes away. She wanted
m to tell her it wasn't true, to tell her it wouldn't
appen. She wanted to be told nothing would happen to
ick and her father, but Diego knew he couldn't give
er false hope. He could only give her the truth. Time
as on their side. If Nick came within the next day,
ranklin could be caught off guard. Franklin might be
xpecting someone to follow Jessica, but he wouldn't be
xpecting pursuit to come so quickly. He would expect it
take time.

Diego's words had done little to ease her worry, he
new, but there was little more he could say or do. He
ould only point to Nick's experience and prowess. It
as little enough to offer as hope, but it had given her
omething to hang onto until the emptiness of sleep
ame to claim her just before the eastern sky began to
eflect the light of a new day. Temporarily at least the
eight of her anxiety had been removed.

Quietly Diego moved from her bunk to walk to the
indow. Outside an armed guard stood, waiting and
eady for any attempt to escape. Diego frowned sourly.
one would be made. He couldn't risk it. Not with
essica so close to him. He could take chances with his
wn life but not with hers.

His gaze shifted to the yard of the camp. He had

studied it thoroughly the evening before when Jess
was gone, thoughts of getting away filtering through
mind. But, it had soon become apparent that even alc
it was next to impossible. Too many men. Too ma
walls. Even if he managed to overpower the guard wi
out drawing any attention to the hut, he would have
make his way around the entire complex before bei
able to reach the horses that were corralled on the otl
side of the camp.

His frown deepened. Escape would be difficu
there was no doubt of that. But, it could be done. Nig
would be the best time. During the day it would
suicide. He shifted restlessly as he stood at the gla
pane of his prison. Perhaps he could try tonight. If
could convince the Confederates that he was willing
stay, he might be able to lull them into a sense of fa'
security.

He glanced back at Jessica. He did not want
leave her behind, but trying to take her with him wou
set the odds against a successful escape. He could mo
more quickly and quietly by himself, and he didi
believe she was in any real danger here. Franklin did n
seem ready to harm her and probably would not. Die
looked away. Time would tell.

Outside in the yard there were several wago
standing where none had been the day before. Th
would be the ones he had heard arrive last night ju
before Jessica had returned.

Diego leaned negligently against the windowsill ar
watched the men carrying the contents of the wagons
the various buildings in the camp. None of the sacks
boxes they were unloading were guns. From wh
Jessica had told him, those lay beneath the floorboar

t of sight, and apparently, that was where the Con-
derates intended to leave them.

Diego let his eyes wander over the bustling activity
the yard. Everyone was doing something. Re-
ranging, cleaning, moving back and forth from the
agons. It was a bad sign. It confirmed what Franklin
d told Jessica the night before. The Confederates
uld be leaving soon.

After they got this shipment settled, the Rebels
uld probably wait an extra day or two for any more
en who were coming to join them. Then they would
ove on to Mexico. Diego suddenly smiled. The going
ross the border would not be easy. The wagons would
t reach Maximilian undetected or unmolested. No,
arez would be looking for the arrival of the guns and
the Confederates in happy anticipation.

From what Diego had heard in the cantina in
edra, Juarez had already beaten the French back a
od distance from the border. Juarez was attempting
drive Maximilian into a retreat to Mexico City. And,
r the present, it looked as if the self-appointed
exican leader might succeed. The Juaristas had gained
strength since the rebellion's beginning, and their
rength was in no way diminishing.

Diego shook his head at the futility of the Con-
derate movement. The French were already on the
n. It would not be long before they were defeated.
erhaps it would take several months for Mexico City to
ll, but once the French were isolated within the city's
alls, the revolution would be over. Juarez would have
on.

The Confederates could do little to stop that
ctory. They were too late. They would get into

Mexico, yes. There was no question of their being a
to cross the border for the Juaristas were far to
south. But at the first sign of trouble behind him, Jua
would send a force back. His men would take care
Franklin as, Diego suspected, they had taken care
him before.

Diego looked across the room again at Jessica.
understood why Franklin had called her to see h
alone. Franklin had known he'd probably be able
bluff her, but he couldn't be so certain about Diego.
had rightly assumed that Jessica would have little r
knowledge of the war in Mexico where Diego, he h
guessed, would probably have more, and Franklin h
used Jessica's lack of knowledge against her in
attempt to get her to talk.

Franklin had led Jessica to believe
Confederate's plans were going well, that their g
shipments were being received by Maximilian and th
the arms were being used to fight Juarez. Diego doubt
this, and his frown returned as he wondered about t
gun shipments.

How many had actually gotten to Maximilia
How many had instead been stopped and confiscated
Juarez and his men? How many Southerners who h
taken the guns into Mexico were still alive? How ma
of the guns the Southerners had brought f
Maximilian's use were actually being used against t
French emperor?

Diego turned back to the window. No, Frankl
had suffered defeat south of the border, Diego was su
War and revolution never brought a clear victory
anyone. Both sides lost, as did those in the middle—
Franklin was. He was a pawn being used in a deac

me by both the French and the Mexican leader. It was
t an ideal position to be in. It was like sitting on a
nce, and it was a place from where a fall was
evitable.

Outside and hidden from Diego's and everyone
se's view, Nick moved his throbbing shoulder with a
nce. The ache had become more of a pain and was
aking his head pound.

Wescott saw the pain register briefly on Nick's
ce. They'd been on the move without rest for several
iys now. Nick needed to rest his arm. "Why don't you
t some sleep? There won't be anything happening here
r awhile," he suggested in a low voice.

Nick looked out at the camp activity from the small
ind-carved hole the two of them had found in the
nyon wall shortly after their arrival. The wagons had
ached the Confederate stronghold just before dawn,
d he and Wescott had jumped from their hideaway at
e end of the train as it had passed between the walls
ading into the camp. There they had waited for the
ipment's arrival to gather enough attention to insure
eir getting inside without being seen, but they hadn't
eeded to wait long.

At that hour, there had been few people awake,
nd those who were had been interested in nothing but
e wagons and the supplies they brought. So while the
onfederates had been busy settling the new arrivals in,
lick and Wescott had slipped inside the camp and
orked their way around the canyon walls behind the
dobe buildings. They had been searching for a safe
lace to hide when they'd stumbled onto the small hole
iey rested in now.

Partially concealed by rock and an overgrowth of

hardy sagebrush that had wedged itself into a cra‐
running beneath it, it was the perfect refuge. There w
room for both men to lie stretched out inside as t
depth of the hole was enough to accommodate the
height, but the low ceiling limited them to lying
sitting. It wasn't the most comfortable position f
them to wait in yet it afforded an excellent view of t
camp. They were slightly elevated in their perch a
could see everything going on while remaining secure
hidden.

Nick nodded reluctant agreement. Even if he did
sleep, he needed to rest. His strength still wasn't what
had been, and it was wise to relax while he could. If th
were to do anything during the night, he had to be rea
physically as well as mentally. "I suppose you're right

Wescott twisted his face into a halfhearted gri
"Don't worry. I'll keep an eye out for your friend a
Jess."

"And the guns."

Wescott turned back to watch the camp. "And t
guns."

Nick studied the determined profile of the ma
beside him momentarily before easing himself down to
completely prone position. With anyone else, Nic
might have been reluctant to sleep, but he had no wor
with Wescott on guard. The man had lost his daught
once because he had sent her away. He wasn't going
lose her again now by letting someone take her away

Jessica walked toward the main house beside Dieg
in the fading evening light. Thomas Franklin and h
wife had invited them to dinner. She and Diego we
being treated as their guests. She grimaced inwardl

e wasn't looking forward to another evening in
anklin's company, but there was little she could do to
oid it.

She heaved a silent sigh of resignation and looked
ound the almost completely silent camp as they went,
intedly ignoring the men who were following them
th rifles firmly in their grips. If only she knew where
ck was, if only she could warn him and her father of
e trap being set for them.

During the day she had found herself searching the
nyon walls for some sign of Nick or her father. She
d watched everyone and everything for some
dication that they were nearby, but there had been
thing to confirm their presence. Only stone walls and
ay uniforms. And, when she hadn't been at the
indow, she had watched Diego do much the same
ing with the same result. Though he would not say so,
e was sure Diego was as worried as her about those who
ere sure to follow them.

Diego was better at covering his concern than her,
ough, and during the slow passage of the day, he had
ade every attempt to occupy her mind with more
easant thoughts. He had told her about his and Nick's
rst meeting, of their subsequent adventures together
d of places they had been. She had to admit, it had
en a good effort. He had succeeded in making her
ugh more than once, but it hadn't been enough. It
adn't been enough to wipe the worry from her mind. It
adn't been enough to dispel her fear for those she
ved, and as they reached the house, a cold chill
uched her. Where would all this end? Would she ever
e Nick and her father again?

Franklin was there to greet them at the door.

"Good evening, Miss Wescott. And you would be *Señ*
Terez . . . Won't you come in?''

Jessica and Diego followed Franklin into the hou
to a room much like that which served as his offic
Though it was slightly larger, it was as bare as the othe
Again there were no paintings on the walls and no ru
on the floors, only a dining table and chairs. Eve
room held just the essentials, it seemed, to serve
purpose, and this particular room was for eating.

As soon as they were seated, dinner bega
Franklin took the head of one end of the table while h
wife sat at the other. Jessica and Diego were seated c
Franklin's right and left, respectively, and were serve
first by a young girl who Jessica realized immediate
must be one of Franklin's children, for the girl look
exactly like her mother, a nondescript woman with pla
brown hair and an equally plain face.

Franklin began jovial conversation immediately b
directing a question to Diego, leaving his wife to ente
tain Jessica, and Mrs. Franklin was quick to fill h
role. She did her best to make small talk with Jessi
while Diego was kept in constant conversation by h
husband. She rattled on endlessly about the plantatio
they had left behind in Virginia, about the balls she ha
once held there and enjoyed, and about the South tha
was no more. As Jessica listened, the older woman
wistful expression and sad brown eyes told Jessica mo
than any words could.

Franklin's wife was caught up in the past and wha
had been. The future was something she was unsure c
and so she had avoided examining it too closely. Jessic
felt a wave of sympathy for Mrs. Franklin even as sh
struggled with her own churning emotions. Th

ranklins had left much behind. Everything they had
wned, everything they had loved was gone. Their lives
ould never be the same again. There was simply no
omparing what their life had been to what it would be.
essica wondered how anyone could give up so much on
he chance of finding a new start in a revolution-torn
ountry.

But even as Jessica sympathized with Mrs. Franklin
nd managed to continue to smile tightly at the
oman's nostalgia, she could not completely tune out
he talk of the two men at the table. Franklin was
ngaging Diego in a conversation laced with questions.
sues of the War between the States and its aftermath
ere at the center of their discussion, and Franklin was
retending curiosity toward Diego's opinions. In
eality, however, he was after more than opinions.
Without asking directly, he was using every method of
ersuasion he knew in an attempt to discover all Diego
new about the Confederate movement.

It was a duel of wits, and Jessica had to remain
ilent while Diego played the game, skillfully avoiding
ny answers to queries calling for more than personal
peculation. His amiable good nature and winning grin
ere part of Diego's fencing strategy and gave Franklin
ause to laugh heartily whenever Diego managed to slip
hrough another of Franklin's verbal traps.

Franklin's laughter grated constantly on Jessica's
erves. Between his enthusiastic good humor and his
vife's endless reminiscing, the dinner seemed inter-
ninable. It was hard to eat. Hard to talk. And Jessica
pent most of her time pushing the food on her plate
round and wishing fervently that the meal would end
nd that the evening would draw to a close. She couldn't
wait to get away from their would-be hosts.

Diego, however, seemed in no particular hurry t
leave. He ate and drank and listened and talked, payin
no mind to time and relaxing in their captor's company
He didn't appear to mind the sparring with words or th
skillfully planned conversation. In fact, he appeared t
enjoy the evening tremendously. He smiled and laughe
and parried Franklin's rhetorical thrusts with laughte
and barbs of his own.

Left to watch, Jessica couldn't understand how h
could be so amiable! And, it wasn't until she was abou
to give up all hopes of ever escaping back to the littl
adobe hut that midnight arrived, and Dawson cam
with it. Jessica didn't think she'd ever been so glad t
see somebody. Dawson's coming was a clear sign tha
she and Diego were going. The ordeal was almost over
At least temporarily. At least for one evening. But sh
wasn't prepared to think of that. Not yet.

Dawson led the way outside, and Jessica was quicl
to follow him amidst the parting chatter Diego and
Franklin exchanged. Stepping into the night with a sigl
of relief, she felt as if her smile was frozen on her face
Her cheek muscles ached from keeping the expressior
firmly in place.

Franklin saw them to the door. "I hope you
enjoyed yourself this evening, Miss Wescott."

Jessica turned back reluctantly, a smile stil
straining her lips. "Of course. I can't think of anywher
else I'd rather be."

Franklin laughed, Dawson grunted, and Diego
took her arm. The door closed as the small group moved
away, and Jessica began to relax. There was no need tc
pretend any more. The charade of pleasantry was over.
But, for how long?

The unconscious question caught Jessica by surprise, and she felt depression settle over her as once again she and Diego were led by Dawson to their small cell while two armed guarded followed on behind. She glanced covertly back at their armed escort. When would this nightmare end? How many more dinners with Franklin would they be forced to endure? When would the Confederate leader get tired of playing with his captives and take more decisive action? How much longer did she and Diego have until Franklin gave up on his attempts to gain information from them? What would happen then?

Jessica hugged herself against the chill night and the chill of fear. She didn't know if she could stand the suspense much longer, the not knowing, the wondering what was coming next and how. What would eventually happen to her and Diego? Her eyes fell eagerly on the adobe hut ahead. For a few hours at least she could be sure of some peace, however fragile. For a few hours she and Diego would be alone and unbothered. There would be no pretending. No forced niceties or veiled conversation. And, perhaps, if they were lucky, there would even be further escape—in the form of obliterating sleep.

They reached the hut, and Dawson pushed the door open and stepped aside, handing the kerosene lamp he'd been carrying to Diego. His gaze fell on Jessica then, and he swept the battered Confederate hat he wore off his head in a gallant gesture. "Have a good night's rest, Miss Wescott," he told her, a roguish grin on his face.

Jessica met his provocatively dancing eyes in the lamp light. "You enjoy taunting me, don't you, Mr. Dawson?"

Dawson grinned. He'd always fancied himself lady's man. Women had always seemed to apprecia his good looks and well-bred manners, and he'd learne to use whatever charm he had to his advantage with th fairer sex. "I guess it's just a fascination with yo Northern women. I can't understand how tho: Yankees can keep you sweet young things in line whe you spout so much fire."

"Meaning we're a bit more temperamental tha you Southern boys are used to?"

"Something like that," he agreed with a widene grin.

Diego chuckled. "If it is fire you are after, *Señc Dawson*, you are going to the right place. The *señorit* in Mexico are raised on it."

"Is that a fact?"

"If you gentlemen will excuse me," Jessic interrupted before Diego could continue. "I don't thin this conversation is meant for my ears."

Diego laughed merrily and turned back to the thre obviously intrigued men while Jessica went inside. Sh was tired and didn't feel up to any more battles wit words. Diego could fight this war alone.

Moving carefully into the dark room, Jessic stepped around the door to make her way to one of th waiting bunks. It was the last step she took.

A hand shot out of the shadows and clamped ove her mouth. A harsh jerk followed, and she was dragge roughly into a restraining embrace. Crushed against body she could not see, her arms were pinned to he sides, and pressure by the hand kept her neck cocked a an awkward angle. She couldn't move!

Panic threatened, and a scream lodged in he

roat. Madly her heart pounded against her ribs. But
en as fear threatened to overwhelm her, reason
revailed. Who could this be? A man certainly, but
ho, and why was he here? She subdued the urge to
ruggle as her mind raced.

Could it be one of the Confederate men in the
amp? Had one of them come to the hut to wait for her
eturn? But why? Even if one of them wanted her to
afisfy a crude need, she was not alone. Diego was in the
ut with her. Diego would defend her. And, what Con-
ederate would want to see the two of them alone? Who
ould want to be locked in with them? The pounding of
er heart slowed with determined calm. No, it didn't
ake sense. This was no Confederate soldier. It
ouldn't be. A blind hope ignited, and her body began
o tremble with it.

Abruptly Diego entered the hut. Laughing and
winging the lamp carelessly in his hand, the door was
ulled to behind him and the bolt was slid into place.
Iis smile vanished immediately, however, when he
ealized he couldn't see Jessica.

Frantically he spun back toward the door. He'd
een her come in! Where could she . . His eyes
uddenly found her, and the cry of alarm on his lips died
s his mouth dropped open in surprise. She was here.
She was in the hut, and she was trapped. Locked in the
rms of Nick.

Nick smiled slowly at his friend, his eyes shining
with laughter.

Diego quickly returned the silent communication,
nd he grinned as Nick slowly released his hold on
Jessica and dropped his gaze to look down at her.

Crying and laughing at the same time, Jessica threw

her arms around his neck. "I knew it was you! I
knew . . ." Her words were suddenly lost as Ni
silenced her hysterical ranting with a hard a
demanding kiss.

It was a long moment before Nick raised his he
again. In his attempt to quiet her, the harsher emotio
brought on by suspense and danger were nearly ove
come by the soft sensations of her yielding lips and t
trembling of her limbs. The days of living with the fe
of never holding her again were wiped away as she clu
to him. She was safe. She hadn't been harmed. F
finally broke away and met Diego's patient gaze. "O
guard?"

"Only one," Diego agreed with a quiet nod.

"He won't be there long," Nick returned, lookir
back down into Jessica's tear-filled eyes. A gentle smi
touched his mouth, and he raised a hand to wipe t
wetness from her cheeks.

A thud sounded outside the door. A scraping soun
followed. The guard was being dragged out of sigh
Diego blew out the light as the bolt was pulled free, an
when the door swung open, Nathan Wescott filled tl
entrance.

With a small cry Jessica slid from Nick's arms t
run to her father. She hugged him silently. There was n
need for words as he returned the quick embrace.

Nick handed Diego the rifle he had propped again
the wall beside him when Jessica had come ir
"Ready?" he whispered with a conspiratorial grin.

Diego smiled back. "Need you ask, *amigo*?"

Wescott took Jessica's hand and led her out tl
door of the hut. Nick and Diego quietly followe

ining them in back of the hut where Nick nodded to
escott before motioning to Diego.

Jessica watched in happy confusion as the men
ave silent signals to one another. It was over! They
ere free! Nick and her father had come to take them
way! But her elation quickly died when suddenly Nick
nd Diego turned to go and her father began leading her
another direction. She tried to stop and protest, but
ne hand holding hers was firm. She was being forced to
o. There would be no argument. She threw an anxious
ance over her shoulder at the two retreating forms of
ick and Diego. Where were they going?

But even as she wanted to ask, she knew there was
o time. Nick obviously had a plan, and he'd taken
iego with him to accomplish it. He knew what he was
oing, and she couldn't ruin it for him—for all of them.
he had to go quietly with her father and leave Nick and
iego behind. She could only hope they would all be
nited again—soon.

Diego followed Nick's lead, crouching behind him
hen he stopped and shadowing him when he moved.
e was nearly as uncertain as Jessica as to what Nick
ad in store for the moments ahead, but there was no
esitation on his part to do what Nick asked. Diego
new Nick had a plan. A plan, he guessed, that would
llow them to accomplish what they'd set out to do
hen they'd left Evans—stop Franklin.

The two men circled the camp quickly and quietly
nd with little fear of being seen. The only guard in the
anyon had been taken care of. The Confederates felt
o need for others inside. They were more concerned
ith the outside, and that's where the men on top of the

canyon walls would be looking. They would
searching for trouble coming from beyond the wal
They would not expect it to develop from within.

Nick stopped by the wagons. Standing side by sid
he knew they were completely unloaded now except f
the guns. Wescott had assured him of that.

When Nick had woken in the late afternoo
Wescott had rapidly explained what had happened
the camp during the day. Through the hours while Ni
had slept, Wescott had watched the high activity of t
Confederates and had observed the unloading
supplies from the wagons. Everything had be
removed except the guns. The weapons had remain
undisturbed and hidden. As for where Jessica and Die
might be, Wescott had seen only one place bei
guarded. An adobe hut. The hut, he had surmised, ha
to be where Jessica and Diego were being held—if the
were indeed inside the Confederate camp. That hopef
assumption had proven correct when Nick and Wesco
had watched as Jessica and Diego were escorted to t
main house earlier in the evening.

With Jessica and Diego's presence confirmed, som
rapid planning took place, but what had followed ha
been easy. Nick and Wescott had waited for darkness t
fall and had left their hideout to make their way into th
camp. They'd been careful of not being observed, bu
there was little need to worry. The only guard had di
appeared as soon as Jessica and Diego had been take
away, and almost all of the other camp inhabitants ha
left their chores in search of their evening meal. Tha
left the area clear for the two men to get to the deserte
adobe hut. Once there, Nick had slipped inside whil
Wescott had waited outside behind the hut.

Yes, getting to Jessica and Diego had been easy. The hard part started now. They had to get out of the camp without being detected. To insure this, they needed a loud and attention-drawing diversion.

Nick turned to look at Diego and whispered one word, "Powder."

Diego grinned immediate acknowledgement and slipped away to the next wagon. He knew what Nick had in mind. He knew what Nick wanted to do.

Poking and prodding, boards were cautiously shoved out of the way as the two men sought the black powder they needed. There was little light to see by with a cloudy sky overhead, and to them, their efforts seemed way too loud in the black of night, but there was no one about to hear the muffled noises they made. They were alone with the wagons and the arms the wagons held.

The powder was stored in small barrels, and both Nick and Diego worked swiftly to gather several of the containers. Once ready the barrels were punctured and the granular contents were spilled in long, snaking lines around the wagons and their cargo.

It was swift and easy work, and when he was satisfied with the results, Nick waved Diego to him and broke open one last barrel. With it, he slowly worked his way toward the canyon wall. He wanted to make it stretch to the narrow entrance to the camp. There he hoped Jessica and Wescott were already waiting.

The last of the powder drained out of the barrel, and Diego touched Nick's arm and pointed silently. Jessica and Wescott were in sight and mounted on horses. They were ready to go.

Nick motioned Diego on. Diego scampered off

quickly, and Nick struck a match. He put it to the black
powder which ignited with a flash of spitting spark
Nick dropped the match and stepped back, watching :
the small ball of fire leapt forward to consume the blac
dust spread across the ground. It wouldn't take long fo
it to reach the waiting wagons.

Nick swung away and broke into a run. It was no
or never. He raced toward the horses. There were thre
of them. Wescott was mounted on one, Jessica o
another, and as Nick reached them, Diego was swingin
into the saddle of the third. Nick hurriedly threw him
self up behind Jessica.

"What about Franklin?" Jessica asked in a hoars
whisper as he took the reins from her.

"To hell with Franklin. Let Evans worry abou
him," Nick snapped and dug his heels into the horse'
sides.

With an only partially obscured moon lighting thei
way, they clattered through the shadowy corrido
leading out of the canyon. It was far from a quiet exit
and cries echoed from the men standing guard on th
walls above them as they went.

Someone yelled as they burst into view, and rifle
barked when they didn't respond to the call but instea
sprinted for the plains beyond the rock walls. Th
bullets whistled shrilly in the night air but went wil
after unclear moving targets. The guards couldn't see
There wasn't enough light, but they continued to fire.

The echo of the shooting shattered the night and
chased them into the desert, but the riders didn't stop
They pushed the horses on as time stretched and ther
broke with the brilliant flash of the first explosion. I
shook the night with a deafening roar. More powde

quickly erupted. The canyon walls shook, and inside the camp flames began to devour the canvas-covered wagons and danced through the air to light the sky and the startled faces of those jarred from sleep. Among them was a short man with a dark beard. He stood in front of the main house beside his handsome first-in-command as part of his dream burned and withered before him.

The ground rocked as kegs of powder continued to burst free of confining barrels, and ammunition sparked to life to whine and scream through the blazing inferno engulfing it. The echo of the destruction boomed from the canyon to the plains surrounding it, but the fleeing riders who had caused the crescendo of chaos did not pause to look back at the damage they had done. They did not look back at the canyon walls to see the once gray cloud cover now reflecting fiery orange. They weren't interested in what lay behind them. They only wanted what lay ahead. Freedom. And they spurred their mounts on over the rolling terrain to the safety offered in the land beyond.

Chapter 27

Dawn found the trio of horses heading north at an easier pace. Around them the desert silence had returned. There were no more explosions renting the air, no gunfire whining after them, and there were no signs of pursuit. But, then, they hadn't really expected any.

With the guns blown up and their prisoners loose, Franklin and his men would have no choice. They would have to run. They would have to leave immediately for Mexico and whatever sanctuary they might be able to find there.

Yes, they were alone with the peace of the desert and with the company of one another, and none of them appeared to mind. Jessica laid back against Nick as they rode, content to have his arm around her. This was all she wanted, and the secret smiles she frequently shared with him as they went told her that he shared her feelings.

Diego and Nathan Wescott kept quiet pace beside

the two, exchanging smiles of their own whenever the
intercepted the silent communication between Jessic
and Nick. They were content, too, and there was n
need to use words to express how they felt. Smile
seemed to say it all.

Before two hours passed from the mornin
however, they realized their solidarity was about to en
A heavy dust cloud was building to the north of them
and it was growing larger as those creating it dre
nearer. The three men viewed the gathering dust wit
disinterested speculation. The cause was, no doubt,
group of riders, possibly the Army troop Evans wou
have sent in response to a message from Tom. If it wa
Evans, the men doubted the government agent would b
able to catch the Confederates. The Rebels had to
much of a head start on fresh horses. By the time thes
riders reached the canyon on tired mounts, it would b
too late. Franklin and his followers would be well o
their way to Mexico.

But, Nick found it hard to care. He met Diego'
gaze with a casual shrug, and Diego grinned. "We hav
visitors, *amigo*."

Nick nodded. "Could be Evans."

"Could be," Diego agreed with a sigh.

"Or, it could be Tom," Wescott put in. "He had
head start on your Evans." He shook his head. "He'
be madder than hell when he finds out he missed all th
action."

"Either way," Nick responded. "We might as wel
wait for whoever it is to join us."

They pulled their horses to a halt, and the four o
them watched the top of the ridge just beyond them. I
wasn't long before they could hear the steady pound o

approaching horses. Whoever was coming was riding in fast and would be with them shortly.

A band of men suddenly topped the rise, hesitated briefly when they saw the four waiting below them, and then hurried on. It only took a moment for the two groups to come together, and when they did, it turned out to be Tom who was leading the second group—not an Army commander.

Tom pulled his horse to a halt before the four and slowly looked from one face to the next. He frowned in puzzlement at their happy expressions. If he didn't know better, he'd have said they were out for a Sunday ride! He finally decided to center his attention on Jessica. "I thought you were being held prisoner."

Jessica smiled. "I was."

Tom's frown deepened, and he looked at Wescott.

"Sorry, Tom. We couldn't wait," Wescott explained with a shrug of his broad shoulders.

"You mean it's over?" Tom asked in livid disappointment.

"Afraid so," Wescott confirmed.

"We came all this way for nothing?" Tom complained with a wave of his hand to the men behind him who were looking disappointed as well.

"If you really want to," Nick offered, "you could try to catch Franklin."

"*Sí*," Diego agreed. "But he is probably very close to the border by now."

"Or," Wescott suggested, "you could go back to Piedra instead and enjoy a day off. Drinks are on me."

Wescott didn't have to ask twice. A unanimous cry of acceptance split the air, and without further discussion, the men swung their horses around and stampeded back over the ridge to the north, leaving Jessica, Nick, Diego and Wescott behind.

"I think I am going to join them," Diego announced after a moment had passed. "It has been a long ride and, I remember seeing some very pretty *señoritas* in Piedra."

Wescott grinned. "I could use a drink myself." He turned to look at Jessica and Nick for a response.

Nick merely shook his head and smiled. "You two just go on ahead. I've got everything I want right here."

Wescott nodded, returning the glowing smile of his daughter. It looked as if he was going to lose her again, but this time he didn't think she'd stay too far away. "I guess you do." And, to Diego, "Shall we go?"

The two men raced off after the others, and Jessica watched them go, waiting until they had disappeared from sight before speaking. "Does this mean you're going to marry me?"

"I thought we were already married," Nick objected with a lopsided grin.

Jessica nodded thoughtfully. "For us it may be enough, but there's Grandmom and Grandfather to consider. They might not see an Apache ceremony as legal, and I don't think they'd want their granddaughter's children to be born out of wedlock."

"Children!" Nick exclaimed. "Are you . . . ?"

Jessica laughed mirthlessly at his reaction, and he squeezed her tightly.

"For that I should make you walk home."

"No!" she squealed in protest as he threatened to push her from the saddle. "Wait! I don't know. I mean, I might be."

Nick looked down at her, critically examining her

flushed face and her slender but softly rounded young body with an intent blue-gray gaze. He sighed heavily as if in defeat. "Yup, I guess you could be."

She smiled and watched him shake his head forlornly.

"I guess I'll have to."

"Have to what?"

"Marry you."

"Promise?"

He didn't answer but lowered his head to hers, letting the reins fall from his hands as he pulled her closer to him.